Westcoast Legacy

To order additional copies, please contact us.
BookSurge, LLC
www.booksurge.com
1-866-308-6235
orders@booksurge.com

Westcoast Legacy

A NOVEL

To John: I hope you enjoy my little Westcoast tale. Regards, Ian Kent

Ian Kent

2004

Christmas, 2004

Westcoast Legacy

Introduction

Who among us has not said, at one time or another, *"Now that would make a great story!"*? Throughout my life, I have found that most of these stories have already been "made", and it's just a matter of pulling them together from the bits and pieces of information available.

Although this story is mainly about the history and heroic efforts of the early settlers in Victoria and the west coast of British Columbia, there is an inter-woven plot about a subject that can kindle fires in the minds of even the most conservative reader, *Spanish Gold!*

As a young boy growing up on this coast, my imagination would conjure up various wild scenarios whenever I heard the stories of Spanish ships exploring the coast, and the rumours and speculations of treasure! Years later, further fuel was added to these imaginative fires when I heard a story of a logger, working in the hills near the Port San Juan area. Apparently one day, while logging an area near the location of part of our story, he stumbled upon a cave formed in the rocky slopes; a cave with a very distinct set of stairs leading down into it! The logger's situation at the time did not allow investigation, and as far as I know, it was never followed up.

Spanish records tell us that *officially*, the first ship built on the west coast of Mexico to sail the northwest was the "Santiago" in 1773. Although this was the first ship built, other Spanish ships had been in the area before this, exploring the coast to California and beyond.

The real mystery starts around 1596, when an

Englishman named Michael Lok returned from Venice with a story about a Greek pilot named Apostolis Valerianos. This man, also known as "Juan de Fuca", had been in the service of the Spanish for many years, one voyage including the Northwest coast of America. The lack of detailed records creates an air of mystery around this voyage, especially about the strait that bears his name. Yet the early Spanish explorers were aware of its location and speculated that this was the long-sought "North-west Passage" or the mythical "Strait of Anian" connecting the Atlantic and Pacific oceans. This would have provided a more direct route back to Spain from the west coast of Spanish America.

During the sixteenth and seventeenth century, the Spanish soldiers plundered *hundreds of tons* of gold and treasures from the civilizations of South and Central America and shipped to Spain. Most of us could not visualize a ton of gold, let alone hundreds of tons!

Is it possible that at least one ship, earlier than the Santiago, Sutil, or others we know of, might have attempted to take its cargo of gold to Spain via the rumoured Northwest Passage, or as we know it today, the Strait of Juan de Fuca? Considering the nature of the west coast of Vancouver Island, (later to become known as the graveyard of the Pacific) it is easy to speculate on the fate of such a ship. Besides dangerous reefs and rocky shores, there are hundreds of coves, inlets and small beaches where a sailing vessel could be driven ashore (and even remain relatively intact) by the storms that frequently pound the coastline. Who knows what hardships the survivors had to endure, hoping to lighten the ship by unloading its infamous cargo to make repairs or re-float the vessel? The duty-bound captain would have the gold safely stored away, possibly in a cave, far from prying eyes and the ambitions of his crew.

The ultimate fate of this hardy group was probably not a happy one, as this coast offers very little opportunity to re-float a vessel once it is driven hard-ashore. More than likely, they eventually perished from starvation and exposure, or possibly experienced a disagreeable meeting with some local natives.

As I've said, the story has already been told, let's just see what we can put together from the tantalizing fragments available to us today.

Ian K. Kent
Tsawwassen, B.C.
Canada.

To my Mother, Olive Belle, the first real pioneer lady in my life.

Chapter 1

London—1850

The late November fog folded around them as they stepped from the cab, piercing their garments like a knife. Margaret Manson paused a moment, adjusting her wool shawl around her shoulders. She looked around at the dull, dirty buildings of Fenchurch Street, barely visible in the mantle of mist that shrouded the area. She trembled visibly as the soggy air intensified the foreboding that grew with each step of this new venture.

"Go ahead Sis. I'll arrange with the cabbie to drop our luggage off at the hotel and return for us later."

Climbing the worn stone steps, she turned to watch her brother, Kenneth Cameron. The tall, good looking man acted with the poise and confidence of the successful businessman he was. His hat covered most of his ruddy brown hair and she smiled as his bushy red moustache bounced up and down as he talked to the driver.

Again the chill racked her body as she thought of her future, and how much she would miss her brother. They had always been very close, Kenneth acting as her protector and confidant when they were children, and later her chief supporter and go-between with her family since her controversial marriage to Adam Manson.

Her thoughts drifted back over twelve years and she wondered again if she had made the right decision. Only sixteen at the time, she had felt the whirlwind romance with Adam, a young shipwright's apprentice two years her senior, was the answer to her prayers, and a way out of the dull, weary life her family had planned for her. Although her rebellious nature had developed at an early age, her better judgement had not, and before she knew it, she was carrying Adam's child. She shivered as she recalled the violent reactions and arguments that followed with her family.

Cast out and almost disowned, she had turned to her brother Kenneth, her life-long pillar of support for solace and encouragement.

"Get ye inside quickly lass, ye'll catch your death out here!" Kenneth's words snapped her back to the present.

The building was a gloomy, grey edifice, ominous in its cloak of fog, yet indistinguishable from the hundreds of others in the district. A small sign beside the entrance proclaimed this to be an office of the "Hudson's Bay Company". Margaret hesitated slightly, took Kenneth's arm, and entered with a distinct feeling of being swallowed alive.

In sharp contrast, the interior was warm and dry, immediately easing her discomfort. An air of busy, yet quiet activity permeated the office. A well stoked, pot-bellied stove radiated heat from the corner, and the occasional twinge of coal-smoke mingled with the odour of the damp wool clothes hanging in the entrance hall.

Kenneth again took charge, and before long, a jovial, rotund, middle-aged man approached them, with an air of authority and complete confidence within his domain.
"Margaret, this is Mr. Barclay, Head Secretary of the Hudson's Bay Company. Mr. Barclay, I have the pleasure and honour to present my sister Margaret . . . er . . . Mrs. Adam Manson."

"Mrs. Manson, I'm delighted! Please have a chair, both

of you!" He turned aside and called in a louder voice. "Johnston, some tea for our guests if you please!" He then turned to Margaret, "Mrs. Manson, you must be frozen! This is beastly weather to welcome someone to London, but I'm very pleased you've arrived and hope your journey from Scotland was pleasant."

Before she had a chance to answer, he continued. "As you already know, I met Adam in September before he shipped out on the "Falmouth". We had arranged his contract and land grant details at that time."

Johnston, the clerk, arrived at that moment, and with a bit of a flourish, presented the trio with tea and cakes. As he poured, Margaret recalled how excited Adam had been when he returned from London to explain his plans for their new life in the far-off colony of Vancouver's Island. She had not even heard of it, but Adam assured her it was a thriving, beautiful country, with bountiful farms surrounding a perfect harbour, on which the Hudson's Bay Company had built "Fort Victoria", named in honour of the Queen. He had appealed to her adventurous nature, and made it sound so simple. Pack up everything and move to a new land, inhabited by savages and a handful of settlers, work for the Company on their farms for five years, and they would receive a land grant of twenty-five acres or more! Mr. Barclay's words brought her back to reality.

"Although it must be very difficult for you, Mrs. Manson, I feel your husband's decision to ship out on an earlier vessel was wise. It is seldom we can recruit settlers with Adam's skills and training as a shipwright, and the opportunity for free passage as ship's carpenter on the Falmouth was too good to ignore." She nodded in agreement as he continued. "Besides, Mrs. Manson, he should have time to get settled in his new duties and arrange lodging for you both when you arrive later."

Kenneth interrupted "My sister also has her two sons, Thomas and Andrew travelling with her, so I sincerely hope sir, ye have made adequate arrangements for them on the Tory."

Mr. Barclay frowned slightly and fumbled with some papers. "Unfortunately, Mr. Cameron, the original conditions for Mrs. Manson's passage on the Tory have changed. The Tory sails tomorrow, with its full complement of cargo and passengers."

He referred to the papers, obviously the cargo manifests and passenger lists. "Last minute arrangements had to include Captain William Mitchell on this voyage, who is going to Fort Victoria to assume command of the Company's steamship "Beaver". Also, I'm afraid, previous arrangements had been made, unknown to me, for a Captain Langford, his wife and five daughters, as well as Captain Cooper and his wife to join the vessel at Gravesend."

Margaret's first thoughts were that is was comforting to think of these men bringing their wives and daughters on such an adventure. Suddenly, she realized what Mr. Barclay had just said. She was stranded! Left here with no way to catch up to her husband, already thousands of miles away!

Her teacup almost upset as she cried out "But Mr. Barclay, I thought . . ." as Kenneth leapt to his feet!

"Now, now, no need to fret," Mr. Barclay went on, "I've already checked the possibility of other vessels, and I've found several options. Unfortunately, most of the departures are not expected for at least another month."

Margaret interrupted again, clearly shaken. "I find that quite unacceptable Mr. Barclay. For one thing, Adam is expecting us to arrive on the Tory. For another, we are not a family of unlimited means, sir. We cannot afford to bide our time in a hotel or rooming house in this damp and gloomy city for another month on the odd chance of obtaining passage on some future vessel!"

"Please, Mrs. Manson," Mr. Barclay broke in abruptly, not accustomed to being chastised by a woman, "I said most of the departures were expected within a month. There is one other ship, leaving within a week, bound for Vancouver's Island."

"Mr. Barclay," interjected Kenneth, "Do I detect a note of hesitation in your voice? Why did ye not mention this ship earlier?"

"Well," he hesitated, "She's a new ship, just in from the Orient, a 350 ton brigantine, somewhat smaller that the Tory. Mind you, she's a fine looking vessel, but one which the Company has never employed before. The captain has a reputation on the docks as being tough, but also an excellent seaman . . . however, very little is known of his background. The ship is presently loading supplies for Fort Victoria and other points on Vancouver's Island, and should be departing within the week." He paused briefly, measuring their reaction.

"If you wish, I can make inquiries for you."

"Thank you sir," said Kenneth, "Ye've been very helpful, but I think we can make the arrangements from this point. If ye would be so kind as to advise me the name of the vessel and whom we should contact?"

After consulting his papers a moment, Mr. Barclay replied, "The captain is Mr. Mark Holland, and the ship is the "Shanghai Lady"."

Chapter 2

Late the following day at the "George and Vulture" Hotel, Margaret paced the confines of her small room, anxiously waiting for Kenneth. Although he had said he wouldn't be back until dinner, her restless nature and concern would not allow her to relax. For the hundredth time, she went to the mirror to straighten her hair and pinch her cheeks.

"If he doesn't return soon, I'll have no hair left, and my cheeks will be black and blue!" she fretted. In truth, she should not have been concerned, for as a woman of 28 years and a mother of two, she had stood up very well. Although of average height, her upright posture and graceful way she carried herself gave the appearance of a much taller woman. Her long auburn hair, piled high on her head increased this illusion and the copper and gold highlights competed with the sparkle of her blue-green eyes.

"The years have been good to me," she thought, brushing off the times of hardships she had endured since her marriage. The early years were the hardest, while Adam completed his apprenticeship and served his indentured time, and she struggled to keep the house and raise their first child, Thomas. Later, as a qualified shipwright, and later still when he started his own business under Margaret's insistence, conditions improved. It was this period Margaret had most enjoyed, taking over the economic management of the business from her more craft-oriented husband. She had been able to rise to the challenge with all her in-born business sense and Scottish frugality.

Over the years they had pinched and saved enough for a major improvement in their lot when fate again intruded. A chance meeting with the Hon. Edward Ellico, of Glenuich, started it all. Mr. Ellico was a director of the Hudson's Bay Company, and when he told Adam of the opportunities available, it wasn't long before they had talked it over and he was on his way to London to make arrangements.

There followed an intense period of activity for almost a year, finishing existing work, selling the business and everything else which they couldn't take to the colony. They shipped most of their supplies and tools on the Falmouth with Adam. Margaret had remained behind to finish the final arrangements, stock additional supplies, clothes, books, and a few luxuries probably not available in the Hudson's Bay stores.

"At least we've done it all ourselves," she thought, "without any help from my stodgy old family!"

Her main concerns were for her children and how they would fare on the long ocean voyage. Healthy and sturdy lads, they loved the sea. As they had spent most of their life in and around ships, this was not surprising.

A knock on the door broke her reverie, and she rushed to open it.

Kenneth burst in, sweeping her off her feet, "Come along lass, I'm starving! I have a lot to tell you, so let's be off to try some of Mrs. Groggan's leg of lamb I smelled roasting downstairs!"

Very little was said during dinner, as Mrs. Groggan fluttered about, chattering all the while. Margaret could hardly contain her curiosity, and the only satisfaction Kenneth provided was to his own appetite.

As the last of the dishes were cleared away and they were enjoying their tea, Margaret couldn't control herself any longer.

"For God's sake, brother, are you going to tell me something or do I have to beat it out of you?"

"Calm yourself, Margaret," Kenneth said, a mischievous look in his eye, "We've a lot to discuss and I scarcely know where to start"

"How about at the beginning, what of the ship?"

"I have found the ship, talked to the captain and you and the boys are booked to sail on her Tuesday or Wednesday next."

She gasped as the enormity of that statement sunk in. "Oh Lord, Kenneth, we're really going!"

"Of course you're going, you silly girl, isn't that what you've been working towards for the past year? 'Tis no time to be having second thoughts, with your husband well on his way and all!"

"No, no, Kenneth, you know what I mean. Please go on and tell me more."

"Well, the ship is a fine little vessel, a brigantine of sorts. She's quite new, and well fitted out. I'm sure you and the boys will take a fancy to her. We've used similar vessels by the firm for shipping coal to the smaller ports up north, and the way she is rigged, she'll beat to windward as easily as running down the trade-winds."

"As for Captain Holland," he continued, "I found him very pleasant and business-like and it appears he runs a tight ship. Barclay's comment about not knowing his background concerned me somewhat, so I asked a few questions around the docks. This man is not the average sailor or British Navy type; in fact, he admitted this was only his second voyage to London. It seems he has spent most of his days in the Orient, India and other God-forsaken places like that! When I introduced myself as a director of the Cameron Coal Company, he didn't bat an eye! Obviously he's never heard of the firm! Most ship-owners would be grovelling in the dirt, hoping to pick up some of our business."

"Ha!" Margaret broke in, "I like him already! Someone who can shatter the ego of the great Kenneth Cameron, of the Cameron Coal Company! I'll wager father must be turning in his grave!"

"Be that as it may," her brother continued, "His knowledge of Britain is of little importance, what's more to the point, he seems a proper gentleman, is a successful ship's captain, and knows his way to Vancouver's Island. He's been there before, you know. He appears to be quite taken with the place, although I can't imagine why!"

"In any case, I've booked passage for you and the boys, two small cabins, quite well appointed. I stopped by the warehouse and asked Parsons to have your freight delivered to the dock-side tomorrow so the can load it aboard. Lastly, I've dispatched a message to Aunt 'Liz to have the boys here at the hotel by Monday next."

"Now," Kenneth paused, watching Margaret's wide eyes, "Is there anything I've forgotten?"

Margaret's mind was in a turmoil. Part of her was anxious about this uncertain future, concern for the well-being and safety of her husband and children. At the same time, her spirit was fired by the promise of change, challenge, and literally, new worlds to conquer! Her thoughts raced for an answer to Kenneth's question.

"No brother-dear, I'm certain you've thought of everything. Oh thank you so much Kenneth, how would I have managed without you?"

Kenneth laughed, "Knowing you, Margaret, you'd have managed very well, although it's probably as well I went alone to arrange your passage. We'll at least get you on-board without incident, then if the captain wants to, he can throw you overboard later!"

They both smiled, knowing Margaret's history of direct and often-times obstinate approach to business dealings. Kenneth's gaze wandered and his eyes took on a far-away look.

"Something troubling you, brother?" Margaret asked.

"No, I was just thinking. When I was on that ship today, I envied you, and almost wished I were going myself."

Margaret said nothing for a moment, finishing her tea, then slowly put her cup down. The tavern was quiet, the servants in the kitchen and other patrons retired for the evening. The candles flickered, catching the glint of a tear in Margaret's eyes as she murmured "Who knows, Kenneth, who knows? Perhaps we'll find a reason one day for you to come."

Chapter 3

Thomas and Andrew's eyes were like saucers as they devoured the dock-side scene before them. Although they had spent most of their short lives hanging around the docks and vessels where their father worked, never had they experienced the sheer magnitude of ships and activity as here on the London waterfront!

The stench hit them without warning. As they stepped out of the cab, the reek of the rubbish and filth in the gutters wrinkled their collective noses in disgust. Then came the penetrating mixtures of fish, fresh and not-so-fresh, drifting from the markets surrounding them. As they picked their way around the stacks of crates across the docks, a dense cloud of acrid black smoke engulfed them from a nearby steamer. Such a variety, yet all intermingled with the ever-present fetid foulness of the Thames.

Andrew clutched his mother's hand tighter as someone yelled from behind and they all jumped from the path of a heavily loaded cart as it clattered by them on its way to one of the ships. The raucous cries of seagulls and other sounds joined the uproar of activity as dock-workers cried out, more carts and wagons rattled and rolled, and the clamour of horse's hooves on the wharf reverberated between the warehouses.

"There she is!" Thomas cried out, running ahead of the others as they approached one of the vessels. To Thomas' eyes, she was a beauty! Despite his tender years, Thomas did have a "good eye" for sailing vessels. Most of his life he had kicked around the docks by himself or with Andrew, and in recent years, had spent most of the time working with his father, learning the shipwright's trade.

The Shanghai Lady was laying alongside the dock, appearing impatient to leave, straining at her mooring lines. In truth, the current flowing past created this impression as it rippled around the hull. Thomas looked her over with a practiced eye, the hull jet-black and wide-waisted, lying low in the water, set off by a saucy sheer capped with a stark white toe rail and teak bulwarks.

From the carved detail in the teak taffrail to the long over-hang of her bow-sprit, he could see detail and workmanship seldom seen in working vessels of this kind. His eyes travelled up the rigging, studying the two slender masts, raked back at a jaunty angle, giving a further appearance of speed, even as she lie at the dock.

A call from his mother arrested his inspection and he returned to her side.

"Hello there!" Kenneth called, "Is the captain on board?"

A large man broke away from a group on deck and moved lightly across to the gangplank where they stood. "Mr. Cameron isn't it? I'm William Guthrie sir, first mate. I'm afraid the captain's ashore just now, won't be back 'til later."

Towering over them, "Billy" Guthrie was an imposing figure. He moved with the swiftness and grace of a ballet dancer, contradicting his initial appearance of being bulky and slow. Six feet tall, Billy rippled with muscle. His head joined his broad shoulders with muscled buttresses rather than a neck. A rough seaman's shirt was straining to reach around his barrel chest and was tucked in his trousers at a surprisingly narrow waist. The well trimmed tail of flaming red hair was pulled back and neatly tied behind his head and a curly bush of a beard surrounded a smile that matched the sparkle of his eyes and belied his intimidating appearance.

Turning to Margaret, he touched his cap and greeted her with his low, growling voice. "Good morning ma'am, you must be Mrs. Manson, and these your boys! Welcome aboard the Shanghai Lady ma'am, if you'd like, I'll show you to your cabins. Leave them bags there and I'll have 'em brought aboard presently." He led the way aft along the silver-grey weathered teak deck towards the main companionway, picking their route around rigging and deckhands busy at work. Before long, they were settled in the two small cabins aft, the boys in one and Margaret in the other.   Each cabin had two narrow bunks on the outboard side, with a small desk and chest of drawers on the other walls, with a hanging locker in the corner for coats and longer items. The furniture and wall panelling glowed with the golden brown of hand-rubbed Burma teak, while the brass fittings and lamp sparkled in contrast. A richly coloured oriental rug partially covered the planked cabin sole, the like of which Margaret had seen only in the finest of homes. She was so pleasantly surprised with the surroundings and the tasteful manner in which the cabin was appointed, she commented to Mr. Guthrie.

He replied, "None o' my doin' ma'am, that's the skipper's ideas. He had all that fancy-work done when she was built. It's all too rich for me, never saw anything like this on any ship I've served on. We don't carry many passengers ma'am, you three will be the only ones on this voyage."

He turned to leave, then stopped. "Your freight is all stowed in the f'w'd hold ma'am, and should be all snug 'til we arrive at Fort Victoria. I must be goin' topsides now ma'am, to see to a few things afore the skipper gets back. Someone will be down later to show you around."

Margaret turned to him, "Thank you so much Mr. Guthrie, you've been very kind."

"Not at all ma'am, please call me 'Billy', everyone else does, and we'll be at sea too long for this 'Mr. Guthrie' stuff!"

"Thanks Billy," Kenneth added, "I'll be leaving the ship as soon as I make my farewells."

Billy turned and quickly disappeared up the companionway.

The farewells were short but tearful, none of them wanting to prolong the agony. The boys were too excited about their new surroundings to get involved with long farewells with their uncle.

Margaret fought to hold back the tears she knew must surely come as she embraced her brother for what might be the last time! Within minutes it was over, and as she watched her brother turn and ascend the companionway, she felt that her last physical link with her old life had been broken.

As the boys raced to explore their own cabin, she looked around what was to be her home for the next few months, and, overwhelmed, Margaret threw herself on her bunk, weeping quietly.

Chapter 4

She awoke to a soft knocking on the cabin door. Confusion slowly gave way to recognition as the sight of her surroundings slowly penetrated her sleepy fog. Remembering where she was, she leaped off the bed to open the door.

She was scarcely prepared for the sight that greeted her, and had to repress a smile. A wiry little man, barely as tall as herself stood before her, a silly grin spread across his gaunt, droll little face.

"George Mullins, bosun, mum, at your service, with the Cap'ns compliments." His high pitched voice well suited his comical countenance and again Margaret had to control her amusement.

"Your lads are topsides, mum, with the Cap'n, an' they 'spec you'll be wantin' some victuals presently! Come along when you've a mind to!"

With that he vanished, leaving Margaret standing at the door with her mouth open. Not wanting to delay further, she quickly turned back into her cabin to refresh herself. Pouring some water from a large, ornately decorated pitcher into the elaborate porcelain basin, she continued to wonder at the luxury of their quarters as she washed. Within minutes she had combed her hair and smoothed out her clothes to make herself presentable.

Arriving on deck she first noticed how quiet it was, in vivid contrast to the tumult when they had arrived. The coolness of the evening tempered the smells, dulling them to a fetid dampness. The lamps had been lit and evening stillness was descending on the waterfront.

"Good Lord," she thought, "I've slept away most of the afternoon!" Only then did she realize the extent to which her pent-up emotions and anxiety had drained her. Her sons spotted her almost immediately and came running to her side.

"Oh come mother," Thomas cried, grabbing her hand, "Captain Holland is showing us his ship!" Approaching the solitary figure on the foredeck, Margaret suddenly wished she had spent a little more time preparing herself.

As the children pulled her closer, the man stood up straight, removing his cap. Bowing slightly, he said, "Good evening Mrs. Manson, my name is Mark Holland. I'm sorry I wasn't here to welcome you aboard earlier." The words rolled out with a resonance and clarity of one accustomed to command, falling on Margaret's ears with a pleasant assurance. Looking up at his face she was astonished to see a young man, not much older than herself. Expecting a much older man to be the owner and captain of such a vessel, she was momentarily at a loss for words. He brushed back a mop of dark curls as he replaced his cap. Margaret felt her heart skip a beat and a flush rise in her cheeks as she looked into his eyes. They were sharp, clear, and the deepest blue she had ever seen. Framed with long, dark lashes and bushy eyebrows, they were accented by tiny, tanned wrinkles in the corners, common to the continual squint of sea-going men.

She forced herself to regain her composure and reply to his greeting. "I'm pleased to meet you Captain Holland. Thank you for entertaining my boys. I'm afraid I have been somewhat of a sluggard, sleeping most of the afternoon away!"

"No problem, ma'am, from my discussions with your brother, I suspect you've been busy lately. As to the boys, they're doin' fine and they've been no trouble at all. The crew has been keepin' an eye on them most of the time and getting along famously."

He turned to the boys, who had been hovering close by, fascinated by their mother's meeting with their new hero. "Can't you boys find something more interesting to do?", dismissing them with a wave of his arm.

He continued "They've already seen most of the ship, so if you'd like, I'd be pleased to show you around." He then pulled a pipe from one pocket and a pouch of tobacco from the other. Slowly and deliberately, he started to fill his pipe, his eyes not leaving hers as he smiled down at her.

"Thank you Captain, I'd like that! My husband is a shipwright you know, but I seldom get to see the details of a working ship." A slight frown flickered across his face, then disappeared as he struck a match and pulled on his pipe. He then turned to her.

"Well I'm sure you'll have ample opportunity to see as much as you wish on this voyage. This vessel will be your entire world for the next four or five months!"

As they started their brief tour, Margaret sensed the deep sense of pride the captain felt for both the ship and the crew. She watched him closely as he moved ahead, his broad shoulders cloaked in a dark blue, double breasted jacket. The brass buttons glistened as he turned to help her as they continued from deck to deck, then later down the companionway stairs. Each time he held out his hand to help her, she felt the warmth and strength through the calluses as the large hand enclosed hers. He smiled again, his teeth flashing white against his dark, well trimmed beard, and Margaret was annoyed with herself for again feeling as giddy as a school-girl.

Before she had a chance to compose herself, the tour

was over. The captain was saying "We'll be sailing on the morning tide ma'am, at first light, so I have some important details to attend to now. Begging your leave ma'am, I'll leave you here in the main salon in the care of our cook, who I'm sure can fix you up with some nourishment!"

Turning toward the galley he bellowed in a deep voice, "Ah Fong! Get your yellow hide out here and meet a real lady!"

A clatter of pots preceded the entrance of a slight Chinese man, who trotted in, pigtail flying, bowing furiously!

"Yessir captain-sir, yessir! How do missee?"

"Mrs. Manson, this is Ah Fong, the ship's cook. Although it's a blow to my ego, he is the most revered and respected man on this vessel! You must remember, that on a voyage of several months, the cook can play a very important part in a person's life! Actually, although I don't like to tell him too often, Ah Fong is one of the best cooks in the business." Turning to the cook, who was still bowing and grinning from ear to ear, he admonished "This is Mrs. Manson, Fong, who will be with us for this voyage. You treat her right or I'll have you strung to the tops'l yard by your pigtail!" With that, he bowed slightly to Margaret and left her standing there, fascinated by this funny little man who obviously wielded considerable power.

"Missee like sit down? Have velly fine loast beef tonight!"

Margaret smiled as she sat at the long table to try some "velly fine loast beef".

Ah Fong continued "You lucky some left, your boys velly hungry, eat like ten men!"   It wasn't long before Margaret realized this was no ordinary ship's fare. The quality and presentation of her meal was the finest she had ever sampled. The meat and vegetables done to perfection, sauces and pastries that would be the envy of any chef. Generous with her praise between mouthfuls, Margaret finally had to push herself away.

Ah Fong kept chattering the whole time, "Not always eat like this, only when in port, good time to get fresh meat and vegetables."

"How long have you worked for Mr. Holland, Ah Fong?" asked Margaret as she watched him pour some tea from a massive tea-pot.

"Oh, many year, missee! He velly good man, good sailor. You likee him." Margaret didn't know if this was a statement or a question, so she declined to answer.

She watched Ah Fong clear the table as she relaxed and sipped a mouthful of tea. She spluttered and convulsively choked it down, "Ah Fong, what is that!"

"Tea, missee," he replied, "you no likee?"

"That's not tea!" she countered.

"Oh yes, missee, is captain's special tea, called 'Lapsang Souchong'. Grown in south part of my country, Fujian Province, not far from Shanghai. Good stuff, but must get used to it. Have many other teas on board if you no likee."

"No, Ah Fong, that's fine. If everyone else drinks it, I'll try at least" she murmured as she tentatively sipped the smoky, tarry tasting brew again.

She lingered for awhile longer, chatting with Ah Fong and sampling the Lapsang Souchong tea, then realizing how late it was, rounded up her boys and chased them off to their cabin.

"Come along Thomas, Andrew. The captain said we're leaving first thing in the morning, and you wouldn't want to miss that would you?"

After settling them down, she retired to her own cabin, her mind awhirl with the activities of the day. A day to remember, she was sure!

Chapter 5

They did miss the departure however, as the day had been too much for them. By the time they awoke, the Shanghai Lady was on a port tack into a northeast breeze, well out from Gravesend. Thomas was still half asleep when he noticed the movement of his bunk as the ship dipped into the swells. Suddenly realizing what was happening, he scrambled to get dressed, waking his brother as he headed out on deck.

The piercing cold of the North Sea wind slapped him in the face as he emerged from the companionway. He felt the deck rise and fall as the Shanghai Lady met the light swells rolling across the North Sea, building slightly as they funnelled into the mouth of the Thames. She moved easily, all sails sheeted taut, pulling together, as she gathered speed toward the open sea. Light clouds of spray flew sporadically over the bow, misting the foredeck. The weak winter sun lay low in the southern sky, providing little comfort against the icy chill. As Thomas buttoned up his jacket and pulled his woollen cap down over his ears, he spotted Alfred Cooper, the second mate, leaning on the lee rail, watching the shoreline and puffing on his pipe.

"Good morning, Mr. Cooper," he cried out.

Alf Cooper turned and chuckled, "Morning? I'm afraid you've slept through the morning lad, it's almost four bells in the forenoon watch! I take it you slept well?" Thomas felt a little sheepish as he nodded, agreeing with Cooper. Not one to let a little ribbing get him down, Thomas continued talking, and before long they were deep in a discussion about the finer points of sailing vessels.

Thomas cast his eyes aloft as he asked "What kind of a rig is she, Mr. Cooper? Mr. Guthrie called her a brig, the captain said brigantine, yet Mr. Mullins said she was a...herm... herma..."

"Hermaphrodite brig?" offered Cooper.

"Yes, that's it! Which one is it?"

"Well, lad," Cooper started, obviously into a subject dear to his heart, "She's all of those, and then some. Those names just mean a certain way the masts are rigged, how many square sails, how many fore'n'aft sails." He paused slightly, gathering his thoughts. "I suppose she'd be called a brigantine now for sure. A hermaphrodite brig usually has a gaff mains'l with a square tops'l above it. We have the gaff mains'l, but we use a fore'n aft sail, a main gaff tops'l above. This gives us better working to weather in lighter airs, but we could change over if we had a mind to."

"It's all so complicated!" noted Thomas.

"Ah lad, you'll get used to it. You see, it depends on where and how you want to sail. Take now f'r instance, you'll notice we only have the for'n'aft sails up now, those four jibs up f'w'd, the stays'ls here between the main and foremast, and the main. That's 'cuz we're beating into the wind. If she weren't quite so breezy, we'd have that main gaff tops'l up too!"

"When do you use the big squaresails then?" Thomas asked.

"Those are the work-horses, but they are only good with the wind abaft the beam, that's behind us, on a run. Later this afternoon, we'll be rounding the point into Dover Straits and start our run down the channel. With this nor'east breeze, most of those sails'll be up and we'll fairly fly!" Thomas nodded and grinned, anticipating the pleasure of such a run.

"You'll get spoiled on this ship lad, 'cuz she'll do things most ships wouldn't even try! You see, when the captain had her built, he wanted her to be fast when running down the trades, yet good for coastal work or beating his way off a lee shore. That's why we have all the extra halyards, sheets and hardware; we can change her rig for the best possible sailing!

As Thomas' eyes studied details Cooper pointed out, he began to understand and appreciate some of the possibilities.

"Come on lad," Cooper offered, "It's as good a time as any for you to start learnin' how it all works!" With that, he started Thomas on a tour of the deck, explaining the terminology and uses for each line and piece of gear. Thomas was fascinated, and a good pupil, a factor that would prove useful to him later.

Mark Holland was pacing the deck near the helmsman, watching the training session in progress with approval. At the same time, his eyes were taking in other things as well, the trim of the sails, the sea condition and the helmsman's course. His attention to these details was rather instinctive and unconscious, as his conscious mind was occupied with the happenings of the previous evening. He was annoyed at himself for assuming when her brother signed them up for the trip that this woman would be much older. After all, she was married with two children, the eldest almost thirteen. Instead of a sedate and mature matron he had expected, he was faced with an attractive, spirited, well developed woman younger than him! His emotions stirred, recalling the firm warmth of her hand as he helped her up the steps. Her rather modest dress did little to hide the curves of her ample breasts, tapering tightly at her narrow waist and flaring again over her hips. By the time he had left her in the salon, he felt he had to escape her flashing smile and sparkling eyes. His thoughts piled up, confused, for it was the first time he could remember being unsure of his feelings and actions. Memories flickered on and off to another time, another place. Dark hair and flashing almond eyes appeared, then faded, leaving feelings of confused guilt.

His attention returned to the vessel, directing the helmsman to turn two points to starboard, starting their slow turn to the south.

"Mr. Guthrie!" he called. "Stand by to set courses!"

Thomas stood back and watched the flurry of activity as the crew prepared to set the large square sails when they had rounded enough to place the wind on their quarter.

One by one, the large canvases boomed into action as they filled, straining at their lines, already notably increasing the ship's speed. As each sail thundered into action, the ship responded with a quiver of delight, eager to be underway down the channel toward the open sea. Thomas finally succumbed to the icy winds, going below, overflowing with news to relate to his mother.

Nightfall found them still coasting down the channel as the crew continued to make the ship ready for the Atlantic. Soon activity on the vessel settled down to a routine that would be maintained for the next few months.

Chapter 6

Two days later, the wind increased to gale proportions. In her cabin, Margaret heard the extra activity on deck as dozens of feet pounded to and fro while sail was shortened and rigging made fast. The wind continued to rise, shrieking through the stays and lines above her, sending a drumming vibration right down to her feet. Staggering out of her cabin, she reeled down the hall to the galley for something to settle her stomach. As she arrived, Ah Fong was calmly sitting in the corner, sipping tea, oblivious to the rattle of pots and dishes that clattered around him.

He jumped up as she entered. "Missee want tea?" he asked.

"Yes please, Fong, maybe it will help my stomach. I don't feel very well."

"Ah so! Then you need Ah Fong special remedy!" With that he scurried around, mixing a brew of steaming liquid in a large mug that he handed to Margaret. "You drink, feel better" he ordered.

Margaret cautiously sniffed at the fumes from the concoction, vaguely familiar, but with an odd, but pleasant aroma. She ventured a sip, and finding it not unpleasant, continued to imbibe the potion. "What is this, Fong?" she asked.

"Ancient Chinese recipe!" he smiled. "Is special tea from ginger root, used much in my country in cooking and for medicines. Velly good for problems here!" he said, patting the front of his apron. In truth, it was good, as Margaret could already feel her queasiness subside, and the warmth dispel her chill.

"I'll have to remember that for the boys in case they don't feel well." she murmured.

"Boys O.K.," Fong countered, "They too busy to feel bad, too much new things to see and do!"

"Yes, they certainly have been occupied," she added, as she steered the conversation to something else on her mind. "I presume the captain has also been occupied, as I haven't seen him at dinner last night, or at breakfast today."

"Oh yes, captain velly busy!" Fong offered, a knowing look in his eyes as he spoke to Margaret. "He not eat here velly much, most-time in his cabin."

"Oh, I see." Margaret replied, feeling somehow disappointed. Her disappointment changed to annoyance as she rebuked herself for acting like a child. After all, she had much more important things to consider.

Her attention turned to Ah Fong as she asked "However do you manage to cook down here Fong, with everything moving about so!"

"I get used to it," he replied, "Learn to move with ship, not fight it!" The conversation continued, Margaret fascinated by this little man whose knowledge and wit was endless. With a well developed understanding of life, he appeared to Margaret more of a philosopher than a cook. In any case, the more time she spent with him the more she felt there was more to him than appeared.

Later in her cabin, Margaret's thoughts were on her husband, Adam, as she wondered how he was managing. She then realized Adam's voyage was still in progress. So much time had passed since he had left, that she often thought of him as already being there, getting things settled for them. Her thoughts wandered, and she found herself comparing Adam to the captain. Shocked at the direction her mind was moving, she leapt to her feet and started pacing the floor, forcing herself to think of other matters. Fortunately, her attention was diverted by young Andrew as he knocked on her cabin door.

"Oh Andrew dear!," she exclaimed, "I almost forgot your classes! Where is Thomas?"

Andrew shrugged his shoulders and replied "I suppose he's up there again working with the men. I don't think he's very interested in this kind of learning just now, Mother." Margaret had made a pact with herself and had forewarned the boys that this voyage was not going to be an idle one. She felt once they were at Fort Victoria, a lot of the boy's time would be taken in helping their father with the running of the farm and other duties. Although they had been told the fort chaplain did manage to hold classes for some of the boys, Margaret felt she could add to their schooling during the many months they would be travelling.

Thomas' education lately had been mainly directed to the shipwright's trade, under the tutelage of his father. He had learned fast, taking an intense interest in the trade, and all things nautical. He had long since surpassed Margaret's fairly extensive knowledge of the tools, materials and techniques required in ships and shipbuilding. His exposure to the crew and sailing of the Shanghai Lady was like an elixir to him, the more he drank of it, the more he wanted.

"Well," she replied to Andrew, "I suppose he's learning a considerable amount about the ship, but we must try to have him carry on these studies as well!" With that she pulled some books from her desk and they both sat down to the task at hand.

Intensely proud of both their children, Margaret was

particularly fond of Andrew, possibly because she had lost most of Thomas's attention to his father. As Thomas and Adam were so much alike and very close, so were Andrew and Margaret. With fair, almost white hair and big blue eyes, Andrew had always been quieter than his older brother.

"Probably more of a thinker," thought Margaret, although Andrew seemed to enjoy things and have a more complete understanding of situations than Thomas ever did at his age. They continued working, Andrew surprising Margaret again at the swiftness with which he grasped the mathematical portions of his studies.

"You certainly are doing well with your sums, Andrew," she complimented him.

"That's the part I enjoy most, Mother," he replied. "I want to be like uncle Kenneth when I grow up, and work with numbers and money!"

Margaret laughed and thought, "I just hope you have the opportunity, Andrew, in this primitive place we are going to!" After a time, they put away the books and just sat there, talking about their new life and what it would be like.

Chapter 7

To Thomas, however, his "new life" was here and now! Farm life on Vancouver's Island was the least of his worries, the last to waste time thinking about. To him, the ship was a living creature whose heartbeat he could feel as she rose and fell to meet each swell or cresting wave. His ear was also becoming attuned to her communications, from the strumming of her rigging by the winds, to the creaks and groans throughout the hull as she strained to keep up with the sails that pulled her. As the days passed he began to feel, sometimes unconsciously, the condition of the seas without even being on deck, by the way she moved. Sometimes a slow and gentle pitch or roll, other times more violent, often shuddering as she crashed into a large swell or dipping into one as she slid down the crest of a following wave. His days were now packed with new experiences. From dawn until dusk he roamed the decks, helping where he could, asking questions, many times getting involved in long discussions about different rigs and rigging, hull shapes and seaworthiness.

About the time the captain was thinking he'd have to put the boy to work to keep him out of everyone's way, Thomas met Jonathan Stone, the ship's carpenter and sail-maker. It was a mutually enjoyable meeting, creating an instant liking of each other from the outset. Jonathan was working one day on the foredeck, wielding a razor-sharp draw-knife on a large spar he was shaping from a long spruce timber. Here was something he understood, thought Thomas, as he introduced himself and offered to help. So it started, a deep friendship between man and boy, drawn together by a common fondness for working wood, and the bond of master and student in a trade.

"As you can see, Thomas," Jonathan said as they continued with the spar, "I've already marked off the taper with those lines. If you'll just give me a hand to turn her in the jig, and clamp it, we'll save a lot of time!" With that, the draw-knife was moving again, peeling off long shavings of the straight-grained wood. They carried on a continuous conversation as they worked, Thomas detailing his brief life history, highlighting his experience and training with his father.

"Well lad," Jonathan remarked, "It sounds like you've had a good start to the trade. Maybe we can carry on with your apprenticeship while you're on board."

Music to his ears! To carry on with the activities he loved so much, while on board a vessel like this was more than he could have hoped for!

"We'll have to do it right though," continued the carpenter. "I'll have a word with the captain. I've needed a helper for some time now, so maybe we can get you signed on proper. There'll be no more wandering around starry-eyed! If you're going to be on my watch, you'll have to step lively, and turn to bright and shiny every morning, or any other time we're needed as far as that goes!"

And so Thomas became an official member of the crew. Jonathan, true to his word, talked with the captain, who after consulting with Margaret, signed Thomas on as apprentice carpenter and sail-maker. They agreed that while Thomas was now a working member of the crew, his wages on arrival at Vancouver's Island would be the return of the passage money Margaret had paid for him. The boy tackled his new duties with an enthusiasm and vigour that only the young can apply. Before long, he was assigned major tasks, which under the master's guidance he completed to the satisfaction of all. The additional duties of sail-maker were new to him, but before long he was turning out small sail repairs, learning the sail-maker's darn, how to whip a rope and make a hand-worked eye on a sail. He studied rigging, learning how to work, parcel and serve both wire and rope. He practiced knots until he could do them behind his back or one handed. All of this he tried to explain and show to his mother and Andrew. Unfortunately, he also called on them to help him practice, until they had to protest that they had their own duties to perform. Margaret was pleased, as it helped her and gave some direction to Thomas' life. She realized that her son would have little taste for farm work once they arrived at their destination.

She mentioned this to Ah Fong one evening after dinner, as she helped him clean up the dishes.

"Don't worry missee, Ah Fong advised, "He very good boy, learn fast, maybe won't have to work farm. Maybe do something else. Jonathan good teacher, he work on this ship when she built. I know him long-time."

At that point, Mark Holland entered, mug in hand.

"Oh, good evening Mrs. Manson" he mumbled. "I didn't expect you to be here, just came down for a cup of tea with Ah Fong."

"Hello captain" she smiled, enjoying his obvious uneasiness at finding her here. "We were just discussing Thomas' work, and how enthusiastic he is about it" she added.

"Oh, he's enjoying it all right," as he poured some tea into his mug, "and doing a find job too, Jonathan has nothing but praise for the lad!"

She caught her breath as she watched his eyes flash brightly when he talked. Forcing herself away from his eyes, she dropped her gaze to his large hands, wrapped around his oversized mug of tea. His voice resonated pleasantly in her ears, creating a vibrating sensation that travelled down through her body. She felt a flush rising in her cheeks, and she blurted out "My, it's terribly warm in here tonight Fong!"

"Not too bad now missee," Ah Fong smiled, obviously aware of her discomfort, and the reason for it. "Get much warmer plenty soon," a knowing glint in his eye.

"Yes," added Mark, unaware of the inference of Fong's words. "We'll be getting into the Tropics soon. Within a couple of weeks, you'll wish it was this cool." He paused, and then added, "Would you care for a stroll on deck, Ma'am, a little fresh air might do you good?"

"No, thank you, Captain" Margaret replied, much too quickly. She instantly berated herself for not having better self-control. "I really should be seeing to the boys and turning in soon myself."

"Fine Ma'am, whatever you think. Good night then." With that he turned and left.   On deck, Mark filled his pipe, pacing back and forth like a caged animal, trying to figure out why this woman annoyed him so much. "Oh well," he thought, "She's not my worry," as he lit his pipe and puffed furiously. Somehow that thought didn't make him feel any better as he continued his pacing.

Chapter 8

Days turned into weeks as the tiny world of the Shanghai Lady worked her way slowly but steadily southward towards the warmer climes and fair winds of the northeast trades. They had passed the infamous Bay of Biscay, well known for its fierce storms and unpredictable weather. Approaching 35 degrees north latitude, almost between the Azores and the island of Madiera, the crew felt they had been fortunate and were looking forward to fair sailing for some time ahead.

It was not to be. Strong frontal winds spawned by a major weather system behind them struck from the northwest. Although they were somewhat prepared by the falling glass and tell-tale weather signs, the ferocity of the squall line shook even the most experienced of them.

Already travelling under shortened sail, the first blast hit them like a brick wall. The fore upper topsail, one of the only two sails left working on the foremast, split lengthwise and exploded like a cannon. The ship shuddered, then heeled over on her port side so quickly they thought she might not recover. She responded to the extra force, driving her forward in a crazy, uncontrolled sleigh-ride down the troughs and through the deep green seas. The noise was terrifying as the rigging shrieked and howled in protest and the remnants of canvas slapped about with an ear-splitting racket. The reverberations travelled down through the hull, almost overpowering the cry of "all hands" as the crew set to their demanding task.

Margaret and Andrew were working in Margaret's cabin

when the first gust hit, pitching them across the small space into the opposite bulkhead. She scrambled to her feet, realizing what was happening as she heard the call for all hands.

"You stay here Andrew, and hold on tight! I'm going to check on Thomas," she cried, staggering about to get her warm clothes on. Anxiety gripped her firmly as she thought about Thomas, knowing the "all hands" call would place him on deck to help Jonathan wherever they could. She reeled down the hall and with some difficulty made her way up the companionway.

On deck, the scene was chaotic. The vessel was leaping and pitching in the mountainous seas, while other waves, impatient with her progress, were breaking behind them, their tops whipped off by the wind, scouring the length of the deck.

The crew knew their jobs, so few orders were required as small groups attended to lines, sheeting what sails were left standing while other men were already aloft, perched precariously on foot-ropes trying to furl the fore lower topsail.

"Let's douse those main stays'ls Billy," she heard the captain direct his mate. "We'll run under inner jib and foretopmast stays'l alone. She's pretty well running hull speed now, hopefully that'll give us some control."

Margaret noticed the two men on the wheel as they laboured to control the ship's wild movements.

A sharp crack detonated above them, and Margaret looked up as an additional clangour of loose metal and wood filled the air. Billy Guthrie was also looking up, and his keen eye narrowed in on the problem.

"Looks like somethin's gone on the fore topmast or upper tops'l yard, skipper" he yelled over the din.

The captain had already come to a similar conclusion and was fast to react.

"Better go aloft Billy, with Jonathan and the lad, and get a line on that yard, in case she lets go!"

Billy moved fast, directing his two work-mates to grab the line and equipment they would need, and started up the weather shrouds.

Margaret gaped incredulously as she watched her eldest son scrambled up the rigging as it swayed and pitched violently.

"You can't send him up there, he's only a boy!" she cried as she turned to face the captain, her hair flying and eyes flashing.

"He's a member of the crew ma'am and he'll go where I send him!" he shot back, obviously annoyed.

"But it's too dangerous! He could be killed... and he's so young!" she protested.

"For God's sake woman," he turned to her, eyes blazing, his voice cutting through her. "Would you get the Hell below and leave this to the crew? There isn't a man aboard that hasn't done what he's doing right now, and probably at a much younger age! I'll thank you to stop meddling in the way this ship is being run!" With that he turned and marched across the deck to help a crewman with a line.

Margaret stood there, stunned, barely feeling the spray as it washed over her, soaking her to the skin. Oblivious to the discomfort, there was no way she could leave while her son was aloft.

Looking up she could see them working, trying to secure the loose fittings on the tops'l yard. She groaned inwardly as she spotted Thomas, hanging on one hand while he helped Jonathan with the other. Another gust hit the ship, and as it reacted, the loose spar swung around, plucking Thomas off his perch, flinging him off as one would flick off a fly.

Margaret screamed as she watched her son cartwheel through the air, down through the rigging to a certain death! Time stood still as her screams echoed in her ears, adding to the tumult of noise around her.

Working on the weather side, Thomas passed down through the rigging of the foremast as he fell to the leeward side. Striking the main stays'l stay, he was deflected forward, slowing his fall, allowing him to grasp a line as he fell. The rope burned through his skin as he clenched it frantically, trying to slow his fall. Finally colliding with the foremast, he flung his arms around it as he found he was still sitting on the main stay. Bruised and badly shaken, he realized he was relatively unhurt. He slowly gathered his wits and cautiously released his death grip on the mast. Trembling severely, he slowly started to make his way back up to Jonathan to complete the task they had started.

Margaret couldn't control herself any longer. She ran across to the captain, hammering his chest with both hands, hysterically screaming at him.

"You monster! You almost killed him! Oh, my God, you almost killed him! I hate you, I hate you!" Sobs racked her body as she clutched at him with uncontrolled anguish.

Mark stepped back, seizing her hands, caught off-guard with her reaction. Realizing her condition, he slapped her across the face, stunning her back to reality.

Turning to the second mate he called, "Alf, get her out of here will you? See her to her cabin and have Fong give her a shot of brandy and make her some tea, then get back up here smartly so we can get this mess under control."

Margaret was sobbing frantically as Alf led her below, feeling a mixture of horror at the near tragedy, anger at the captain and shame at her own reaction.

Chapter 9

The storm raged for over two days, pushing the small vessel at break-neck speeds on her south-west course. For both the ship and her crew, it was an exhausting run. With the initial damage repaired, they continued with sails either reefed or furled completely. Soon, life on board became almost routine as they rushed along on their hair-raising ride.

Mark Holland was pleased with their progress as he came on deck the morning of the third day. The seas had calmed noticeably and the winds had shifted around to the northeast at a more reasonable force, marking the start of the trade winds they were seeking.

The skies had cleared enough for a star sighting at dawn, and later a sun shot. These were the first good sightings he had managed to get for several days, sightings that pin-pointed their position just 30 degrees north of the equator. They had run over 500 miles in the last two days, placing them well ahead of what they had hoped. Dark shadows surrounded his blood-shot eyes as he checked his figures and plotted his position. Few of the crew had much sleep, the captain least of all.

Billy Guthrie, his mate and long-time friend had been watching him, a concerned look in his eyes. Billy's sleep had suffered too, but no matter what time of the day or night he had come topsides, the captain had been there, pacing the deck, helping with the wheel, checking the rigging, always with an eye to the weather.

Billy stepped forward as Mark told him of their

progress during the storm. "That's great skipper, I figure we were pretty lucky, coming through as well as we did. Things could have been a lot worse. I thought for sure the lad Thomas was a goner when that yard took him out!"

"Yes, we were lucky," Mark agreed. "It's a good thing he's so young and flexible, I don't think any of us would've gotten away that easy, at least not without a few broken bones!" Mark shook his head again in disbelief as he recalled the incident. "The lad's got spunk though. Did you notice he didn't quit? Just crawled back up there until they finished the job. He'll be a good man to have around!" Billy nodded seriously, re-living the horror he had felt as he watched the boy fall.

"He'll be a little sore for a while I 'spect" he added. Concerned with Mark's well-being, he continued. "It's my watch now skipper. The weather seems to have settled down some, so why don't you go below for some shut-eye?"

"Thanks Billy," Mark mumbled, "I think I will. Call me in a few hours, sooner if anything changes."

As he turned and left, Billy moved to check the helmsman's course, still thinking of Mark. "Bloody fool won't turn in until he's written up his log and done all his bloody course calculations" he murmured to himself. He had worked with Mark for almost twenty years. He thought back, recalling how they had both shipped out as boys on an old bark skippered by Mark's father. They had worked the South China Sea, down to Australia and back to India. Mark had always been the serious one, studying navigation, mathematics and all the subjects that were still a mystery to Billy. Over the years, a bond had developed between the two men as they worked, played, laughed and cried together. Mark's all-consuming desire to succeed and eventually own his own ship had driven him to challenge impossible odds, involving both of them in a few situations from which only mutual trust, teamwork, skill and experience allowed them to escape.

Billy's thoughts snapped back to the present as he bellowed to his watch, "Come-on lads, the picnic is over! Let's get some sail up and get the Lady moving again!"

The crew worked with a will, relieved that the storm had subsided, looking forward to the clear sailing of the trade winds. Before long, the large main and main tops'l were set, followed by the large square sails. One by one they unfurled, booming into action as the wind inflated them. Sheets and braces were adjusted to rob the wind of as much energy as possible, pushing the craft faster on its journey.

The storm eased over-night, also easing the ship's violent motion. Margaret awoke with a voracious appetite and could scarcely wait to get some breakfast. She was finishing a large breakfast with Andrew as Ah Fong bustled about, pressing them with more treats. Margaret felt almost ashamed as she wolfed down her food, the first in three days. She hadn't realized how weak she was until she swung out of her bunk that morning. Her legs were wobbly and getting dressed was a real chore. Besides the constant, violent action of the ship for the past three days, she had been worried sick about Thomas and was still in a state of shock over his near disaster. Andrew had seen none of the events, so he carried on as if storms were an every-day occurrence. Once over the initial shock, Thomas had bounced back and carried on. He was kept too busy to think about it much, and too exhausted after his long watches to let anything interfere with his sleep. Margaret had to refuse again as Ah Fong pressed even more food on to her.

"Please Fong, if I eat another bite, I won't be able to move!" Ah Fong fussed around, concerned about her health, scolding her for not eating recently.

"Missee go for walk now, top-sides. Get fresh air and sunshine. Velly nice weather now!" He noticed the pained look on Margaret's face and added "Billy on watch now."

"Maybe I will" she said, somewhat relieved at Ah Fong's words. She looked at the little Chinaman again, wondering at the keen perception of this man. As she came on deck, she immediately felt better. The sun warmed her skin, adding to the internal glow of a good breakfast. Billy spotted her right away, giving her a cheery greeting. She moved over to the big man as he leaned on the taffrail, puffing on his pipe.

"Good morning Billy" she answered as she took up position beside him, turning to let the sun beat down on her face. "It definitely is much warmer weather today" she added.

"Sure is ma'am" he agreed. "Should be like this for some time now as we catch the trades. Hopefully, she'll stay like this until we get down to the southern oceans." He stepped forward briefly to bark an order to a seaman then turned to her saying "Glad to see you feeling better ma'am, we were a mite worried about you."

"I guess I'm just not used to it all yet Billy, especially the violence of a storm like that" she said, feeling a tremor pass through her body as once more she recalled the terror.

"Well, no need to worry ma'am, you've got a good ship under you, with one of the best crews and captain afloat!"

She snorted and mumbled something about the Captain that Billy didn't hear, but could guess it's nature.

"Don't you be too hard on the captain ma'am. It's a damn lonely job, beggin' your pardon, but Mark is one of the finest, both as a captain and as a man!"

"But anyone who would send a boy up there" she cried, pointing upward to the foremast, "to take those risks..."

Billy didn't let her finish. "Hold it ma'am, maybe we'd better get somethin' straight right off! You talk about risks, if he hadn't done what he did, it would have been a bigger risk. If that spar had cut loose, God knows what could have happened. It could have dropped, taking God knows what with it, then killing who knows how many on deck.... maybe even yourself. A loose spar on deck can do a lot of other damage that might have endangered the ship. No, someone had to go up there. The rest of the crew had their hands full, so it was up to Thomas, Jonathan and me." He chuckled as he added "And I don't think you should talk about Thomas as being a 'boy' anymore. I figure after that chore, he's all growed up now, and as good a man as most. Besides... most of us were younger than he is when we started, even Mark!"

She thought about his words, and although painful, they did make sense. However logical, they did little to ease her pain or lessen her hatred of the captain. "I'll just be glad when it's all over Billy, when we arrive at Fort Victoria."

Chapter 10

A more deliberate routine returned to the ship as she devoured the miles towards the equator. As the days passed, the sun grew noticeably warmer, relieved only by the constant breezes that pushed them. The cloudless skies and empty horizons offered nothing to attract the eye or interest the mind, so the ship's company turned to within their little world, occupying their time with watch duties and what entertainment they could muster.

During her tours on deck and conversations with the crew, Margaret saw all forms of crafts and hobbies that the men worked on during the time they were not on watch. She was intrigued by the scrimshaw work, delicate drawings and designs scratched into bone, ivory or whale's teeth to form all manner of useful articles from buttons to pastry cutters. The woodcarving and whittling also fascinated her, as some seamen produced beautiful or often-times whimsical figure from rather ordinary looking pieces of wood. What interested her even more, possibly because Thomas was now learning it, was the beautiful work done with ropes and rather plain looking twine or string. Jonathan, a master at the art, had shown them how various combinations and series of knots can develop to form either a very useful or delicately attractive art object. The sail-maker had examples of intricately woven ropes, handles, bags, covers for other objects, all fashioned from the common hemp and twine available in his rigging loft.

"I can see now" offered Margaret, "who has done all the fancy work I see all over the ship!"

"Yes," Jonathan admitted, "But it's not only good to look at, it serves a useful purpose."

Thomas hung on his every word, obviously idolizing the man, trying to garner a new lesson from everything he said.

As the days passed, Margaret saw little of the captain, but learned a little more about him each day during her little chats with the members of the crew. Rather than the usual feeling of resentment towards ships' captains, and especially ships' owners, the crew held him in high regard, with a feeling of respect and even comradeship. Although the discussions and anecdotes gave her a better understanding of the man, she gleaned very little information about his past. She couldn't decide whether they didn't know much, or just would not say anything. As she sat reading or sewing in her cabin, she felt irritated by the apparent conflict of her hate for the man, and the undue amount of time she spent thinking of him. She hated to admit that a small glimmer of respect for him had appeared, a glimmer that appeared to grow a little each day. She resolved that she would have to face him and clear up their differences, at least in her own mind.   H e r opportunity came that evening. She had deliberately come on deck when she knew he would be taking his sextant sightings on some evening stars. The air was warm, but refreshing in contrast with the torrid sun that had beaten down on them all day. Light airs moved the ship silently along, only a slight ripple of her wake audible from the deck. The sunset was hypnotic, casting a calm stillness over the vessel as everyone moved very quietly and suppressed their conversations to a hush.

She watched the captain as he braced himself against the starboard taffrail, sextant in hand, peering at a star above the western horizon, barely visible in the glow of the receding sun. As he turned to write down his sightings in a notebook, he noticed Margaret watching him. A momentary feeling of confusion passed through him, not knowing what to expect from this volatile woman. She looked peaceful enough tonight he thought, so he offered a smile and greeted her.

"Good evening, Mrs. Manson. I hope you're enjoying this pleasant evening".

"Thank you, yes, captain, it is lovely!" she returned, her initial plans and enmity forgotten. She continued "Just what do you see through that thing captain, and however does it tell you where we are?"

"Well it's quite simple really," he answered, feeling more comfortable with a subject he could discuss. "We know where the sun and stars should be positioned at any given time of day, information recorded in the nautical almanac. By measuring the angles and calculating our position relative to the stars, we can then determine our location on the chart. The sextant just measures the angles or heights of the stars above the horizon. Once we know that, and the time at which we take the sighting, we can calculate the rest."

She watched his face as he talked, fascinated by the sparkle of his eyes and flash of his teeth, contrasted by the glow of his tanned skin in the deepening sunset.

"Would you like to look through the sextant?" he offered. "You'll find it's not really very interesting."

"Oh could I?" she asked, now totally involved in the process. She moved closer as he showed her how to hold the sextant and peer through its small telescope eyepiece. He moved behind her closely, holding her left hand with his to steady the instrument, explaining how to adjust the scale with her right hand. As he moved his right arm around her, he drew closer and Margaret could feel the heat of his body penetrate her clothes and smell the heavy, manly scent about him. Her heart quickened, and she felt a flush rise in her cheeks as she tried to concentrate on what he was saying. Her body was tingling and her legs felt weak as he moved back and forth around her, trying to explain the details. Just as she thought she might faint, he broke away, obviously disturbed and aroused himself by the proximity of their bodies. The lull in the conversation was welcomed by both of them as he returned the sextant to its case and took it below for safe-keeping in his cabin.

He returned shortly, fumbling with his pipe, again going through the ceremony of filling, lighting and puffing, a ceremony he used whenever he needed time to think.

Soon, they had both regained sufficient composure to continue their conversation, although with an underlying feeling neither of them could understand.

They talked well into the evening, each fascinated by the other, as the ship continued its southward trek. The helmsman, standing at the wheel, suppressed a smile as he witnessed these events, feeling almost cheated as all he got from the conversations was a low mumble, punctuated at intervals by laughter.

Ah Fong, standing in the shadows forward of the mainmast, smiled knowingly and went below.

Chapter 11

The taffrail log ticked off the miles steadily as the weeks turned into months. Time became meaningless as their passage was tallied by landmarks rather than man-made increments. These land-marks, visible or not, became major milestones in Margaret's ship-board life. Names like Tropic of Cancer, Cape Verde Islands and later the St. Peter and St. Paul Rocks, all sounded so foreign and exciting to her as she was told of their passing.

They recognized a much larger event on the day they crossed the invisible line of the equator. This event stimulated a small celebration by all aboard including a few pranks by the crew to initiate their newest recruits to Neptune's realm.

Margaret loved it all, and always enjoyed joining in the festivities both in the larger events like this or the sing-songs and story telling that could develop at any time on deck during quiet times. Although they were not involved with the work, both she and Andrew joined in with the sea shanties sung during many of the strenuous duties on board. She could see how the rhythm and cadence of the songs helped coordinate the crew's efforts.

She particularly looked forward to the quiet evening talks with Mark, as they idled away their time on deck, marking the passage of the sunset. The days were hot, as the fiery tropic sun blazed down on them, broiling the decks like a stove-top. It became almost unbearable in the sun, and only slightly more comfortable in her stuffy cabin or the stifling heat of the salon, next to the galley. In her mind, this was the excuse she used for her enjoyment of her evening forays, during the period of cooler air and fresh breezes.

Mark enjoyed similar feelings as he too looked forward to the cool breezes at sunset. He would watch her hair flash gold and copper in the glow of the descending sun as she recounted stories of her childhood, her family and especially her brother. Mark noted very little was said about her husband, Adam, and he did little to encourage more. He couldn't help wonder however, what type of relationship they had, and as he grew to know Margaret better, he grew more and more envious of Adam.

The more they talked, the more Margaret realized he knew a lot about her, but she knew very little about him. Oh, there were many stories, stories of adventures and voyages to far-off places, his escapades with Billy, details about the ship, but never anything about his childhood or his family. When she pressed him with specific questions, they would be passed off as unimportant, or he would change the subject to something else. She was also puzzled at her own outspoken approach to him, and how easy she found it to sit and talk for hours while they devoured mug after mug of his infamous tea. She could not recall ever being able to talk to Adam like this, and began to resent her husband's straight-laced and business-like approach to their relationship.

One sultry evening, well off the coast of Brazil, a heavy rain squall descended upon them. It was a welcome change from the torrid heat of the day, and when many crew members rushed on deck to strip and enjoy the shower and wash their clothes in the fresh water, Margaret was obliged to go below. As she descended the companionway, she collided with Mark, who was on his way up.

"I thought you'd be topsides, enjoying this shower after all the heat today" he asked.

"I would" she answered, "But I'm afraid the crew would be a little embarrassed to have a woman on deck just now, to say nothing of my feelings."

"Of course" he murmured, realizing the situation. "Well, if you wish, we can watch the squall pass from my cabin windows, without bothering the crew." Without thinking, she agreed, anxious to see the private sanctuary of this mysterious man. He opened the door, and stepping aside with a theatrical flair, bowed and waved her inside.

As she entered, she suddenly realized just how little she knew about him. The cabin was large, running the full width of the vessel at the stern. The overall impact of the rich interior took her breath away as her eyes scanned the room. The bulkheads on each side were filled with books, all stowed neatly in shelves, held in place with removable teak cross-bars. The panelling on the walls glowed with the golden sheen of a hand-rubbed, oiled finish. It was similar in style to the wood in her cabin, but obviously had been hand-picked for particular grain patterns in the shimmering Burmese teak. She crossed the luxurious carpet to his navigation area, where a chart was anchored to the large table, surrounded by the tools of plotting and navigation. Other charts and reference materials were neatly stowed in cleverly designed racks. Another large table dominated the centre of the cabin, surrounded by several chairs, all ornately carved with oriental figures. Soft light from a large hanging brass lamp cast a glow over the area. The opposite side was more of a personal nature, including a small wash stand, mirror, hanging locker, and in the corner close to the stern, a small bed. The large windows in the transom were tied open, allowing the cool breezes and fresh air from the rain to waft through the cabin.

Margaret rushed over to one of the windows to look out. "My goodness, you have the best view in the house" she laughed.

"As befitting a man of my status" he returned, laughing with her.

"I had no idea Mark, your cabin is absolutely lovely!" She felt strangely at ease as she stood there beside him, looking out the large transom windows over the receding ocean. The main part of the squall had passed, only light showers remained as the broken clouds flashed fragments of sunlight over their foaming wake. As they watched, the sun dipped to the horizon, peeking under the remaining clouds and painted the wave-tops with highlights of red and gold.

Margaret, held spellbound by the striking interplay of colours, breathed a heavy sigh as the last light faded and the tropic night closed over them. She felt Mark's closeness, and as she turned to face him, her hand brushed his. A thrill shot through her like an electric shock as they stood, almost touching, face to face. Before she could recover, his arms were around her, his lips on hers. The brief instant of shock melted quickly in the heat of his kiss, and she eagerly responded. Her heart pounded, feeding the fervour that gripped them, each feeling the eager release of pent-up energies. His tongue probed hers as she opened her mouth with a moan, consumed by her feverish desire. Hands groped wildly, then more tenderly as they explored each other's body. Something in the corner of Margaret's mind told her this was wrong, but the rest of her body and spirit cried out that this was what was meant to be. Their eager bodies tingled and skin became flushed as new areas were discovered and explored. His fingers fumbled briefly with the laces of her dress and in seconds it fell. She helped with the rest of her garments as he unbuttoned his shirt and trousers, dropping them to the floor. Their naked bodies touched, melting together. His kisses smothered her as his lips explored down her neck, dipping further into the deep valley between her breasts, caressing the soft mounds, finally nuzzling the erect nipples that waited in feverish anticipation. They moved to the bed, toppling into it in a fervid embrace. She moaned ecstatically as he delicately touched and stroked her body, adding fuel to the already fiercely burning fires. The passions built and just as she thought she could wait no longer, he entered her, tenderly at first, then passionately as they eagerly clutched the other's body. All the pent-up feelings and desires of months surfaced, firing the flames to an incandescent, seething climax, racking their bodies with spasms of relief. Physically and emotionally spent, their moist bodies lay entwined, breathing heavily, as they let the cool night air drift over them.

Mark was the first to move. Stepping out of bed, he padded across the room, naked, opened a small locker, and removed a bottle of sherry and two glasses. Returning to the bed, he poured them both a drink, and offered one to Margaret.

"Madam . . ." he began.

"Really Mark," she interrupted, smiling demurely, "I would think we should be on a first-name basis by now."

He laughed, that wonderful, deep-throated laugh that Margaret had grown to love.

"Yes, I suppose you could say that," he chuckled. "Well Maggie . . ."

"Maggie?" she exclaimed! "Where did you get Maggie?"

"Why, don't you like it?" he asked.

"No . . ., I mean yes, it's quite alright, it's just that nobody has called me that since my father died, years ago."

"Well then, Maggie it is! Madam is much too formal, under the circumstances. Margaret seems much too lady-like, now that I know what a little vixen you are . . ." as he leered down at her body " . . . and Mrs. Manson tends to remind me of an unpleasant fact we will both have to face." The last comment didn't escape her, but oddly, it didn't upset her.

"I know Mark," she murmured, "I should feel ashamed and horrified at my actions tonight, but I don't! You've shown me a love I've never had, feelings and emotions that have never been aroused. All this, and yet I feel calmer and more at peace with myself than ever before. I'm glad it happened, and as long as we're together on this ship, I'm going to make the most of it!"

He moved to her, eyes moist in the dim light, and wrapped her lips in his. The taste of sherry heightened the sensation as they moved together. They made love again, slower, more deliberate, with a poignant tenderness that left them both drained.

Chapter 12

It was as though Margaret had passed another major landmark in her life. Her entire outlook was altered; she became alive again to the world around her. She arose each morning feeling more alert and driven with purpose than she had in years, retiring at night with a genuine feeling of accomplishment.

The love between her and Mark flourished, continuing to grow with an intensity neither could deny, both willing and eager to enjoy the present and not be concerned about the future.

The weeks slid by as they continued their journey down the coast of South America, every day bringing them closer to the day of reckoning.

One day, as Margaret moved down the passageway to the salon, she heard voices, talking in Chinese! Knowing Ah Fong was the only Chinaman on board, it piqued her curiosity. As she entered the room, Ah Fong was just finishing what he had to say, to none other than Mark Holland! They both turned as she entered. Mark was obviously distressed, and quickly excusing himself, left for his cabin. Margaret stood there, mouth open in disbelief.

"Fong," she said, gathering her wits, "You never told me Mark could speak Chinese!"

"Well, I suppose Madam," he answered, without a trace of accent, "That is because you never asked."

Margaret's mind whirled as the words penetrated her already confused mind. She looked at the little man, standing there, smiling politely.

"Wha . . . what did you say?"

"I believe you heard, Madam."

"But where . . . how . . . what happened to you? Where is the 'How so, Missee,'" she stammered.

"I suspect Mrs. Manson, that it is time you learned that things are not always what they seem," he continued.

"I can see that" she mumbled, getting more confused by the minute. "Where did you learn to speak like that, and why this charade?" she asked.

"It's a long story, Mrs. Manson, and I feel the Captain should be the one to tell you" he offered. With that, he turned back to his little galley, leaving Margaret standing there, mouth agape.

She whirled out of the salon, and in seconds was pounding on the Captain's door.

"Come in, Maggie," she heard him call. She opened the door, stepping inside. "I've been waiting for you," he said. She was visibly distressed.

"Just what is going on Mark?" she asked. "First I hear you speaking Chinese to Fong, then he talks to me like a proper English gentleman!"

He reached out, taking both her hands in his. With a light kiss on her pouting lips, he directed her over to a chair.

"Sit down Maggie, I suppose it's time I explained a few things to you, things I should have told you a long time ago." She sat down and watched him, her curiosity now burning. He paced the floor, slowly repeating the ceremony of pulling out his tobacco pouch, filling his pipe, carefully tamping it down, then lighting it, puffing furiously as he gathered his thoughts.

"I suppose it all started when I was born" he began.

"It usually does" she smiled, instantly regretting her sarcasm.

"Be quiet woman!" he shot back. "Its hard enough to get this out! . . . As I was saying, my Mother died when I was born, a fact that impacted my life substantially." He paused, puffing nervously on his pipe, creating clouds of the aromatic smoke.

He continued "You see, my Father was a sea-faring man, away from home for months at a time. With my Mother dead, my Father had no choice but to hire a wet nurse for me, one who could later care for me while he was away. The lady he picked for this chore was his number one concubine . . . his mistress." He paused, watching Margaret's face, trying to gauge her reactions to his tale. "As it turned out, this woman was also Ah Fong's mother."

Bewilderment still dominated her mind as Mark's story unravelled. As she struggled to keep up with his words, the meaning of the last statement slowly penetrated Margaret's baffled mind.

"You mean . . ." she started, trying to fit the puzzle together.

"Yes, Maggie, Ah Fong is my half-brother!"

Margaret's thoughts were now in a complete turmoil. Mark puffed a few more times on his pipe and continued.

"The early part of my childhood was entirely Chinese. Fong and I were raised as brothers, learning the language and customs of the streets of Shanghai and Wusung. Our uncle, one of my mother's brothers, was in the silk trade and we lived most of the time in his home in Shanghai." He paused again, totally immersed in his memories as he tried to put together his story. "You see, 'Shanghai' means 'above the sea' or 'by the sea', even though it's several miles up the river from Wusung. This probably accounts for my obsession with the sea and ships. As we grew up, we often travelled with uncle on the Grand Canal, and river routes from Foochow to Nanking, learning other dialects and trading skills in the silk and tea business." He stopped, eyes focussed on some distant shore. "Margaret, you've no idea what it's like to sail up the mighty Yangtze River!"

She could see the obsession he had for ships and the sea, as well as the love he had for his childhood home.

"Later, my Father realized what was happening and hired a tutor, one of the finest available from Europe, to continue our education. Thus, we both learned English, mathematics and everything any British school has to offer." Margaret remained quiet, fascinated by this unfolding tale, not wanting to break his train of thought.

"When I was older, I started travelling with my father on the ships." He stopped, temporarily lost in thought. "I suppose that's about the time I met Billy. We shipped out together for the first time with my father and have been together ever since." He paused, and Margaret was afraid he had finished.

"What of your father, this ship, and why your little charade?" she asked.

"My Father loved the sea, but never had his own ship. All his earnings went to support and educate Fong and me. That must have cost him a lot, both in money and lost dreams. I always felt guilty for that. I could see the sweat and time he put into his job, making fortunes for the East India Company, the Jardines, and Symes, Muir and Company, with nothing for him but small shares of the profits. When I was eighteen, working as first mate with my Father, we were caught in a typhoon off Malaysia in the South China Sea. It was probably the worst storm that any of us had ever seen, and that's when Billy and I both learned the importance of obedience and teamwork on board a ship. For three days we fought to stay alive and keep the ship afloat. In the end, we managed to save the ship, but lost my Father." He paused again, in deep thought. Margaret could feel the pain of years pour out into the silence.

"I continued working for the company, eventually skippering several of their ships for a few years after that. With the knowledge and training I had received from my uncle, Billy and I worked out a few schemes on those trips to make a little extra money for ourselves. At first it was just pocket money, but during the last couple of years, I made enough to build my own ship."

He paused again, his gaze proudly scanning the cabin, soaking up the pleasures of his proud achievement.

Again Margaret realized how little she knew about him. "What of your other friends, other childhood friends. Did you have any young lady friends?" she asked, suddenly curious about the more personal side of this man.

He looked at her briefly, then quickly looked away, a small twinge of guilt pulling him.

"What is it Mark? Did I touch something?" Margaret asked, now even more curious.

"No," he answered slowly. "Well, yes . . . I suppose there was one . . . but it never amounted to anything, no real commitments." As he paused, Margaret realized that would be all she would learn about that subject.

"While I was at sea with Billy," he continued, picking up the threads of his story, "Fong stayed in Shanghai, learning other trades which have served him well. The pidgin English he uses is just a helpful little trick he learned years ago. You see, no one trusts a Chinaman who goes around talking like 'a proper English gentleman' as you put it.

Later, after my ship was built, Fong decided to come with me, signing on as cook."

Mark started pacing the cabin, disturbed by the memories. "By the time I returned, I had been away for four years, and that was the first news they had about my father's death. The loss was too much for 'Mother', as I called her, and she died within a week. When the ship was launched, she was christened in honour of the finest woman I had ever known, the 'Shanghai Lady'."

Chapter 13

Margaret sat quietly at first, confounded by the story and all its implications. Then the questions came and they talked long into the night, Mark relating more anecdotes of his childhood, filling in the gaps in his unusual background. As she listened, she heard the answers to many of the questions and little puzzles that had plagued her since she had arrived on board.

The following day, she cornered Ah Fong in the galley, and was again rewarded with a rich tapestry of details; enough to make her head spin.

The stories continued from that point on, intertwined sagas of two lives with a most unusual background. She particularly enjoyed the evening she got both of them together to relate old events. Annoyed occasionally by periodic lapses into Chinese, punctuated by bursts of laughter, she realized there would always be a relationship here she could never be a part of as well as small personal details she would never learn. As the time passed, a bond of kinship grew between Margaret and the two men.

The ship moved on, and day by day, they grew closer to the southern tip of South America and the dreaded Cape Horn. The atmosphere on board grew serious, as the temperature dropped and they experienced more frequent storms and contrary winds. Crew members grew more solemn as the ship was prepared, cargo and rigging checked and double-checked, making ready for the rounding.

The actual rounding was an anticlimax. They carefully and peacefully sailed past the desolate headlands on their starboard beam, encountering only light winds and reasonable seas. They were soon in the Pacific Ocean, another major milestone in their journey. Margaret realized their northerly progress now was the last long leg of the voyage.

Another event, however, had seized Margaret's attention even more. Rather it was a non-event, as her monthly "women's problem" did not appear. During the following few weeks, as they continued northward into the tropics again, she was gripped by anxiety, her fears finally confirmed as the second month went by without a sign.

For several days, she stayed below, fretting over this new problem. She had mixed feelings as she imagined various scenarios during which she would explain the situation to Adam. No matter how logical they seemed to her, she knew he would not accept any excuses she could make, and she feared the possible actions he might take. At first, the thought of being thrown out in a strange country frightened her, then it became tolerable as she considered the shame she would feel once her sons discovered the truth.

She finally became resigned to the fact that they would all know once the baby started to show, so she would just have to face each obstacle as it came.

She decided, however, not to tell Mark. Hopefully he would be gone again shortly after their arrival, and would never have to know. The thought tore through her, body and soul, leaving her shaken and desolate.

Their love for each other had grown beyond anything they could have foreseen, clouding their reason and overshadowing the future they would have to face. She finally composed herself, resolving to take each day as it came, hoping for the best.

She rejoined the ship's company, and again began to enjoy the adventure as each passing day brought them closer to their destination.

Her manner, however, was not as spirited as it had been, and her attitude somewhat subdued.

Mark took this as a sign of her concern with her reunion with her husband, not suspecting the deeper problem.

He too, was troubled, as he carried on his day-to-day duties, checking off each day's run on his charts. He had never felt so deeply for a woman before. Little flings and one night stands in far-off ports were easy to forget once he was at sea with a fine ship under his feet.

This was different, and he knew it wasn't going to be easy, leaving this woman to God knows what kind of a life.

He began to look at his own life a little closer, and consider what his future held. He had always had some driving force, some goal to strive for, if only the next port of call. He found his perspective now changed, his past achievements fading in the glowing light of Maggie's love.

To divert his attention to other matters, he spent more time pouring over his charts and reference material, updating them with new information he had picked up in London.

Late one evening, a soft knock on his door distracted him.

"Enter" he called out. Margaret stepped over the threshold, a tired and haggard look on her face.

"Maggie, dear!" he greeted her, "Aren't you a sight tonight? You look like you're carrying the problems of the world on your shoulders!"

She smiled in return, already feeling his vitality picking up her spirits.

"Oh Mark, I'm just concerned with our new life at Fort

Victoria. The more I think about it, the more I feel I'm not ready for this."

"Oh Maggie, of course you are" he replied, obviously trying to make light of their personal involvement. "You've got the spirit and strength to do anything you want! Regardless what may happen, I picture you as a survivor!"

Maggie chuckled at this and replied. "I know what you mean Mark, but I'm not sure I like your choice of words, especially that 'survivor' part. It makes it all sound so difficult and primitive."

She paused a moment, then continued. "You've been there before, what can you tell me about Vancouver's Island and Fort Victoria?"

"Well, Maggie, you've come at a good time." He gestured towards the navigation table and said, "I was just updating some charts of the area from my notes, so I can show you some areas we'll pass, and your final destination."

Maggie watched intently as he traced their proposed route from the Pacific Ocean into a wide strait leading around the southern tip of Vancouver's Island.

"You can see," he continued, "Vancouver's Island is quite large, about two hundred and forty miles long, and up to seventy miles wide, almost a quarter of the size of Great Britain."

She nodded with some surprise, not realizing the island was that large.

"Once we round this point," he continued, pointing to the chart, "we'll turn east along this strait."

She interrupted "That sounds like a Spanish name. I thought this was British territory."

He laughed and replied, "Yes, it is now Maggie, but the Spaniards were here first, and you'll find a lot of Spanish names around here. Actually, 'Juan de Fuca' was a Greek, or Cephalonian pilot whose real name was Apostolos Valerianos, reputed to have been travelling on a Spanish ship some two hundred and sixty years ago up as far as this area. Not much is known or recorded about him, but after this strait was 'rediscovered' by the Spanish ships in about 1774, it was named after him. The Spanish made several voyages up from Mexico before Captain Cook and William Bligh arrived in the "Resolution" and "Discovery" in 1778, then later in 1792 by George Vancouver who gave the island his name."

He became quiet, gazing at the chart, studying the irregular coastline intently.

"What's the matter, Mark?" she asked, curious as to his sudden silence. "Is something wrong?"

"No, no . . . I'm sorry," he continued, "I was just thinking of something . . . a story I heard years ago during my travels."

He reached over to a shelf and pulled out another chart and unrolled it on the table, anchoring its corners down with small lead weights. As he adjusted the lamp for better light, she could see it was a map of the entire world, covered with arrows and notes drawn on all the ocean spaces, marking trade winds and favoured routes of travel.

"When the Spaniards first came to this area, about three hundred years ago," pointing to Mexico and the north part of South America, "they plundered great civilizations, destroyed their temples, burnt their libraries, and stole all their treasures. For years, virtually hundreds of tons of gold and silver were taken, melted down into bars or Spanish coins, and put on Spanish ships to be shipped back to Spain."

Margaret listened intently, fascinated by the story, the man and the ambience of the situation.

"You see, all the gold had to be carried overland to either here or here," pointing his finger to the ports on the Caribbean coast. "Then they could load it on their galleons for shipment back to Spain." He paused a moment, searching the western coastline of Mexico, then continued ". . . right here, see? San Blas, Mexico. In 1773 the Spanish built the first ship on the west coast, the 'Santiago', which sailed into this area in 1774."

He smiled at her, and, putting his finger to his lips, he continued, "The first official ship that is! Also, there were other Spanish ships which had sailed around the Horn, and had gone on to discover the California area. There is some speculation about earlier ships, but no official records. You must realize that records do not become officially established or even recorded until the ship has returned and reported about their voyage. You see, Juan de Fuca's discovery of this strait was known at that time, but little was known about where it led. Some thought it could be the "North-west Passage" or the fabled "Straits of Anian" which many were convinced was a connection between the Pacific and Atlantic Oceans."

Margaret watched him, realizing he was building up to something. His hands swept over the chart, pointing out various features as he continued. "The whole point of the story, the way I heard it, is this. There are some who feel that the Spanish had earlier ships, and that at least one, loaded with treasure from the west coast, sailed in this direction trying to find a shorter route back to Spain! An immense gamble for the right man, so considering the possible gains, a bold, adventurous captain might try it . . . but he lost the gamble. The ship never arrived in Spain, so God knows what happened to them. It's either at the bottom of the ocean or wrecked along this coastline close to where you are headed right now!

Margaret sat there, stunned by the possibilities.

"You mean there could be . . ." she started.

He interrupted her, "Now Maggie, don't get too excited, it's just an old story, probably no truth in it at all. We only know the Spanish kept returning to this area for quite some time, and after a few encounters with the British in the late 1700's they left and haven't been here since."

Margaret studied the chart, noting the Spanish names of Juan de Fuca, Esteban Point, Flores Island and Port San Juan, as her imagination wandered.

Chapter 14

At the same time, several thousand miles away, Adam Manson examined the same coastline. Rather than looking at a chart, he was standing on the deck of the "Falmouth", gazing over the Strait of Juan de Fuca trying to pick out details on the distant shoreline. As he watched, it would fade from view, reappear, then fade again, obscured by the rain that increased by the moment. Soon everything was cloaked from view.

He had arrived on deck a short time earlier to see the great point of land called Cape Flattery and Tatoosh Island on their starboard side, the last landmark before turning east towards Fort Victoria. He could make out the large mountain range in the background with magnificent snow covered peaks appearing occasionally between the clouds.

The wind had increased over the past hour, bringing the rains and hastening nightfall. Adam buttoned his coat tighter and adjusted his oilskins for better protection against the sheets of rain that now pelted down on them. Rain conceived in the tropical areas of the Sandwich Islands, growing and developing over thousands of miles, building to a major storm front as it approached the island coastline.

The crew worked quickly, shortening sail as the gusts grew stronger. However eager the crew felt with only about seventy miles to go to their destination, they did not relish the thought of arriving in the middle of the night during a major blow. The captain ordered sail shortened to storm conditions, both to ease the handling of the vessel and to delay their arrival until daylight hours.

Adam quickly stepped down the companionway into the fo'c'sle, out of the wind and rain. He then pulled a small package from deep inside his coat and unwrapped the oilskins that contained his diary. Once protected from the weather, he jotted down some notes on the passing landmark, noting the date and time of day, as it truly was a momentous occasion to be turning onto the last run!

As he carefully rewrapped the small book and replaced it in his pocket, some yelling and activity on the foredeck snapped his attention back to the ship, drawing him quickly topsides. Torrents of rain pounded him, the individual drops searing his skin like stone pellets.

The blasts of wind hit more frequently, until there was no relief between the gusts as the crew worked desperately to furl the large sections of canvas. As they attempted to douse the fore topsail, the halyard had jammed at the foot of the mast. The men above were helpless as another crew below struggled to free the halyard, and still control the straining sheets and braces.

Another gust pummelled them, as the wind screamed with anguish through the rigging. Adam suddenly realized the screams came from one of his crew-mates, as he saw him lifted off the deck, his arm caught in a bight of the starboard sheet that had been slack up to then.

The scream echoed in his ears as he watched in horror as the man rose, then stopped abruptly, arrested by another line. The scream also stopped, but the arm continued to rise, torn violently from the man's body. Blood spurted, exploding into red clouds, spraying the length of the deck as the man fell, his limp body crumpling onto the deck with a sickening thud.

Nobody moved. Time stopped as they all gaped, unable to accept what had happened.

Sharp commands aroused them, as the Captain tried to direct their feverish attempts to control the barque's onward flight.

In the confusion, other lines had worked loose, and Adam rushed forward to help, trying to avoid the grisly sight of other crew members removing the man's body.

Another line had caught under the bow of the longboat tied down on the deck, lifting it and snapping its lashings. The smaller but very heavy craft now careened dangerously back and forth across the deck as the vessel rolled and pitched violently in the building seas. Adam grabbed an extra line, approaching the boat with caution, waiting for an opportunity to get the line around it to slow it down. Another man approached from the opposite side with the same idea. Sheets of salt spray battered them, clouding their vision with stinging drops. They continued to waltz around the boat timing their movements to get as close as possible, yet quick to jump out of the way when it skidded off in another direction.

Adam was the first to get a line on it, then suddenly wished he hadn't. Before he could snub the line, the boat took off again, jerking him with it. He quickly loosened the line, again regretting the move as it burned through his hands, then stopped. He grabbed it again, only to see the boat heading towards him. He dropped the line quickly and again jumped out of the way.

The wind was deafening as it roared and shrieked through the maze above them. The barque reared and plunged as they slowly turned eastward, then eased slightly as the helmsman turned to bring the wind over the stern to ease the ship's motion and help them secure the boat. She turned too far, rolling to her port side in an uncontrolled gybe, skidding down a massive swell, the wind now pushing from the starboard quarter.

Adam grabbed the line again, frantically looking for a spare pin on the rail or a cleat to snub it down. He felt the ship lurch and he started to slip easily across the deck. He looked down, suddenly realizing he was sliding through the gory pool of blood!

With no time to recover, he gained speed and was flung across the deck, towards the careening boat. The port rail was now awash, the vessel pushed to her limit. Adam and the boat both arrived at the rail together, colliding simultaneously as they were both lifted by the momentum and flung overboard, lost to the sea.

The other crewman rushed to the rail, trying for a glimpse of Adam, but could see nothing in the gloom but angry seas and breaking whitecaps as the barque crashed onward.

Chapter 15

Mark rolled up the chart, stowed it away, and pulled another one from the rack.

"To get back to your original question Maggie," he continued, "This should give you a better idea of the area around Fort Victoria."

She watched as he unrolled a small chart showing a diagram of the harbour and surrounding land.

"Why is it called "Cammusan Harbour" she asked, reading the notes on the side of the map.

Mark replied, "James Douglas, the Chief Factor for the Hudson's Bay Company told me it was the original Indian name. It has also been called Camosan or Camosack, but they all call it Fort Victoria now."

He continued, pointing out features on the small map. "You can see there is good sheltered anchorage here, close to the fort, and deep enough for ships of this size or larger. When I was here last year, only the Fort and a few other small buildings were finished around this area, but I'd wager there will be a lot more by now. Most of the building activity was going on in the outlying areas, at the company farms. That's probably where you will be living."

She shuddered as she heard those words, the stark reality of her future again hitting home.   M   a   r   k continued, recounting details of the areas as he jumped from chart to chart, island to island.

"It all looks rugged and primitive now Maggie, but there's a big future in this country, and fortunes to be made!"

The words echoed in her head as she tried desperately to raise her enthusiasm to meet the challenge.

The miles dropped behind them as the weeks passed. Once more they crossed the equator, but this time without the festivities of the first crossing as they were now all experienced sailors with at least one crossing to their credit. They now counted time backwards, crossing off each day from their estimates of the number of weeks before they arrived.

Margaret worked constantly on small projects to keep her mind occupied. She continued with Andrew's lessons, which kept her busy and provided a satisfactory outlet for her frustration.

One afternoon Andrew arrived, a smug look on his face, with his hands held behind his back.

"I've got something to show you Mother, but first you must give me a large sum to do," he said. The request puzzled Margaret at first, but as it was part of his studies, she wrote down some figures.

Andrew took them and, removing his hand from behind him, produced an odd looking wooden rack on which dozens of coloured beads were strung. With this strange device in front of him, he started to move beads back and forth on their slides, glancing at the figures she had written. Before she had a chance to inquire what he was doing, he wrote the answer down and handed it to her. She looked at the figures, adding them up to check his answer.

"That's correct!" she exclaimed, "How in the world did you do that?" she asked.

"Ah Fong taught me" he answered, "This belongs to him. He calls it an "abacus". He says they all use them in China. Come and see, Ah Fong can show you!" And with that he was off down to the galley.

Margaret followed, fascinated by this device, and once more by the little man that owned it.

This started a whole new diversion, as Ah Fong taught them both the art, or was it a science, of using the abacus. Ah Fong's fingers would fly, the beads clicking up and down, solving the most complex problems Margaret could provide.

Margaret found herself spending more time each day in the galley with Ah Fong, drinking large amounts of tea, listening to more tales of his childhood as well as learning other interesting facts and philosophies. She started learning the tricks of using certain spices and herbs in the cooking, many of which were totally unknown to her.

What fascinated Margaret the most was Ah Fong's philosophy and outlook on life, as well as his endless wit. As she was exposed to his teachings more and more, she felt herself change, a profound sense of inner peace developing within her. Mark had noticed the change, liking the difference. Often Margaret would quote some of Ah Fong's maxims in their discussions, causing Mark to laugh.

"I see Ah Fong's been teaching you the wisdom of the old ones. You've learned well and I must say I approve! Fong studied the old writings for many more years than I did, mainly during the years when Billy and I were out to sea. He has turned into quite a philosopher."

Margaret agreed, "But you must admit Mark, his approach makes a lot sense, and I do feel so much better within myself since I've been listening to his ideas."

"Yes, that's true," he replied, noting her recent air of self-confidence.

He then moved across the cabin to his chart table, leading Margaret by the hand.

"I'm sure you won't mind if I change the subject Maggie, but I have something here you might want to see." With that he pointed to the chart, to a cross marked just south west of the Strait of Juan de Fuca.

"There is our position at our noon-sight today, we should be well into the strait by dawn tomorrow!"

Margaret's hand flew to her mouth, stifling a small cry, as she stared down at the chart.

"So near..." she looked up into his eyes, feeling her legs go weak. "Oh Mark, I had no idea we were so close, the time has moved so quickly these last few weeks!"

"Well, we've made pretty good speed with these westerlies recently, and they should hold steady until we're there" he replied, now feeling cheated of more time with her.

"Oh God Mark, I don't want to loose you now! What am I going to do?" she asked, her eyes brimming with tears.

"I don't know Maggie," he replied, "The only thing you can do is take things one day at a time. Who knows, this could be the beginning of a wonderful new life for you."

They came together, embracing with the desperate fervour of those who are parting, possibly forever. Their love exploded once more as they clung feverishly to each other throughout the long night.

Chapter 16

Both Margaret and the boys were up before dawn, tired but elated with the prospect of their arrival. Ah Fong had laid out a large breakfast, but they were too excited to eat.

"You eat good now, might be long time to next meal" he chattered. "Going to be big day for all of you!"

They did manage to put away most of it, surprising themselves with their own appetite once they got started.

Thomas went off to attend his duties, while Margaret and Andrew bundled up to go on deck as first light broke.

The eastern sky glowed ahead of them as the west winds pushed the vessel briskly along a wide strait, bordered by land on either side.

Looking to the south, Margaret was stunned by the sight. The wide body of water merged with the distant shoreline in the morning mist, melting upward into the hazy blue hills. The not yet risen sun was already casting a rosy flush on snow capped peaks of the magnificent mountain range dominating the southern shore, stretching as far as she could see.

Her eyes followed the land towards the sun, pausing directly ahead, where the silhouette of a majestic snow-covered peak dominated the eastern horizon. She gasped in wonder as the sun finally broke over the mountains, beaming golden across the water, silhouetting the forward rigging of the ship in a crazy cat's-cradle of lines.

Her gaze moved on, to the nearest shore on her left. Tree covered slopes rose from the water, some steep, some sloping gently as they climbed to high mountains cloaked in clouds. The shoreline presented a rugged, rocky facade, tormented by the crashing waves she could see in the increasing light.

She moved aft to where Mark stood, close to the helmsman.

"Well, Maggie," he asked, "What do you think?"

"Oh Mark, it's all so beautiful and yet so frightening. It looks so rugged and untamed!" she exclaimed.

"It is that, my dear. That's why we're here, to try to tame some of it!"

She gazed intently along the coast. "I don't see any sign of life, no houses or anything."

"You won't see much out here, not yet." he explained. "Nobody lives out here, except maybe the occasional Indian camp. We'll be coming up to Sooke Harbour pretty soon, then you'll see one of your stalwart Britishers at work.

"Who is that?" she asked.

Mark chuckled softly as he replied, "None other than Captain W. Colquhon Grant! I met him during my last trip. An officer and a gentleman to be sure, but honestly, I don't believe he's the type to survive this kind of life. Apparently, he had arrived here just before I met him... in '49 I think, coaxed out with some other settlers by the Hudson's Bay Company. You see, Maggie, the more people, the more labourers you bring, the larger the land grant you can get, so Grant arrived with eight labourers. He also brought coach and carriage harnesses with him, but there aren't any roads yet to speak of." He smiled again as he continued, "And in typical British tradition he brought some cricket sets with him, although so far I haven't seen any cricket fields built. Officially, he was brought out as Colonial Surveyor, but he resigned last spring. I think he's rather disillusioned and will leave before long."

Margaret smiled as she listened, vividly picturing the English gentleman, completely out of his element.

They coasted along, moving even closer to the island's shoreline to their right. They revelled in the warmth of the sunny weather as the miles slipped by. The massive boulders and cliffs at the edge of the sea gave way to higher hills behind, eventually rising to a low mountain range that disappeared in the distance. The lower levels were covered with grasses, shrubs, and interesting trees with reddish coloured trunks. On the higher slopes, the vegetation changed to larger coniferous trees... firs, hemlocks and cedars.

By noon they had passed the place called "Sooke", with rocky shorelines alive with colonies of sea lions, either swimming around for fish, or basking on the rocks in the spring sun.   Turning almost north towards another headland, Mark moved closer to Margaret as he murmured "That's it Maggie, almost dead ahead!"

She concentrated her attention in that direction. "But I can't see anything" she cried.

"Not yet," he replied, "The Fort is on the inner harbour, and you won't see it until we're almost there. Off to the left, up ahead, is the harbour called "Esquimalt", another Indian name, I think."

"You appear to know a lot about this area for the few times you've been here, Mark," Margaret noted.

"That's part of the job," he explained, "I have to meet people, know the area and the names, as well as knowing what's going on if I want to do any business, to keep this ship busy!" He paused, then pointed off the starboard bow. "See on that point of land almost dead ahead, you can see one of the first farms established here by the Beckleys. They have been producing wheat, beef and butter for years now, stocking ships that arrive, and even shipping up to Alaska. One of the first things we'll be doing after we unload is replenishing our fresh food supply."

Margaret could see the Beckley's fields in the distance. The surrounding area was spotted by small clusters of trees, many covered with blooms. The gentle farm landscape contrasted sharply with the rugged beauty of the coastline they had been passing and in some ways, reminded her of the rolling hills and farms of home.

"Where are you planning to go after that Mark?" she asked, almost afraid of the answer.

"Just a short trip first, around that point of land to the right, and up the coast a few miles to a sawmill to load lumber for San Francisco, then returning here."

Margaret thought about this, wondering when she would see him again, if ever. She had become accustomed to the ship-board life, and did not relish the thought of her future prospects on the farm.

The miles slipped by, and later that afternoon, the "Shanghai Lady" drifted through the narrow entrance to the harbour. Within minutes, she had rounded up, sails doused, and the anchor cut loose.

As the clangourous rattle of the chain died out, a muted hush descended on the ship like the final curtain of a great play.

They had arrived.

Chapter 17

Fort Victoria—1851

The silence exploded into a flurry of activity throughout the ship. Sails were furled, lines made fast, and the smell of burning hemp signalled the end of the long journey as the anchor rode hissed through the hawse-pipe. The long boat was rigged and lowered over the side. Margaret's eyes scanned the scene around her.

The "Shanghai Lady" was anchored in a small, perfectly sheltered harbour, almost totally enclosed and protected from the winds of Juan de Fuca Strait. Large flocks of ducks and various sea birds scattered the water's surface, staying a safe distance from the ship. Her gaze finally approached the shoreline.

The Fort itself dominated the scene, standing high above them on the top of a rocky bluff. Roughly 300 feet square, the stockade stood almost 20 feet high, consisting of cedar logs driven into the ground. A two-storied bastion stood at the south-west corner, closest to them, cannon bays peering out over the harbour.

Few other buildings were visible. A scattering of small huts and log cabins faded off to the south, lost in the bushes that ran up to the end of a shallow bay. North of the fort a few more cabins sprawled amongst the trees. The bare rocky shore of a long inlet extended north out of sight. The Songhees Indian settlement occupied the west side of the inlet, dominated by a large longhouse and surrounded by small cabins, shelters and salmon drying racks along the shore.

The raucous cries of sea-gulls filled the air as they moved quickly from the drying racks to circle the ship, looking for hand-outs.

Her attention drawn back to the ship, she watched as Mark and several of the crew were already pulling briskly towards the small wharf near the fort, where two men waited their arrival. She watched until they landed, greetings echoing in the small harbour, then they disappeared up the hill to the fort.

Looking around again, she wondered where Adam was, shivering slightly in the fading daylight as she thought of the unpleasant scene that loomed nearer.

Many hours and many mugs of tea later, her patience was slowly wearing away.

"What in the world is keeping them, Fong?" she asked, feeling more frustrated with each passing minute.

"Calm yourself, Madam," he replied, pouring more tea. "These things take time, and they have a lot of news to catch up with! I would suggest you have some supper, they could be there until late tonight."

After supper, as some crew members came off watch and arrived to eat, Margaret made sure Andrew was safe in his cabin then returned to talk with Ah Fong.

Later that evening, small noises and muffled voices interrupted them, as the group returned to the ship. Controlling her urge to rush out and talk to Mark, Margaret sat patiently while the crew secured the boat, tended to final details, and left an anchor-watch topsides. Margaret looked up as footsteps shuffled down the companionway and approached the salon.

As Mark entered, she sensed a change in the man. The

fatigue of the long voyage tugged at his broad shoulders and cast shadows around his deep blue eyes. His face was sombre with a determined set of his jaw as he cast an apprehensive glance at Margaret and called out to Ah Fong for brandy for them all. She studied his face closely, and a sense of foreboding shivered through her body.

"Margaret" he croaked, then stopped, visibly shaken. He cleared his throat, then continued. "Margaret, I'm afraid I have bad news."

A hundred thoughts rushed through her mind at once. "Adam!" she cried, "Has something happened to Adam? Where is he?"

"Oh Maggie, I'm so sorry" Mark continued, obviously uncomfortable with this unpleasant chore. "Adam never made it" he blurted out, "He was washed overboard with the longboat on the last day, just as the "Falmouth" was entering the Strait of Juan de Fuca. It was just at nightfall, a squall hit the ship, and they haven't seen him since."

As the words penetrated her consciousness, she shivered violently, trying to deny their meaning. Her mug rattled on the table and she clutched it frantically with both hands, trying to control the shaking. She was barely aware of Mark peeling her fingers from the mug, replacing it with a glass of brandy, urging her to drink it. She gulped it down, aware of the raw, burning sensation as it flowed down her throat. In the seconds it took for the sensation to grow, her thoughts cleared and a dozen questions came and went, unanswered. The desired yet dreaded meeting with Adam would never take place, yet another, greater problem had taken its place.

Suddenly her thoughts focussed on something else and she cried out. "My God! Our savings! We won't have enough money! Where..."

"Maggie, it's all right," Mark interrupted, "All his tools and the freight you shipped out with him is safely stored in the Fort."

"No, no," she cried, "You don't understand! Except for the small amount I brought, Adam had all our savings, and all the money from selling our business."

"Well then, I suppose it will be in his personal kit, which is also stored with his equipment" Mark offered.

"Oh Mark, I wish it were that easy" Margaret explained. "You see, before he left, we talked about where to put the money. We didn't want to take a chance on it being lost or stolen, so we decided he should keep it with him all the time. To do that, I sewed all the money into his coat, throughout the padded lining."

"You mean..." Mark started.

"Yes, don't you see? . . . it's all so ironic, Adam never lost the money, but both are lost to me." She buried her face in her hands, sobbing violently. Mark put his hand on her shoulder, trying to comfort her. He looked at Fong with a bewildered look, neither knowing how to handle the situation.

"Come along Maggie," he offered. "Drink up another tot of that brandy, and I'll see you to your cabin. I think a good night's sleep will help, and we can sort this out in the morning."

Sleep did not come easy for her. Too many thoughts raced through her mind, too many questions, and too many uncertainties. Her feelings over the loss of her husband were mixed. Rather than grief, a sense of shock filled her as this circumstance was totally unexpected. As she considered this lack of grief, she realized she really hadn't loved Adam, at least not in the way she had grown to love Mark. She suddenly realized she was free to love Mark, free to do whatever she wanted, then just as suddenly felt guilty as she remembered Thomas and Andrew, and the more significant problem of survival for them all! Her business sense took over and she was considering various options when the brandy induced fog overcame her, dropping her into a deep, undisturbed sleep.

Chapter 18

Pounding footsteps penetrated her sleepy fog and she rolled over, trying to bury her head in her pillow. The ship was quiet, and utterly still. Something was different. It took several seconds before she realized it was the first time in months that her bunk wasn't moving. It felt so good, she turned over again, trying to go back to sleep. The footsteps pounded again, this time bringing her wide awake as the problems she faced returned.

Activity on deck increased, as preparations were made for unloading the freight. Muffled orders mingled with the cries of seagulls, clanging of chains and the barking of dogs on the opposite shore. Further sleep now hopeless, Margaret decided she might as well get moving as well. After dressing, she headed down the hall to have her breakfast, as she had done every morning for several months.

This morning, however, was different. No longer concerned with the every day ship-board life, and the anticipation of their arrival, the larger problem of survival took precedence. Fortunately, Margaret's resolute nature and inborn business sense took over. She had done it before and she could do it again.

Her memories drifted back to when they had first started their business back home in Greenock, and how they had struggled for so long before making a decent living.

This was different, she realized. There wasn't even an established village and reasonable population here to support a business. Yet something inside told her that this too represented opportunity. Surely the population would grow, and to be one of the first businesses established should assuredly be an advantage. What business? Where would they live? What of Adam's contract with the Hudson's Bay Company? Her mind was reeling with these questions as she entered the salon.

"Good morning, Madame" Ah Fong smiled at her. "I trust you slept well?" The smile abruptly left his face. "Please accept my condolences, I'm so sorry your plans haven't turned out well for you."

"Thank you, Fong. Yes, I slept very well, thanks to you and Mark." she said sarcastically. "Two brandies! ...I must say!"

"Sometimes is necessary, missee!" Fong smiled, lapsing into his Chinese sing-song voice.

She laughed, already feeling better as Fong hustled into the galley to fix her breakfast.

Few words were wasted during breakfast, but later, over tea, Ah Fong asked about her future.

"What are you planning to do now Madame?"

"Fong, for God's sake, please stop calling me 'Madame'. Call me Margaret or Maggie or whatever!"

"I think," Ah Fong replied, "that under the circumstances it would not be appropriate for me to use such a familiar name, so I will refer to you as 'Mrs. Manson' until such time I can think of a more apt title."

"Oh, Lord!" Margaret fretted, once again amused with Fong's sense of propriety. She continued "I really don't know yet what I'm going to do, Fong. I'm certainly not returning to London. I've decided that this is our new home, so we'll just have to make the best of it! We don't even have a place to stay, or much money, but I'm sure something will come up."

"Madame, if you don't mind me saying so, you're much better off than most settlers that arrive here."

"In what way Fong?" she asked.

"Well, for one, I assume you do have some cash, which most of these people don't have when they arrive. Most arrive with the clothes on their back and a five year contract as a farm worker."

Margaret thought about that, thinking about Adam's contract. Only their own hard work, saving and planning over the years had changed this situation, providing them with a much better foundation on which to build.

Ah Fong continued. "Second, you have a shipment of freight on board that I assume consists of goods required by people starting out here. That alone represents a fair opportunity."

"Why, of course!" Margaret interrupted. "We can..."

"Please, Madame, I'm not finished! Third, I understand you also have a large shipment of goods and tools in storage here that arrived on the "Falmouth", the first shipment sent out with your late husband. Surely all of that means you are already a relatively wealthy lady here!"

Margaret sat there, letting Fong's words sink in. "Relatively wealthy" meant nothing to her as she had no idea yet what it would take for them to carry on here. Mentally, she began to calculate values of goods and tally up the various tools and equipment. Ideas formed and possibilities developed, but she realized she had to know more about Fort Victoria and the people around the area.

Her thoughts were interrupted as Mark entered the room. Surprised to see her up and around, he mumbled some greetings, obviously feeling ill at ease.

Margaret didn't notice. Consumed with her prospects for the future, she attacked with enthusiasm.

"Mark, when can I go ashore and meet some people and see the area?" she asked, her face lit up, eyes flashing.

Mark gaped at her for a moment, surprised by the question. Expecting a woman grieving over her loss and fretting over her future, here was a spirited girl anxious to get on with the job at hand! He should have known better, he thought. He smiled at her and replied.

"Well Maggie, we can get you to shore any time you're ready. I'll be going ashore myself in a few minutes to discuss the cargo manifests with Mr. Douglas, so you can come then if you wish."

"Good!" she replied. "I'll be ready right away, I just have to talk to the boys first," and with that she was off.

The discussion with the boys was short. Thomas took the news like a man, but Margaret could see he was visibly shaken. Adam and Thomas had been very close, working together for so long. The time Thomas had spent on the ship with a new instructor and new mates helped ease the pain.

Andrew was a real surprise. Margaret expected someone so young would be despondent or at least cry over the loss of his father. Instead, Andrew took the news in a very calm manner, as if it happened every day. He accepted the situation and was eager to get back to whatever he was doing. At first, Margaret was shocked at this response, then realized Andrew had never really spent a lot of time with his father and had not seen him for over six months, and she supposed his memory was already fading for his father.

After the boys left to go on deck to watch the unloading,

Margaret scurried around, making herself presentable to meet the dignitaries ashore.

Arriving on deck, she found Mark and several crew members waiting for her. Ah Fong came rushing out, issuing orders about getting some fresh meat and supplies. Margaret felt a renewed sense of excitement and adventure as she stepped from the ship that had been her home since leaving England over four months ago.

Chapter 19

As they rowed ashore, Margaret again surveyed her surroundings. The land around the harbour glowed in the golden radiance of the spring sun glistening brightly off the water, warming her spirits. Large flocks of ducks moved slowly away as they approached, then suddenly took flight, their wings beating the surface of the harbour with a high pitched cadence. The rugged beauty took her breath away as massive rocks rose around them from the harbour. The craggy sentinels held dainty halos of wild flowers and blossoming shrubs.

"Spring certainly comes much earlier here" she commented, the warm April sun reminding her more of the summer weather back home.

Within minutes they had arrived at the small dock and were on their way up the path to the Fort. The main gate, overlooking the harbour, consisted of a wall of twenty foot high pickets, much like the rest of the stockade. Furious barking of the Fort dogs greeted them as the gate swung open, revealing a large area, like a village square, surrounded by buildings. A couple of large, two story dwelling houses faced them from the rear wall, while six more buildings of equal size, three on each side, stood against the side walls. A smaller building was tucked into the rear left corner and a bell tower stood in the centre of the enclosure. In contrast with the natural beauty outside the Fort, the entire area looked dirty and unkempt. The passing winter and spring rains had turned the area into a quagmire, and constant traffic had churned the mud on the pathways to an almost impassable state. Picking their way along some planks that had been thrown down, they were escorted to one of the main buildings, through the large area used as the main trading floor and storage area. The room was divided into small sections piled high with trade goods, tools, blankets, clothes, sacks of flour and beans. Barrels of salt beef and salmon from Fort Langley lined one wall, while the rear of the room was piled high with bundles of furs. The musty stench of the hides permeated the room, mingling with the fishy smell of the salmon barrels. Navigating around the piles and through the assortment, they entered another room, into the presence of the Chief Factor.

James Douglas rose from his desk and approached them, his tall frame slightly bowed. Rather dark complexioned with thinning hair, Margaret guessed he would be in his late forties. A grave looking man, he carried himself with an air of dignity, an air slightly tarnished by the rather seedy looking London clothes he wore.

Mark greeted him enthusiastically, then turned to formally introduced Margaret.

Mr. Douglas bowed slightly at the introduction. "Mrs. Manson, I'm sorry your arrival at Fort Victoria could not have been a happier occasion." His dark eyes looked directly into Margaret's and she felt warmth and compassion she later learned was not often visible in this rugged man. He continued "But you are most welcome. If there is anything we can do to help, please don't hesitate to ask."

"Thank you, Mr. Douglas...." she replied, not knowing where to start.

He didn't give her the chance as he continued. "First, we'll have to find lodging for you and the boys, then we can discuss your future, your husband's contract and see where we can help you."

Finished dealing with Margaret, he quickly turned to Mark. "Now Mr. Holland, let's get at those papers so your crew can unload right away, I'm sure you won't want to stay around here any longer than necessary!"

Feeling a little rebuffed, Margaret relaxed and looked around the room that served both as an office and domestic purposes. Her attention had been held by Mr. Douglas since they had arrived and she now realized the other person watching her from the corner desk was a young woman! The first woman she had seen in over four months! Anxious to talk to her, Margaret moved closer and introduced herself.

A petite young girl with dark hair and flashing eyes, Cecilia Douglas was Mr. Douglas' eldest daughter, who often helped him with clerical work and acted as his private secretary. From this meeting, an immediate friendship developed, Margaret's straight forward, spirited approach complementing Cecilia's animated youth.

The girls were deeply engaged in their gossip and chatting when Mark finished his business and asked if she wanted to return to the ship.

"My goodness no!" Cecilia cried out. "She has just arrived and she hasn't seen anything but this dirty old fort!" She turned to her father and pleaded "Father, could we borrow John for awhile so I can show Mrs. Manson around?"

"I think that's a capital idea" he replied. Turning to Mark, he added "It looks like you've lost your passenger for the afternoon, Mr. Holland. If you wish, you can return for her later, and you are all invited to be my guests for dinner this evening."

Looking rather upstaged and disappointed, Mark thanked the Factor and, bidding farewell to the girls, returned to his ship. Cecilia rushed about and within minutes had commandeered a young clerk in the service, John Ogilvy, who saddled up some horses for them.

It was all Margaret needed to reinforce her decision to stay. The weather was perfect. The sun provided considerable warmth to their spirits as well as their bodies, while light breezes off the ocean refreshed them from time to time. For hours they rode through acres of clover, fields filled with wild flowers, and along trails that skirted the cliffs and beaches. Even the most peaceful of these vistas was enveloped in a cover of sound. Sounds of bees working their floral routes, sounds of the remarkable variety of birds, from the tiny humming birds strumming from flower to flower, to the raucous cries of the gulls and herons by the cliffs near Beacon Hill.

Cecilia proudly showed Margaret the area where her father planned to build a new house for his family, just past the low mud flats at the east end of the harbour among tall stands of stately oak trees. She excitedly tried to explain the house with its two stories, glass windows and all of the fine things you might expect in an English manor back home.

Margaret saw for herself the areas Mark had described, the glorious views from Beacon Hill, the beauty of Clover Point and the lush productivity of Beckley's farm.

At the farm they were treated with tea and fresh baked bread, fresh butter and preserves from local berries and fruit. Margaret revelled in the luxurious change from ship's fare, but enjoyed the discussions that followed even more. She gained an insight into the type of life they lived here, the products and equipment they needed, as well as a better understanding of the workings of the "Puget Sound Agricultural Company". The Puget Sound Agricultural Company was a company formed in London several years before to manage the farms and encourage colonization. The shareholders were almost exclusively Hudson's Bay Company officers, so the policies followed those of the Company. They were attempting to set up a system similar to what had worked in Britain, with indentured servants or labourers working under a five-year contract for the farm manager or bailiff, who acted in the role of a country squire.

The Hudson's Bay Company owned all the land around the fort and as well, had claimed most of the good land within five or ten miles of the fort for their farms. They were large farms, from several hundred to a thousand acres each, which limited the farming of small areas by individual settlers.

Margaret began to see a pattern, a monopoly held by the Hudson's Bay Company that she would have to contend with if she expected to start any private enterprise. Some ideas began to develop, and not wanting to waste an opportunity, Margaret mentioned some of the equipment and supplies they had brought. She was pleasantly surprised at the response and agreed to meet with them at a later time to discuss possibilities.

Chapter 20

Upon returning to the Fort, Margaret was surprised to find the Shanghai Lady tied close to the shore, hard against the rocky outcroppings. To steady her from the wind and current, long lines ran from the bow and stern to trees on shore and to iron rings anchored in the rock outcroppings near the Fort. A long heavy plank bridged the gap between ship and shore, bouncing and bending precariously with the traffic as the cargo was walked across.

Cecilia explained, "Many of the ships do that if the tide is right. This afternoon the tide is quite high, so they have a few hours to tie up close by the rocks and unload directly to shore. It's a lot easier than bringing it all ashore in boats and canoes."

Margaret watched as the crew worked along with the men from the Fort, helped by dark skinned workers who she learned were either local Songhees Indians or Kanakas from the Sandwich Islands.

Cecilia proved to be an excellent guide, showing Margaret the area around the Fort, as well as the buildings within the actual Fort enclosure. In addition to the chief factor's house, there were large store houses, a carpenter's shop, a blacksmith's shop, Indian shop, a "Batchelor's Hall" and a kitchen/mess-hall in the rear corner. Margaret was fascinated by this complete "village" within the confines of the stockade.

Completing their tour, they noticed the unloading activity had ceased and the Shanghai Lady was being towed back to her original anchoring spot. Realizing how late it was, Cecilia clutched Margaret's hand and led her back to their house.

"Oh Margaret, how the time has flown, we've had such a wonderful afternoon! I must go and help mother prepare dinner as our guests will be arriving soon. Please come to meet mother, you can freshen up there."

They went in, chattering all the while about their outing, Cecilia's lively enthusiasm sweeping Margaret along. Once inside, the aromas of fresh baked bread, roast and vegetables permeated the kitchen. A short dark-haired woman was bustling around, obviously in control of the situation.

Cecilia pulled Margaret along like a new playmate and presented her to her mother, Amelia Douglas. Shorter than Margaret, Amelia's stocky frame displayed the strength and energy she was known for. Margaret felt the warmth and kindness in her dark eyes as they talked and had a cup of tea together. Teasing Cecilia about her laziness during the afternoon, Amelia directed Cecilia to get busy and help her sister set the table. She then turned back to Margaret, quietly continuing with their conversation. The more they talked, the more Margaret liked this woman, as she represented the strength and capability Margaret most respected in women, in contrast with some of the cringing flowers she had seen back home.

Their talk continued until James Douglas arrived with Mark and some other men. Shortly after, other guests arrived and the meal was served.

Mark's eyes flashed across the table at her and his warm smile filled Margaret with an intense longing. She could scarcely wait to tell him of all her activities this day, but controlled herself, listening to the conversations, learning of the day-to-day activities of the colony.

Margaret was impressed and intrigued by the stories told of the Fort's beginnings and the early days of trading with the local natives. The Company's business also took them on excursions to Fort Langley, several miles up the Fraser River. She listened carefully as they related their experiences, the difficult times as well as humorous events.

The guests included Roderick Finlayson, a man in his early thirties who had been at the Fort since it was built, and who had assumed command of the Fort seven years previous. Also present were the Fort Chaplin, Reverend Robert Staines and his wife Emma. Margaret learned that Rev. Staines held school in the Fort for some of the boys, but as the evening wore on, she developed a dislike for the man, who appeared to her to be all show and no substance. His wife Emma was the epitome of a proper English lady who apparently spent much of her time instructing the young girls of the Fort in proper manners and deportment. Margaret sensed that Emma disapproved of her sitting there, chatting, laughing and enjoying herself, rather than mourning the loss of her husband.

It was also apparent that Emma was not very comfortable in the presence of Amelia Douglas. She learned later that Emma Staines did not really approve of all the Indian and half-breed wives and daughters in the colony and had made it her mission in life to "civilize" them all.

The evening proved entertaining and informative for Margaret, and when the men retired for brandy and cigars, the girls continued with further tales of gossip and local colour.

It was late that evening when the affair finally broke up, Mark borrowing a lantern to light the way down to the boat for Margaret. The moon provided more light as it glistened across the still harbour, silhouetting the ship and casting long shadows on the shore.

Margaret watched his dark outline as Mark rowed the boat, both completely involved with their own thoughts. The pain and turmoil that had started the day seemed so distant now as Margaret calmly reviewed the day, seeing a plan and purpose forming out of the confusion.

Once on board, Mark led her to his cabin, locking the door behind them. He wrapped his strong arms around her, holding her tight.

"Maggie" he said finally, "You can't stay here! Please come with me, marry me!" He kissed her feverishly, and she felt herself start to weaken, returning his kisses.

"Oh Mark, I love you so much, but I can't leave! Don't you see? This is my future home here, not sailing around the world all the time. I have my boys to care for and a new life to build!"

"But what are you going to do?" he asked, frustrated. "Where are you going to live?" She paused a moment, strengthening her resolve as she stared up into his deep blue eyes. How easy it would be, she thought, just to give up and go with this man she loved so much. The spirit within her rebelled and she felt her confidence return. She smiled at Mark and continued.

"I haven't been idle today while you've been playing at ship's captain" she started, joking with him. "I've already arranged to stay in the Fort until I can build my own house. I'm moving off the ship tomorrow, so you can get on with your job. Mr. Douglas told me there are lots held by the Company that I can either rent or purchase. The boys are capable enough to help me clear some land and build a house."

"But how are you going to live?" Mark asked, concerned with her combination of innocence and fighting spirit.

Margaret was quick to reply.

"My first business tomorrow is to arrange for the sale or trade of some of our supplies for a horse. That will supply us with transportation and help in clearing our lot. We also have some items needed by Beckley's farm, so we won't be going hungry."

"But that won't last forever, Maggie," Mark protested. "You must have some income to carry on."

"Well . . ." she said, now on uncertain ground, " . . .I'm still working on that. I have a few ideas, but there are more details I haven't quite figured out." She paused a moment, staring blankly at Mark, an idea forming deep within her.

"What's the matter Maggie?" Mark asked, sensing the change.

"Mark . . ., how would you like to go into business with me?" she asked, not yet sure of what she was proposing.

"But why . . . how? I already have my own business, right here on this ship!" he replied.

"But that's just it, don't you see?" she cried, the concept becoming clearer in her mind as she continued. "These people need supplies, hardware and items they can't grow or manufacture locally. You have a ship that can bring them in from other areas. My part of the business will be to run a store and sell those items here."

Mark shook his head, astounded at the boldness of this woman.

"The Company already runs a store here, a virtual monopoly. You can't hope to compete with them!" he said, trying to reason with her.

"Oh but I can!" Margaret replied, quite sure of herself now. "Rather than compete, we can supplement the goods they have. Have you seen what they offer in the company stores? They are only concerned with the basic trade goods, the necessities. The people here are looking for other things, things to make life more civilized and comfortable."

"Well . . . I suppose. Maybe you have a point there" Mark conceded, still not convinced.

"In any case," Margaret continued, "We'll both have some time to think about it as you mentioned you'll only be away for a short time on this trip."

"Yes, we'll leave day after tomorrow, early, to catch the tide around Discovery Island. We shouldn't be more than a week before returning here, then off to San Francisco."

"That's perfect!" she cried, "That will give me time to look things over and we can discuss it further when you return."

Mark nodded, not quite sure what he was committing himself to, unavoidably swept up in her enthusiasm. They talked long into the night until their pent-up emotions brought them together in a feverish yet tender conflict of passion.

Chapter 21

The following morning Margaret and the boys were all up early, packing their gear to move ashore. Margaret shared a room with Cecilia in the Factor's house while Thomas and Andrew moved in with some other boys in the "dormitory" or attic of the Bachelor's Hall. Many of the boys from the out-lying farms were boarded here for short times to receive their schooling from Reverend Staines.

Not one to waste time, Margaret rode out to Beckley's farm with Cecilia and John Ogilvie again, this time to start some serious bartering for her own horse and supplies. She drove a hard bargain, and by the time they returned, she owned a rather plain but strong horse, complete with a saddle and sufficient tack and harness to handle most of the jobs she had in mind. In addition, she had a commitment for a supply of vegetables and dairy products for the months to come, as well as feed for the horse to supplement the local grazing. In return, Margaret would supply a new plough, a crate of miscellaneous farm tools as well as several books on botany and agriculture. She felt the recent changes in her life had eliminated her need for books in this field.

She spent more time sorting out their supplies with the boys, listing what they would keep and what they would sell. Thomas naturally claimed all of his father's shipwright's tools, something that would help them build their new home.

The following day, she talked with Mr. Douglas about land available in the area. She was pleasantly surprised to find that lots sold for ten to twenty pounds, a fraction of the cost of land back home. Even better, some land in the surrounding area sold in twenty acre parcels for only a pound an acre! Not wanting to waste money on renting land she agreed to buy a lot from the Company. Captain Grant, the Colonial Surveyor, had done very little surveying on the lots around the Fort, but there was enough done to allow them finally to select a small plot up the inlet, not far from the Fort. Margaret was pleased to find land fronting on the harbour, on the main trail leading to Sooke and the larger farms. She promised herself she would buy more land if her situation ever improved.

The weather stayed mild, lifting their spirits as they trudged out each morning from the Fort to work on their small plot of land. Margaret supplied the directions and outline of what would be required and Thomas provided the know-how and expertise in cutting the timber and rigging the lines for skidding it out.

The first day they stepped off the outlines of their house and started cutting down the trees needed to clear the space. It was hard work for all of them, taking turns on the axe or cross-cut saw, but very rewarding, as one-by-one, the large trees came crashing down. They then trimmed the branches, sawed them into manageable lengths and rigged the horse to skid them out to a more suitable place. It was Andrew's job to peel the smaller logs, leaving them slippery and smooth, perfect for their home.

On the third day, they almost gave up. Their bodies cried out in agony as they hiked down the trail, broken and bleeding blisters making their hands almost useless. The sticky residues of pitch from the tall firs and pines had glued their fingers together and covered them with patches of dirt and pieces of bark. Sheer will and determination drove them on, and by the end of a week they had a small area cleared and a fairly good stack of logs piled up to one side. Margaret groaned as she realized they would still require another week or two of this kind of work to clear the area she wanted. As well as skidding logs, Thomas had rigged tackle for pulling small stumps out with the horse, and had constructed a rough sled to haul rocks up from the beach for their foundation blocks. A large bonfire was kept constantly burning to dispose of the trimmed branches and underbrush cleared from the area.

Margaret soon realized they just didn't have enough manpower to tackle this kind of project or even enough of the right type of logs to build a log house! Most of the logs were irregular shaped, oversized logs with too many twists and curves to be used in a log house.

She then started trying to find a supply of cut lumber to supplement their efforts. They had decided they could do the main frame-work using the smaller logs, but would need sawn lumber to complete it. Apparently all the other settlers and farms wanted the same, so lumber was a scarce commodity. A small sawmill at Millstream near Esquimalt had been operating for a few years, but its production was limited, and almost all taken by the Company for their own construction, including the new house under construction by James Douglas. The remainder was snapped up by the other farms in the area, so a stranger had little or no chance! Margaret realized this was going to be their biggest problem, one that could slow their building almost to a halt if they had to hand-hew and cut their own rough timber. She continued to think about the problem, but did not let it slow them down at this stage of their planning.

A few days later they had marked off the outline of their new home on the ground with wooden stakes and string.

Initially, there would only be three rooms. The largest room, facing the trail would be the storeroom, which also would serve as their store. The other two smaller rooms at the rear, overlooking the harbour would be their living quarters. A small outhouse was already under construction and Thomas had further plans to build another shed for some chickens, so they could have a ready supply of eggs.

When they returned to the Fort late that day, Mr. Douglas took Margaret aside for a private word.

"Mrs. Manson," he began, "I really don't know how to tell you this . . . or even if I should."

"Tell me what, Mr. Douglas?" Margaret asked, intrigued by his manner.

"Well, I don't want to get your hopes up too much, after all you've been through . . ." He hesitated again. Margaret was surprised, knowing James Douglas was not one normally at a loss for words.

"Please Mr. Douglas, what is it?"

"Well," he continued, "I've just been talking with someone from Captain Grant's farm at Sooke . . . that's way out to the west of us . . ."

"Yes, yes, I know where it is, please Mr. Douglas . . ."

"Well, it seems some Indians had passed through recently from the West Coast, around Port San Juan, and they had a story about a white man who had washed up alive with a long-boat on one of the beaches."

Margaret's eyes grew enormous as she stared at the Chief Factor, temporarily speechless.

"Oh my God . . . it's Adam!" Margaret cried, cold shivers running through her. "Is he alive, where is he?" Suddenly, she felt weak, her world starting to crumble again, her thoughts and feelings in a turmoil.

"Well Mrs. Manson," the Factor continued, "That's the

problem with some of these rumours. We never do get the complete story. Apparently, whoever it was has survived and was living with one of the Indian tribes until well enough to travel. That's all we know, I'm afraid. We don't know who he is, if he's still alive, or even if it's true."

Margaret's mind was racing as she mumbled her thanks and went back into the kitchen for a cup of tea with Cecilia. Cecilia had already heard the story and was bubbling over to talk to Margaret.

"Oh Margaret, wouldn't it be wonderful if it were Adam, and he was alive?" she cried, obviously enthralled with the possibility.

"Yes, I suppose it would . . ." Margaret murmured, not totally reassured. She sipped her tea, a blank stare on her face as she struggled with her thoughts.

Cecilia studied her, at first confused with Margaret's reaction. Her eyes grew wide and a smile slowly spread across her face as an idea formed in her mind. She leaned close to Margaret's ear.

"Oh . . . my . . . " she mumbled. ". . . It's . . . it's that captain isn't it, that handsome captain from the ship you came on! Is that it Margaret? You can tell me, I'll keep your secret!" she whispered, enjoying her little conspiracy.

It shook Margaret at first, the idea of someone knowing about their relationship. She looked into Cecilia's eyes, unsure of what to say. Seeing only caring and innocence she relented, nodding her head silently.

"Oh my goodness!" Cecilia cried, looking around quickly, then dropping down to a whisper again.

"Oh my, Margaret, that certainly does complicate things doesn't it?" she said.

They continued to discuss the problem, Margaret supplying only enough information to satisfy Cecilia's curiosity. It felt good to be able to confide in someone about some of her troubles, but she wasn't ready yet to tell all.

Margaret retired early that evening, deep in thought about her life and the other tiny life within her. Although the thought crossed her mind that she was being punished for her sins, it wasn't long before she fell into the deep, untroubled sleep of the innocent.

Chapter 22

"Ship ho!", Thomas' cry rang out through the trees. They dropped their tools and rushed to the shore, looking down the inlet towards the main harbour. Margaret's heart skipped a beat as she recognized the sleek lines of the Shanghai Lady swinging around, coming up into the wind to drop anchor.

She immediately declared a holiday and they rushed up the trail back to the fort. By the time they arrived, the small boat was already pulling to shore. Margaret gasped as she saw Mark in the stern sheets, looking their way. She was such a mess! When she tried to straighten her hair tied under a scarf, she found small leaves, bark and other unidentified articles stuck on with ample doses of pine pitch. The pine pitch had also found its way onto her old work clothes, along with the stains of the black earth from her stump digging. Without time to even wash up, she whimpered slightly as she saw Mark strolling up the path! She flushed red under the grime as he approached her, a broad smile wrinkling his face.

"Well I'll be scuppered!" he chuckled, "It is Mrs. Manson, is it not? I hardly recognized you" he continued, breaking into a deep laugh.

Looking down at herself, she realized how funny the situation was and joined in his laughter.

"Oh Mark, I must be a mess!" she said, trying without success to brush some of the dirt off her clothes. He stood back, once more looking her over with a more critical eye.

"Actually," he said, more serious, "You look great! I think this life agrees with you."

His eyes surveyed her body and her tanned skin flushed red under his attention. She had lost the softness acquired during the voyage. Her body now was trimmer, more muscular, enhancing her femininity rather than diminishing it.

Mark greeted the boys, who had been waiting patiently, receiving in return a complete but rapid summary of their activities since their last meeting.

Mark listened with interest then turned to include Margaret and said "Well, it sounds like you have a good start, so you'll probably be interested in something I've brought for you." He took Margaret's hand and led her back to the edge of the hill, overlooking the harbour.

"See there Maggie?" he pointed to the ship, "On deck... the lumber? When we were loading all that good lumber at Jensen's Mill for San Francisco, I thought you could probably use some. I know it's in damn short supply around here."

Looking down on the ship, she could now see what she had missed before. A large stack of fresh-cut lumber was tied down on the foredeck, with smaller piles tucked here and there behind deck houses, all tied down securely.

Mark continued, "Of course, our main shipment is stowed in the hold for sea, so we stacked as much as we could on deck for you. There's a high tide later today, so we can move up the inlet closer to your lot and unload it."

Margaret was speechless. This would solve their lumber problem and they could build without any further delays.

Mark explained "I thought if we were going to be partners in this new venture, I'd better contribute my share!" causing Margaret to remember something.

"Mark," she said, in a low voice, "There's some news I think you should hear."

"What's that Maggie?"

"Come along, lets go for a walk. I'll show you what we've been doing while you were away, and there are a few things I must tell you."

The boys ran down to the wharf to visit the ship as Margaret led him down the trail, relating the story as told to her by Mr. Douglas.

As she finished her account, Mark stopped suddenly, grabbing her arm, spinning her around to face him. His eyes flashed as they bored into her, penetrating the depths of her soul.

"Maggie," his words cutting her, "What do you think . . . how do you feel about this?"

"Oh Mark, you know how I feel . . . Oh God, my entire life's a mess, not knowing one way or another."

"What if . . ."

"If Adam is alive, then I'll just have to face that decision. All I know for now, is that I have to carry on as I planned. I can't change my life again on the basis of a vague rumour."

"But what about us?" he protested.

"Well, if its all right with you, we'll carry on as planned, I will sell . . ."

"Damn it woman!" he barked at her, "I'm not talking about the business, I'm talking about us, our love and life together!"

"Oh Mark!" she murmured, reaching for him. "You know how much I love you, but I can't control the future. Adam's still my husband if he's alive. That I cannot change, no matter how much I would like to! Once we know for sure, maybe then we can make plans."

He wrapped his arms around her, holding her tight. They stood there, basking in the pleasure of their closeness. As she tilted her head back to look up at him, his lips met hers.

Suddenly realizing where they were, she broke off, pushing him away.

"Please Mark, somebody might see us," she said, blushing. In a determined effort to change the direction of their thoughts, she clutched his hand and pulled him down the trail. "Come on, Mr. Holland, take a look at what real work is!"

Like a small child she scampered around the plot of land, pointing out each tree and stump as another conquest, finally arriving at the staked out area for the house.

"Where's the bedroom?" Mark asked, a broad smile creasing his face.

"Oh, be serious Mark!" she scolded. "It will be so good to start building! Thank you so much for thinking about the lumber."

"Actually," he said, "There's more."

"More? What do you mean?"

"Well, you remember Jonathan Stone?"

"Yes, of course I do, he's your carpenter on the Lady."

"Yes, . . .well . . . not any more. Jonathan is going to stay here with you for the time we're away on this trip. He's been talking for years about settling down somewhere on shore. This will give him a chance to see what it's like. Anyway, he'll stay and give you a hand with the house."

Margaret couldn't believe her ears. "Oh, that's wonderful Mark! But what . . .who's going to be your carpenter?"

"Old George Mullins," Mark replied, "He spent years as a shipwright in the navy before he joined the Lady, so he knows the craft."

Overjoyed, Margaret realized their project could now move ahead quickly with the help of Jonathan. Mark asked more questions about her plans, and they discussed further possibilities.

"Here is a list of goods I've been working on," Margaret said, pulling a tattered piece of paper from her pocket. "Do you think you could get this stuff in San Francisco at a reasonable price?"

He looked over the list.

"I'm not sure, Maggie. The gold rush has created a terrible shortage of things down there, but the situation might be improving by now. God knows they've been bringing in supplies for years now. The last time I was there, more than two hundred ships filled that harbour... what a mess!"

"That many?" Margaret interrupted, surprised at the number. "Oh Mark," she continued, "Do you think we could ever have something like that happen here?"

Mark laughed, "Not for some time Maggie . . . unless we have a big gold rush here as well."

"Well," she said, her face alive with promise, "Mr.Douglas told me they found gold up north on one of the islands, but it never amounted to anything. Maybe they'll find more somewhere."   They walked back to the fort, engrossed in their plans for the future.

Later that day, the Lady was towed up the inlet, and again tied close by the rocky shoreline. All the crew members pitched in. Within a few hours, a large pile of timbers, boards and split cedar shakes were stacked on one side of their building site.

Thomas and Jonathan were deep in conversation as they paced around the site, gesturing wildly, obviously planning their attack.

As the daylight faded, the ship was returned to its anchorage and they all went aboard for a special treat prepared by Ah Fong. The farewells were longer this time as the Shanghai Lady would be away for almost a month. It was almost midnight when the trio returned to the Fort with heavy hearts and exhausted bodies.

Chapter 23

Thomas and Jonathan were up and away at first light, determined to get an early start. By the time Margaret and Andrew arrived, the men had already erected a small framework.

"Why are you building the chicken-house?" she cried, confused by their priorities.

"Because it's the quickest," replied Thomas. "Jonathan is going to sleep here while we build the house."

"And besides, Mrs. Manson, we can lock up our tools here each night," added Jonathon. "And we won't have to carry them out from the Fort each morning."

It made sense to Margaret, so she pitched in and helped wherever she could. By the end of the first day, they stood back to admire their first efforts, a modest but sturdy little chicken-house. The small building would serve in the meantime as a storage shed and sleeping quarters for Jonathan.

Work progressed rapidly on the main building, attracting considerable attention from the local population as they passed by. Margaret seized every opportunity to inform them all of her plans, probing further into their needs and what goods they had to trade.

The local Indians also took an interest in her activity, arriving on foot, but usually by canoe from across the inlet. She was careful however, not to interfere or try to compete directly with the Company trade at the fort. She felt frustrated by this restriction, promising herself she would look into it further.

The main structure was built with a high peaked roof, which provided a large attic storage area. This area covered the living area, but was open to the front store area with access stairs built in. By the third week, they were nailing down cedar shakes on the roof, almost completing the structure.

Learning some tricks from the Indians, Andrew had been gathering empty clam shells, which he cooked in large, hot fires on the beach. The resultant lumpy lime powder was then mixed with water, making a very satisfactory white-wash. Applied to the exterior, the building sparkled white in the sun. James Douglas had done something similar in his new house, but instead of white-wash, he had the Songhees gather clam shells that they had turned into an acceptable plaster, which was now being applied to the interior of their new house.

Jonathan showed them some further tricks as he bartered for some dogfish oil from the Indians. This is a smelly oil which the Indians make from rendering down of the livers of a local small mud-shark that the locals normally called dogfish. Into the oil, he mixed red lead from the shipwright's supplies, providing them with an ample supply of a very durable, rust coloured paint that they applied to the trim around the doors and windows of the house.

"My goodness, doesn't it look grand?" Margaret cried as they all stood back on the trail, admiring their work.

"Ah . . . I don't know. What do you think Thomas, maybe there's something missing?" said Jonathan, with a sly wink to Thomas.

"What do you mean?" said Margaret, "It looks wonderful!"

"Just a minute, mother," said Thomas as the two of them

disappeared behind the chicken house. They appeared again shortly, struggling with a long cedar plank. When they were positioned in front of the building, they flipped the plank over, revealing a smooth surface, polished with oil, on which the deeply carved letters declared:

"MANSON & HOLLAND"

and in smaller letters:

"General Merchandise."

Margaret gasped, her hands flung up in total surprise.

"Oh my God! it's lovely!... Oh boys, I just love it! Thank you so much... Oh my... we must hang it up proper, right up there, where everyone passing by can see it."

The two men were already at work, and it soon dominated the area directly above the front entrance.

The next few days were occupied with moving their supplies and equipment that had been stored in the Fort into the new home, building furniture and shelves for storage.

Their timing was perfect, for as the last of their supplies were moved from the Fort, the cry of "Ship Ho" rang out again. This time it was the Tory, the original ship they had planned to travel on from England.

A farmer from Beckley's farm had spotted her coasting along Juan de Fuca Strait and brought the word, causing considerable excitement and activity around the fort. A crowd gathered on the bank to watch her manoeuvre into the inner harbour. Margaret, Jonathan and the boys picked a choice spot close by and settled down to watch the arrival, which had been expected for some time.

The Tory, an old barque of some 500 tons, had lived up to her reputation of being slow, as she had left England a week before the Shanghai Lady.

It was a momentous occasion for the colony, as some

of the new bailiffs and their recruits were arriving, many with families. Margaret watched with mixed feelings as the ship rounded up for anchoring, many of the families on deck. Her heart went out to the women standing at the rail, looking out at the Fort. She knew their feelings, the uncertainty they were experiencing.

Activity at the Fort increased as more flags were raised, the cannon bays opened and the nine-pounder rolled out. A crowd gathered at the fort and along the bank, more people than Margaret had seen since arriving. She watched closer as the crew stood ready to drop the anchor. A silence had descended on the crowd, watching in anticipation.

Suddenly all hell broke loose with the splash and clatter of the anchor and chain. The nine-pounder boomed from the Fort and a cheer rose from the crowd. A blood-chilling scream over-shadowed the cheers, yanking Margaret around in alarm, looking back to the Fort. She was not alone as others were equally disturbed by the scream, but eventually, thinking that somebody had been rather over zealous in his cheering, returned their attention to the Tory. It was much later that Margaret learned the ironic story; the Fort cannon had claimed it's first casualty. Poor Charles Fish, a young worker at the Fort had unfortunately become the victim of a freak accident. The cannon fired in salute had blown his arm off and he died later. The incident was doubly sad as his two brothers had just arrived on the Tory.

Small boats pulled out from the wharf to meet the ship, and canoes from the Songhees village circled the harbour. They hadn't seen this much activity since their arrival, and the word was already circulating about a celebration and dance planned for that evening.

Jonathan moved closer to her, "Well Mrs. Manson, it looks like you have a few more customers on that load!"

"My goodness yes, Jonathan. I hope Mark gets back soon so we have some more stock to offer them"

"I figure he should've been back by now, it's been almost a month and it usually doesn't take that long. Maybe he . . ." as he watched, Margaret's face paled and her eyes grew wide. "What . . .?"

"That man . . . that Indian over there, Jonathan . . . he's wearing Adam's coat!"

"Where . . .?"

"There!" she screamed, pushing past some spectators, annoyed glances cast her way. Jonathan and Thomas followed quickly, grabbing the fellow from behind.

A brief struggle followed, the man more surprised than trying to resist. Confusion followed as he could speak very little English, so they marched him up to the Fort to find someone who could translate.

Margaret trembled as she witnessed the long account that followed, told twice through a translator. The man's name was Hay-hay Kane, an Indian from the West Coast. He had been travelling for almost a month to visit a relative in the Songhees tribe, a journey he took almost every year. He told the story of a white man who had been washed ashore in a small boat over two months previously. Badly injured, he was cared for by a small group of Indians hunting in the area. The constant travelling had been too much for him and he had finally perished. Not wanting to waste a sturdy garment, one of the Indians claimed it and later traded it to Kane, the story teller now in front of them.

Satisfied with his story, they released the man and handed the grimy coat to Margaret.

She shuddered violently as it touched her hands, the smell of death and month's of filth filling her nostrils. Tears streamed down her face as she looked down at the final confirmation of her husband's death. Her mind raced, consumed not by sorrow, but by what the coat represented. Seemingly overcome by her grief, she rushed into Cecilia's room, slamming the door behind her. Respecting her need for privacy, the group finally dispersed, glad to return to the celebration of the arrival of the Tory.

Chapter 24

The strain of months of uncertainty gripped her as she collapsed on the bed, weeping violently. The filthy garment beside her represented death . . . yet life as well. Thoughts of the money she had sewn in the lining so many months before consumed her now as she felt the stiffness through the heavy Scottish weave.

Unable to wait any longer, she grabbed a pair of Cecilia's scissors and, hands trembling, started snipping away at the stitching. Within minutes she had access to one area and could already see a small packet within. She continued cutting, and soon had several of the slim money-packets before her. Her excitement grew as she realized what this represented to her and the boys, the savings from a previous life that gave hope to their future.

As she handled the garment, she could feel a bulky item in a lower pocket. Reaching in, she pulled out a larger packet, wrapped in oilskin and tied with string.

"Oh, my God, it's Adam's journal," Margaret muttered to herself, realizing what it was. With trembling hands she carefully unwrapped the covering, removing a small, leather-bound journal.

A clink on the floor startled her as some objects fell from the package. Picking them up, she saw they were large coins that had been wrapped up with the journal. Rubbing the grimy surface of one coin, she gasped as she realized they were solid gold! She held one up for inspection, polishing it further with her sleeve. She didn't recognize the strange markings stamped on its surface, but the colour and weight were unmistakable.

She sat there, staring blankly at the coins until her hands stopped shaking. Her mind was whirling with questions . . . what kind of coins were they, where did they come from, how did Adam get them, and above all, how much were they worth? She realized they were valuable, but would have to know more about them before she told anyone.

Her eyes fell on the journal. "Of course!" she cried, realizing some of the answers could lie there. She inspected the book closer. Although now dry, it had obviously been thoroughly soaked at one time. The leather binding was deteriorating and the entire book was tattered and stained with mildew and mould. She laid it on the table and carefully opened it. The opening page declared this to be the journal of Adam Manson, etc. . . . . She skipped on.

"*October 5, 1850, The Barque "Falmouth". We embarked this day . . .*"

There followed an almost daily entry describing the day-to-day life on board the ship, Adam's work and occasional sketches of the ship's equipment and new ideas. Her eyes misting with memories of Adam the journal awoke, Margaret kept thumbing through the pages, finding no reference to the coins.

A familiar name caught her eye.

"*March 15, 1851. 4 bells, dogwatch. Cape Flattery on our starboard side, and Vancouver's Island dead ahead. Will soon be turning into Juan de Fuca Strait. Weather worsening.*" The rest of the page was blank and Margaret realized that was the last entry on board the Falmouth. Not a word about the coins. Frustrated and confused, she started to close the book. The page flipped over, exposing further entries!

"Of course!" she thought. "He just skipped a page." The remaining entries were very faint, almost unreadable, written while the pages were quite damp, if not wet.

It started "...*Date—unknown ...Place... unknown, somewhere on southwest Vancouver's Island. Living with band of savages near beach... saved me when boat wrecked on rocks. Broken ribs, arm and hand. Unconscious for how many days? Now travelling along river, east or southeast by the looks of sun, band hunting.*" Margaret shivered again as she thought how difficult it must have been for him to write. She carefully turned the page, now brittle with decay.

"*Day 2, have climbed large hill or mountain, many trees. Moving southeast all day. Country now more open, fields, can see mountains across water, probably Juan de Fuca Strait. Arm bound tightly and improving, hand very sore, probably infected.*"

There followed a small sketch of what must have been the view from their camp, high on a hill, showing some shoreline in the foreground and mountains in the background. Scattered among the notes were small diagrams that Margaret finally realized were maps, each small section forming part of a whole! Margaret continued, now completely involved in Adam's account.

"*Day 4, missed a day, exhausted, travelling high country then down steep ravine to river. Crossed another river today. Continuing southeast. Hand worse, now red and swollen. Should be removed, but cannot make them understand.*"

The writing was becoming fainter and harder to make out. Adam's writing hand as well was becoming shaky, the sketches remained fairly clear but many of the words were nothing more than a wild scrawl.

"*Day 5 . . . or 6??? Country flat plateau, fields and swamps. Crossed many creeks and rivers. Arrived some sacred place wh . . . cave and steps. Good work . . .not savage*" The words were much worse now, his fever increasing and his hand obviously shaking badly.

"*Camped near cave, large hill, two smaller peaks to north . . .*

good landmark." Margaret looked quickly at the sketch that outlined the unusual shape of the peaks described in the text. More faded notes described the cave location and surrounding terrain. *"Water near... Cave sacred to savages, frightened, ... filled ... tons of gold ... silver bars ... Spanish coins."* Margaret stopped, staring at the words "Spanish coins." She grabbed the coins, looking at them closely. "Of course!" she thought "Spanish coins ... gold ... oh my God, Adam, you must have found it!" thinking back to the story Mark had told her months ago! She shivered, the impact of the words wrenching her entire existence. "You didn't even know ... and you found it!"

She tried to read further, but was disappointed. Obviously Adam had tried to make a further entry, but the writing deteriorated further into an illegible scrawl, then nothing. She thumbed through the final pages. All blank. Adam had wrapped up the journal, planning to continue the following day; a day that never came.

Sitting back to collect her thoughts, she stared at the odd collection of items she had just inherited, a stack of money packets from their savings, which until now had seemed so important, representing all their wealth. Next came a small stack of gold coins, which she realized only hinted at the greater treasures described in the mouldy little journal. Last came that very same mouldy little journal, possibly the most valuable of the three.

Chapter 25

"Margaret . . . Margaret . . . are you all right?" Cecilia's voice and gentle knock interrupted her day dreaming. She quickly wrapped up the money packets and Adam's journal in the coat, slipping the coins into her pocket.

"Yes, quite all right, Cecilia, please come in."

Cecilia opened the door gingerly, eyes wide.

"Oh Margaret, I'm so sorry. I just heard what happened." Her eyes dropped to the filthy bundle Margaret clutched to her breast. Looking up again she was surprised by what she saw. Here was not a grieving widow, but a determined young woman with a sparkle in her eyes and a trace of a smile on her face. Margaret then told her the tale of the coat, their savings and Adam's journal, leaving out any reference to the coins. Cecilia was delighted with the account, as well as Margaret's good fortune.

"Please, Cecilia, not a word about all this. We'll just have to see how it all turns out."

The shouting and rejoicing had increased, and as they left the Fort, they were swept up in the activity. Over one hundred new settlers had arrived on the Tory, many of them families with the same hopes and fears Margaret had when she arrived a short time ago.

Wandering around, she finally found Thomas and Andrew. Taking the boys aside, she related the same tale to them about their father, again leaving out any reference to the coins. They appeared unaffected by the confirmation of their father's death. Like Margaret, they had completed that chapter of their life, and were anxious to get on with a new one.

While they unloaded the ship, Margaret slipped away to their new home, where she carefully hid away her new treasures, becoming very anxious now to share her secret with Mark.

Returning to the Fort, she arrived just in time to watch some of the new labourers unloading a piano from the ship. Curious about who would bring such a luxury, she asked Thomas and Jonathan, who were equally fascinated by the chore.

"It belongs to the Langfords" Thomas explained. "Captain Langford and his wife Flora."

"And that's not all" added Jonathan, a large smile creasing his face, "They also brought five daughters with them!"

With a glance at Jonathan, Thomas continued, "Captain Langford is a bailiff for one of the company farms. Oh Mother, we must stay for the dance tonight, it should be a grand affair!"

And a grand affair it was, and a fitting welcome for the newcomers. Many of the local farmers and residents of the fort turned out for the occasion. They crowded the buildings, taking turns in the mess-hall at the steaming bowls of vegetables, savoury roasts of mutton and local venison, grouse, fresh baked salmon and many other delights the passengers and crew hadn't enjoyed for months.

Margaret became thankful she hadn't come on the Tory as she learned the details of their journey. After being at sea for a short time, the slow old bark had been delayed by a storm in the Bay of Biscay and they were forced to go ashore in Cape Verde for more supplies. Soon after that, their food had turned bad, the cheese and biscuits full of weevils, and their water scarce and putrid.

Margaret shuddered as she tried to imagine over a hundred people surviving in the confines of an old ship under conditions like that. She thought back on their own voyage, almost luxurious in comparison to the stories she was now hearing. Silently, she thanked Ah Fong for his skill and culinary management during her voyage.

Mr. Douglas and Amy, with Mr. Finlayson, entertained the bailiffs and their wives, all of them turning out for the dance and welcoming speeches later. Mrs. Langford and Mrs. Duncan, who also had a piano on the Tory, took turns on the piano, while Aubry Dean played a flute. Other instruments appeared and the entire Fort resounded with the festivities late into the night. After Margaret had chased Thomas and Andrew home to bed, she enjoyed herself immensely, meeting many of the new families, who in turn were equally fascinated by her story and anxious to help.

Although it was a social gathering, Margaret's business sense could not relax as she gleaned as much information as possible which might help in her trade. She made mental lists of goods she required, determined to satisfy the settler's every need if possible. As they would be dealing with the Hudson's Bay Company for the majority of their needs, she tried to offer other items, more luxury items that the company might not have. She also had the advantage now of having a considerable amount of goods and equipment in stock, ready to be picked up, where usually, the HBC would have to order some of the larger items from London.

The festivities faded as dawn paled the eastern sky. Margaret and Jonathan wandered down the trail to the house, both still bubbling over with the events of the day. Entering her room, she quickly undressed by the feeble light of the rising sun and collapsed into a dreamless sleep.

Chapter 26

Incessant hammering and the raspy sounds of a crosscut saw rattled in and out of her dreams. She slowly became aware the sounds were real and not something she was imagining. Still exhausted from the previous day, she forced her body into an upright position to survey her surroundings. The sun was high, already warming the house.

The voices of Thomas and Jonathan filtered in between hammering sessions from behind the house. Hauling herself from the bed, she poked at the fire and put on the kettle for tea. While it heated, she went out the back door to see what the activity was about.

Thomas and Jonathan had previously cleared off a good sized area close to the shoreline, and were in the process of erecting the corner poles of a sizeable building.

"What in the world are you two up to?" she asked. Thomas finished nailing a corner brace and turned to her.

"It's going to be our work-shop Mother, Jonathan and I are going to build a boat."

"A boat?"

"Well, just a small rowboat for now, but maybe we'll start on some larger ones later. There aren't many small work-boats around here, and almost everyone we've talked to would like one."

"Well, it sounds like a good idea," Margaret said, not really convinced. "But what are you going to use for lumber?"

"We've saved enough of the good boards from Mark's

last shipment. When we need more, we'll go with him on his next trip and hand-pick the stuff we need. The local oak, fir, and red and yellow cedar grown around here are perfect for this type of boat."

She went back into the house, returning shortly with her tea. Sitting on a stump nearby with the sun warming her back, she soaked up the scene around her. A light breeze from the inlet drifted up to them, carrying the salty aromas of the shoreline and beach life of the low tide. Margaret breathed deeply, relishing the pungent smells of the sea, remote yet reminiscent of home. Bees and flies added their buzzing to a constant background of small sounds as they went about their business in the thousands of flowers and blooming shrubs along the bank. Small birds whistled and chirped their contributions to this chorus and a squirrel scolded them all from his perch high in a fir tree.

Margaret basked in this ambience as she surveyed the skeleton structure before her. They had erected tall poles at the four corners on foundation plates of flat rock, with the front end facing the water much higher than the others. Cross-pieces and bracing had been notched and pegged into place, and Thomas was already nailing rough boards to one wall. Jonathan was busy cutting notches in longer poles he was positioning fore and aft along the roof. Similar to their house, this would later be covered with long shingles or shakes split from large blocks of the local red cedar, an aromatic and very long lasting wood used regularly by the local natives in their lodge houses and large dugout canoes. The lean-to type building was simple and fast to build, and easy to expand later if necessary.

She watched a little longer, then returned to the store to help Andrew, who was busy sweeping up and preparing for what he thought might be a busy day.

After doing what she could, she sat down and composed a long letter to her brother Kenneth. As this was the first ship returning to London since they had arrived, she did not want to miss the opportunity. She described her voyage out in detail, only hinting at her feelings towards Mark. Adam's loss and unusual tale was told, again not mentioning the coins.

She finished her letter with a challenge, which she was sure Kenneth would accept.

She wrote, "I have learned dear brother, from Mr. Douglas and others in the Fort, that considerable effort is being made to investigate areas further up Vancouver's Island where coal has been found. An Indian Chief from the area known as Nanymo Bay recently arrived here with his canoe filled with coal of excellent quality. I am sure Kenneth, if that is what they are picking up on the surface, a man of your knowledge and ability could easily make his fortune. You might think about that as you struggle to manage what you have there." She continued with further details of their life, finishing with yet another challenge. "By the way, Kenneth, your young friend from Ayrshire, Robert Dunsmuir, was contracted last year by the Hudson's Bay Company to work on the coal exploration and mining. His wife Joan has recently arrived in Fort Vancouver on the tea clipper "Pekin", and is expected here soon."

Margaret smiled as she penned her best wishes and completed the letter. Mentioning Kenneth's old friend and rival, Robert Dunsmuir, should be enough to get him moving, she thought. She then composed a long list of supplies, mainly related to the boat-building trade, which she asked her brother to send on the next available ship. If the boys were going to build boats, they would need more hardware. Closing off, she then sealed the letter carefully and walked up to the fort to arrange for it to leave with the next mail shipment.

Chapter 27

The days passed swiftly as the entire family slipped into the routine of their individual chores. Thomas was already nailing the last of the cedar shakes on the roof of their new boat shed. Open at the front facing the inlet, the structure was wide and high, well braced to protect and hold rigid the delicate framework of their first boat. Construction of this boat was already underway as Jonathan was busy hewing a long fir log into a rectangular shape that would serve as the keel.

Welcoming any excuse for a break, they later gathered down at the harbour to watch the Tory weigh anchor for her long journey back to London. The Company steamship Beaver puffed and belched smoke as it manoeuvred alongside the old barque, her crew lining the rails, ready with a line to help her out of the harbour. Clouds of smoke poured out of her stack as they threw some more wood into her furnace, firing the boiler that drove her seventy horsepower engines. Shots rang out from the Fort as the HBC cannons fired their traditional five gun salute as the vessel left. This policy had been adopted and used not only at Fort Victoria, but at all the company's posts along the coast. It served not only to keep up the dignity of the Hudson's Bay Company, but to impress the Indians.

They all watched as the Beaver's new Captain, William Mitchell, exchanged a few last minute farewells over the rail with Captain Duncan on the Tory. Other exchanges to and from the shore finally faded, leaving the crew of the aging vessel looking longingly back at the Fort, obviously not relishing the thoughts of their return voyage.

As the two vessels moved down the channel and turned out into the strait, Margaret wondered when the next ship would arrive to again add some spice to their daily routine. It seemed as though their only connection with their past lives was the irregular arrival of the ships from time to time, usually from London or another British port.

As it turned out however, she didn't have to wait long. Within days the HBC brig "Mare Dare" arrived from Fort Vancouver.   Upon   hearing   this,   Margaret wasted little time in tracking down Joan Dunsmuir, wife of her brother's competitor. Although they had met only once before, each greeted the other enthusiastically, both hungry for companionship, and a common link to more civilized times.

Margaret's welcome included many details of Fort life that she had only recently learned herself that would help the Dunsmuirs start on their new venture in the colony. At the same time, however, Margaret tried cautiously to dig out bits of information about Robert Dunsmuir's involvement in the coal mining explorations for the Company. She wanted to glean as many details as possible, not only for her own possible use, but also to pass on to her brother. Unfortunately, she found that Joan Dunsmuir knew very little more than what Margaret had already learned from Mr. Douglas and others around the Fort.

The two enjoyed each other's company, meeting regularly both socially or at Margaret's store. They would talk for hours about friends and places they both knew. Joan recounted the interesting tale of her trip from Scotland to Fort Vancouver on the tea clipper Pekin. As Joan described the clipper ship, Margaret listened intently, comparing the details to her own voyage. The sheer size and speed of these great vessels fascinated Margaret as she recalled the ones she had seen being built in the large shipyards back home.

She in turn captivated Joan with the account of her own journey and subsequent adventures and mishaps since she had arrived, up to the present time, thus explaining why she was now the proud owner of her own store.

At the store, business continued to grow, slowly at first, then more quickly as the word spread among the settlers about the tools and equipment Margaret had for sale. They were also very interested in the items Margaret promised would come, many placing specific orders for hard-to-get items.

Stock of items in the store was running low, and Margaret worried more each day about how her business would survive until the Shanghai Lady returned. She found it particularly frustrating now, as she had all the money from their savings, but no place to spend it on new stock. Thomas and Jonathan tried their best to help, taking time from their boat building to fill the occasional order for small furniture items, kitchen accessories and toys they could build.

She would often sit down for tea with Jonathan, using his experience to figure out when the Lady should return. Many times, they calculated the times required for each stage of the trip, allowing for reasonable delays, normal loading times and other chores that could possibly slow them down. They always arrived at a time much shorter than what had already passed. As each day went by with no sign of a vessel on the straits, they became more concerned, trying to think of reasonable explanations to justify why she should be so long overdue.

Worry or not, life and labour continued, as they struggled with their chores. Improvements continued on the store, both inside and out. Areas were partitioned off, extra shelving built to hold the stock they didn't have. More of the land was cleared, cords of wood cut and stacked for burning the following winter. All this activity left very little time for worry as the group struggled from dawn to dusk each day with their own projects, dropping with exhaustion each night.

One morning they awoke to a blustery, cool, almost gale-force westerly blowing in from the ocean. The tall trees around them groaned and creaked as they strained against the wind, while small branches, cones and leaves pelted them from above. They were just completing their breakfast when a rider galloped by, calling out the news of a sail in sight, heading in from the Pacific.

Margaret needed no further excuse, immediately heading to the shed to saddle up her horse.

"I'll meet you all at the Fort later," she shot over her shoulder as she mounted up. Reining the horse to turn him around, she dug in her heels, goading the animal into an immediate gallop. "I'll just ride ahead to see what ship it is," knowing in her heart it must be Mark.

The horse responded with a will, glad to be out in the brisk weather, straining against the wind. Within minutes she galloped past the Fort and headed down Kanaka Road towards James Bay. Around the bay, she rode swiftly down the trail past Beckley's Farm towards Shoal Point, where she would have a good view of the straits as the ship approached.

Chapter 28

The wind whipped at her clothes and the salt spray stung her cheeks as she pulled up on the point, overlooking the water. Large swells rolled in from the Pacific, in some places curling with a mighty roar onto the shallowing shore, and in other places mixing with shorter, angrier waves as they both died furiously on the rocky coast in a crash of sound and spray.

Looking out into the Straits of Juan de Fuca to the west, she could see a break in the clouds, blue sky and sunny weather coming later that day.

Margaret's gaze immediately spotted the ship, her eyes filling with tears as she recognized the sleek lines of the Shanghai Lady. The ship had already turned in from the straits and was reaching down the entrance between Ogden and McLaughlin Points, the wind hard on her port quarter. Low in the water, lee rail almost awash, the little brigantine fairly flew, devouring the waves ahead of her. Most of the sails were still set, each one pulling and straining as she approached the point, anxious to get home to a safe anchorage.

Margaret watched in admiration as the last of the large square-sails were doused and furled, main-sheet tightened and jib-sheets slackened as she turned around the point for her final run into the harbour.

Wiping the tears from her eyes, Margaret recognized Mark at the wheel, all his attention ahead of the ship or up into the rigging. She waved frantically, but was ignored as the vessel passed, everyone intent on their immediate duties.

"My God, how I love that man!" Margaret thought as she watched his broad shoulders and strong arms braced against the kick of the wheel.

Relief poured through her as her worries and anxieties of past weeks were washed away by the sight of him. Her residual feelings of shame gave way to a resolve to tell him about the young life that stirred within her.

A gust of wind tugged at her, snapping her back to reality as she realized the ship was well past her and almost into the inner harbour. Spinning her horse around, she again broke into a gallop, retracing her route back to the fort, now afraid she wouldn't be there to meet him.

As she pulled up she noticed her family was among the small group that had gathered on the wharf, all watching the Lady's long-boat being lowered over the side. A few others from the fort joined them, led by Mr. Douglas and his new secretary, Richard Golledge, a young clerk who had arrived on the Tory. Catching sight of Margaret, Mr. Douglas angled over to where she was standing with her horse.

"Good morning, Mrs. Manson," he boomed, a broad smile lighting his usually dark countenance. Margaret thought she detected a twinkle in his eye as he continued.

"I take it you are anxious for news from San Francisco?"

"Why yes, Mr. Douglas" she replied immediately, not to be taken in by his private joke.

"I understand the gold-rush has had a considerable impact on the supplies market, and Captain Holland had several orders to fill for our store."

"Of course, Mrs. Manson, I understand," he responded quickly, not wanting to match wits and words with this strong willed young woman.

They stood in silence as the long-boat broke away from the larger ship and started pulling to shore. The wind at their backs helped their labours as it whipped up small waves in the inlet. Ducks and cormorants moved noisily out of their way and seagulls that had followed the ship in still circled, screaming plaintively, always hoping for a handout.

Margaret's heart pounded uncontrollably as she watched Mark, then almost stopped when their eyes met. A large smile contrasted sharply with his sun-browned face, and she felt her body tremble and turn weak.

They were soon alongside the wharf, greeting each other enthusiastically. Jonathan and the boys welcomed Mark warmly but briefly, realizing he would be too busy with others to spend much time with them. Instead they grabbed their old friend, Alfred Cooper, Mark's second mate, who hopefully would fill them in on the details of their voyage.

After Mr. Douglas had welcomed Mark and introduced his new secretary, Mark turned to Margaret. With some difficulty she controlled the shake in her voice as they greeted each other formally, their eyes meeting, hungering for more.

Sensing her discomfort, Mark provided her with a way out of their dilemma.

"Mrs. Manson," he started, "As we have a lot of business to discuss regarding the merchandise I have for you, could we perhaps meet later after I have finished with Mr. Douglas? We shouldn't be much more than an hour."

Relieved, Margaret seized the opportunity, "Why of course, Captain Holland. Please come by the store for tea later, and we can discuss things then."

With that they separated, Mark heading up to the Fort

with Mr. Douglas and Mr. Golledge. Margaret mounted her horse again and set off down the road, anxious to be ready for Mark when he arrived later.

As she approached the store, she noticed the boys busy at the boat shed showing Alfred all they had done while he was away. Thomas came running when he spotted her, flushed with excitement.

"Oh Mother!" he cried, "Could we invite the crew over for dinner tonight? It's been so long, and we all have so much to talk about! The weather's much better already and it should be sunny and warm by this afternoon. Jonathan and I could spit that hind-quarter of venison we got yesterday and roast it over an alder fire."

"We'll need more than a hind quarter to feed the whole crew" she countered, surprised but pleased with the idea. Thoughts raced through her head as a plan started to take shape.

"I think that's a wonderful idea Thomas," she started. "But . . ." her mind racing, "If we are going to do it, let's do it right! Call the boys in and let's put our heads together!"

Thomas was off like a shot, yelling the news to his mates.

Before long, they all gathered around Margaret in the large room at the front of the store, eager to participate in this impromptu celebration.

"Now, let's see!" Margaret started her long list of duties. "Andrew, I want you to ride over to Beckley's Farm . . . Jonathan, we'll need a long table . . ."

Chapter 29

When Mark strolled down the road and approached the store later that day, he was ready for his promised cup of tea. Looking forward to seeing Margaret again, he was scarcely prepared for the sight that greeted his eyes. Besides being pleasantly surprised at the grand white-washed edifice with its splendid carved sign, he couldn't believe the beehive of activity around the site.

Thomas and Alfred were adding alder logs to an already large bonfire some distance from the building, preparing the hot bed of coals over which to roast their venison. Already the heady fragrance of the alder smoke drifted through the trees. Jonathan directed other members of his crew in building two long tables from the rough cedar planks, complete with benches for seating on each side.

Billie Guthrie appeared from behind the store, a massive plank under each arm.

"Well, it's about time you showed up Mark," he chuckled. "Some people will do anything to get out of a little work!"

"Billie," Mark started, rather confused with all the activity. "Just what is going on here, and who's looking after the Lady? It looks like the whole crew is here!"

"Don't you worry none Mark, I left a couple of lads on watch. The wind has almost died off completely, so she'll be O.K." He continued his explanation, beaming with delight. "Mrs. Manson and her lads decided to have us all over for a little shin-dig this evenin', so we all came along to help with the preparations! You go on ahead into the store, you'll find the missus there!"

Mark laughed to himself as he turned to enter the store. "What a woman!" he thought, longing to see her again.

Entering the store, he was again caught up in the turmoil of activity. A quick glance around took in the almost bare shelves, crates and boxes pushed back to make room for yet another long table down the middle of the room, already set with dishes and cutlery, buffet style for the feast later. Noticing the activity at the rear of the building, obviously the kitchen, he bellowed out a greeting over the din.

"Ahoy there! Anyone home?" he called. Looking around some more, he got the distinct feeling that some of these preparations had been planned and started before the ship had arrived.

Margaret's head poked around the corner, followed by Ah Fong's. Her eyes lit up as she recognized him.

"Oh Mark, you're here!" she cried as she ran to him, hair tousled and spots of flour on her face. He scooped her up in his arms, swung her around once, then set her down as he firmly embraced her, kissing her feverishly. She returned the kiss longingly, then noticing all activity in the store had stopped, she pried herself away.

"Mark, please!" her cheeks turning red under the patches of flour. "Everyone is watching."

"I don't care Maggie, I want them all to know that I love you and I want to marry you!"

"Mark, what . . .?"

"I'm sorry Maggie, I can't help it. This isn't the way I'd planned it, but just seeing you again, I got carried away." He paused, taking her hands in his, and continued.

"Mr. Douglas told me the news about Adam. I didn't know the man, so I can't say I'm sorry for that Maggie. It's a rough way to go, but it at least clears the deck for us, and I don't mind who knows it," looking around at the others.

Smiles and nods encouraged them and a small cheer and round of applause rose from the group. Margaret blushed brightly as she looked around, then back to Mark, for once at a loss for words.

"Well, woman?" Mark continued brusquely, mocking her. "Don't you have anything to say? Are you going to marry me or not?"

Finally gaining some composure, Margaret broke into a large smile. Clasping his hands firmly she answered.

"Oh Mark, of course I'll marry you!" breaking out laughing. Mark joined her and before long, the entire group was laughing and cheering for them. One by one, they came over to congratulate them and wish them well. As the confusion settled down, Mark turned to Margaret again.

"I must say Maggie, when you invite someone in for a cup of tea, you really do it up grand!" gesturing around at the preparations going on. "But I really wouldn't mind just a cup of tea for now, it's been a long session with Mr. Douglas" he added.

"Oh Mark!" she cried, "I clean forgot about the tea, come into the kitchen and we'll see what we can do. We have so much to talk about, I want to know all about your trip."

They entered the small room where Ah Fong was busy pulling out some loaves of fresh-baked bread, adding them to an already large collection of breads and pastries. The aroma of the fresh bread filled the room, making more than one mouth water. Andrew sat in the corner, peeling a large pile of potatoes and carrots, all additions for the feast. Ah Fong turned to them with the tea pot in his hand.

"I really feel the occasion calls for something more than this, but that can come later." He smiled as he poured their tea.

"Oh I'm so pleased you're here, Ah Fong," Margaret said thankfully.

"Ah so! Big business missee should have chinee cook!" he mocked, laughing again.

"Oh, Ah Fong," she returned, "you know what I mean!"

"Yes, missee, I do. Now if you two can't find anything better to do, we need all the room we can get, so please take your tea and at least get out of our way!"

Chapter 30

Shuffled out the back door by Ah Fong, they walked together down the path to the boat shed near the water. As the activity was centred around the store and Thomas' big fire-pit, they finally found themselves alone.

It was one of Margaret's favourite spots, a place where she could sit in the evening, overlooking the inlet, dreaming of the future and making her plans. The pungent scent of yellow and red cedar shavings all over the floor of the shed mingled with the salty odours of the rocky shoreline. Occasional puffs of alder wood smoke laced with the tantalizing aroma of smoked salmon drifted lazily across from the Songhees Indian village on the west side of the inlet.

The wind had died, the air still. The late afternoon sun warmed their skin as they brushed away sawdust and shavings from the front step and sat down together, overlooking the water.   "Well, I must say Maggie," Mark started, sipping his tea, "You've certainly got a good start." He looked around in the shed. "I see you are also in the boat building business."

"Thomas and Jonathon started that," she replied. "We've had a lot of interest, the boys should do well. They want to talk to you about getting some more lumber. I've written to Kenneth and ordered a lot of hardware that he can find easier in the chandleries back home." She paused a moment, then suddenly remembering something, she turned to Mark.

"Now it's your turn, Mark. Please tell me about your

trip, what took you so long, we were worried sick, and did you manage to get any of the goods we needed..."

"Hold on woman!" Mark interrupted. "Let's take your questions one at a time!" He put down his cup, gathering his thoughts. Pulling out his pipe, he slowly filled it, then lit up as he launched himself into a long discourse about his voyage.

"Maggie, you just wouldn't believe the situation in San Francisco now! Literally hundreds of ships are lying at anchor in the Bay, abandoned by their crews . . . gone to the gold fields! Although most people think the rush has reached its peak, there is still a shortage of everything down there. Business opportunities are incredible! If anything like that happens around here Maggie, you'll make a fortune!"

"We will make a fortune," Margaret corrected.

Mark continued in more detail, describing the activity and turmoil of the city to the south, growing too fast for its own good.

"James Douglas wouldn't recognize his "Yerba Buena" now, it's a fair size city. In any case, Maggie," he carried on, "I've managed to round up an entire ship-load of supplies that I think you'll find will suit your needs perfectly. It just took a lot more time and travel than we originally planned. Most of the best supplies had come directly from Europe on a ship that had been dis-masted in a gale off Santa Barbara. After our poor success in San Francisco, we carried on farther south, hoping to have better results in Los Angeles. We came across this ship in trouble, trying to make her way into port with a jury-rigged mast. We helped her out and . . . well sort of struck a bargain for a load of goods." His eyes twinkled as he smiled at his recollections. Margaret had the distinct feeling the other ship probably had very little bargaining power during that transaction. She said nothing, waiting for him to continue.

"After we loaded, we headed straight back here" he concluded. "We even brought along a few extra passengers."

"Passengers?" Margaret asked. "Who were your passengers, I didn't notice them."

"Well actually only one man and two donkeys," Mark replied, laughing. "One Charles Croghan, a prospector who was travelling from South America up to San Francisco to join the gold-rush. When he found out how busy it was in San Francisco and how many people were already there looking for gold, he decided he would carry on with us to try his hand at some new territory."

"And the two donkeys?" Margaret asked, a puzzled look on her face.

"Apparently the most important piece of prospecting equipment," Mark explained. "They're used for packing your gear, very good for rough ground where horses run into trouble."

Margaret thought about this, already thinking of a similar use for the donkeys.

Mark continued, "I certainly hope you've been making some money at this venture Maggie. This load took everything I made on that load of lumber and then some! We're going to need more money if we hope to continue."

Margaret broke into a smile, feeling more comfortable with herself now that she could make her contribution. "It so happens, Captain Holland, we are making money!" She paused a moment, watching his face. "Not only that, but we've recovered our savings that Adam had with him on his voyage!"

"But how . . . I thought . . . Mr. Douglas didn't explain everything." he stammered.

"There are some things that happen around here that Mr. Douglas doesn't know," Margaret countered. With that she opened a small handbag she had carried from the house, emptying the packets of money on the step beside Mark. His eyes opened wide, his jaw gaped as he saw the money.

"My God, Maggie! Do you realize what this means?" he started.

"And that's not all!" she added as she went on to tell the long tale of Adam's fate. As she came to the part about the Spanish gold, she pulled out the coins, dropping them into his hand, once again enjoying the shock and surprise she saw in his face.

"Spanish . . ." he stammered.

"'Just an old story' eh?" she mocked, repeating his words from their voyage. "'Probably no truth in it at all', isn't that what you said," she laughed.

"Yes, but . . .My God! . . . who would have thought?"

"You did obviously!" she shot back. "Isn't that why you had all those charts and books? Haven't you been digging out all this old information for years?"

"Yes, but . . ." he stammered, knowing he was repeating himself, but at a loss for words.

"Oh Mark!" she cried, clutching him fiercely, "This could be our big chance! I haven't told anyone else about the coins, not even the boys!"

"Hold on Maggie, I agree it could be done, but we'll have to take a good look at the whole situation. You said yourself that Adam's journal didn't provide much information about the specific location. That west coast is a big area, and pretty wild too! A person could wander around there for years and never find a thing. We'd have to have a lot more information about the area, the Indians and the lay of the land before we could even attempt it. Even then, we'd have to put together a pretty good sized expedition to explore the area."

Not wanting to agree, she had to give in. Part of her had hoped Mark would immediately want to set off for the coast. Common sense told her this was not the way it would be done and experience then told her this man did not make rash decisions, and any moves of this magnitude would be well planned and thought out ahead of time. They talked further, agreeing to keep the project secret, but to continue to dig out whatever information they could for a possible attempt in the future.

Her jaw set hard, she grasped Mark's hands, her eyes cold with determination.

"One way or the other Mark, I'm going after that gold!"

"I'm sure you will," Mark replied soberly, concerned with the icy resolve in Margaret's voice.

Returning to business, Mark gave her a brief summary of the goods he had brought, delighting Margaret with their quality and variety.

"Oh Mark, it sounds wonderful. Can we unload at high-tide tomorrow afternoon?" she asked.

"My plans exactly" he answered. They talked on, relishing each other's company. The sun dropped lower, skimming the tree-tops on the opposite shore. As sounds of laughter and revelry grew louder from around the house, they suddenly realized how late it had become.

"Oh Mark, I'm enjoying this so much, but I really think we should get back. The rest of them will wonder what became of us!"

"Before we go young lady, I must tell you, I expect you to accompany me to my cabin tonight after the festivities."

"Whatever for?" she laughed, as she took his arm and

headed back up the trail. They had only gone a few steps when Margaret stopped abruptly, her hand flew to her mouth.

"Oh my God!", she cried, "I almost forgot!"

"What is it Maggie?" he returned, suddenly concerned.

"The most important thing of all" she smiled. Lowering her voice, she whispered "We're going to have a baby!"

Again, Mark's chin dropped, eyes wide. "How . . .when . . .?" he stammered.

"I'm sure you know how, Captain Holland," she laughed, "and you should have a pretty good idea about when!"

"Oh my God!" partially recovering. "Maggie, what are we going to do?"

"Get married, that's what!" she said firmly, clutching his arm, turning toward the house. They continued up the trail, both bubbling with delight, and wondering how Ah Fong would receive this news.

"I must say Maggie," Mark stated as they approached the house, "Since I've met you my life certainly hasn't been dull, it doesn't have a chance!"

Chapter 31

The warmth of the still summer evening closed around them as they left the cool air of the inlet and walked toward the house. Showers of sparks erupted from the fire-pit as someone threw on another log. The young lad turning the spit sat red-faced and perspiring, staring into the hot coals, mesmerized by their intensity. A fiddle and an accordion tried feeble attempts to play the same tune amongst outbursts of joking and laughter.

Ah Fong, obviously upset about something, ran from the house with Thomas hard on his heels.

"You watch Thomas, I'll show you how to cook it properly!" he admonished. Using a long wooden spoon, he scooped generous quantities of a dark liquid from a pot, pouring it over the large roast as it turned on the spit. "This is not a roast of beef or pork with lots of fat and natural juices. This venison is a game meat, very lean and possibly quite dry. This basting will help to seal in the juices and give extra flavour to the roast, otherwise it will all dry up."

Thomas nodded, then tried it himself as Ah Fong shuffled back into the kitchen, muttering to himself.

"It looks like Ah Fong is getting the crew whipped into shape," Mark commented as they walked among the group, heading towards the house. As they approached the door, a stranger staggered out, mug in hand.

"Charlie!" Mark exclaimed, reaching out to steady the man. "It looks like you're having a good time!" Turning to Margaret, he continued, "Maggie, this is the passenger I told you about . . .Charlie Croghan. Charlie, this is my wife-to-be, Margaret Manson."

A dazzling smile greeted her from under a mop of unruly rusty hair. The smile turned to a lewd grin as his dark eyes squinted slightly as they roamed up and down her body, pausing occasionally to enjoy some of her more prominent curves. Margaret flushed hotly, feeling almost violated by such scrutiny.

"My pleasure, ma'am," he blurted, bowing low . . . a little too low for his condition as he lost his balance and collapsed unceremoniously into a pile. Mark pulled Margaret aside quickly, avoiding the struggling body on the ground.

"Come along Maggie, poor Charlie has had a little too much already. Maybe you can meet him again under better circumstances, he's really not such a bad chap."

Margaret wasn't too sure about 'poor Charlie', still feeling unsettled by their meeting, but tried to put it out of her mind as they carried on towards the house.

"Oh look Mark!" Margaret exclaimed, "The Douglas' are here, and there's Reverend and Mrs. Staines." They moved closer to greet them. The chief factor turned as they approached, bowing slightly to Margaret.

"Good evening Mrs. Manson. I understand congratulations are in order! I'm very pleased to offer you our warmest best wishes, and sincerely hope you are very happy together!" Stooping his tall frame slightly closer to Margaret, he added, "I must say young lady, you certainly do not waste any time starting an enterprise once you've made up your mind! You're just the type of person we need in the colony to get things done!"

Turning to Reverend Staines, he continued.

"What do you think Reverend, after all you'll be marrying these two, rather soon I would think," chuckling softly.

Reverend Staines had been watching Margaret and

Mark, a sullen smirk on his face as he watched the couple receive congratulations from their friends. He turned to James Douglas, obviously uncomfortable about being called upon to comment on the events. He seized the opportunity to continue his lamentations about Fort life and his opinions of the chief factor's ability to manage it.

"As I've said many times before sir," he started, "I think the unorganized and savage nature of this colony runs contrary to accepted civilized Christian behaviour. Mrs. Manson has already created enough confusion in this Colony by starting up this . . . this merchandising operation! She should not be too hasty with any further decisions."

"Now Robert," Mr. Douglas interjected, "Let's not get into that again. You know very well that situations here often force us to make quick decisions and take actions as a matter of survival. It is my opinion that Mrs. Manson is a survivor, and we are very pleased to have her and her family here as part of our society!"

His rebuke silenced the Reverend. Margaret felt uncomfortable, not aware of the gossip that had been circulating among the fort women about her. Separate and alone, she had been different from the beginning. Now, rather than trying harder to fit into the mould of British society, she had become a common trades-woman, running a business virtually by herself, almost unheard of. She glanced around, her eyes resting on Emma Staines. Always the perfect lady, Emma approached Margaret, smiling warmly.

"Don't take Robert too seriously Margaret. He means well, but is constantly frustrated with the hardships and short-comings of life here." She clasped Margaret's hands firmly as she wished them well. "I'm sure he's looking forward to your marriage as much as you are. He hasn't had much opportunity to perform many real Christian marriages," hinting at her constant dislike for the common practice in the colonies for men to live with a mate chosen from the local natives or half-breeds, many times without the sanctity of marriage. Margaret thanked her, feeling a little better for the words of encouragement.

Cecilia Douglas and her mother Amelia waited patiently until Margaret had finished talking with Emma. Not wanting to add fuel to the fires of resentment, Amelia had purposely stayed out of the discussion, knowing her marriage to James was one of those not completely approved of by Emma Staines.

When James Douglas first married young Amelia Connelly back in 1828 in Fort St. James, their marriage was "in the custom of the country," where a couple just started their life together without any real formal ceremony. Knowing this type of marriage was not always accepted by others, they re-married again later, in a civil ceremony when they moved to Fort Vancouver, and yet a third time in a church ceremony in 1837. Amelia could never understand why these efforts never seemed to satisfy the Staines' strict Victorian standards and Christian ethic.

"Oh Margaret," Cecilia cried excitedly, "I'm so glad for you. I know you'll be so happy!" Bubbling with enthusiasm, she whispered in Margaret's ear, "Oh goodness, I'm so glad you got him, he's so handsome!" They both looked around for Mark, at first not seeing him. Outbursts of laughter in the corner attracted their attention as they noticed Mark surrounded by other men, both settlers and crewmen.

"I've a feeling you can forget about your love tonight Margaret," Cecilia giggled, "It looks like the men have Mark well in hand and probably won't release him until morning."

Margaret had little chance to lament her loss for the remainder of the evening as the festivities gained momentum. What started as an impromptu dinner for the crew had developed into a full-fledged engagement celebration for the happy couple.

Ah Fong was priceless, running about organizing and directing the cooking and serving, the boys and several crew-members drafted as cooks and waiters. The word had spread fast to the fort and some local farms. Not wanting to miss any opportunity for a social occasion, many of the local residents had shown up, loaded with fruit, vegetables, pies, pastries and all forms of local game and fish. Ah Fong bowed politely as he welcomed them and accepted their gifts, incorporating as much of it as possible into the menu. Another fiddle and a flute joined in, adding to the musical capabilities and dance repertoire to everyone's delight.

The festivities continued throughout the night, with only slight pauses as the children were sent to bed exhausted, or men were sent up to the Fort stores for more spirits. Margaret completely lost track of Mark, last seeing him surrounded by a group of drunken friends, wandering back up the path to the Fort. The sun was creeping over the hill behind the Fort as the last merry-makers said their farewells and left.

Margaret faced Ah Fong over a cup of tea, both exhausted. She looked around her, missing Mark and depressed by the mess around her.

"Let's go to bed Ah Fong, I think we should be in better condition before we attack this mess!" Ah Fong nodded in agreement as he cleared an area in the corner of the store large enough to spread some blankets.

"I'll sleep here tonight and help you in the morning" he said, obviously very pleased with the events of the day.

Chapter 32

A loud crash shattered the silence of their sleep.

"Hullo the house!" Mark's voice boomed through from the store. Fatigue glued Margaret's eyes shut as she tried to raise herself to a semi-conscious state. Her mind slowly cleared, but her body screamed out for more sleep. She peered out the window and moaned as she noted the sun had barely risen a few more hours since she had gone to bed.

A loud knock on her door was followed by a challenge.

"Are you going to sleep all day, Maggie?"

"I'll be right out Mark," she answered, quickly pulling on some clothes.

Entering the store, she was pleasantly surprised to see all signs of the previous night's merrymaking all cleaned up and everything in order.

Ah Fong turned to her with a smile, bowing.

"Good morning, Madam" he grinned, "I trust you slept well."

"My God, Fong," she mumbled, "What time is it? I feel like I've hardly slept at all! And you, you noisy thing," turning to Mark, "I thought you would be lost for the day in the fog of a hangover, judging from when I last saw you early this morning."

Mark chuckled as he came to her, kissing her lightly. "Well now Maggie," now laughing heartily, "It just shows you have a little more to learn about your beloved . . . which reminds me," he continued, looking her over closely. "Aren't you a sight! And on your wedding day too! It's as well I came by, otherwise you might have slept through the ceremony!"

"What . . ." she stammered, her thoughts still not clear.

"Well Maggie," Mark explained, "If we're to be married, I figured why not right away? I've had a few words with Reverend Staines and Mr. Douglas, and they agreed we should be married today, before noon!" He paused, looking at her seriously.

"If you agree, of course," he added.

The essence of his words finally sunk in, filling her with mixed emotions.

"But Mark, so soon . . . what am I to wear . . . what . . .?"

"Oh come now Maggie, you have some fine dresses, you'll think of something. At least this way you won't have to worry about anything. We've already had the celebration, just get yourself ready and we'll go up to the fort and make it official."

Ah Fong grinned again, thoroughly enjoying the events unfolding as they were. Margaret's mind whirled as conflicting ideas and feelings clashed head-on. This was certainly not the way she had dreamed it would happen. Before she had time to raise another protest, Mark continued.

"Before you come up with any more excuses, consider this. Directly after the marriage, we'll be returning here for one of the hardest day's work you've ever put in! The crew will be coming ashore to help Thomas and Jonathon build another storeroom on the side of the store. We're going to need it for all the extra supplies we have to unload on this evening's high tide."   This was something Margaret could understand and agree to. It helped calm her, settling her thoughts into a more organized pattern.

Mark continued. "And in case you think it stops there,

you're wrong! That's just the beginning. You're coming aboard with me tonight and we're sailing at first light in the morning."   "Why . . . where . . . I can't Mark, someone has to be here for the store."

"That's all arranged, Maggie," he stopped her. "The boys can look after everything while we're gone. Besides, it was their idea. They suggested we take a little voyage together as a married couple, and while we're at it, we might drop in at Jensen's Mill and pickup a load of lumber for their boat yard!"

"Oh, I see," Margaret laughter, suddenly seeing the humour in all the confusion and underlying schemes. "I might have known the boys would have another motive. Well Mark, I must say this is all very sudden, but I can see you boys have it all planned, and I have to agree it sounds quite lovely." As she thought about it, she hadn't stopped working since she had arrived, months before! The idea of spending some time with Mark on the Shanghai Lady appealed to her. She waved at Mark as if to sweep him out the door, "Now if you'll just get out of here, I'll see if I can't find something to wear to my wedding." She shook her head, scarcely believing what she was saying.

"I'll come by in about an hour and walk you up to the Fort," Mark threw back as he strode out the door.

"An hour?" she yelled at him, "That soon?" Mark ignored her, already on his way up the trail.

"Ah Fong," Margaret cried, "Could you please get some water on to boil, I'll try to find a dress, then I'm going to have a nice long bath!"

"Yes, madam, right away" he answered, already moving.

Margaret hustled back to her bedroom, her mind in a turmoil as she rummaged through her trunks, looking for a dress.

Chapter 33

The ceremony was quiet and efficient, almost an anti-climax to the events of the past two days.

In addition to Reverend Staines and Emma, the Douglas family was also present. Cecilia enjoyed the event, helping Margaret and fussing over her hair, bubbling with excitement as she chattered away. Margaret noticed Joan Dunsmuir talking to the new surveyor Joseph Pemberton, as well as James Yates and his wife.

After the ceremony, refreshments were served as the newlyweds were congratulated and toasted by all present.

In the discussions that followed, Margaret learned that Joseph Pemberton had been very busy since arriving from England. Already he had re-surveyed most of Grant's work, as well as laying out a plan for the town-site, divided into lots.

She also learned from Mrs. Yates that James, her husband, had already purchased some lots and was planning to build a house. Margaret felt close to the Yates, their fate being very similar to her own. Similar to Adam, James Yates had signed on as ship's carpenter with the Hudson's Bay Company, contracted to serve a certain amount of time for the Company. After arriving at the Fort, however, he had a serious falling out with the Company. Serious enough that he just packed his gear, left Fort Victoria and struck out for California by himself to try his luck in the gold fields. Left behind, Mrs. Yates survived as best she could, often mending clothes and taking in laundry to earn some money. When James returned for her, Fort officials threw him in jail for violation of his agreement. After a month, still refusing to work for the Company, he was finally released and allowed to assume the status of an independent settler.

As they talked, Margaret learned that James was planning to import spirits and wines to the colony, another commodity controlled by the Company monopoly.

She was heavily involved in the conversation when Mark finally put his hand on her arm and steered her towards the door.

"Come along Mrs. Holland," he laughed, "If I know you, you'll be here all day talking business! We must get back to see how the lads are doing at the store."

Margaret followed, almost reluctantly leaving the group, now deeply involved in a debate over the future of the colony. The words "Mrs. Holland" finally penetrated her thoughts, snatching her back to the present.

She grabbed Mark's hand as they left, smiling up at him.

"Oh Mark, I'm so happy!" she paused, shaking her head. "I'm also slightly confused. Events are moving so fast. I hope we've made the right decision."

"Of course we have Maggie," he answered, his teeth flashing in a wide smile. "You're the best thing that's ever happened to me, and I'll not risk losing you by hesitating now!"

"'Mrs. Holland'," she mused. "I like the sound of that Mark. You have me now for a fact, complete with a ready-made family!" pulling the boys closer to her.

"Aye, that's true enough," he laughed, "But I couldn't ask for a better lot!"

They carried on quietly down the road towards the store, each lost in thought as the changes in their lives kept coming at a furious rate.

A tumult of activity greeted them as they approached the store. A large floor area was already being planked over next to the main building. They were framing a large wall section at one end of the floor, almost ready to raise it. Other crew members were carrying boards, hewing timbers, and clearing more bush around the store, all steered by Jonathan or Thomas.

"My Goodness, they'll be finished before you know it!" Margaret cried, surprised at their progress.

"Well, they'd better," Mark agreed, "We'll be unloading at high tide this evening, so as long as we have it framed and roofed by then, we'll be in good shape. The lads can finish the rest while we're away."

"These boys will be getting hungry soon, I'd better make sure we have some food ready" Margaret said as she went into the store, looking for Ah Fong.

She needn't have worried, Ah Fong was already busy, trays of breads, meats and leftovers from the previous night already covered the tables, ready for the hungry crew.

The work continued through the hot summer afternoon, with short breaks for eating, or a cold dip in the inlet. The sun was sliding down the western sky when they manoeuvred the Shanghai Lady up the inlet and against the rocky shore, anxious to take advantage of the short unloading time available to them.

As the goods piled up in the store and the new storage room, Margaret was astonished but very pleased with the variety and quantity of material.

With some reluctance she packed her bag and left the store in the care of Thomas and Andrew, heading down to the ship with the exhausted crew.

The full moon was high in the southern sky when they finally dropped anchor in the outer harbour. Fragments of moonlight, broken by the surface ripples, echoed silently up through the rigging, casting an almost magical air over the deck.

The newlyweds stood by the rail, mesmerized by the interplay of light and darkness on the water's surface. The slow undulations of the ripples held their gaze like a spell, deeper and deeper as the movement slowed and the wavelets died. Their minds transfixed, they felt themselves drawn into the depths, darker every minute.

The surface exploded, a million drops sparkling with captured moonlight, releasing the spell instantly.

"My God Mark! What was that!" Margaret cried as she jumped back into his arms.

"It's only a seal, Maggie, out looking for a late night snack," he laughed. "I must say though, it startled me as well!"

She turned to him, looking up into his eyes, like the dark water reflecting the sparkle of moonlight. Mark looked down, aching with the love he felt for her.

"I think we'd better go below Maggie, we've had a long day and I still have a little unfinished business to discuss with you!"

She squeezed him a little harder as they walked to the companionway. Upon entering his cabin, Mark moved quickly aft to the windows, opening them wide to let the cool night air clear out the heat of the day.

"That's better!" he said, turning to Margaret, his eyes devouring her. "Come here Mrs. Holland, let's get down to that unfinished business!"

Margaret moved to him, trembling slightly, her body quivering with anticipation.

"Oh Mark," she whispered, "How I've missed you so," melting into his arms.

Tender kisses grew more passionate as hands groped and clothes melted away, expanding into a frenzied joining of their bodies in a climax of love. The activities of recent days added to sheer exhaustion finally overcame their passion, dropping them both into a deep sleep.

Chapter 34

Margaret awoke to the familiar sounds and movement of the ship under sail. A stiff westerly drove the vessel hard on its easterly course down the Straits past Discovery Island. Sunlit whitecaps, whipped up by the breeze, danced on the deep royal blue of the Straits. Soon after she watched the island pass on her port side she heard more activity on deck and felt the changing angle of her surroundings as the vessel gybed around on her new course to the north.

She dressed quickly, not wanting to miss any of this new territory they were now entering.

Breaking her fast with some of Ah Fong's fresh baked rolls and butter, she gulped down some tea and headed topsides to enjoy the view.

A quick glance around spotted Mark near the rail on the after-deck, pulling on his pipe as he watched the men trim the jib sheets for a little more speed. The sun was almost directly behind them now, feeling much warmer as the cool breeze had dropped slightly after they had rounded the point.

Mark spied her almost immediately and beckoned her closer. Several crew members greeted her cheerfully, obviously pleased with her return to the ship. A large form suddenly appeared before her, bowing slightly.

"Top of the mornin' ma'am," Billy Guthrie's teeth flashed as a large grin spread across his face.

"Oh, Billy!" she exclaimed, moving forward quickly and wrapping the large man in her embrace. "I've missed you, you big brute!" she laughed.

He backed off quickly, his face flushing as red as his long hair. An angry scowl from the large man quickly stifled a few snorts and chuckles from the crew. He turned back to Margaret, still glowing brightly.

"I'm sure glad you managed to throw a hitch on the skipper Ma'am. Maybe you can sheet him in a mite, I figure he's been running too slack and flogging around in the wind too long!"   It took Margaret a few seconds to decipher Billy's sailing jargon. Catching his meaning she nodded in agreement.

"I sure hope so, Billy. By-the-way, please thank the men for all their help yesterday at the store, it would have taken us weeks to do what you boys did in a day!"

"Any time Ma'am, our pleasure" he returned, allowing her to pass. Mark had watched the meeting, enjoying Billy's discomfiture immensely.

"Good morning, Mrs. Holland," he grinned as she approached. "I trust you slept well?"

"Very well, Captain Holland," she replied formally, mainly for the benefit of the helmsman, who stood at the wheel with a large grin. Mark also noticed the grin.

"Mind your course there, lad, or you'll have us on the rocks!" he barked. The man at the wheel straightened his back, eyes dead ahead, obviously enjoying the situation.

"Mr. Guthrie!" Mark bellowed, somewhat abashed with the attention Margaret was drawing. "I'm sure your crew has better things to do than stand around grinning like schoolboys when a girl walks by!"

"Aye, Captain," he replied, hardly able to suppress his own smile. He strode down the deck, barking orders fore and aft. The crew willingly set to, hustling around, straightening lines and generally making themselves look busy.

Margaret beamed at Mark, flattered at the attention.

"I don't recall your crew being quite so flighty Mark, they always struck me before as rather serious types," she quipped.

He laughed heartily, delighting in the feeling of warmth and acceptance the crew held for Margaret.

"Ah Maggie, my dear, it's the spell you weave over men; seems like we're all caught up in it," he laughed as he pulled her to him, kissing her fiercely.

"Mark, really!" she objected feebly, pushing him away.

"Come now Maggie, it's all legal and above-board. You're part owner of this ship now. You might as well enjoy yourself while you're aboard, we'll only be out for a few days."

Margaret relaxed, her arms resting on the smooth teak rail. Her eyes scanned the shoreline on their port-side, then moved forward to the islands they were approaching.

"Just where are we going Mark?" she asked, "In fact where are we now?"

"Well Maggie, we're now heading north in Haro Strait, just passing Gordon Head and heading towards Sallas Island that you can see just ahead." He paused a moment, then added quietly, "There's another Spanish name for you Maggie. Haro Strait was named over sixty years ago by one of the early Spanish sailors who explored this area about the same time as George Vancouver."   T h e mention of Spanish explorers brought vivid memories back to Margaret, as she thought again about the coins and other riches that lay hidden, waiting for her. A sudden idea entered her mind.

"Mark," she murmured, still collecting her thoughts. "Do you think we might some day take a little trip around to the west coast, maybe as far as Port San Juan?"

His head snapped around as he heard the words, their meaning clear.

"I know what you're thinking Maggie, I don't think it would do any good." He paused, sensing disappointment in Margaret's eyes. "But then again," he added, "I don't suppose it would do any harm, and besides, it's a beautiful area. Yes, I suppose we could do that, if for no other reason than to show you just how rugged, wild and big that area is!"

Margaret broke into a smile, threw her arms around him and kissed him soundly.

"Thank you, Mark. You know how much that means to me!"

"Belay that woman!" he cried, backing off. "Let's maintain some propriety here," he said, blushing slightly.

"Now who's worried?" she laughed. "Besides, you said yourself I'm part owner of this vessel, and if I feel like kissing the Captain, I will!"

Chapter 35

The ship pivoted slowly around her anchor chain as the last of the evening breeze died. The sun had already dropped into the trees on the far shore, casting long shadows across the small cove when Ah Fong called them for supper.

Clouds of steam poured from the galley as Ah Fong fished fresh cooked crab out of the massive pot, rationing them out first to the line of hungry crew members who had volunteered their time that afternoon to catch them.

Margaret and Mark joined the queue, eager to share in the sea-bounty they had harvested. Besides the crab, bowls of steamed clams and mussels smothered in a delicately spiced cream sauce lined the counter with an assortment of fresh vegetables from the farms near the fort. The crowning touch was the large salmon Alf Cooper had caught that afternoon, much to the delight of all aboard.

After brushing it with butter and sweet basil, Ah Fong had wrapped the entire salmon in long bands of seaweed leaves and baked it whole in the big galley oven.

Loading their plates with generous portions, they worked their way past the crew and back to Mark's cabin. As Margaret set up a little dining area below the open window at the stern, Mark poured some wine.

"Good Lord, Maggie," he exclaimed as he noticed her plate. "If you finish that you shouldn't be hungry for sometime."

Somewhat abashed, Margaret smiled broadly as she replied. "You must remember Mark, I'm eating for two now," as she patted her tummy, which only slightly showed signs of the life within.

"It is a little embarrassing though, as I'm eating like a horse lately, yet always hungry!"

"I'm not surprised you're eating like a horse," he laughed, "You've been working like one for sometime now. I think this trip will give you at least a small rest that you sorely need."   The conversation tapered off as there was little time or indeed inclination to talk as they became further involved in their meal. Crab legs were cracked noisily, the succulent meat tenderly picked out, then sucked greedily for the last juicy morsel. Clams and mussels were pried, cracked, slurped and munched amid the rattle of cutlery and glasses. Noisy as it was, this culinary cacophony was at times lost in the raucous screaming of the seagulls outside the window. Each time some shells or empty crab legs were thrown out, either by themselves or those on deck, the squawking and battling would start anew.

Later, as they sat back sipping their wine, the conversation eventually came full-circle back to business.

"But Maggie," Mark pleaded, "If we want to maintain our stock of trade goods, and have the flexibility to buy goods whenever we can get a good deal, I've got to deliver at least one more load of lumber and furs back to China. It's our best source of cash to keep us going."

"I know Mark," she replied, "But you've only just returned from your last trip, and besides, we've just been married."

"Maggie, believe me, if there was any other way," he groaned. "Besides, if you want me back before the baby comes, I'll have to leave soon."

Margaret said nothing as she made some rapid mental

calculations. "It's only the end of July now, and the baby isn't expected until at least mid-November. That's over three months, almost four Mark, are you going to be away that long?"

"At least, Maggie," he returned. "Normally, if this was a normal trading trip, we could do it in half that time. In fact, if we have good winds we might be back much sooner. Our turnaround time in Shanghai should be very brief, but we have several other contacts to make, a few debts to call. Ah Fong has some personal business there that shouldn't take too much time. I'm hoping if we can leave by the end of this week, we'll be back by early November."   M a r g a r e t said nothing as the implications of that statement sunk in. She shivered as she thought of being without Mark for three months.

"You'll be fine, Maggie," he said quickly, seeing her distress. "The boys and Jonathan will be here to help and keep you company, and the business will keep you so busy you'll scarcely notice we've been gone."

"I hope so Mark," she cried. "Oh I'll miss you so!" she murmured, clutching him desperately as they comforted each other.

A warm breeze wafted through the open window as the Shanghai Lady swung slowly in the small cove.

"Looks like good winds tomorrow," Mark noted as he studied the evening sky. "We should be at Jensen's Mill by mid-morning and have enough of a load by the day after. That should get us back in Fort Victoria within three days."

Tears filled her eyes as she realized how little time they had together. She trembled as the falling darkness outside the window worsened her already despondent mood.

Turning from the open window, she lit the lamp,

bringing a warm glow to the cabin. Mark watched her hungrily as she turned to him, cheeks blushed with colour.

"Come here, Captain Holland," she whispered as she pulled him towards the bed. A couple of quick pulls on the ties and her gown fell to the floor, her body tingling, ready for him. "We don't have much time, and I want to make sure you'll remember me enough to want to come back soon!"

Chapter 36

Before long, their little excursion was over and they were back in Fort Victoria. The time had passed so quickly, Margaret scarcely felt she had been away.

The reality of the situation hit her again as she waved goodbye once more to the Shanghai Lady, drifting out of the harbour in a light morning breeze. Months would pass before she saw Mark again she thought, tears streaming down her face.

"Come along Mother," Thomas' arm encircled her shoulders. Seeing her distress, he tried to divert her attention. "They'll be back before you know it" he added. "In the meantime Mother, we have a business to run. I have to stop by the Fort to pick up some fittings from Mr. Beauchamp. Why don't you come along and visit Miss Douglas?"

The thought of talking with Cecilia again appealed to Margaret, as it had been some time since they had visited.

"Thank you, Thomas" she said quietly, wiping away her tears. "That's a splendid idea, and just what I need."

Beauchamp, the burly French-Canadian blacksmith, was already busy at his anvil when they arrived. An early morning start meant he could ease off during the summer afternoon heat, exaggerated by the heat of the forge.

"Bonjour Madame," he greeted her, his broad smile flashing from an already sooty face.

"Good morning Mr. Beauchamp," she replied. "I see you've got an early start!"

"Mais oui, Madame. But of course, your beeg son here, Thomas, he keep me busy, no?"

Thomas laughed, slapping Beauchamp on the back.

"But of course, Mr. Beauchamp," he mocked, "If we didn't keep you busy, you'd be just sitting around, nothing to do."

"Mon Dieu," Beauchamp moaned, "I weesh that true. Mr. Douglas has so much work... 'specially on his new house, you have so much work, the farmers have so much work, I have no time for Beauchamp!"

They all laughed, the big blacksmith obviously enjoying both his work and his new-found popularity in the colony. Even the children enjoyed him, bringing small clay balls to him to fire in his forge into hard little marbles for their games.

Margaret left them talking over some details of the fittings Thomas needed, and headed over to the chief factor's residence.   Amelia greeted her at the door, clearly glad to see her.   "Come in Margaret," she said quietly. "I didn't realize you were back. Please sit down and I'll put on some tea." Calling for Cecilia, Amelia bustled around, preparing tea and cookies.   Cecilia arrived out of breath. "Oh, My Goodness Margaret, you're back! We didn't expect you for a fortnight at least. Someone said last night Shanghai Lady had arrived, but as I didn't see her this morning, I thought they must have been mistaken. Where . . . Margaret . . . is something wrong?" she asked, noticing Margaret's quiet manner.

"No, nothing's wrong Cecilia dear. Well, nothing other than Mark has left again, this time for the Orient. He shan't be back until November."

"Oh you poor creature," Cecilia moaned. "Just when you get one problem solved, you're faced with another."

Amelia interrupted at this point to pour the tea. Looking Margaret over very closely, Amelia turned to her daughter saying, "Cecilia, I think Margaret has more problems than you even suspect." Turning to Margaret, she asked "When do you expect the baby dear?"

Cecilia's mouth gaped in surprise as Margaret answered "Probably mid-November, Amelia. I certainly hope Mark will be back by then."

"And you never said a word!" Cecilia exclaimed. "How could you keep this a secret Margaret?"

"How could I not?" she answered. "After all, the circumstances have been rather difficult lately, and not everybody is as broad-minded as you."

"I mean from me, silly," Cecilia laughed. "I thought we shared all the secrets. Oh, Margaret, I'm so glad for you. I think that's so wonderful!"

"It must be a joy to be so young and innocent," Amelia said quietly, smiling at Cecilia's remarks. "Everything is so simple and wonderful."

"Oh Mother, Margaret knows what I mean, don't you Margaret?"

"Yes dear, I know," Margaret replied, "But your Mother is right. At sixteen or seventeen years old, problems of life appear so different from when you are older."

Cecilia carried on, not really listening to Margaret. "Oh, it will be interesting to see who has the baby first, you or Mrs. Langford." Turning to her mother she said "Mother, we must ask Father again about getting a doctor for the colony, more and more we're going to need one."

Amelia answered, more to Margaret than to her daughter, "I've already asked him, and I think they're going to bring that nice Dr. Helmcken back from Fort Rupert possibly within a few months."

That information was encouraging to Margaret, but she knew she couldn't depend on it. She would just have to wait to see what happens when the time came.

"Oh Margaret" Cecilia continued, determined to apprise Margaret of all the news. "Have you heard about Father? He is to become Governor of the colony next week when Mr. Blanshard leaves for England."

"Oh wonderful!" Margaret exclaimed. "He will make an admirable Governor, with all his experience as chief factor as well as his other accomplishments." She paused a moment, thinking over the rest of Cecilia's news. "How is Richard Blanshard leaving for England? I haven't seen any ships arrive lately."

"He'll be going back on H.M.S. Daphne, one of the navy ships now in Esquimalt. She's due to leave next Monday, September first."

The news surprised Margaret as she realized she would have to hurry if she wanted to get another letter ready to send to her brother.

Chapter 37

Business at the store settled into a routine. The extra stock of supplies now stored in the new addition to the store helped fill a lot of the previous requests she had been taking from the farmers. Payment for the goods varied considerably. In addition to cash, they accepted trades for farm goods such as vegetables, fruit, milk and cheese. In addition, they had their choice of roasts of mutton or venison, as well as fish and furs from the Indians.

Margaret knew trading for furs with the Indians was in direct competition with the Hudson's Bay Company, but she hoped nobody would mind her small activity in this area. Her discussions with Mark taught her that the furs would bring very high prices in China, so the business was more actively sought now than before.

One day during some active bargaining with a group of Songhees Indians, Margaret noticed one Indian standing apart from the rest, watching her closely, almost afraid to get involved. Although normally she could scarcely tell most of them apart, she recognized this one almost immediately.

"Kane . . ." she blurted, finally, recalling his unusual name. "Hay-hay Kane!" The Indian jumped back, at first surprised to hear his name. Realizing she meant no harm, he smiled.   "Yes . . . Hay-hay Kane" he repeated proudly, poking his chest with his finger. "You remember Kane, woman who take Kane's coat."

Margaret smiled at his words, then realized how it looked from his point of view. He had traded with the other

Indians, in good faith, something of value for the coat only to have it ripped off his back, virtually stolen by her!

Thinking quickly, she beckoned to Kane. "Come along Kane, we must set the record straight." Glancing back, she noticed Kane hadn't moved. He stood watching her, not completely understanding her words and definitely very wary of this fiery haired white woman that had already caused him considerable trouble. Margaret turned back to him, realizing the situation. "Kane, please come with me" she said softly. Thinking quickly of a reason that would seem reasonable to Kane, she continued.

"The old coat I took from you belonged to my husband and carried his spirit. We must now find a better coat, more fitting for a man like Hay-hay Kane!"

Whether or not he understood all the words or the general idea, Kane appeared to agree, smiling broadly as he followed Margaret into the back of the store. Digging into the back of a closet, she finally found a few of Adam's coats she had been saving for the boys.

"Here" she said, showing him a selection of about a half-dozen coats and jackets. "Kane pick one that he likes."

Kane's eyes opened wide as he scanned the selection, settling immediately on a heavy tweed jacket with leather trim. Recognizing it as one of Adam's favourites, Margaret smiled sadly, realizing the choice was very appropriate under the circumstances. Kane turned to her, clutching the coat, an uncertain look on his face. Margaret nodded, trying to reassure him.

"Yes, Kane, you may have that one . . . much better coat for Kane. Trade for old one I took from Kane?" she asked.

"Yes, good trade" he replied proudly, slipping on the coat. "Lady keep old coat."

They returned to the main part of the store, Kane

immediately going to his friend to show off his new coat. Margaret smiled as she watched, feeling much better now, as if a debt had been paid.

The two Indians were talking furiously in their own language, occasionally looking or gesturing towards Margaret. Understanding nothing, she tried to ignore them and carry on with some other work, casting an occasional glance their way in an outwardly disinterested manner. She was not surprised therefore, when the two started moving towards her, Kane impatiently pulling his friend.

Kane spoke first, pushing his friend in front of Margaret. "This my friend, Pel Shaymoot."

"Pel Shaymoot," Margaret repeated his name as she held out her hand, "How do you do?"   "Do   fine" he answered. "How do . . . lady . . . Manson?" he asked tentatively.

"Mrs. Manson," she corrected, " . . . er . . . I mean Mrs. Holland" she stammered again. The two looked at her strangely as she carried on, trying to explain in simple terms why her name had been recently changed. The two listened closely, staring at her blankly until she finished. A long pause followed as they digested these words .

Kane spoke first. Margaret couldn't tell whether he understood, or just passed off her explanation as more of the white-man's crazy ways.

"Kane not call you "Cluz-ma" or woman, now call you "Tlul-cul-ma"... pretty woman!" he spit out the words of his own language. Each time Margaret tried to repeat some of his words, Kane would either smile or appear confused at her inability to manage the gutteral sounds of the native tongues. She had particular trouble with the 'tsh' or 'ch' sounds that Kane seemed to spit out with ease. On Margaret's insistence, Kane tried to coach her on the correct pronunciation. She tried vainly to copy him, placing her tongue against the back of her upper teeth and cough the sounds out of each side of her mouth.

Proudly prancing around with his new coat, Kane continued talking, proud to practice his newly acquired language. Margaret noticed that he didn't seem to have the same problem with her language. From the broken conversation that followed, Margaret learned that Kane was from one of the West Coast tribes, but travelled to the Victoria and Saanich area quite often and many times joined his friends in the local "Teechamitsa" tribe. His friend, Pel Shaymoot, also belonged to the Teechamitsa, living in the local Songhees village. They had been friends for several years, hunting and fishing together each summer.

More direct questioning by Margaret extracted a few more details surrounding Adam's death. According to Kane, the Indians that Adam was travelling with when he died were most likely of the Pacheenaht tribe, but different in that they travelled more than usual on the West Coast, depending on their success at hunting and fishing. Margaret felt the old excitement grow again as Kane described the area where he met them as he was travelling to Victoria. From the description of the shape of the large bay and surrounding area, it could only be Port San Juan. If the Indians were then travelling north, Adam's last resting place as well as the gold, must be somewhere not too far south of Port San Juan!

Chapter 38

The ship's stem sliced through the murky water as the Shanghai Lady drifted smoothly up the river. The warm southeast breeze off the East China Sea made their job easier, making the brief sail up the river from Wusung to Shanghai even shorter and more pleasant.

"Billy, let's douse the courses before we round the bend." he said quietly to the large man. Billy Guthrie barked out a few commands and the crew responded immediately to furl the remaining large square sails. Mark glanced around, moving the large wheel slightly to allow for the current. He felt comfortable, at home, every twist and turn of the Whangpu River familiar to him. Peering ahead, he could now see the outflow of Soochow Creek, appearing from behind the north end of the foreign settlement, beside the British Consulate building. The surrounding fields and rice paddies changed quickly to the bustling activity of houses and business hongs along the river. Already he could see more changes as the settlement continued to grow, astonishing him each time he returned to his birthplace.

His memories floated back to the day almost ten years before, when he returned home after a four year absence. How things had changed! Leaving as a young seaman on a ship with his father, he had returned as captain, but without his father. At the mouth of the river they had passed the Wusung forts, still bearing the wounds of the British shelling a couple of years before. The activity on the docks had not suffered, the opium receiving stations at Wusung almost as busy as the other freight shipments there and in Shanghai. He still remembered his shock at the changes to Shanghai, the old fields and ditches on the north side of the walled town now designated as the "foreign settlement" site by Consul Balfour. During the following couple of years he had watched the buildings grow, both residential as well as merchant houses and at least two Protestant missionaries.

Activity on deck brought him back to the present. Sheets were slackened on the fore'n aft sails, easing their speed as Mark swung the wheel hard over to port, turning the ship a full ninety degrees as they rounded Putung Point and headed south in front of the city. The "Bund", the long, heavily populated embankment of the river spread out along their starboard side, dominating the entire shoreline. Mark knew Chinese, English and Portuguese, but he could never figure out how they managed to pick an Indian name, Hindi he thought, for the area of the town now populated by the better class residences, clubs, consulates and large Hongs. The British Consulate was the first, prominently established on the point near Soochow Creek. A short time later he could see the Chinese Custom House, overlooking the busy waterfront scene. Dozens of ships, British, Portuguese and American were either anchored along the shore or tied up to the docks, either loading or unloading their cargos. A couple of British warships anchored in the river added a note of austerity to the scene. Coalers, barges, lighters and a variety of junks and sampans added to the confusion, criss-crossing the river as well as running from the foreign settlement to the old Chinese walled city. Both the old and new section spread before them, the city that the Chinese called "Chiang-hai kuan", and the foreign devils called Shanghai.

Continuing along the Bund, they passed many of the

Hong warehouses, eventually coming to the splendid building of Ch'i-ch'ang, the Chinese name for the large trading firm of Russell and Company. A few blocks later as they passed the French Consulate and approached the walled city, the small boat traffic of junks and sampans increased, making passage appear impossible. Mark remained calm, used to the confusion and the crowded waterways. Billy shook his head, admiring his comrade and captain as he deftly steered the large vessel through the maze, calling out orders to shorten sail and stand by the anchor.

Within minutes, they had dropped the forward anchor, drifted back far enough to set another one aft, holding the vessel in the river just off the docks at the old city. Billie shook his head again, amazed they had not either run down one of the boats or at least dropped their anchor through one.

As the crew busied themselves with the ship, Mark looked around, absorbing the atmosphere and kindling memories of his childhood. The warm, damp air drifted past them, carrying the dank smells of the docks and the shops spread out for miles. It was hard to distinguish where the shops on the shore stopped and the river sampans and small houseboats began.

"Wu Chang!" Mark called out as he recognized the man in the small sampan sculling towards them. Within minutes the little boat was alongside, the man leaping aboard the Lady. Mark greeted him warmly, lapsing into the crude dialect used by dock workers and coolies. Before long they were in Mark's cabin, drinking to each other's health. Ah Fong joined them, anxious to glean the latest news from the city. They talked far into the night, recalling old adventures as well as filling in with the new.

"Wu Chang, old friend," Mark asked later that night. "I must talk with P'an Ming-kuan," using the Chinese name for the merchant known to the foreigners as Mingqua. As Tai-pan of one of the largest Hongs in the city, Chung-ho hang, Mingqua could provide Mark with some of the goods he needed and help him arrange for additional goods in other cities.

"I'll arrange a meeting tomorrow." Wu Chang answered. Looking at Mark closely, Wu Chang continued "You look different my friend. Travel to the foreign devil's lands has changed you."

Ah Fong glanced quickly toward Mark, waiting for his answer.

"I suppose I'm just tired." Mark replied, trying to pass off the remark.

"Well then, you'd better get some rest tonight, because I know a little cousin who will anxious to see you tomorrow night" he laughed slyly.

The memories of flashing eyes stabbed him again as he realized he could not avoid the subject.

"Wu Chang . . . you must tell Mei Feng . . . I cannot see her again. I have met another woman, we are married." There, he thought, it's out. Relief filled him as he realized how long he had been dreading this moment.

Silence descended on the group as the words penetrated Wu Chang's mind. Slowly, as the meaning dawned on him, his eyes became slits, boring into Mark's.

"Old friend" he started, "We have known each other too long to risk our friendship over such trivial matters as a woman! But Mei Feng is my cousin. I cannot see her disgraced, even by you!"

"Hold on there Wu!" Mark interrupted. "Mei Feng and I were only friends, there were never any promises made."

Wu Chang leapt up from the table. "Maybe no promises by you, Mark, but sharing her bed signifies something, even to a foreign devil!"

Mark started to object, hurt by Wu Chang's words. It was the first time he had ever referred to Mark as a foreign devil. Before he could say anything, Wu Chang turned to leave.

"I'll set up the meeting as I promised with Mingqua, but you'll have to deal with Mei Feng yourself!" Without another word, he slammed the door and his footsteps faded up the companionway.

Chapter 39

It was late that evening when Margaret finally found herself alone in her room. Her hands trembled as she pulled Adam's log-book from her trunk and slowly unwrapped it. The musty smell of the mouldy pages surrounded her as she studied the rough maps and sketches Adam had struggled to make. She finally decided none of it would make any sense until she could be there, to see for herself. Before she fell asleep, a seed of a plan started to grow in her mind.

During the weeks that followed, the challenge of her family and business diverted Margaret's thoughts of the west coast. From time to time throughout the rest of the summer, she spent as much time as she could with Hay-Hay Kane whenever he came by the store. As far as his knowledge of English would allow, he tried to explain to Margaret details of his life and customs. Apparently his mother was from the Seshart tribe up near Barkley's sound. His father was a Nitinat, a tribe from further south on the west coast. Kane was raised into a life of travelling, not only between these two locations, but as far south as Sooke and north to the village of Yuquot, or what the white man called "Nootka". Kane continued this nomadic life as an adult, venturing further a-field each year, using his skills as a hunter and fisherman both to survive and get trade goods as needed. Kane considered himself "Mowachaht" or "People of the Deer". His journeys sometimes took him over the mountains from the west coast to the area of the Cowichan tribe, north of Fort Victoria. Other times he would follow the coast then cut across the south end of the island.

It was on this route that he met the group of Indians that had Adam's coat. From what she could gather, they were part of the Pacheenaht tribe near the San Juan harbour area. Kane explained that they had been travelling steadily for sometime and were "quina-jac" or without food. Having just bagged a fine "mowach" or deer, Kane struck a bargain with them, trading his deer for the coat. From his comments, or more from his hesitations, Margaret gathered that Kane did not feel comfortable with the Pacheenaht, and was glad to leave them. Upon trying to glean more information about either the Indians or the area around Port San Juan, Kane became very vague and close-mouthed, providing nothing specific enough to be of any use to Margaret. More and more she realized the chore would not be easy, again confirming her thoughts that she would have to visit the area and study it for herself. She continued, however, to listen, learn, and piece together bits of information in the weeks that followed.

It was during this period that Margaret had her second meeting with Charlie Croghan, almost two months after the first. It was a warm, sunny day and Margaret had walked far up the inlet, almost where the Esquimalt trail headed west around the end of the inlet. After refreshing herself at a small stream, she picked a few wild flowers then stretched out on a grassy knoll to relax before returning. It was a pleasant spot, cool breezes drifted off the water, rippling the grass around her.

She heard them coming long before she saw them, Charlie and his two donkeys, clip-clopping along the rocky trail beside the inlet. He spotted her immediately as they approached the clear area where Margaret rested.

"Well, Hello" he called, "aren't you a lovely sight for a weary man?" He tied his animals to a tree-branch and turned to Margaret. Weeks of stubble had grown into a scruffy beard, peppered with the same dust and dirt that covered his clothes.

"Mrs. Manson . . . er, I suppose it's Mrs. Holland now, how do you do ma'am, we really never had much time to talk during our last meeting."

"There was enough time, Mr. Croghan," Margaret interrupted, "But I'm afraid you were in no condition to talk at the time."

"Alas, yes," he replied, "The evils of demon-rum, I'm afraid that after so long at sea, your little celebration was too much for me." His smile flashed again, dimpling his tanned cheeks and wrinkling the corners of his eyes. "I hope you won't hold that against me," he continued. "Perhaps we can start again," bowing low.

His undisguised charm and appeal melted away any animosity Margaret held for the man and she stepped forward, offering her hand.

"How do you do, Mr. Croghan," she offered.

"I do just fine" he replied, grasping her hand tightly, his gaze slipping down the front of her blouse, open several buttons from the summer heat. Flushing hotly, Margaret tried to move back.

"Please Mr. Croghan, you can let go of my hand now." A momentary feeling of panic went through her as his other hand reached towards her blouse.

"Well, well . . ." he muttered as he grasped the coin she had tied around her neck, snapping the light cord. "What do we have here?" releasing her hand. His eyes glazed slightly as he looked closely at the coin, licking his lips.

"Spanish!" he exclaimed. "Where did you get a Spanish gold coin, up here in this God-forsaken place? I've seen a few of these down in South America, but sure didn't expect to see one up here!"

"Please give that back to me" Margaret asked anxiously. He took another look at the coin before handing it back. "It was a gift from my late husband," she said as she retied the coin around her neck.

"Your late husband?" he repeated, digesting this new information. "And I don't suppose you know how he came upon it?" he asked.

"How should I know," she shot back, suddenly suspicious of his interest. "He's dead."

She watched his face closely as he digested this piece of information, a shiver of apprehension running up her spine.

He looked at her again, licking his lips once more as he appraised her curves. "It's too bad, I hear your Captain has been off to sea since you were married . . . such a waste!" He started to move towards her again, then suddenly stopped, looking over Margaret's shoulder.

The familiar voice of Hay-Hay Kane greeted them from behind her. "You have trouble with this man, Tlul-cul-ma?"

She realized Kane was being seriously protective and it would only take a slight nod of her head to start a quarrel that could turn very ugly.

"No, No," she quickly replied. "It's nothing, Kane. He's just been out in the bush too long," wondering if she would regret those words.

Charlie had already spotted Pel Shaymoot and another of Kane's friends standing near. Knowing any further advances would be a waste of time, he graciously excused himself, backing quickly to his gear.

"Until we meet again then, Mrs. Holland." bowing low. She nodded back, intrigued by this enigmatic man.

Quickly turning, Charlie strode over to his donkeys and

was soon leading them down the trail. A venomous glance to Hay-Hay Kane told her the matter was not completely over.

Chapter 40

The rising sun found Mark and Ah Fong aboard a small harbour sampan, serving as a water taxi to shore. Weaving through the maze of other small boats, floating houses and waving laundry took the skill and patience only a native boatman could muster. The damp morning air was rich and heavy, filled with the smells of smoke, a variety of foods and cooking techniques, thousands of sweaty bodies and the fetid stench of excrement that the river had not yet washed away. To Mark it was like perfume, the overpowering essence of his childhood memories.

Arriving at a small dock, they paid the boatman and headed up towards the city, stopping only briefly to break their fast at a small food stall. Already gangs of coolies trotted by, heavy loads swaying from the long bamboo poles on their shoulders. A couple of half naked children ran by, chased by a local merchant cursing the two and questioning their parentage. Mark smiled at Ah Fong, both remembering two other young urchins from another time.

Taller than most, Mark looked over the mass spread out before him. Hawkers and farm workers vied for attention, trying to sell their wares. Dark heads and the ever-present wide straw hats with the conical crowns bobbed along, strung up and down the shoreline in front of the walled city.

The two men headed immediately to the little east gate of the city, into the old part of town seldom visited by foreigners. Once in, they parted, each man on his own quest. Mark headed directly up a narrow street to a small shop operated by his old friend Wu Chang. He couldn't help thinking about the night before, hoping the incident wouldn't jeopardize their long friendship. Feelings of guilt about Wu's cousin, Mei Feng, had been replaced by stubborn independence.

They had all grown up together, played in the streets together, and later gone their own ways. A chance meeting with Mei Feng years later had shocked Mark. The skinny urchin he had played with as a child had developed into a beautiful woman, a "Sing-song" girl at one of Shanghai's exclusive clubs. Further encounters led to an inevitable passionate affair, fuelled by Mark's abstinence of several months at sea and Mei Feng's delicate beauty and consumate skill as a sing-song girl. During the following three years, Mark had returned to Shanghai several times, each filled with the torrid lovemaking of two souls looking for comfort and companionship. Never during this period had any promises been demanded or made. The comments of the night before left Mark confused, wondering what had changed, what demands Mei Feng would now place on him.

Arriving at Wu Chang's shop, Mark stooped to enter the low doorway. His eye caught a brief flicker and he ducked to one side, the small knife flashing by his ear, thudding into the door post beside him.

"What the . . .!" he spotted Mei Feng behind the counter, fire in her eyes.

"So . . . foreign devil show up!" Speaking English, the final insult, she moved from behind the counter towards him, eyes flashing at him, defiant and full of scorn. "What you want in Shanghai Mister Captain sir . . . your new wife not treat you so good?"

"Mei Feng, please, let me explain." he started in

Shanghainese. She continued to advance, finally lunging for her knife, trying to pull it out of the wood. Mark grabbed her hand, pulling it from the knife. "Stop that, you little vixen!" He struggled with her as she screamed and sobbed epithets at him, finally collapsing in his arms. He could feel the warmth of her small body as she clung to him, her heady perfume clouding his judgement. Memories of other times flooded back as her soft curves aroused feelings, wearing away at his resolve. Shaking his head, he suddenly remembered why he was there. Pushing her away slightly, he tried to comfort her, starting to explain his side of the story. Both actions were wrong. She tore herself away, cursing him soundly in the foulest gutter language she could muster.

"You never leave Shanghai alive!" she screamed, turning quickly and disappearing into the back of the shop.

Mark stood there, stunned by her performance. Barely recovered, he looked up as Wu Chang entered, his face rigid and cold. Handing Mark a slip of paper, he also turned and retreated into the living quarters behind the shop.

Knowing there was nothing to be gained by further discussion, Mark left the shop, determined to get on with his business. He didn't notice the dark eyes that watched him from the side of the building, or see the slim form that headed down the narrow alley on a mission of revenge.

Opening the folded paper, he read the Chinese characters that listed the time and place for his meeting with Mingqua, surprised to see it was to be at the Hong warehouse in the foreign settlement.

Heading out the north gate, he crossed the little creek of Yang Ching Pang and headed down the Maloo to Kiangse Road. With time to kill, he wandered along the embankment, enthralled by the changes that had taken place, the buildings that had gone up since his last trip.

As it neared the time for his meeting, he headed for the large warehouse operated by one of the largest Hongs in the city, the Chung-ho hang, officially known as P'an Wen-tao. As he approached the building, he was challenged by a large burly guard. The man was not Chinese, but understood the language. Mark assumed he was Parsee, as many of that race were active in trading on the China coast. The guard wasted little time in ushering Mark into the presence of the Hong merchant, talking with his comprador in the large warehouse. The old man was stooped slightly, making him appear smaller than he was. He turned, looking closely at Mark, his eyes squinting against the brightness of the outside light behind the tall man. Sparse white hair drooped down over a wrinkled face, a living map of his troubled life.

"P'an Ming-kuan" Mark started with the man's formal name.

"Mark, please," the man answered casually, "Come into my office, we must have tea."

Mark's head spun, not expecting this sort of informality. He knew these affairs usually involved long, dragged out formalities and carefully worded negotiations.

"I'm sorry sir . . ." he started, not sure of what to say. He knew he had never dealt directly with the man before, so did not understand the casual nature of his greeting.

"Relax Mark," Mingqua added as they entered his office, calling for tea. "I can understand your confusion. Although we have never met, I've known you since you were a boy."

"You have?" Mark asked, trying to place the man's face.

"Yes. You see, I knew your father many years ago. Very well I might add. He did some favours for me a long time ago, so I have been in his debt for some time. I have watched you grow up and become a man, and watched when you faced life without your father." He paused briefly while the tea was poured, then continued. "You have done well, and all the better as you stayed within the bounds of civilized decency."

"What do you mean?" Mark stumbled, astonished at the man's comments. "What do you know of . . .?" he never finished.

"Opium! The British curse that enslaved the Chinese population and caused years of grief, wars and bloodshed. Patna from Bengal, grown under the control of the East India Company, Malwa from Dauman and Bombay. All making fortunes for Jardine, Matheson, Lyall, Dent and the entire group. Contrary to this standard British method of trading and making a fortune, you have done it without resorting to the opium trade, an admirable job."

"That's just because I've grown up here, I've seen too many of my friends destroyed by the drug." he explained.

"Exactly!" Mingqua exclaimed. "Perhaps if more of the opium traders were forced to see the results of their trade, we might develop more friendships and legitimate trade."

Mark's head was spinning, totally confused by the turn of events. This was definitely not what he expected from the meeting.

"In any case," Mingqua continued, "This is not what you have come for today. In what way may I be of service to you?"

Totally astonished, Mark finally collected his wits enough to present his trade requirements to the merchant. They discussed the details of Mark's list, establishing what he could obtain there, and where he could get the rest. By the end of the day, they had decided he would travel to the other ports first, while Mingqua traded some of Mark's goods and gathered the remaining cargo for loading on his return.

Eventually relaxed enough to enjoy his encounter, Mark began to like the old man. The day quickly passed as they mixed business and old stories of times past. Late that evening they ended the visit with a large meal, more tea and a few stories about his father that gave Mark a different view of the man he had loved so well.

Chapter 41

Mark was almost back to the ship when he remembered he had not asked Mingqua what favour his father had done for him, what task had held him in debt for so many years? He would find out when he returned from Chinkiang, their next stop.

Chinkiang and Nanking were both busy ports just over a hundred miles further up the Yangtze River, serving Kiangsu, Anhwei and northern Chekiang provinces. Mingqua had suggested they visit there first, being closer to the silk and tea trade routes. They could then stop again at Shanghai on their return. Although Mark was very familiar with the Grand Canal that ran from Chinkiang southeast to very close to Shanghai on its way to Hangchow, he knew he could sail directly up the Yangtze much faster than dealing with the canal boats.

Knowing Ah Fong would be occupied for some time, he sent a messenger to tell him of their plans. He then met with Billie to prepare to sail on the morning tide. It was late that evening when he finally turned in, exhausted and confused by the day's activities.

By mid-morning the following day they had already passed Wusung and turned up the mighty Yangtze River, heading almost west towards Chinkiang. Very near to its mouth, the huge river was miles wide, even though they were only in the southern portion of the river after it had split and flowed around the large island on their starboard side. Always awed by its size, Mark was again astonished by the amount of traffic the river carried. River barges, fishing vessels, small harbour sampans and larger sailing ones dotted the horizon. Large seagoing junks ploughed their way up the large water course, inbound from distant ports. British warships, cargo vessels and Portuguese traders appeared from time to time, heading down to the ocean, on their way home with their exotic oriental cargos.

Later in the day they watched in awe as a massive junk sailed down the river, dwarfing their small ship.

"She's got to be somewhere between three to four thousand tons!" Billy exclaimed as they all stared from the port taffrail.

"All of that," Mark agreed. "She's the size of a regular square-rigged ship to be sure." The two sails were huge, a ruddy coloured fabric battened with long bamboo poles. They appeared so flat, barely filled, yet the vessel cut the water at a speed that made them all envious as she sliced by them, on her way to the East China Sea and beyond.

They completed their business in Chinkiang quickly. The small amount of goods required by their small ship was loaded briskly and efficiently, getting them back to Shanghai within a week. This time he docked along the Bund, near Mingqua's large warehouse, ready to load the remaining goods.

"Well my young friend," the old man said after they had enjoyed their tea. "The rest will be loaded tomorrow, which only leaves the last item on your list."

"The book?" Mark asked, referring to a special volume recently printed that Mark desperately wanted.

"Of course" Mingqua answered. "As you know, Chekiang province alone has over two hundred and sixty-seven individual book collectors."

Mark braced himself for what must eventually be a long discourse on how difficult it was to track down his volume.

He was pleasantly surprised when the old man came straight to the point.

"I think your best chance is in Ningpo." he said slowly.

Mark knew Ningpo, the busy port at the south end of Hangchow Bay, near the opium receiving ports at Chusan.

"The most outstanding private collection in the country is the T'ien-i-ko of the Fan family. I have dispatched a message to them, but have not received a reply" he continued.

"Do you think they will have the volume?" Mark asked tentatively.

"If anyone has it, they will. The last catalogue I saw almost forty years ago listed over four thousand valuable works."

Encouraged, Mark relaxed, eager to complete his business and return to Fort Victoria. Remembering Mingqua's comments about his father during the last visit, Mark asked the old man about it.

"It was a small thing at the time, some help with a little problem I had" he explained.

"What kind of problem?" Mark asked cautiously, knowing he would never learn the details.

"The type of problem that would seem petty to you now, but was vital at the time, the kind of problem that can be repaid only in kind." The old man paused, looking closely at Mark. "Included in the freight to be loaded on your ship are two large cartons . . . they're well marked. These must be opened as soon as you reach Wusung and start down into Hangchow Bay."

"But what is it, why the mystery?" Mark interrupted.

"No mystery," he answered, "Just some cautionary measures . . . something you might need if you run into pirates in Hangchow Bay."

Mark nodded, no stranger to pirates and their attacks on helpless traders along the coast.

Mingqua continued. "When you leave, head straight down the river, do not bother to stop at the Customs House."

"But the tariffs . . . I'll never make it out, or I'll never be able to return!" Mark argued, not sure what to say.

"Never mind. It's all taken care of. As I said, your father helped me, now I must help you. If anyone is planning to follow you, this will give you additional time as well."

Mark nodded, realizing what the man was telling him.

"The third item I will give you to clear my account is a small piece of advice."

"Advice?" Mark asked, again intrigued by the old man's words.

"Word has reached me that you have recently had trouble with a certain young lady, a sing-song girl?"

"Yes . . . but what do you know of that?" Mark asked, amazed at the merchant's intelligence gathering.

"If I were you, I would be careful returning to the ship tonight, or any other time on the streets before you leave. Apparently your young lady has been dealing with some characters you would not like to meet."

"What have you heard?" Mark asked quickly, now very interested.

"Nothing specific, so I don't know whether they want to attack you alone, or your ship later . . . or both!"

Mark groaned, thinking not so much of himself, but the precious cargo Ah Fong was taking back across the ocean.

Their business completed, Mark thanked the old man for his help, realizing he might never see him again. "I also want to thank you for the stories about my father, you have supplied a side of him I never knew." Mark added.

"Remember" the old man reminded Mark as he left, "Watch your back!"

Mark did, but the short trip to the ship was uneventful. He was glad he had not anchored further up the river by the old city.

The following day was busy, loading the final cargo and preparing for the long ocean trip home after they completed their side trip to Ningpo. Mark took Billy aside and told him of Mingqua's warning. They decided they would wait until the following day to leave, so they could travel across Hangchow Bay in the daylight.

That evening Mark headed up into the old city to pick up Ah Fong and help load the last of his things. Rather than walk, he hired a rickshaw to make the trip as quickly as possible.

Heading up Nanking Road, Mark expected the coolie to turn left to head down to the north gate. Instead, the man continued along Nanking Road towards the Race Course. Mark barked at the man, telling him to turn around. They continued without turning, the coolie deaf to Mark's commands. Annoyance turned instantly to concern as Mark realized how vulnerable he was, heading out alone to an area deserted this time of night. Reaching out, he grabbed the man's long black queue that hung down under his little cap, snapping the man's head back painfully. Letting go of the rickshaw handles, the coolie slipped out of Mark's grip and dropped to the ground, rolling over and coming up beside him, a long knife in his hand. The move was fast and unexpected, catching Mark unprepared. The knife appeared from nowhere, arching towards his throat. His hands went up defensively as he ducked to one side, trying to roll off the rickshaw. Something hot touched his face, continuing down to his shoulder. He dove to the ground, grinding painfully into the gravel surface. Before he could turn around to defend himself, the coolie was again on him, his knife raised for another attack. The knife dropped fast for a sure kill just as Mark got his arm from under him. Self-preservation and the street fighting experience of his childhood finally took control of his body. His arm went up, locking the coolie's wrist in a vise-grip. Twisting his arm slightly as it continued to descend, he guided the knife into the man's own stomach.

The man's eyes widened, the savage sneer replaced by astonishment, then pain, as the long blade tore into his bowels.

Mark dragged the body over to the side of the road and rolled it into the filthy ditch. The rickshaw followed. Reaching up to the side of his face, he could feel the blood trickling down, joining the gaping wound on his shoulder. Although not serious, he was concerned about what that filthy knife might have left in his wounds and decided to head back to the ship for medical attention. Ah Fong would have to wait until the next morning.

Chapter 42

The leaves were falling in late September when Kane came by the store with some strangers to tell her that he was leaving.

"Why?" she asked. "Where are you going?"

Pointing to the others he said "These friends...of Seshart tribe. Return now before storms come. Visit 'V-mec-zo'...mother." He smiled at Margaret, then back at his friends, obviously very proud that he could talk with this white woman in her own tongue. The two other Indians were watching him closely, impressed with his skills. Kane looked at Margaret closely, concern on his face.

"Tlul-cul-ma, you be careful when Kane away, not go near Charlie-man."

Margaret smiled at his concern. "Yes, Kane," she replied, "I'll be careful." She had not seen "Charlie-man" since the last incident, but heard he was working for the Company for the fall and winter for a grubstake for the following year's prospecting. She did not expect to run into him again for some time.

"Kane come back later, when sun shine warm again" he explained.

"In the spring?" Margaret asked.

"Yes, spring . . . when new life begins."

With that he left, leaving Margaret wondering about their life and their journey. Almost envious of their freedom to be able just to walk away to visit the area she so much wanted to see. She resolved that come what may, she would make the same trip the following summer.

Later that day she visited Cecilia Douglas at the Fort.

"Can you answer some questions for me Cecilia" she asked, "about the Indians around here?"

"I'll try Margaret," she answered. "What I can't tell you, I'm sure Father can . . . can't you Father?" she asked the tall man, giving him a hug. Turning to Margaret, she added "He's been so busy these days with our new house. Can you believe it, we should be moving in later this month?" Margaret was surprised, being so wrapped up in her own business, she had not been keeping track of the progress on the Douglas home. An impressive two story structure, the house dominated the area at the end of what was now called 'James Bay'. The name sounded more civilized to the colonists than 'Whosaykum', the Songhees name for the place, meaning 'the muddy place', referring to the shoal area and mud flats at the east end of the harbour. The last time Margaret had seen it, the new roof was already on and they were installing some glass windows from England.

"Oh I'm so glad for you all, I haven't seen it lately, but it looked just lovely the last time. It must be grand inside."

Turning to the Chief Factor, she continued, not really sure what she wanted to know. "Do you know anything about this Hay-Hay Kane? Kane sounds like an English name, at least it doesn't sound like the other Indian names I've heard."

"Well Mrs. Holland" James Douglas answered, "Since we met Kane that first day, I thought he looked familiar . . . like possibly I had met him before. Remember that day when the Tory arrived?"

"Yes, I remember."

"Well I finally figured out where I had met him. Just the other day I looked it up in the Company records. Kane was one of about a dozen signatories of the Teechamitsa tribe who signed the sales agreement when we purchased all of the land from Esquimalt to Saanich from them last year . . . April I think. We have their mark on the sales document for the Company.

"The Company bought all of that land from the Indians?"

"Why yes, of course. We paid the grand sum of twenty seven pounds, ten shillings. You see Mrs. Holland, if the land is officially purchased, we have fewer problems later with the natives claiming we stole their land."

"Yes, I see, but for so little . . .?"

"In any case," he continued, "to get back to your original question . . . Kane's probably an adopted name. Many Indians use the white man's names, usually with part of their own. As you know, most white men cannot pronounce the sounds of the real Indian names. Sometimes parents will give their children combination names. In this case, it sounds like a name he borrowed from Paul Kane."

"Who is Paul Kane?" Margaret asked. "I don't remember anybody around here called that."

"No, he's not living here" Mr. Douglas replied. "At least not now. Paul Kane is an artist, one of those fellows that travels around, drawing and painting everything. He was here a few years back . . . spring of '47 as I recall. He canoed up from Fort Nisqually, then spent a few months travelling around, drawing and painting . . . Indians mainly. I can't recall what became of him . . . just moved on I guess."

Margaret thought about this a moment before she continued. "What can you tell me about the "Pacheenaht" tribe from the west coast?" she probed.

James Douglas looked at her, somewhat surprised at her question.

"Well, Mrs. Holland, you do pose some interesting

questions, although I can't see why in the world you would want to know that."

Margaret replied quickly, not wanting her curiosity to seem to obvious. "I just wondered," she said, "Kane mentioned that he thought it was the Pacheenaht tribe that cared for Adam after he was washed ashore. At least it was a Pacheenaht that had Adam's coat when Kane met them."

"Well, Mrs. Holland," he started, "you first have to realize that these natives or "savages" as some newcomers refer to them, have a very complex society of their own. Each group or tribe tends to remain close to their own home territory, although they travel at different times of the year for better hunting and fishing. Most of the time they are friendly with other tribes, trade and inter-marriage being quite common." He paused a moment, watching Margaret closely as he spoke again.   "They can, however, be quite savage, attacking other tribes with war parties, massacres and taking of slaves."

Margaret's eyes opened wide, surprised to hear this. Ever since she had arrived, she had dealt with these people, assuming they were all the gentle, proud people she had begun to know.   "Of course, you know of the Songhees" Mr. Douglas continued. "They are part of the local Teechamitsa tribe, similar to the Cowichan or Salish people. Even these even-tempered groups have been known to go on war raids, stealing slaves from the others. The west coast of the island has many tribes, all the way up the coast. The Pacheenaht are mainly around the Port San Juan area. I've met a few, but know very little about them. I don't suppose they're much different from the rest."

Margaret listened avidly as the Chief Factor continued.

"Further up the coast you find the Nitinat, around a big

tidal lake in that area with the same name. Then come the Oiaht, Seshart, Opitchesaht, Toquaht, Ucluelet, Ahousaht and many others I can't recall."

"I had no idea" Margaret exclaimed, "There were so many."

"Oh that's only a few" Mr. Douglas laughed. "They represent just a small sample of the tribes on the island's west coast. There are also those on the east coast of the island, the Cowichan, Koksila, up to the Comox. Over in British Columbia near Fort Langley there are others, as well as up the coast to the Queen Charlotte Islands!"

"So many" Margaret mumbled.

"And more" Douglas replied. "As for your first question about the Pacheenaht, they have always appeared to me as pretty steadfast and reliable in trade. You must remember Mrs. Holland that as you deal with these people, Pacheenaht or any other tribe, they have their own rules and beliefs and lack the traditions and what we consider as the controlling influences of English society. Above all, remember they can become quite savage if provoked or cheated in any way."

Margaret remembered these words, especially the comments about how volatile and savage the Indians could be. She could still see the look in Kane's eyes during the confrontation with Charlie Croghan. As well, the words ran through her mind each time she dealt with the Indians at the store, creating a cautious, almost unnatural atmosphere.

Chapter 43

The rising sun was in their eyes as they drifted easily around Putung Point, catching the early morning land breeze down the Whangpu River to Wusung. Mark eased the wheel over slightly, cringing a little as the bandages on his shoulder pulled at his wound. Arriving back at the ship after midnight, he was greeted with relief and concern. He needn't have worried about Ah Fong as his friend was already safely aboard with his cargo. Expecting him to return hours before, Billie was ready to take a search-party ashore to look for him.. His wounds were quickly washed and dressed, Ah Fong carefully stitching up the large gash in his shoulder.

"You won't be quite as pretty now for your new bride," Ah Fong kidded him, checking the long cut down his cheek. "There's not much we can do about that cut on your face. It's not too deep, so it shouldn't be any problem."

By noon they were clear of the Yangtze River, well into the East China Sea heading almost due south down Hangchow Bay. The sun was high and hot, directly in front of them as they scanned the horizons for trouble. Following Mingqua's instructions, Mark had the two large crates brought on deck to be opened as soon as they had cleared Wusung.

The first crate was opened and the cotton packing pulled aside, revealing a half-dozen small muskets and the same number of long rifles, made for accurate, long-range shooting. All the weapons had been polished and were ready for use, complete with extra flints, wads, balls and a small keg of powder. The weapons were quickly passed around to the crew, the rifles supplied to the known marksmen among them. Mark wanted every man prepared to defend both the ship and himself, knowing what their fate would be if they were captured.

The second crate was a pleasant surprise. "No wonder this damn thing was so heavy!" Billy complained as he stared down at the small cannon in the crate. "Jeez Mark, this one's bigger than the little falconet you have in your cabin. Looks like about a four pounder . . . a minion, only shorter."

Mark looked down at the weapon and agreed, knowing a regular minion was almost nine feet long. It was a deadly little piece capable of firing a four pound ball with considerable accuracy. "You're right Billy, it's almost half the length of a minion. Probably not quite as accurate, but it could be a handy piece in a short range skirmish. Concern wrinkled his brow. Mingqua knew a lot more than what he told Mark. He must have been pretty sure they would be running into some serious trouble before they got away from the China coast.

"Looky-here Mark," Billy exclaimed, "There's even some rockets down under this powder keg. We've got enough powder here to blow up the whole ship!"

"Careful, Billy." Mark said. "Get that little baby mounted on the taffrail where it will at least cover our ass! Maybe you can figure out some chain or grape-shot as well as those four pound balls, something designed to take out some riggin'. Then we'll get the falconet from below and mount it up on the bow, just in case."

Before long, they had their small cannons mounted, ammunition prepared below and ready to carry topsides if required. Practice runs were tried, defensive tactics discussed and rehearsed. The rest of the day was consumed by the practice runs and lookout duty. Many of the crew grumbled about the extra risk to go to Ningpo just to pick up a book. They felt they could have been well out into the ocean by now, instead of trapped in the large bay. Mark was also concerned about their location, constantly plotting their position on the chart and covering escape routes with Billy.

It was dusk when they docked at Ningpo, the crew eager to enjoy their last night in port before the long journey home. Mark immediately sent a message to the Fan family, advising of his arrival early the following morning.

They were ready for him as he arrived at dawn. Apparently Mingqua's directive had also been received, making a much greater impression than Mark's. Within minutes he had completed his business and was on his way back to the ship.

"Let's go Billy! Get your crew alive and let's get the hell out of here! I want to be well clear of Chusan and into the Eastern Sea by nightfall."

He didn't have to say more, Billy was ready. Lines cast off, they once more enjoyed the early off-shore breeze to help them get underway from the docks and pick their way through the traffic. Ningpo harbour was crowded with vessels of all sizes. Sampans were everywhere, constantly ferrying trade goods or people to and from the docks to larger vessels. Dozens of fishing boats were manoeuvring for position to bring their overnight catches to the markets along the waterfront. Junks and lorchas from Macao and Manila, both legitimate traders and barbarous racketeers mixed with their Chinese and British counterparts. A sense of order was barely maintained by the presence of a British frigate anchored in the harbour, together with the armed lorcha "Adamaster", sent by the Macao government and manned by the Portuguese navy. Mark had learned that earlier that year Macao had sent another ship, the corvette "Dom Joao I" to Ningpo to help control the piracy on the sea and violence on shore against the Chinese citizens. Italians, Spanish Manilamen, some Fukienese, and a few other dregs of Asia had all been involved in the racketeering and violence.

The traffic quickly dissipated as they continued northeast, heading for the tip of Chusan Island and the open sea. The off-shore breeze had died, replaced by a light easterly on their starboard side as they beat towards Chusan under fore'n aft sails alone. By mid-morning they were almost alone as they started around the easy end of the island.

"I hate to tell you this Mark, but I have a feeling we're being followed."

Mark looked at Billy quickly, then checked behind them. He had noticed the lorcha earlier as they left the harbour, but it was then one of many.

"Why do you think so Billy?" he asked his mate.

"Well, she's been matching our speed ever since we left port, almost like she's waiting to make her move. Look at her hull . . . very fast, European design, not just one of these Macao tubs." Mark studied the boat carefully. "Now look at those sails, those battens, that high mast... they're all built for speed. How about the crew? Hard to tell from here, but seems to be only a few doin' the work and a lot of extra men hanging around on deck."

Mark watched closely, agreeing with Billy. "You're right Billy! Let's get the hell out of here! As soon as we get around the island, just past that fishing boat ahead, we should be able to get the courses up and give her a run."

Billy moved quickly, his crew eager to put some miles between the ship and this hostile shore. A stiff south-easterly blew up the coast on the seaward side of the island. As soon as they could get clear of the island, they could take advantage of that wind and nothing could catch them.

Mark swung the wheel a little more, glancing over his shoulder at the lorcha. He was surprised to see it had gained on them a little more since he talked with Billy. Sheets were eased slightly as he turned the wheel a little more, waiting until they were clear of the fishing boat on their starboard bow.

"Damn!" he mumbled, watching the activity on the fishing boat. "Now's not the time to raise your sails, you're just going to get in my way!" he muttered under his breath, another quick glance over his shoulder to check the lorcha.

The truth of the scheme suddenly dawned on him as the side of their companionway hatch exploded in a shower of splinters! Turning quickly, he could see the fishing boat, now under sail off their bow, the smoke from the shot barely clear of its rigging! Another shot went whistling by his head. Just as quickly, Billy was barking orders and two marksmen started to return fire on the smaller boat while another manned the falconet on the bow.

Quickly estimating the distance, Mark decided it was worth a try. Swinging the wheel hard over, he headed straight for the smaller vessel, not yet up to speed. Expecting their quarry to run back into the bay, the pirates were caught off guard when the larger vessel bore down directly toward them. Rifle and cannon-fire pinned them down, hampering efforts to raise more sail and avoid the encounter. The lorcha behind them realized what was happening and started to open fire, still a little far away for accurate shots. Mark left the lorcha to his crew, concentrating on the one enemy before him. He could feel the ship respond with more speed as parts of the southeaster caught them.

The smaller boat didn't have much of a chance as the sharp prow of the Shanghai Lady took her revenge, slicing the vessel in two. The much larger brigantine slid over the wreckage with barely a shudder of satisfaction, leaving the remains behind them. A cheer went up from the crew as they all headed to the stern to watch their attackers swim for their lives. Looking over the stern they were suddenly pelted with small arms fire from the lorcha, now closing fast.

"Jeez Mark, that thing is fast!" Billy exclaimed, noticing how close they had come to their ship. Manning the minion himself, Billy took aim again, trying to get the range. He could see some of their faces, standing at the rail, eager to deal with their quarry face to face. His second shot tore through the lorch's rigging, accurate but doing very little damage.

"I've got her range now!" Billy exclaimed as he called for version of grape-shot. His riflemen were trying eagerly to pick off individuals on the enemy ship without getting picked off themselves the constant rain of musket balls.

A larger cloud of smoke appeared on the lorcha as a mass of material went screaming by their heads, blowing apart the end of the fore upper topsail yard. A scream from a crewmember added to the confusion as a piece of metal tore through his arm.

"Christ, he's using grapeshot too!" screamed Billy, oddly shocked that the pirates would use exactly what he was loading for them. "Try this on for size, you bastards!"

he yelled as he fired the minion, loaded with an odd assortment of nails, pieces of chain and whatever was available to fit into the three inch calibre gun.

His range tested, Billy's shot was effective, tearing a large hole in the lorcha's main sail. Losing much of their driving power, they quickly started to fall behind. Another shot from the lorcha sailed by, missing their rigging entirely.

"That's our chance!" Mark yelled. "Get everything up you can Billy. We've got the wind now, so let's get some distance between us before they have a chance to recover. Hopefully it will be dark and we'll be out of sight before they can patch that sail."

Nothing more was said as the crew scrambled aloft to set the large courses that would put on the speed they needed. By nightfall, the lorcha had dropped over the horizon behind them as the southeast wind carried them quickly out into the East China Sea, on their way back to Fort Victoria.

Chapter 44

As the days and weeks passed however, she relaxed more, realizing she knew many of the Songhees by name. Her business with them increased as her reputation for fair dealing in her trading spread to others arriving in the area.

A blustery autumn storm in early October was driving wind and rain in from the Pacific when a ship was sighted, moving in fast along the Straits of Juan de Fuca towards the Fort.

It was the "Norman Morison", the same ship that had brought 80 passengers to the colony the previous year, including the company doctor, John Helmcken. This year's cargo was mainly goods for the trading post, but also included 35 more passengers. As soon as Margaret heard this, she wasted little time in heading up to the Fort to meet and welcome the newcomers.   The meeting was a curious, even humorous one. Margaret felt she had something to offer as she had experienced the same uprooting of her life, the long ocean voyage as well as the worry and uncertainty of the new life and could now help others, if only in spirit. The passengers, however, were cold and tired from the voyage, especially battling fall storms up the west-coast for the past two weeks. Their spirits picked up as they watched this pretty, very pregnant lady hustle around trying to ease their fears and apprehension, inviting most of them to drop by her store for tea. As they learned more of the details of Margaret's plight, they felt much better about their own situation.

After enjoying some much needed rest, most of the

newcomers were eager to see more of the colony. By the end of October the new colonists had dispersed, settled into work at various farms and projects around the area, some as free and independent settlers and some working for the Puget Sound Agricultural Company. Although Margaret held special feelings towards the indentured workers of the P.S.A.C., she knew most of her business would come from either the independent settlers or the bailiffs. The managers of the P.S.A.C. farms tended to be very loyal to the Hudson's Bay Company for most of their supplies. Although officially they were not directly affiliated, most of the P.S.A.C. directors were also Hudson's Bay Company directors and the two organizations reeked of patronage and monopoly. Margaret did what she could, supplying speciality items and material not normally stocked by the Hudson's Bay Company, being careful not to antagonize Mr. Douglas or other trading officers at the Company store.

By early November, the approaching arrival of her baby began to worry Margaret. She had not heard any definite time when Dr. Helmcken was returning from Fort Rupert. Amelia Douglas and a few of the other women had tried to comfort her with stories of their knowledge of midwifery. In previous years, Amelia had delivered Cecilia's younger sisters Agnes, Jane and Alice as well as her son James earlier this year.

Margaret's discussions with Mrs. Langford, who also was expecting very soon, reflected her own concern. The Langford's farm was several miles away from the fort, but at least she had her daughters to help if necessary. Offers of help from the Songhees women also did little to ease her anxiety. She had hoped Mark would be back before the baby was born, not for any help he could offer, but for the moral support she so sorely needed. Thomas and Jonathan were usually so busy working on their new boat and Andrew was always off playing somewhere, she received very little comfort or companionship from them. More often recently she asked Thomas to keep his eye on the store while she walked up to the Fort to have tea with Cecilia and her mother, with the comfort and conversation the meeting provided.

It was during such a session that cries of a ship sighting echoed within the fort. Margaret's heart skipped a beat as she quickly put down her tea and reached for her cloak.

"Oh Cecilia, it just has to be Mark! I must go" she said as she left the house quickly and headed towards the wharf.

The wind was strong and gusty, blowing sheets of spray and rain down the length of the inner harbour towards the fort, often obscuring the view of the harbour completely.

The wind eased momentarily and the rain stopped, clearing the view of the inner harbour as the Shanghai Lady crept in under a small jib and double reefed mains'l. Margaret watched with delight as the vessel rounded up and dropped anchor almost directly in front of where she stood. As carefully as she could, she rushed down to the wharf to be first to greet whoever came ashore. Luckily someone spotted her right away, and after a flurry of activity on board, they lowered a boat that George Mullins and Mark pulled ashore quickly to pick her up.

"Oh Mark!" she squealed, meeting him as he stepped out of the boat, "am I glad to see you."

"Ah Maggie, it's so good to see you too. I see we're not too late" he said as he lightly patted her stomach. "But it looks like something could happen any time."

"Any time" she agreed, "and Dr. Helmcken hasn't returned from Fort Rupert yet, so I'm hoping there are no complications." She looked at him closer, spotting the long scar down the side of his cheek, almost healed. "Oh Mark, what happened . . . how . . .?"

"Don't worry Maggie, it's almost healed now. Just a little argument with a fellow in Shanghai . . . nothing too serious."

"It looks pretty serious to me." she answered, only partially accepting his answer.

"Well, enough about my little cut, let's get you on aboard" he suggested, taking her arm. "If you can make it. We just might have something on the Lady that could help."

Before she had a chance to ask any questions, George Mullins took her other arm as they helped her into the boat and headed out towards the ship.

"Good day Mum," he chirped, a large grin wrinkling his comical little face. "I'm some pleased to see you again Mum, and I 'spec the crew will be too . . . almost as much as the Cap'n." He grinned even more as he watched Mark redden slightly.

"Oh George, I'm so glad you're all back" she cried as they approached the Lady, her rails lined with expectant faces. After a few short moments and some delicate manoeuvres, Margaret found herself on deck, surrounded by the crew.

The ring of men parted as Billy Guthrie's large form moved towards her. Tears of joy mingled with the light rain as they shared the moment. Margaret flushed with embarrassment as she received more attention than she had in months. Mark finally intervened, taking her arm again and started leading her aft. Looking around, she seemed puzzled at first, then suddenly realized what was different. Normally the wood-work was polished and smooth, pleasing to the eye as well as the hand. Now gaping holes were still visible, not yet patched. Sections of cabin planking that had been blown apart had been hastily patched for sea, visible scars on a beautiful lady.

She turned to Mark again, her eyes wide with fright. "What are those holes Mark? What happened to the cabin . . . wha . . .?"

"Don't worry Maggie, we just had a bit of a rough trip, we'll have her fixed up in no time."

Looking again at the long scar on his face, Margaret was not taken in by his little show of bravado. Rather than pursue it further, she decided to leave it for now and find out more later.

"Come along Maggie," Mark said quietly. "There's someone else who will be glad to see you, down in my cabin."

"In your cabin?" she repeated, puzzled by his comment. "Ah Fong is the only one left. Why is he in your cabin?" she asked suddenly, "Is he ill . . . or injured?"

"No, no, nothing like that Maggie. He just asked me to bring you down there when you came on board." They were descending the companionway by then and as they approached Mark's cabin, he stepped forward quickly, knocked lightly and opened the door, stepping back to allow Margaret to enter. Ah Fong stood directly in front of her, smiling slightly.

"Ah Fong" she cried as she moved forward, arms outstretched to embrace him. He stepped back quickly as she approached, greeting her formally.

"Hello Mrs. Holland, it's good to see you again" he said. Before she had a chance to collect her wits or reply to this, he continued.

"It is with great pleasure I have the honour to introduce

you to my mother-in-law, Li Ching," he chanted, turning towards the slightly bowed figure near his side.

Before Margaret could grasp the implications of that statement Ah Fong then turned to his other side and said "And with even more pleasure, I would like you to meet my wife, Po Lyan."

Chapter 45

Margaret froze, mouth gaping. Her mind in a whirl, she slowly turned her head, scanning the three people in front of her, not knowing what to say. She then turned to Mark, a puzzled look on her face. His large grin only told her that he was enjoying the moment immensely.

Finally finding her tongue she stammered "But when . . . who . . . how . . . Oh God, but you two are always full of surprises!" Suddenly realizing the circumstance, she remembered her manners and turned first to the older woman. Shorter than Ah Fong, Li Ching had a slightly stooped, fragile looking body. She was dressed very simply and austere in black. Her silver-grey hair, pulled back tightly from her face and tied in a bun at the back of head, appeared to be pulling her face tightly over her high cheekbones, giving her a taut, very smooth complexion. A collection of small wrinkles around her dark half-closed eyes belied the severity of her appearance, reacting pleasantly each time she smiled.

"How do you do . . . Li Ching?" she said hesitantly. "My name is Margaret Holland" she continued.

Ah Fong stepped closer, bowed slightly to the older woman and said to Margaret "Li Ching means "beautiful or graceful vapour" in English. He then turned to the woman, chattering in Chinese, obviously interpreting Margaret's words. The woman listened, smiling slightly, watching Margaret. As Ah Fong finished the old woman nodded politely to Margaret then turned to Ah Fong. Gesturing wildly and pointing at Margaret, she walked towards Ah

Fong, talking so rapidly he backed up slightly, not prepared for such an outburst. As she finished, Ah Fong smiled, turning to Margaret.

"She says you're in no condition to be climbing around on ships, we should have all have gone ashore to meet you. I'm afraid Mark and I are in a lot of trouble for bringing you out here."

"Oh no, it's all right," Margaret protested. "Please tell her I'm fine. I was down at the wharf so it was only natural I come out, and besides, this isn't my first baby, so I know what to expect." She paused slightly while Ah Fong translated again. Continuing, she added "Please tell her too that I think her name is lovely. I didn't realize you actually had meanings for your names. In English we don't have meanings to names, just the names. Tell me Ah Fong, what does your wife's name mean . . . and as a matter of interest, what does your name mean?"

Ah Fong answered "Ah Fong is only a common use name, what you would call a nick-name, and thus has very little meaning. You would find my real name quite unpronounceable. Po Lyan means 'valuable water lily' or possibly 'precious lotus' in English."

Intrigued by these names, Margaret turned to the younger woman. Taller than her mother, Po Lyan differed in other ways as well. The long, tight fitting red silk dress stressed her slim figure, making her appear even taller. The high collar that supported the long ivory neck added to the illusion. Her dark hair was pulled back from her tiny round face, but instead of being tied in a bun, was braided into a long queue which swung over her shoulder and hung down between her small breasts. Struck by her simple beauty and how young she looked, Margaret noticed her tiny lips trembling and her dark eyes wide with apprehension.

Either the voyage or the prospect of meeting strangers of a new race of people terrified her.

"Oh Po Lyan," Margaret started, extending her hands in friendship. "Come dear, don't be afraid," grasping her hands. Turning to Ah Fong, Margaret had mixed feelings as she berated them both. "Fong, she's positively lovely . . . but so young! Can't you two see she's scared stiff? Both of you get out of here and leave us alone. Could you please bring us some tea?"

The two men left the room sheepishly as Margaret guided the young girl over to a settee and sat her down. Li Ching approached, rattling away in Chinese, obviously upset with the girl, scolding her. When Ah Fong returned with the tea, he served as translator, clearing up some confusion and calming some of Po Lyan's fears. Margaret learned that she had been learning some English from Ah Fong during the voyage and was anxious to practice what she knew. As she talked with Margaret, sometimes directly, sometimes through Ah Fong's translation, Po Lyan began to realize that this barbarian woman from this primitive land could be friendly and almost civilized, and she began to like her. Margaret in turn, took an immediate liking to Po Lyan, feeling sympathetic to her feelings of fear and uncertainty in a strange land. For the older woman, she reserved judgment, not understanding the harsh words and actions she had been giving her daughter. As the atmosphere relaxed, they even invited Mark back into the room. Margaret felt almost out of place as the only one who couldn't speak Chinese. Po Lyan seemed to understand and was eager to practice her English on Margaret as well as learn more. As afternoon quickly darkened to evening, they all moved to the main salon to continue the conversation as supper was prepared. It was about halfway through supper when the first pain rippled through her. Margaret cringed slightly, then it was gone. She looked around her, but nobody else had noticed, except Li Ching. The woman looked at Margaret, a question written on her face. Margaret raised her finger to her lips to keep her hushed. It was like a signal, not to be quiet as Margaret intended, but for all hell to break loose.

Li Ching jumped up, jabbering away, pointing at Margaret. Three heads turned to Margaret, and everyone started talking at once, jumping up from the table.

"Relax," Margaret tried to calm them. "It's only the first one, we've got lots of time!" Nobody believed her, hustling her back to Mark's cabin. Li Ching took over, her experience and skill obvious at once. Mark was the first to go. The last thing Li Ching wanted was a worried husband hanging around, so she sent him ashore to notify the boys. Ah Fong was sent to the galley to boil water and Po Lyan assisted with Margaret, trying to talk with her late into the evening as the pains became closer together.

Chapter 46

A series of small cries shattered the Sunday morning silence as they echoed from the Shanghai Lady, flickered easily across the inner harbour and bounced along the shoreline. As the silence was subdued by the tiny cries, so they in turn were overcome by a series of larger cries, first from the proud father, then from each of the crew as the news spread.

And so the first day dawned for "Victoria Elizabeth", daughter of Margaret and Mark Holland, on November twenty third, 1851 on board the brigantine Shanghai Lady.

The word spread quickly and by day-beak, the crew had already ferried several visitors from the Fort wharf out to the Lady to see the new arrival and pass on their best wishes. The boys and Jonathan came first, aroused by a messenger sent ashore for that purpose. Cecilia came later, spending most of the morning helping where she could and talking with Po Lyan as Margaret slept.

Later, Mark talked with Margaret as she nursed the baby.

"She's definitely a little beauty" he murmured, looking down at the infant, now snuggled in Margaret's arms. The curly dark hair, pert little nose and stubborn chin clearly announced who her parents were, and her already defiant nature provided a clue to what they could expect in the future.

Li Ching had taken charge of the situation right from the beginning of Margaret's pains the evening before. Several weeks of travel from China as a passenger with virtually nothing to do had primed her for the opportunity to show these barbarians her skills and experience as a midwife. Using Ah Fong as a translator, she established some very strict rules about visiting rights to the mother and her new baby.

By the end of the first day, Mark had almost lost control of his vessel.

"I tell you Maggie," he whispered to her during a rare moment alone, "This can't go on much longer. I'm going to have to do something."

"Oh Mark, don't worry" she laughed. "This is her way of proving her worth, her big chance to show the rest of us how little we know about these matters. Her daughter has been attracting all the attention ever since they arrived. Li Ching has been standing in her shadow and has been nothing so far. This is her chance to . . . what do you call it . . . save face?" Mark nodded in agreement, wondering why he hadn't seen this. Margaret continued "Once I'm on my feet and back home, it will all return to normal."

"I hope so Maggie," Mark mumbled doubtfully.

Margaret stayed on board the Shanghai Lady a few more days, giving her some time to get to know both Li Ching and Po Lyan a little better. Although quite well and capable of going home earlier, she welcomed the time to rest, recover her strength and again get used to the routine of caring for a newborn baby.

In truth, she had little to do in that area as Li Ching took charge, handling everything except the nursing. This gave Margaret time to write again to her brother. The letter this time was long indeed, filled with all of the news about their business, Ah Fong's new family, as well as additional news she had gathered about the coal mining up the island. It also gave her more time to spend with the boys when they came to visit, time she had been missing lately, everyone so busy. She enjoyed much of her time with Ah Fong's new family.

Although a little timid at first, Po Lyan's wit and charm soon captured Margaret as it had captured the others. Struggling to improve her English, she was often the cause of many laughs during their discussions. At first the situation embarrassed her, making her hesitant to try again. Once she realized she was among friends, her new family, who wanted to help her, she opened up and progressed very rapidly. Her intuitive mind grasped meanings and word associations rapidly, locking them into a memory that lost nothing.

Margaret was fascinated by her and equally fascinated with her impact on Ah Fong. Many times during their discussions Margaret would watch Ah Fong whenever Po Lyan was talking. He obviously worshipped the young woman, trying to help her wherever he could, laughing with her, pain clouding his face whenever she struggled with the language or was the object of a joke. Ah Fong knew the importance of learning English, so he tried to impress this on Po Lyan, making her speak English whenever possible.

In contrast, Li Ching had decided that the language spoken by these barbarians was not worth the effort. Her daughter's husband spoke Shanghainese, as did his best friend Mark, so she felt the rest of them could too. It made communicating a little more difficult as an interpreter had to be present, usually Ah Fong or Mark, but as time progressed, Po Lyan started filling this function.

It wasn't until Margaret's last evening on board the Lady that she finally managed to catch Mark alone in his cabin with time enough to sit down and talk business.

Chapter 47

"My God Mark, I don't believe what's happened in the last few days," she exclaimed. "Since you've returned, we haven't had a moment to talk about your trip. It's obvious from Ah Fong's new family that you must have been busy over there!"

Mark nodded as he poured them some sherry. "More than you'll ever know" he thought to himself. He then continued aloud "Well Maggie, having a baby within a few hours of our arrival hasn't simplified life either."

Margaret agreed, laughing with him. Thinking about other things, she turned serious. "Do you think now you can tell me what really happened out there Mark? What kind of a trip did you really have?"

Mark recounted a brief outline of the voyage, his dealings in Shanghai, minimizing his encounter with the coolie as a chance robbery attempt. He then mentioned briefly their problems with the pirates, trying to pass the incident off as a rather casual affair.

"Oh Mark! Do you take me for a fool? I saw the damage to your ship . . . that didn't happen accidentally, or by some small incident!"

Mark eventually calmed her down, supplying only enough details to satisfy her curiosity. He then continued with the business part of his discussion. "As far as our business is concerned, the voyage was a very profitable one. Unfortunately, we'll only see about half the profits right away, the rest won't come 'til later."

"How is that Mark?" she asked.

"A lot of the cargo will have to wait until our next trip to England. Most of it consists of bales of raw silk which nobody can use here, but is worth a fortune in London. We'll have to off-load all the silk here while we take the rest of our cargo to San Francisco." He hesitated, recalling their slim escape, considering the wisdom of further trips. Finally he said "I feel if we make one more trip to China, we'll then have a full load of silk that we can take back to England."

Margaret listened, fascinated by Mark's accounting of his exotic cargo.

"While Ah Fong stayed in Shanghai helping his wife and mother-in-law pack up, we did a little travelling around, mainly between Shanghai and Chinkiang. The silk is the finest available and should bring an excellent price in London. Most of it is from Kiangsu and northern Chekiang, all within about 150 miles of Shanghai, but we also managed to pick up some beautiful yellow silk from Szechwan and some fine white silk from the Canton delta." He paused again thoughtfully, thinking back on his encounter with Mingqua. "The best part Maggie is that we were paid an old debt by an old friend of my father. I don't know how, but we managed to get the entire load out of the country without getting involved with all the export duties!"

"You never told me your father still had friends there Mark. What kind of debt?" Margaret interrupted, not missing anything.

"I didn't know either. It just happened that the Hong I dealt with had been involved with my father, years ago." Mark continued, filling in a few of the details, but leaving out most of the dangerous parts.

Apparently the explanation satisfied her as she carried

on with her questions. "You said most of it was silk. What else do you have?" she asked, captivated by his account.

"Well, to start," he continued, "We have over 500 piculs of tea and several of cassia."

"Wait a minute" she interrupted, "I'm just a poor Scottish lass! What's a picul and what's cassia?"

"A picul is a measure they use for tea and other dry goods. It's about 133 pounds, or about 15 piculs to the ton. As for cassia, that's a type of cinnamon" he answered, amused at her interest in every detail. "We can leave some of the tea here and take the rest to San Francisco with our next lumber shipment. Last year the British tea market was opened up to the American tea clippers, so I think they'll be concentrating on getting their cargoes back to England, rather than bothering with the small market in San Francisco."

"What did you get for trade goods for the store?" she asked, still worried about what they were going to sell to the local people.

"Don't worry Maggie, beside the silk, tea and cassia, we have rice, soy beans, bolts of woven silks and satins, sandlewood and gunpowder. We also managed a little trading with a Portuguese for some cotton from India and some camphor, rattans and spices from the islands of Malaysia."

The words rang in Margaret's ears, thrilling her with the exotic flavours and images they conjured up.

"Our furs brought the best price," Mark continued. "In spite of our little working arrangement with the company, I think we should try to lay our hands on as many furs as we can before our next trip to the Orient. We also still have some silver and gold left over, which will help us to stock up with tools and hardware back in England." Mark paused again, the next item bringing back memories of their perilous little side trip to Ningpo. "I also managed to find two volumes of a special geography of the world, "Ying-huan chih-leuh" written by Hsu Chi-yu. It was just printed last year and I've been wanting to get a copy. I also promised a friend in London that I would try to get a copy of it for him as well."

Margaret stared at him, again dumbfounded by the way the Chinese words rolled off his tongue, as well as his enthusiastic interest and knowledge of books, maps and the like. She realized it was this knowledge that provided the details for the story he had passed on to her that day months ago, the story that partially explained Adam's coins, the story that had fired her dreams and imagination to heights she never thought possible.

Chapter 48

A weak late November sun crept over the trees to find them already up and about, preparing to move back to the store. After the enjoyment of a few days off, Mark's crew was eager and hard at work, readying the ship for unloading.

"We have a high tide later this morning Margaret, so we'll move the Lady up the inlet to off-load most of the cargo" Mark informed her. "I can see Maggie, that if we keep this up, we'll have to build our own wharf. Maybe a small pier down on the shoreline behind the store so we won't have to limit our loading times to the high tide periods."

Margaret agreed, promising to talk to Jonathan and Thomas about it.

For the present, Margaret had her own problems, Li Ching and Po Lyan. They had all decided the two would move in with Margaret and her family. Actually Margaret was very pleased with the plan. As Ah Fong would be travelling with Mark most of the time, they had decided this arrangement was best for everyone. Besides, Margaret was glad of the company and the help.

A work crew, directed by Jonathan Stone, had been busy for several days adding two more small rooms on the store for the newcomers, as well as re-arranging the storage area to provide room for their new goods.

Using the two high tides each day, it still took them two days to unload all the silk and rest of the trade goods. Only a portion of the tea was taken off, so most of it was still on board when the Shanghai Lady sailed out of the harbour to pick up another load of lumber. They planned to return to the Fort within a week to prepare to take it all to San Francisco.

Margaret enjoyed her time with Po Lyan, helping her struggle with her English pronunciation, wishing she knew some Chinese to help her out on the word meanings. It was during this time Margaret learned more about Mark, more of his background and childhood. They struggled together, searching for the words as a more complete picture of the man developed. Po Lyan and her mother had known Mark for years, known about his affair with Mei Feng, and the recent troubles in Shanghai. Margaret listened, again fascinated with the strange account of their activities ashore as well as their encounter with the pirates. Almost sworn to secrecy, Margaret promised she would not reveal to Mark what they had told her.

Margaret's visits with Cecilia resumed as well, visits that now included Po Lyan, who enjoyed both the social outing as well as the opportunity to practice her English.

"Guess what, Margaret," Cecilia teased one day. "We're finally going to have our own doctor! Remember, some time ago Father recalled Doctor Helmcken from Fort Rupert? We've just heard that he's almost finished there and he should be here within a week!"

The news was certainly welcome. Although too late for the birth of her child, Margaret knew that Mrs. Langford was expecting very soon. She was sure the doctor would be welcome by many of the other settlers as well.

During another visit the following week, a cry echoed outside the Fort that the company steamship Beaver was steaming into the harbour. Normally, this was not big news, as the Beaver was constantly coming and going, transporting people and trade goods between Fort Victoria, Fort Langley, Fort Rupert and other spots on the coast.

"Oh Maggie" exclaimed Cecilia, "The Beaver has just come down from Fort Rupert, so I'll wager Dr. Helmcken is aboard."

Curiosity getting the best of them, they bundled up warmly against the cold December wind and headed off down to the wharf.

The air was crisp and clear, offering a stunning view of the straits and the snow covered mountain range to the south. Low in the southern sky, the weak winter sun offered little protection against the brisk westerly that blew in from the Pacific.

As they arrived, the Beaver was already steaming up to the wharf, crewmen ready to leap off, mooring lines ready.

Margaret and Cecilia joined her father as the little steamer puffed and snorted to a halt alongside the dock. The crew had no sooner secured the vessel when a tall man stepped out of the cabin and crossed the deck towards them. The small, black leather bag he carried immediately gave away his identity.

James Douglas stepped forward to greet him. "John my boy, good to see you back. How was the trip down?"

"Fine, Mr. Douglas" he answered, laughing, "Although we could have done without the last few miles coming around Discovery Island. I must say they were a little brisk in this wind" he observed. He then turned his attention to the girls as the Chief Factor introduced them.

"John, I'd like you to meet my eldest daughter, Cecilia. I don't believe you two had a chance to meet when you came through last time, on your way to Fort Rupert."

John Helmcken stepped forward, bowing slightly to Cecelia. A broad smile spread across his face, contrasting with his ruddy complexion, dark beard and bushy moustache.

"How do you do, Miss Douglas" he beamed. "I'm very pleased to make your acquaintance."

Cecilia flushed hotly, mumbling something in return, visibly dazzled by this dashing young doctor.

"And this, John," Mr. Douglas continued, turning to Margaret, "Is Mrs. Margaret Holland, one of our newer settlers. Mrs. Holland is the proprietor of that store down the road a piece, while her husband has a brigantine to keep her supplied with goods." He paused a moment as the two greeted each other, then continued. "Actually, John, they're giving the Company some competition, trading, selling goods, importing tea and silk from China. I wager we'll regret ever letting her join the colony" he laughed.

Cecilia was still spell-bound by the young doctor, thinking that he was the most handsome man she had ever laid eyes on. In truth, at 27 years of age, John Sebastian Helmcken was a very presentable young man. Upon completion of four years of study at Guy's Hospital in London, John had become a member of the Royal College of Surgeons. He had also served as ship's doctor for the Hudson's Bay Company on a voyage to York Factory. Shortly after, he had accepted an offer to take the post of doctor and clerk at Fort Vancouver on the Columbia River, which started with a five month journey around the Horn on the Norman Morison. However, upon his arrival at Fort Victoria, instead of sending him down to Fort Vancouver as planned, they immediately sent him to Fort Rupert on the northern end of Vancouver's Island in the dual capacity of magistrate and Company surgeon. Stories had been circulating about three deserters from the Norman Morison, reputed to have headed to the Fort Rupert area.

Later that year, during July, he had heard the deserters had been murdered by some Indians, suspected to be the strong willed Kwakuitl from the north. This had resulted in Mr. Helmcken asking the navy ship H.M.S. Daedalus to aid in their capture.

Although they were all very pleased that John Helmcken had now returned to Fort Victoria as Company doctor, Cecilia was glowing.

"I think you rather fancy the man" Margaret whispered to her as the men left, heading up the slope to the Fort.

"Oh Maggie" Cecilia gasped, "You have no idea!"

Thinking back to her own situation a few months ago, Margaret replied "Oh, I think I do Cecilia. I think I do."

Chapter 49

Cecilia's attraction for the new doctor continued to glow, fanned into flames by the occasional glance of encouragement. As Company surgeon, John Helmcken was billeted in the bachelor's hall at the Fort and visited the Douglas home periodically, ostensibly to report to the Chief Factor.

Margaret was not sure whether Cecilia's father was fooled by this little subterfuge, but in any case he allowed the visits to continue. The first real chance the two had to get close and talk to each other was during the Christmas dance, held a few weeks after John's arrival.

The Shanghai Lady had returned from Jensen's Mill with a good load of lumber that would sail for San Francisco immediately after Christmas. Mark and Margaret had been looking forward to the dance at the Fort as it gave them both a break from their normal work and routine, as well as a chance to meet more of the settlers.

When they arrived, festivities were already in full swing. A piano, two fiddles and a flute battled for attention at one end of the hall, providing an interesting background for the dance.

"Well, look who we have here," a familiar voice hailed them as they entered. Charlie Croghan steadied himself against the wall, his finger waving toward them.

"The newlyweds," he continued. "Good evening, Mrs. Holland," he added graciously.

"Good evening, Mr. Croghan. Hardly newlyweds, I might add." Margaret answered, fascinated by the man's almost constant state of intoxication, yet tempered with good manners and undisguised charm.

"Hello Charlie" Mark greeted him. "How've you been keepin', you old coot? I hear you've been doing some prospecting for the Company lately."

"Not so good, Mark, at least not with the prospectin'. Since they found that coal up at Nanymo Bay, that's all they want me to look for." Shifting to a more upright stance, he took a deep breath and continued. "Goddammit Mark, I'm a gold prospector! A man can't change horses that fast after all the years I've been in that saddle. I keep tellin' Douglas there's gold around here, we just have to look for it. I've even found some colours in some local creeks, but he's not havin' any of it!"

"Don't worry Charlie, you'll have your chance," Mark consoled him. "At least you're getting to know the lay of the land . . . never know when that will come in handy."

Never know indeed, Margaret thought. A few more prospects were added to the undeveloped plan she carried in the back of her mind. Here was a man with experience, knowledge and two donkeys, all equipped to do the job she longed to do!

They carried on into the hall, talking with some people they already knew as well as meeting others for the first time. As they walked around, the musicians tried a waltz and Margaret found herself swept on to the floor in Mark's arms. As they circled, she approached Mark with a question.

"Mark, this might sound crazy . . . but . . . do you think your Charlie Croghan might be a good man to lead our little expedition?"

"What . . . Oh . . ." Mark looked around quickly. He continued thoughtfully, "Well Maggie, I don't know . . . you might have a point there. Charlie doesn't really know that area, but I'm sure he knows more than we do about that kind of travel and how to survive in the bush."

"Maybe we should talk to him", Margaret said hopefully, encouraged by Mark's words.

"Not yet Maggie, you know it's too early. As we discussed, I think we should keep this under our hats until we have our plans figured out a little more".

With some disappointment Margaret tucked the idea away with the rest of the plan, with a promise to herself to examine the possibility further. As they danced around the floor, her thoughts were slowly pulled back to the present. Mark proved to be an excellent dancer and as they whirled and dipped, their bodies would occasionally meet, held tighter and longer than necessary by two people in love.

From time to time, they couldn't help looking over to the Douglas family, where Cecilia and John Helmcken were quietly talking in the corner. Margaret could see Cecilia was radiant, her eyes wide as she soaked up everything John had to offer.

Cecilia's mother spent most of her time beside her husband James, talking with settlers as they came by. Margaret could see that Amelia was definitely aware of the conversation between her daughter and the new doctor, obviously pleased with the prospects of a match.

It was during the early morning hours as most of the dancers were refreshing themselves at the punch bowl when it happened. The first low rumblings were scarcely noticed by most, blending in with the sound of the few dancers still on the floor. As the dishes and glasses started to rattle and the punch bowl started marching to the edge of the table they realized something more serious was happening.

Mark recognized it first and reacted quickly.

"Earthquake!" he yelled, grabbing Margaret and pulling her out the side door of the hall into the frosty night. The rumblings grew to a roar, a roar that seemed to be coming from everywhere at once. A few people started to stagger to the doors, but it was over before most of them really had a chance to react. Their faces reflected mixed feelings, varying from confusion to sheer terror. The facade of civilized control can be stripped from a man very fast by moving and shaking the solid earth beneath him.

"What in God's name was that?" Margaret asked as they re-entered the hall, visibly shaken.

"Only a little tremor I guess," Mark replied. "We were lucky."

Like most of the settlers, Margaret was not familiar with earthquakes and had found the experience terrifying. Mark had been through enough of them in China and Japan to recognize them very quickly. James Douglas also knew of them from his California days and was calmly explaining them to the other colonists.

"We must be in a similar geological area to California," Mark added. "Probably links us all the way up the Russian Aleutians and over to Japan. They have small tremors quite regularly. It's the big ones that are really scary" he added.

"The big ones?"

"Yes Maggie, sometimes they destroy whole towns, hundreds, sometimes thousands of people are killed. The ground rolls and shakes, sometimes opening up and swallowing people or entire buildings!" He paused a moment, a troubled look in his eyes. "And then comes the tsunami" he added.

"Soo-nammy?" Margaret queried, suddenly worried, seeing Mark's concern.

"Tidal waves, big ones!" he replied. "It's a Japanese word. When an earthquake happens somewhere under the ocean, it can make the beginnings of large waves. They can travel for hundreds of miles, sometimes washing away an entire village or seaport!"

Margaret listened to this in horror, reinforced by the terror she had just felt with the small tremor.

"My God, it must be terrible" she murmured. "When I think of how much that one scared me."

The dance soon resumed, but somehow without the energy and enthusiasm of before. It wasn't long and everyone was making their excuses and heading home into the cold dark night, their thoughts on things other than the festivities of the dance.

Chapter 50

True to his word, Hay-Hay Kane returned to Fort Victoria as the spring blossoms were appearing. He stopped only briefly at the Songhees village to visit his friend, Pel Shaymoot, as well as paying his respects to Chief Tsil-al-Thach. After a short visit, he continued down to the beach with his friend to be ferried across to the Fort side of the inlet.

Thomas and Jonathan were caulking the final plank of Jonathan's new schooner at the boat shed when they heard Kane hailing them from across the inlet. Dropping their tools, they headed down to the beach, walking down the ramp to their new wharf. Standing on the dock, they watched as Kane's friend paddled him both across the glassy inlet in the sleek little dugout. They were soon gliding up to the dock, Kane's smile beaming as they greeted each other.

The new wharf had caught Kane's eye and Thomas and Jonathan were quick to show off their handiwork. They continued up the ramp to the boat house, trying to fill in the gaps of almost half a year within minutes. The sleek lines of the schooner's hull were not lost on Kane as they watched him looking over the new vessel. The heavy aroma of red cedar and pungent essence of yellow cedar assailed them as they waded through piles of shavings. The smells of the wood were flavoured with Stockholm tar from the oakum used in caulking the planks. They pointed out construction features to Kane as they walked around the smooth form, almost complete in its cradle. He seemed fascinated by the white man's method of building a boat. He couldn't understand why they wanted to cut the tree up into small pieces and then try to put them back together again when a man could just cut the vessel you needed directly out of a large tree. Jonathan's new schooner was barely over forty feet long, small enough for their limited capability, but large enough to be used for some coastal freight work. Kane was interested only in its construction, not its size as he was familiar with the Haida hunting or war canoes which ran up to fifty or sixty feet long.

Later, at the store, Kane was very pleased to greet Margaret again.

"Kla-how-ya Tlul-cul-ma, . . . Hello, pretty woman . . . missus Holland."

"Hello Kane," Margaret replied warmly, so pleased to see him again. "How are you, how was your mother, how . . ." Kane interrupted her, overwhelmed by the questions.

"Please missus . . . please. Kane will tell . . . slowly please," he pleaded, trying to slow the outpouring of Margaret's questions. Soon they were both settled with some tea and cookies that Kane enjoyed, sharing their experiences of the winter. The most important information Margaret learned from Kane was some additional details of Adam's fate.

As suspected, the Falmouth's boat had entered the large bay at Port San Juan. Having missed the rocky shoreline of the outer coast, the vessel had almost reached the relative safety of the sandy shore at the end of the bay. From what Kane could learn, the boat must have lost control in the surf at the end of the bay, surf that rolls in constantly, even on still days. That night the sea must have been whipped to a frenzy by the storm. With little or no control, the small boat was tossed on to the large outcroppings of rock on the south side of the bay, just short of the beach. Quickly torn to pieces by the sharp rocks, the small boat gave up its lone passenger, leaving him to the mercy of the barnacle covered crags along the shore. Barely alive, he was found early the next morning, washed high up on the beach.

Margaret knew the rest of the story from Kane's previous accounts as well as Adam's journal. Although she had suspected such a fate, Margaret was morbidly fascinated by the confirmation of some of the details assembled from the information Kane had gleaned over the winter.

Interrupted by a cry, Margaret rushed back to her living quarters to check the baby. Li-Ching was already there, preparing the baby for Margaret to nurse her. She brought the baby out to show Kane, who had never seen a white baby before. He was equally fascinated by Li-Ching, who reminded him of some of some of the old women of his own race.

Later, when Po Lyan had also returned from visiting Cecilia at the Fort, Kane remarked to Margaret "Many changes, Tlul-cul-ma. Kane away . . . you get new baby . . . new family . . . bigger store . . . new boat."

"Yes Kane, many changes," Margaret had to agree. "Hopefully lots more to come," she added, thinking not only of their own situation, but of the growth of the colony. Mr. Pemberton, the new surveyor, had been very busy. He had just completed a new town plan and sent it off to HBC Headquarters in London. The plan divided all of the land around the Fort into blocks of lots, separated by streets, all laid out like a regular town. The area included all the land right from James Bay, near the Douglas' new home, up Kanaka Road to the Fort. One of the changes discussed was to change the name of Kanaka Road to Humbolt Street, but the decision was not yet final. The plan continued to follow the shoreline of the inlet and along what was now called Store Street, carrying on to Margaret's store and beyond.

The Company coal miners up at Wintuhuysen Inlet, or Nanymo Bay, had also made progress, proud of their first shipments of coal to San Francisco. James Douglas was convinced the coal prospects of that area had a great future and he was pressing young Robert Dunsmuir, the Ayrshire coal mining authority, to find some bigger reserves of the material. He had written to headquarters in London, asking for more miners, coal experts and equipment. The promise of gold deposits had diminished somewhat, the Fort Rupert and Queen Charlotte finds dwindling to impractical amounts. Despite Charlie Croghan's pleas, very little manpower or effort was being expended on the search for gold. By this time, more gold was coming into Fort Victoria from California, through the normal trading activity between the two centres.

For their own behalf, Margaret and Mark were trying to increase this flow of gold northward, but by investing in their large inventories of tea and silk was cutting down their profits from short term trading with San Francisco.

Thomas and Jonathan's boat building activity was moderately successful, but would not pay large dividends until it became self-sufficient. This was one of the reasons they had decided to build the larger schooner instead of more of the smaller workboats like the first one. Jonathan figured once they had their own vessel, one large enough to handle some freight, they could be making additional money through that activity when boats were not being built. It would also allow them to head around to Jensen's Mill anytime they required more lumber, or run some across from Millstream without having to wait for the

Shanghai Lady or another available ship. Jonathan had used all of his savings for the venture, as well as making an agreement with Margaret for a promise of shipping availability of the small vessel. They were all looking forward to the day they would launch her, a day Jonathan assured them would be very soon.

Chapter 51

They launched Jonathan's schooner late in May, during the high tide one warm spring evening. Jonathan and Thomas had worked hard all day with a couple of Songhees friends. They skidded the empty hull out of the boat shed and partially down the beach on some logs while the tide was low. Although the empty hull was much lighter without ballast, moving it was still a formidable task.

Once the vessel was in place near the low water level, they had nothing to do but wait for the tide to come up. With a tidal range of almost ten feet that day, and the vessel's draft of almost six feet, they knew they had a few hours to wait before she would float.

They watched the water level creep slowly up the beach. As the first wavelets lapped at the bottom of the keel, a small cheer went up, turning quickly to laughter as they realized the insignificance of the event.

That evening after supper, a small group of family, friends and the occasional well-wisher gathered, watching patiently as the rising sea slowly covered each plank of the sleek hull.

Before long, the stern of the boat, being furthest out from the shore in deeper water, started to float. One-by-one, the wooden braces that had held the hull erect toppled and drifted away as the vessel floated higher. Soon, the entire hull was afloat, riding high and moving gently with the small ripples in the inlet.

This stimulated a much larger cry as the small gathering cheered, congratulating the young builders on the fine job.

They immediately pulled the vessel over to the dock where Reverend Staines gave the blessing and Margaret performed the official launching ceremony. She accomplished this, to the delight of some onlookers, by breaking a small bottle of home-made berry wine across the oak stem.

Christened the "Maggie M.", the stout little vessel thus started its life with the sea. Jonathan's design maximized freight carrying capacity, so she appeared quite wide in the beam and deep of hull. The long straight keel made her easy to beach for repairs or scraping her bottom as well as effortless to handle once the sails were set. Her rig would be a standard fore'n aft topsail schooner rig, with most of the rigging salvaged from lines and old sails from the Shanghai Lady. Mark had donated the old gear as he allowed that though most of it was no longer suitable for ocean voyages, it would be adequate for coastal work. To sharpen his sail-maker's skills, Thomas had been given the task of changing, cutting and re-sewing the large pieces of canvas.

Once in the water, the vessel provided even more of a challenge to its builders, who now worked harder and longer hours to complete their work. Once they had erected the masts and completed the standing rigging, the carpentry work on cabins, cargo holds and spars stretched their resources and stamina even further.

By early summer, shortly after the Shanghai Lady had returned from another San Francisco trip, the builders announced they were ready for her maiden voyage.

Mark and Margaret were eager to join Thomas and Jonathan for her initial sail around the harbour, testing her response to the light breeze and ability to tack quickly within the confines of the small inlet.

Later that day, a few of the more experienced sailors

took her out into the Straits of Juan de Fuca for a more vigorous shakedown in the brisk westerly which almost daily blew in from the Pacific. To most of them, the lighter vessel provided a welcome change from the much larger Shanghai Lady. This was more of a sport, the smaller vessel being a lot more tender, but much quicker to respond, sometimes a little quicker than they thought. They continued to make small changes to the running rigging as they sailed, and by late afternoon they returned, exhausted but jubilant at the success of their venture.

"I think if we just move that turning block for the jumbo jib sheet a little further aft . . ." Thomas continued babbling his suggestions to Jonathan as they tied her up to the wharf. "And then we can . . ." he went on, immersed in the subject.

Their temporary crew abandoned them to their obsession, heading up to the store where Margaret had invited them to return for supper.

Li Ching and Po Lyan had been busy all afternoon, preparing supper for the lot of them, eager to please Ah Fong and his friends. Margaret's life had gone through yet another change since Victoria or "Vickie" had been born. Years before, when Thomas and Andrew were just babies, her workload had increased considerably, adding to their problems as she and Adam strived to build their business. Now it was different. She found herself with much more time to accomplish the tasks she wanted to do, more time to visit, read and work on her plans. Li Ching had completely taken over her duties as mother and Margaret found it difficult to even spend a little time with her new baby.

The extra time gave her more opportunity to think as well, to think about the gold coins, to think about the west coast and how she should plan her venture. Her discussions with Kane had taught her a fair amount about both the area she planned to visit as well as the people who lived there. She also realized she did not know enough and would require some expert help. During their talks, Kane had expressed his willingness to act as guide and interpreter for Margaret when the time came. She had referred to the excursion as an exploration trip to visit the Indians and see first hand where her husband had died. Kane had accepted this as a convincing reason to make the journey.

The other problem that had plagued her for a time was the need for some pack animals for the supplies. She had her horse, but the animal was not trained to travel in that kind of country and could not carry what they would need. This left her with only one alternative, one she had tried to avoid, Charlie Croghan. Charlie had two donkeys, equipped and experienced in this type of work. The only problem was, Charlie came with them. Although not fond of Charlie, Margaret had to admit he was the ideal choice to lead such a venture. He had the experience, knowledge and ability to travel and stay alive in that kind of country. The longer she thought about it, the more she was convinced that Charlie would have to be the one! Once she talked herself into it, she could hardly wait to discuss it with Mark.

Her opportunity came a few days later when Mark returned from Jensen's Mill.

"Well he's experienced enough to give it a good shot" Mark commented as Margaret enthusiastically explained her plan. "From some stories he's told me, he's had more than his share of tight situations and it sounds like he can surely handle himself in almost any type of country."

"Then it's settled" she announced firmly. "I'll talk to him

the next time he's in town and we'll try to set up a time, possibly right after you get back from your next trip?" she said hopefully, watching Mark's face closely to see what the reaction would be.

"Hold on Maggie," he countered, feeling he had just been trapped. "You'll have to wait until later this summer. We'll be heading to China again on this trip, so we won't be back until late August, more than three month's from now!"

She couldn't believe her ears! Although she felt a twinge of disappointment at being delayed several months, this was more than covered by the feeling of elation and victory as Mark had at least not rejected her proposal outright.

"Well that's probably as well," she continued, trying to keep the discussion centred on the subject at hand. "It will most likely take that long to get everything arranged, and figure out what supplies we need. I'll talk with Charlie and Kane to get their opinion on what we'll need."

"Just be careful Maggie," Mark added. "Don't commit yourself too much until we have a better idea of the time."

He knew he needn't have worried as Margaret was fully capable of making arrangements and dealing with the likes of Charlie Croghan.

Chapter 52

Several days later, they were all down at the wharf to say goodbye to the Shanghai Lady and her crew. As this was not a local trading venture or a quick trip to San Francisco, concern and despondent feelings dominated the scene. Even at this time of the year a trip of several thousand miles to the Orient could be a risky proposition, requiring every resource the ship and her crew could provide. Threats to their safety came in many forms, from major storms off the west coast of Vancouver's Island or typhoons in the China Sea to savage pirates along the China coast. Considering what Margaret had learned about their problems during the last trip, she was hesitant indeed to agree to another voyage.

Margaret's concerns were twofold. Her burning love for Mark occupied her mind constantly and the chance of losing him on one of these voyages always terrified her. The overall responsibility for her family was the driving force that not only kept her going, but sharpened her mind as well. The more she worked on the problems of everyday survival, the less she worried about Mark.

Tearful farewells faded as they stood on the shore, waving at the receding form of the Shanghai Lady as she sailed out of the harbour towards the open Pacific. When the familiar shape had disappeared in the early morning mists of Juan de Fuca Straits, Margaret felt the pressure of her duties land squarely on her shoulders. Her concerns had now turned into a threefold situation, as the planning of her west coast expedition was now included in her load.

Luckily, this new problem was one she loved as it now occupied most of her waking thoughts. Both the demands of setting it up and organizing the details as well as the unknown challenge of the trip itself excited her, making it more like a game than a chore. The most difficult part of the project at this point was trying to keep it secret. She knew eventually she would have to announce some reason for them all to be taking off on an expedition to the west coast, but she felt it would better to keep it to herself for as long as she could.

Her first chance to talk with Kane came a few days later. When she explained her plans further about making the journey later that summer, he was delighted.

"Good time, Tlul-cul-ma. Not so much rain, many berries and food."

"That's good Kane, we'll need all the help we can get. I'm trying to plan what we'll need for the trip so I'd appreciate your help."

Margaret found Kane a big help. His knowledge of the area, people and local vegetation was invaluable in planning a rough schedule of their trip. Kane was not pleased to hear about "Charlie-man" coming.

"We need his donkeys Kane," Margaret tried to explain. "It's the only way we can carry what we need for food and shelter for the time we will be there." She did not mention the chance of finding anything to carry back. Kane could not fully understand why they needed to carry so much. He had travelled the area many times carrying no more than what his two hands could hold. He accepted Margaret's explanation with some reservations, but Margaret knew the relationship between the two men would be very touchy. She wondered what Charlie's reaction would be as she still hadn't talked to him yet. From the reports she got from the Fort, Charlie was still out near Sooke prospecting and was expected back soon.

Late one evening she was explaining the planned expedition to the rest of the family. "I didn't tell you before, but your father left some notes with the money we found in his old coat." She paused for a moment in her story to explain to Li Ching and Po Lyan the details behind the death of her husband. "I can't explain too much just now. I can only say we must return to the area he travelled to investigate something he found on the west coast."

Looks of confusion crossed more than one face as questions surfaced.

"What do you . . ." A sharp jolt hit the house, abruptly cutting the discussion short. A low rumble followed, rapidly increasing to a roar. The house trembled slightly at the first shock, then started shaking again, violently rattling everything around them. Po Lyan screamed as they jumped up, confused and terrified.

"Outside quickly," Margaret yelled, remembering Mark's actions. "Andrew!" she yelled, "Help Po Lyan . . ."

Thomas was at her side. "Come on, let's get out of here" as he grabbed her arm.

"I've got to get the baby," she shrieked at Thomas, pushing Li Ching towards the door. Staggering towards the bedroom, flying objects assailed them from the shelves and furniture bounced around the floor. Almost clubbed by the violently swinging door of the bedroom, she grabbed Vickie from her bed and headed back to the rear of the house with Thomas.

By the time she was out, the tremor had died off, leaving everyone shaken and terrified outside the house.

Thomas was the first to speak. "My God that was a lot

worse than the last one we had last winter. I just hope they don't get any worse than that!"

Margaret agreed, checking everyone to make sure they were all right. Po Lyan still trembled violently as her mother tried to comfort her. The darkening evening still echoed with voices from the Songhees village across the inlet and the occasional yell from down near the Fort.

Terror subsided to nervous laughter as they all started talking at once, comparing feelings and fears. Margaret was facing the inlet talking to Thomas when she saw his eyes grow wide.

"Wha . . . what's that light, flickering in the house . . ." he mumbled, already heading towards the house, fearing the worse. Margaret wheeled around, a silent scream on her lips as she quickly realized what had happened.

"Fire!" Thomas' cry rang out, filling them all with the universal terror of their worst enemy.

"Grab some buckets . . . get down to the inlet." someone yelled.

Thomas ran out of the house, looking towards Margaret. "It's the lamp . . . the kerosene already has everything going. Let's try to get something out of the store!"

Margaret handed Vickie to Li Ching. "Here, move away and take care of her!" she admonished, hoping she would understand. She then joined Po Lyan and Jonathan carrying water from the inlet in a futile attempt to wet down parts of the burning building. Thomas and Andrew were pulling bales of silk and cases of tea out of the store that was already filling with smoke.

Margaret suddenly remembered Adam's journal. Without the journal she would never find the gold! Dropping her bucket, she ran towards the house.

"Mrs. Holland, you can't go in there," Jonathan screamed, trying to grab her arm.

Margaret twisted away, plunging into the smoke filled rear door, immediately tripping over a chair in the thick smoke. Lying on the floor trying to get her bearings, she realized being low on the floor was the only way she could survive. The air coming in the door was moving across the floor, fanning the flames into the store. The heat was already intense, as she could smell her hair burning. Moving on her hands and knees, she crawled towards her bedroom, where the journal was hidden away. The smoke burned her eyes, choking her whenever she raised her head slightly. Crawling as quickly as she could on her belly, she finally gained the bedroom. Fooled into thinking the smoke wasn't as thick here, so she stood up to get into the cupboard. The false impression was short lived as some clothes ignited near the door and acrid fumes enveloped her. Her eyes burnt as she fumbled around in the cupboard with a handkerchief over her mouth, smoke too thick now to see anything. Just as she knew she had to give up, she felt the familiar shape of the journal, wrapped in its oil-skin covering. Shoving in down in her blouse, she turned quickly to retreat. Too late. The entire doorway was now ablaze, fueled more fiercely by the clothes and personal items lying around. Panic struck, thoughts of a useless death flashed through her mind.

Suddenly, she remembered the window. Turning quickly, she crawled towards the wall that held the small window frame. As she didn't have any glass, she had used some oiled paper in the window to let extra light into the room. She struggled to open it, choking on the dense smoke. Coughing violently, she sucked in more of the deadly fumes. She clawed at the frame, trying a feeble punch at the paper window as everything turned black.

Chapter 53

Vague points of light moved in the darkness, foiling attempts to define shapes and forms. Violent coughs racked her body again as she turned and vomited on the dusty ground beside her.

Slowly, the lights and colours took shape and the sounds became familiar voices.

"What . . . where . . ." she rasped, pain constricting her throat again.

"Relax, Mom," Andrew's familiar voice calmed her. "Don't try to talk, you'll just hurt yourself more. You're lucky to be alive, Jonathan pulled you out of that window just in time."

Margaret nodded her head, attempting a smile as she remembered her predicament. Suddenly, she recalled why she was in the building and her hand went to her blouse . . . nothing! Andrew spotted her panic and took her hand.

"Don't worry Mom, Thomas has Dad's journal. It fell out of your blouse when Jonathan pulled you out, so he took it for safekeeping."

Margaret's relief settled her down. Looking around, she then tried to examine the situation without asking any more questions.

It was still dark, but the glow of the fire lit up the area with a ruddy haze. Margaret suddenly realized the glow was coming from the remains of her new home and store!

"Oh . . . my God . . ." she whimpered. "It's all gone." Pain stabbed her in the chest as she coughed again. "Vickie . . . where's Vickie?" she mumbled.

"She's fine . . . Miss Douglas took her up to the Fort with Po Lyan and Li Ching."

"How bad is it Andrew?" she whispered, fearing the worst.

"Well, the boat house and tool shed are still fine, so Thomas didn't lose any of his tools. We've lost the house, as well as the store. They managed to salvage a few cases of the silk and tea, but very little . . . the fire spread so fast."

Margaret's hopes collapsed. They had just lost most of the freight from the last China trip. Their main reserve, their savings to be sold back in London . . . all gone. Tears filled her eyes, overflowing down her cheeks, cutting clean channels in the sooty surface.

Andrew continued. "Most of the Fort people came to help, as well as Kane and some of his friends, but they were all too late. The kerosene from the lamp must have spread and got the fire going too quickly, and everything was so dry. When Jonathan pulled you out, he carried you over here, so you could get some fresh air off the inlet. When Dr. Helmcken arrived, he suggested we not move you, but let you relax and clear your breathing."

As if on cue, John Helmcken leaned over her, his large moustache spreading in a wide smile.

"Well Mrs. Holland, I see you've decided to join us again."

"Hello John . . ." She started hesitantly.

"No, no." he interjected. "Try not to talk for now, give your lungs a chance to clear out." He pulled out his stethoscope and checked her breathing. "The smoke did most of your damage" he continued. "That and a little singed hair, but no serious burns. We had only one small injury from the earthquake . . . a brick fell off one of the chimneys at the Fort and bounced off some poor fellow's head . . . must have had a tough head because he's fine now, only a big headache. Here, we've been patching up small burns all night but luckily nothing serious."

"We? . . . Doctor" Margaret asked.

"Cecil . . . er . . . Miss Douglas has been helping me all night and has proved to be a very capable nurse."

Margaret smiled in spite of her discomfort. She had enjoyed watching their romance grow over the past six months and often wondered when they would decide to marry. She made a note to discuss the matter with Cecilia the next time they had tea.

Propping herself up into a sitting position, she could see the remains of her home, now a pile of smouldering embers. Visible in the smoky darkness beyond the ashes was a pitiful stack of goods that had been pulled free of the fire . . . so little for so much work. Spotting Jonathan nearby, she motioned for him to come over near her.

"Well Jonathan," she whispered, "I understand I have you to thank for being here, as well as all your help in saving some of our goods."

"Oh Mrs. Holland," he blushed, "Don't you bother talking just now. I did what any of us would have." He looked around at the rest of the volunteers cleaning up, ready to go home. "Just so's you don't worry none, you and the baby'll be stayin' at the Fort tonight with Miss Douglas . . . as well as Li Ching and Polly-Ann."

"Polly-Ann?" Margaret asked.

"Sorry," Jonathan mumbled, "That's what her name sounds like when you say it fast, so that's what I call her."

Margaret thought about the name. "Po Lyan . . . Polly-Ann. I can see your point Jonathan."

Jonathan continued "Thomas, Andrew 'n I will be

bunkin' down in the Maggie M. Come daylight tomorrow, we'll figure out what we can do until we rebuild."

The words "until we rebuild" jolted Margaret's resolve. Everything they had worked for had brought them forward, ever closer to setting up a comfortable business and life in this new world. They had not wasted any time on dwelling on the possibility of losing it all. She could see now they had not protected themselves . . . had "put all their eggs in one basket." As she lay there, she resolved never to let the same thing happen again, she would always have a reserve, an alternate supply to draw upon.

"How are you feeling now Mrs. Holland," John Helmcken's voice interupted her thoughts. "Do you think you can make it up to the Fort? There's not much you can do here now until the morning, so you might as well get some rest."

Margaret had no choice but to agree as she struggled upright and slowly shuffled up the trail towards the Fort.

The next day dawned bright and warm on the little settlement as the small group stood around the smouldering remains of their home and business. After a fitful few hours in strange beds, they gathered early that morning to survey the damage.

Thomas sifted through the still hot ashes picking out the iron parts of picks, shovels and ploughs... items they could salvage and rebuild. Margaret and Po Lyan carefully picked through the remains of the kitchen area to salvage some cast iron pots and other utensils that survived the fire. Jonathan and Andrew were occupied in the boathouse for a short time, finally returning to the group.

"Mrs. Holland, if you don't mind, we have some suggestions to make for our next step" Jonathan announced.

"We?" Margaret inquired.

"Yes, Thomas, Andrew and myself . . . we got to talkin' last night, and we figured it out this mornin'. We'll stay on the Maggie M. . . . we have our bunks all set up there anyway. You and Vickie, as well as Polly-Ann and her mother, will have to set up house-keeping in the boathouse. We figure we have enough extra lumber to board in the front of it today and put in one partition. The place is big enough, you'll just have to decide how to arrange it all. As for the store, we don't have to worry too much because there's nothing to sell."

They talked for a short time, trying out different ideas, but finally settled on Jonathan's suggestion as the best alternative. Before long, they were hard at work helping Jonathan and Thomas board in the front of the boat house and install the extra partition.

By the time they had the front wall finished, people started to show up from all over the colony, ready to help. Some had brought food, others had brought extra lumber or some pieces of furniture. Others just came to offer their help.

"We know you'll have more goods coming for the store in a few months Margaret, but we had to help you through this time."

"We love your store, so we can't let your business fail because of this." These comments and many like them made Margaret realize that she wasn't alone, she had many friends in the colony.

By the end of the day, the whole family was again settled on a temporary basis in the large boathouse, recently occupied by Jonathan's schooner.

"Tomorrow we'll have to build a small fire-place for

cooking" Thomas was saying as they sat around eating the food delivered to them earlier in the day.

"And making tea" Margaret added. "By the way, Thomas, what kind of tea did you manage to salvage from the fire?"

"Don't worry Mom, we got at least one case of Lapsang, so you'll have your tea! We also got several cases of other teas, several bales of silk, a case of that cinnamon stuff and several sacks of rice."

"Well I'm sure we can use the rice during the next few months." Margaret answered.   Recovered from the first shock, they would find many things would be needed during the next few months.

Chapter 54

The days that followed reminded Margaret of her arrival, over a year earlier. Almost homeless and without her husband, she felt she was starting over, organizing her family . . . much larger now, and trying to plan for their future.

The conditions now however, were much different. Thomas and Andrew had grown and matured, both now able to handle more of the chores and responsibilities. Jonathan was her mainstay, a big help with the extra physical labour required, but also for just being there to talk with when needed.

Li Ching and Po Lyan had surprised Margaret. Their resilience and capability of coping with the disaster showed a strength of character and range of experience not suspected in such frail souls.

Their first order of business was arranging trade agreements with the local farms. They had tea, silk, cinnamon and some rice to trade for vegetables, meat and flour as required. At least they would eat well for the summer, with promises for additional goods throughout the winter.   Thomas worked on the remains of the tools, replacing handles and repairing them as much as possible with the help of Beauchamp, the blacksmith.

A week later, Jonathan and Thomas announced they were heading up to Jensen's Mill to pick up some lumber.

"We'll need a lot more lumber if we hope to rebuild." Thomas explained. "The Company is using every board put out by the Millstream mill, so we'll never get any of that. We'll take some of our goods up to them, with promises for more, and we'll see how much we can carry on the Maggie M."

While they were gone, Margaret took the coins from the journal and, except the one she carried around her neck, took them up to the Fort. James Douglas weighed them and credited her account with the equivalent value for additional goods. Although somewhat surprised to see the Spanish coins at Fort Victoria, the Chief Factor was familiar with them from his days in California and treated them as any other trade currency.

Margaret's frustration from her loss increased as the days passed. Once she had arranged for food and shelter, her main duties were accomplished and she was left with little to do. Having almost lost the journal in the fire, she promised herself it would not happen again. One warm day when Li Ching and Po Lyan were visiting the Fort, she welcomed the chance to stay home. Alone, she carefully copied the section of Adam's journal describing his experiences on the West Coast. Carefully, she copied each sketch, including every detail and line she could make out, as she didn't know how important each piece would be. By writing the notes and redrawing the sketches, she learned additional details and became more confident about the important landmarks involved. Once satisfied she had a complete and true copy, she carefully rewrapped the journal very tightly, then sealed the package with melted tallow, making it waterproof. She then went out behind Thomas' new fireplace where they did their cooking and hammered loose one of the rocks attached to the base. She then dug out a small depression in the sand beneath the main part of the fireplace. Mixing up some extra mortar, she inserted the small package into the cavity and sealed the rock back in place, protecting the precious volume from any further chance of destruction from fire or theft.

Carefully brushing away any evidence of her activity, she returned into the house. She then assembled her new pages into a small package that she tucked into an inside pocket of her jacket, buttoned in so it would not accidentally fall out. As she performed these small but important jobs, a plan began to form in her mind, a plan to curb her frustration and help them out of their present predicament. Having lost most of their savings, she felt she could not face Mark again unless she did something to compensate for the loss. Instead of waiting to make their expedition when he returned, she would make it while he was away! The thought both thrilled and frightened her, as there were many unknowns to face, many obstacles to overcome. As she thought out each step, she became more determined that she could do it. She already had Kane's support. If she could recruit Charlie and his mules, take Thomas or Jonathan along for help, they could probably be in and out of the area before Mark returned in just over two months. Excited by the possibilities, she immediately headed up to the Fort to inquire on the whereabouts of Mr. Croghan.

"He's somewhere up near Sooke Lake" Mr. Douglas explained to her, "But, he should be back any time now. I asked him to be back by mid June, which will be pretty soon."

"Is there any chance of hiring him myself?" Margaret asked, "Or is he tied to the Company some sort of contract?"

"No, we have no hold on him, he's free to go where he wants. We were only grubstaking him to prospect a few of the local hills, mainly on the chance of some coal deposits around here." He paused for moment, then looked at Margaret curiously. "And what, may I ask, would you be needing him for, Mrs. Holland?"

"Oh we're planning a little expedition to the West Coast to see the area where Adam, my late husband, died and we need Mr. Croghan's help, as well as his mules."

If the Chief Factor suspected any connection to the Spanish coins, he said nothing.

"In the meantime Mr. Douglas, I would like to draw upon your experience and trade stock to supply our little outing. I'm sure you would have a reasonable idea of what we would need for a few weeks travelling that area."

"Well, Mrs. Holland, I have some idea, but if I were you, I'd rely more on Charlie's recommendations, with some help from your friend Kane."

Margaret took his advice, purchasing some of the main items right away and making notes on his additional recommendations. She then struck out to find Kane, both to advise him of her change in plans, but also to ask for his advice on what they should bring. By the time Charlie showed up a few days later, she already had over half her supplies.

"And what would you be needin' to go into that area for, Mrs. Holland?" Charlie asked suspiciously after Margaret had approached him with her idea. Knowing this man would not be satisfied with a weak story about visiting the site of her husband's death, Margaret was ready with what she thought would be a plausible story.

"During Adam's time with the Indians on the West Coast," she started, "he was trying to recover from his injuries and was incoherent and hallucinating much of the time. He was well enough however, to keep up his journal from time to time, and some entries in the journal refer to possible gold deposits in some areas they travelled."

Before she had a chance to continue, Charlie jumped on her last words. "Gold deposits" he asked, "How would he recognize any gold deposits?"

"Believe me Mr. Croghan," Margaret lied calmly, "Adam was familiar with geology and would more than likely recognize reasonable gold deposits . . . and besides, the Indians had referred to the white man's desire for such material." Hoping Charlie would not detect her deception, she carried on, explaining to him what she wanted to do, why she needed his mules, and when she wanted to go.

"Why do you want to come?" he asked. "You can't keep up in that country. Why don't you just give me his notes and I'll go and check it out?"

"No Mr. Croghan, we'll go together or not at all. I'll keep up, don't worry. What I want from you right now is your commitment to me that you will carry out your duties as best you can . . . under my direction! Second, I'll need your help to put together the rest of our supplies, I've already started with the basics. By the way, do you think we could carry your mules on board the Maggie M. out to Port San Juan and land them ashore? This would cut several weeks off our trip as we wouldn't have to travel over the mountains from Cowichan or along the sea past Sooke."

He thought about her last statements carefully then answered. "Yes Mrs. Holland, I'll probably regret this decision, but I'll be glad to assist you in this little venture. To answer your question about carrying the mules by boat, I don't see any problem, we've done it many times before. In South America and even in California it was common to take our animals up the river to the deposits on river boats.

However, before we get into any of the details, I must ask, what's in it for me?"

"As you know Mr. Croghan," Margaret replied, "We have just experienced a bit of a set-back and I can't offer any cash money at this point. I can however, promise a reasonable compensation upon return as my husband will be returning from the Orient shortly after."

"Reasonable compensation?" he laughed. "Just what the hell does that mean?"

Margaret hesitated, not sure of what to say, disliking the man even more.

"I'll tell you what, Mrs. Manson," he continued, "I'll agree to go on the condition that we share, fifty-fifty, any new gold deposits we find."

Margaret seized the chance. "Twenty-five seventy-five" she offered.

"Sixty-forty" he countered.

"Done!" she agreed.

And so the West Coast expedition was formed. Plans continued and equipment and supplies were stocked as they waited for the return of the Maggie M.

Chapter 55

"The Quest"

They didn't have to wait long, as the little schooner sailed into the harbour a few days later, her decks laden with lumber. Margaret met them at their wharf, surprised at the quantity of lumber they had tied down in every possible location, both above and below decks.

"I can see you had a good trip" she offered as she welcomed them home.

"We did, although sailing back was a little tricky with all this wood in the way" Thomas replied.

They started to unload almost immediately, not wanting to waste any time. By the time the schooner was empty, they had a sizable stack of lumber on the shore, ready for the new building.

Later, as they sat together talking over tea, Margaret brought up the subject of her expedition.

"But I thought we were going to wait until Mark got back." Thomas asked, surprised at the change of plans.

"We were," answered Margaret, "But I've changed my mind. I want to go right away, maybe we'll have some good news for Mark when he does come home."

"Mother," Thomas whispered quietly to her. "I read Dad's journal after the fire, so I know what you're after. Don't you think this is a little wild? What are you going to tell everyone else?"

Margaret was slightly shaken by this revelation. "I didn't know you had read the journal Thomas, I hope you keep that to yourself" she replied quietly. She went on to explain to Thomas and the rest of them what she had told Charlie, they would be searching for some possible gold deposits mentioned in Adam's journal. When it came to the part of transporting the mules, Jonathan objected, but they decided they should talk again with Charlie to find out the best way to do it.

"You'll have to remember Mrs. Holland," Jonathan pleaded, "The Maggie's a fairly small schooner. With what . . . at least five or six of us on board with all your supplies below and two mules on deck, we'll have a pretty good load to travel around to the West Coast. We better make sure we pick a good day to do it, or we'll be in more trouble!"

Margaret agreed, hoping the weather would stay fair at least for the next week. "How long will it take us to get there, Jonathan?" she asked.

"With any luck and with an early start, we should be able to do it all it one day, as I don't relish trying to keep those mules calm for any longer period."

Surprised at this, Margaret quickened the pace of her planning and packing. Charlie was a big help, showing Jonathan the best way to load and secure the animals for the voyage. The biggest problem was going to be unloading them once they arrived at Port San Juan. From what Kane had told them, there were some areas along the side of the bay where the vessel might come alongside the rocks close enough to unload the animals. Failing this, they'll be slung overboard and lowered into the water and allowed to swim to shore.

Several days later, they were all packed and ready to go. They planned to load the mules very early the following morning, just before their departure. Margaret talked long into the evening with her family, covering as many possible problems as they could. Li Ching was very pleased to be in charge of looking after Vickie with Po Lyan's help, a duty they would both take very seriously. Andrew would come with them for the boat trip, but would return to look after their interests in the store. Thomas would be part of the main group and Jonathan would transport them, then return to work with Andrew on rebuilding what they could on the new building. Kane would be their guide for the territory and translator if they met any of the local natives.

Early the following morning, they loaded the mules and prepared to leave. After a tearful farewell, they took advantage of the light off-shore breeze and drifted out of the harbour and headed westward along the Strait of Juan de Fuca. Margaret looked back towards the Fort, vividly remembering her arrival the previous year. So much had happened since then. She wondered if as much would happen in the next year, shuddering at the chance of even more disasters. Mile by mile, as they sailed smoothly along in the early morning, she watched the shoreline carefully. It was so different now than the first time she saw it. Then, it was strange and unknown land. Now it was home. The trees and other plants were more familiar, the shoreline not so threatening, but more appealing in their rugged beauty. The early morning smells of the ocean had also become familiar to her and she could now recognize the separate fragrances of beached seaweeds, the tidal flats, the mussels and barnacles high on the rocks.

A wisp of smoke drifted from the shore as they passed a farm on the shore near Sooke, conjuring up memories of the outdoor fires and cookouts they had last summer.

Thomas popped his head up from below. "Tea is ready if you'd like." he announced. With that he started passing up large mugs of tea that Margaret handed out to the group. Thomas then took over the tiller from Jonathan, who welcomed the break as he had been up earlier than all of them, preparing his small vessel for the voyage. Charlie kept a close watch on his animals, making sure they would remain steady during the rougher water they would experience later in the day. Kane remained quiet, only offering information on the passing landmarks if Margaret asked a specific question. At first Margaret thought it had something to do with the boat, but later realized Kane did not feel comfortable around Charlie. She hoped this would not become a problem later in their trip.

By noon, they were well past Sooke and Jordan River, still favoured by following wind. The ocean swells had increased, causing the little schooner to dip and roll somewhat, but still very comfortable. The shoreline here had become very rocky, sometimes with high, precipitous cliffs dropping off to the water, other times notched out by a creek or small river which drained the high country beyond. At times the shore was bare, other times covered with trees and flowering vegetation.

"We've done very well" Jonathan announced as they enjoyed some of the food she had prepared for the voyage. "At this rate, we should be turning into the bay at Port San Juan by mid-afternoon."

This was good news to them all, as the thought of a rough voyage with the mules had been foremost in everyone's mind.

True to his word, Jonathan was soon easing the tiller over, bringing the schooner around for a run into the large bay at Port San Juan. Surrounded by rocks on both sides, the long bay reached three or four miles into the island, ending in a long sandy beach, almost the full width of the eastern end of the inlet. Jonathan dropped most of the sails well before they approached the end of the bay, slowing the vessel's speed to allow them more time to visually check the shoreline conditions. They could now hear and see the surf pounding on the beach at the end of the bay, something they wanted to avoid at all costs. Before they had moved too close to the shore, Jonathan swung the vessel around and hoisted another sail, mainly to test the wind and confirm their ability to escape from the bay if they had to. Turning again, the asked Kane for his help on a possible off-loading point. Checking possible locations on the south shore, they finally spotted a small cove that appeared protected from the incoming ocean swells. They decided to anchor and disembark from there.

As the anchor splashed down in the clatter of chain, Margaret suddenly realized this was what she had been wishing for and planning for over a year! Looking around, she also remembered this was the area that Adam came ashore, probably where he received his injuries. She shuddered slightly, wondering just where his boat had crashed ashore. She then thought how frightening it must have been, being blown into this bay by a fierce gale, out of control and in the dark of night.

Once anchored, Margaret was surprised when Jonathan sent Thomas into the tender boat with a tow line from the schooner. They payed out the anchor line over the bow as Thomas pulled hard on the oars, pulling the schooner's stern closer the shoreline.

"This way we can get closer to the shore without risking being stranded there." Jonathan explained. "When we are ready to go, we'll cast off our shoreline and pull up on our anchorline, pulling us out into deeper water, ready to go."

The entire operation fascinated Margaret as the vessel

moved closer to the shore. Finally, when they felt they were close enough, Thomas tied the line around a large rock on the shore, holding the vessel in the desired position. Within minutes he had returned and they were loading supplies into the small tender and rowing them ashore, each time with one of the passengers. Charlie remained on board to help rig the mules for slinging over the side. One by one, they hoisted the large animals over the rail in large slings and lowered into the water, where they were turned loose to swim ashore. Thomas then rowed their owner ashore to gather them up and prepare them for loading. By late afternoon they had unloaded everything and were ready to start.

"We'd better get away from the beach and find some place to make camp as soon as we can" Charlie advised, "It could take us awhile and I don't want to get caught in the dark with a green crew."

They all agreed, saying their farewells and making arrangements to meet at the same spot four to five weeks later. Jonathan had rowed Thomas ashore and now turned the little tender out towards his schooner. Within minutes, they had pulled themselves back to their original anchoring point and were hoisting sails to leave the inlet, leaving the small group of explorers alone on the shore.

Chapter 56

Standing alone at the high water line, they could feel the solitude of the place descend upon them. Dense foliage of the surrounding forest absorbed the muted roar of the surf on the east end of the bay, creating an eery background whisper. The setting sun washed the entire area in an umber glow as it dipped into the Pacific behind them.

"We'd better get moving" Charlie's voice broke their reverie. "It'll be dark here before you know it and we've got to get up from the beach and find a place to make camp for tonight."

With that they picked up their packs and followed Charlie's mules as he led them through the piled driftwood along the shore to find a suitable campsite. Following some of Margaret's general information and desired direction, Kane suggested they carry on to a good campsite he knew about a mile farther, following the river's edge. Based on what Margaret had gleaned in Fort Victoria, the large river that emptied into the bay ahead of them was the San Juan River. As she studied the river and its surroundings, she knew this was the one that Adam had mentioned in his journal when he had started to travel with the natives.

They continued, almost immediately leaving the area of driftwood near the shoreline and began to follow the sandy bars and gravel banks of the river. They soon found a beautiful grassy area at the edge of the trees overlooking a wide section where the river meandered back and forth across the valley floor. Before long, they had unpacked the mules and set up their small camp, the first of many. Once the tent was pitched and a small fire started, they paused to inspect their surroundings more closely before it got dark.

The sheer proportions of the rain forest growth enthralled them. Vast areas of salal bushes covered the forest floor while huge fern plants dominated the banks near the river. They were fascinated by the size of the huge fir trees that grew on the slopes above them and the giant cedars scattered along the lower land near the river. They picked one of the larger ones near their camp to investigate, its long branches spread out over them. The four of them all held hands and tried to surround one of the sylvan monsters, laughing as they realized they couldn't even reach halfway around.

Kane and Thomas spotted some large trout in the river, but rather than spend the effort to catch some, they decided only to warm up some food they had brought with them and make a pot of tea. It had been a long, eventful day and they looked forward to a good night's sleep.

Margaret felt a little uneasy and couldn't help looking around from time to time, expecting to see some of the local Indians. Mentioning this to Kane, she found that he had expected a reception as well.

"Probably gone to Nitinat for summer fishing" he suggested.

This sounded reasonable to Margaret as she had heard the story before about how these people customarily move around to different locations from one season to another, depending on the food supply.

Before long they had secured the mules and settled down for the night. Margaret must have been tired, because once she had curled up in her allotted corner of the tent, she did not stir until morning.

The entire company slept late. Being on the west side

of the mountain and surrounded by the dark rainforest, the sunlight was late creeping into their camp. Only the raucous cries of the crows and large ravens managed to cut through their heavy slumber.

Charlie was one of the first up, roused by the braying of his mules, obviously scolding him for sleeping late. By the time they were all up, Kane, who had risen earlier than any of them, showed up with several fine looking trout he had just speared in the river.

"Well" Margaret announced, "I guess we all know what we're having for breakfast." She stirred the fire and sent Thomas down to the river for a pot of water for their tea. They were all elated that the expedition was off to such a fine start as they enjoyed the delicious trout for their morning meal.

"We'd better get moving" Charlie grunted, a little angry with himself. "If we keep up this pace, it will take us all year to get anything checked out."

Margaret partially agreed, feeling they had needed the extra rest and good meal to prepare them in both mind and body for the work ahead. Charlie had taken extra time to show them all the methods he preferred for setting up camp and how to unpack the large tent they shared. Now he showed them all some hints on packing and preparing for the trail ahead. Because of the skill and experience necessary, he packed the mules himself. So far, Margaret was pleased with Charlie's pleasant manner and extra help he eagerly provided the entire company. She couldn't help notice however, the frequent glances he gave her, looking her over like he was taking inventory.

On the move again, they continued along the river, making the travelling much easier. The river was low and most of the time they spent travelling in the riverbed, only occasionally being forced by a twist in the river to move up along the bank. As they travelled, she discussed their next move with Kane and Charlie.

"Adam's notes said that once they started to move, they followed this river for about a day, hunting, before they headed up the mountain... more south, to more flat country." she noted.

"Hunting . . . slow travel, maybe not go far." Kane noted. He then suggested "Few more miles, good spot to go up hill . . . near big creek."

Charlie looked around, surveying the possibilities with this information. "Well, sounds good to me. We got a pretty late start, so maybe we'll stay down here tonight and move on up the hill in the morning. That way, we won't get caught in some rough country when it gets dark."

Margaret had to agree, although she was anxious to get up to the higher country. She couldn't help noticing Charlie's fixation, almost fear of being caught out when it gets dark.

They estimated they had travelled about five miles before they spotted the good sized creek coming down the hill from the south. After confirming the location with Kane, they set up their camp high on the bank, this time with extra time to catch their fresh trout again for supper.

"Might as well eat them now," Charlie commented, "We might not see any good trout once we're up in the higher country where the creeks are a lot smaller. By the way folks," he announced, "If you haven't already noticed, it looks like we're in for some rain. Those clouds have been building up most of the afternoon and it's my guess we'll be see'n a lot of it soon. I suggest we prepare now, cut our ditches and get ready for it!"

With that, they all checked their gear, checked the tent

fastenings, then dug a small ditch around the tent to allow the runoff to drain away from the tent before it soaked in.

They were eating their supper when the rain started, hesitantly at first, the first drops kicking up small puffs of dust as they hit the dry riverbed. Darkness closed in fast as the clouds surrounded them. The first thunder clap came simultaneously with the lightning, startling them all and terrifying the animals. Then the rain started. Like the heavens had opened, great sheets of rain pelted them. The large trees offered some shelter, but before long, everything was dripping or pouring with streams of water.

From everything Margaret had been told about this country by others, the only words she could think of was "Welcome to the West Coast!"

Chapter 57

The night was not kind. The full force of a west coast storm descended upon them. Pleased and complacent with their progress so far, they had been fools to think it could last. Winter or summer, it made no difference to these storms, the ferocity and amount of rain remained the same. Some seasons just produced them more often.

It was not a restful night. The first few hours were filled with the fire and noise of the violent thunder storm accompanying the rain. They spent the remainder of the night checking for leaks in tent, moving their gear and trying to divert streams of water around their bedrolls.

As the misty light of a new day started to illuminate their surroundings, four very tired and soggy members crawled out of the tent to greet the day. The clouds were down almost to river level, obscuring the tops of the trees. The air was cool and fresh, scrubbed by the overnight rain. Each waft of air or light breeze carried the damp, musty smell of the forest.

Packing took on a whole new meaning as Margaret tried her best to keep items dry as she stuffed them away and started to make some breakfast.

After struggling with trying to start the fire several times, Kane finally came to her rescue and showed her a few west coast tricks for starting fires in the pouring rain.

"Look here, Tlul-cul-ma," Kane showed Margaret as he dug at the base of one of the large trees. "'most always dry, even in winter when everything very wet." Margaret was fascinated by the large quantities of very dry twigs, small branches and leaves Kane had pulled from the thick mat of dead vegetation collected at the base of the tree. Kane then showed her how to keep it dry while he prepared some tinder from dry dust shaved from a piece of wood. Stooping down by the fire, he struck his flint with the back of his knife, producing a shower of sparks that ignited the tinder immediately. Carefully nursing the small flame, he fed it some larger shavings, then twigs and dry leaves. Before long, he had added larger branches and a respectable cooking fire was well under way. Kane walked over to one of the large fir trees, cutting something from the surface of the giant. "If you want big smoke fire, put this on." he said, as he cut a small piece of pitch from the lump and threw it on the fire. The flames immediately blazed up, violently consuming the volatile substance. Margaret's fascination turned to respect for her native friend, obviously a good source of wood-lore and survival tricks. Margaret continued to listen to Kane as he frequently passed on information and tips as each problem arose. He gave her an extra piece of the flint he carried, with a sharp remark about how much better it was than the white man's matches she had been trying to use.

"Flint not fall apart when wet," he commented, having seen Margaret's matches get wet. She smiled again, thanking him.

By the time Charlie had packed up the donkeys, Margaret had a pot of tea and some hot oatmeal ready for all of them. The tangy aroma of the wood smoke mingled with the musty odour of damp clothes as they gathered around the fire for a little warmth and comfort. Charlie was impressed by her tenacity and resourcefulness, commenting on the breakfast.

"You've done a fine job, Missus Holland, you and that

noble savage of yours. We'll need a good meal for what's ahead, I think it's going to be a rough one, heading up that hill." He turned to the rest of the crew, trying to speed up the packing. "Come on folks, let's eat up and get going, we've got a long, wet day ahead of us!"

Wet it was, as the rain continued to pour the rest of the day, soaking their clothes more and more as they struggled up the slope. Each of them carried his or her personal pack, a small pack of the items they would need during the day, extra clothes and items they did not want to pack away on the donkey. The rain now soaked their packs until the water ran out, dribbling down their neck and back. Margaret could feel the water running down inside her shirt, then down her legs, creating an uncomfortable sensation. As her heavy wool trousers became soaked, the constant rubbing of the fabric against her skin now added to the discomfort, painfully chafing her skin.

Attempting to follow the general direction of the creek, they found they had to travel high up on one side bank as the creek was flowing a little more vigorously now, swollen by the rain. The donkeys had no trouble, plodding along on the soft ground, their hoofs easily digging in for a better grip. The rest of the crew became more cautious as the soft blanket of matted earth and fir needles on the surface would loosen from time to time as they walked on it, causing it to slide down towards the creek.

By the middle of the day they estimated they had only travelled about a mile and were barely halfway up the hill. From time to time as the vegetation and the low cloud allowed, they could look back and down across the valley of the San Juan River, spread out below them. They stopped briefly for a quick meal of hard biscuit and jerky. The rain continued, drowning any hope of a comfortable meal, so they were moving again shortly.

About mid afternoon the ground was starting to level out, making the walking a little easier. Margaret moved almost automatically now, head down, putting one foot after the other, listening to the clumping of the donkey's hooves followed by each of the group's boots as they went "squish, squish" at each step. Filled with water, the leather had softened to a pliable consistency that added to the slippery, satisfying "squish" as they were stepped on.

The clumping stopped first. By the time Margaret noticed the squishing had also stopped, she was grabbed from behind and thrown down. Her face was ground into the leaves and dirt as her arms were held behind her, a knee in her back. Twisting around to see what was happening, she could see Charlie struggling in the grip of two Indians, his hands still firmly gripping the lines holding the donkeys. Her captor loosened his hold slightly so she could turn around and sit up, hurt and confused.

"What . . . who . . ." she started before a hand whipped across her face, knocking her down again with what was obviously an order to be quiet.

Both Kane and Thomas were struggling with their captors, all of them caught off-guard by the ambush. As Kane was wearing white man's clothes and his big hat, the natives must have thought he was another white man. When he started to speak to them in the local tongue, the situation changed only slightly. Margaret was pulled to her feet but still held secure. Kane spoke again, trying to find out the reason behind the ambush. Some words snapped back, but Kane appeared as confused as ever.

"They are Pacheenaht . . . but not Pacheenaht." he translated, confused. "Not sure why they attack."

"Maybe they're renegades or some outcast group." Charlie ventured, before he too was silenced with a hand across his face.

The talking continued, Kane questioning them repeatedly, not satisfied with the answers he was getting. The leader of the group suddenly became impatient with the talking and barked out some orders. The others immediately started tying them up, their hands behind their backs. Thomas twisted loose, swinging at one of his captors. The swing went wild and he was grabbed again from behind, his arms twisted fiercely behind his back. Still struggling, he dropped to the ground, rolling over and escaping their grip. The leader strode towards the melee, his "cheetoolth", a vicious war club made from a whale bone, raised high above his head. Margaret screamed as she saw Thomas still struggling with two of the Indians, not aware of the deadly weapon descending on his head.

It was over quickly. Part of Thomas' scalp peeled back in a shower of blood as the cheetoolth ricocheted off his head. Sobbing violently, Margaret felt sickened and helpless as they dragged his body over to the bank and kicked it over, where it rolled down towards the creek.

Subdued, the group meekly submitted to being tied up. Within minutes they were again moving, marching along, not as explorers, but captives of unfriendly savages. Margaret continued to sob violently. First her husband, then her son lost... possibly at the hands of the same group!

They continued until almost nightfall before making camp. The land had now levelled off, making the walk much easier. Rather than allow them to make camp or even pitch their tent, each of them was tied to a tree and left for the night. The previous night, which they had complained so loudly about, now seemed like heaven compared to what they had to face now.

Not surprising, the exhaustion and pain of bruised

bodies finally overcame their hunger and terror and they fell into a fitful sleep.

Chapter 58

The rain eased slightly during the night, providing little comfort to the three captives. Early morning light found them all awake, their pain and misery again surmounting their fatigue. Checking the renegade group, Margaret noticed that some were missing and passed on this information to the others.

"Three men go hunting, first light." Kane explained. "I listen, not sure what they do. Now they have big problem, not sure what to do with us."

As Margaret thought about his words, several of the options frightened her. As grief shuddered through her again, she sobbed uncontrollably with the pain and anguish of her loss. How could her life go so wrong, she thought, just when she thought she had everything under control?

Charlie started to say something but was cut short by one of the sentries. At that point, the hunters returned, a small "mowach", or deer slung between them. Within minutes, they had cut off a hind quarter and hung it over the fire on a long pole. While one man turned the spit, another cut out the heart and liver of the animal, which they then passed around to share, raw and dripping blood. Margaret gagged and shivered as she watched closely, both terrified by her captors yet fascinated by them. Watching the large piece of meat sizzling over the fire, she suddenly remembered how hungry she was, not having anything to eat since the small meal at noon the day before. Before long, the tantalizing aroma of the roast venison drifted over to the group, now salivating at the prospect of a hot meal. It intrigued Margaret how quickly they could put aside the pain and suffering of captivity when another commonplace discomfort, hunger, became of primary importance. The other captors must have also been feeling the pangs of hunger as all eyes were riveted on the turning roast.

Margaret watched the Pacheenaht renegades intently, hoping to learn something that could help them, if not now, then perhaps later. The leader was the tallest of the group and obviously respected, even feared by the others. His face was similar to Kane's, full and wide, covered with pock marks. The deep scars marked him as a lucky man, as he had survived the small-pox, where thousands of other coastal Indians had not. The deadly disease brought by the white man many years before had almost exterminated their entire race, another reason the Indians did not fully trust these white skinned devils. Naming him "Pock Face" in her own mind, she watched him closely as he strode about the camp, the huge whalebone war club slung around his neck. She could see his dark eyes flash defiantly each time he looked at them, his nostrils flaring. Where Kane always tied his long black hair neatly behind his head, this man's hair was stringy, matted and sticking out in all directions like it was glued together with some greasy substance. Then she remembered. Now that the rain had stopped, she could smell it, the overpowering reek of oolichan grease. James Douglas had told her that many of the coastal tribes used the oil from the oolichan or "candle fish" so named because a dried fish can actually be lit and used as a candle. At certain times of the year, large runs of this fish appear and the Indians catch them by the thousands, enough to fill large pits dug in the ground, then wait until they start to rot. As the mass of fish decompose to thick soup, large amounts of oil float to the surface. This is then skimmed off and stored for the rest of the year. It is used for many things, one of the main ones being oil for their lamps. Other uses include internally with food, and externally as a beauty aid, insect repellant, or as a water-proofing and hair grooming aid. Margaret could see they were all using this grease, the stench now becoming overwhelming as their bodies were warmed by the fire.

Kane tried again to strike up a conversation with the group, but without success. From what Kane could remember, one of the men in this group had traded with him with Adam's coat, a year before. He could not remember any of the others. It was possible this was the group that Adam had travelled with, and that his coat had been salvaged by the man Kane remembered.

The thought excited Margaret, as this also meant that this renegade band also would know where the gold was located. Unfortunately, they were in no position to find out as they couldn't even talk with them.

Before long, they had decided the venison was cooked and started cutting it up, each of them grabbing a piece. Loosening their bonds, they passed some to their captors as well. At least they are feeding us, Margaret thought. It would be unbearable to watch them eat the roast after they had all watched it cooking. They devoured the venison voraciously, surprising themselves at their own savagery. Amused at their actions, the Indians cut off more strips and threw them their way. Margaret couldn't remember when she had enjoyed a piece of meat more. Venison had been a regular staple on their diet for the past year, but she couldn't recall any of it being this good.

Their hunger sated, they sat quiet while the renegades cut up the rest of the deer, taking only another quarter and the hide. Kane had been listening closely to their conversations and now told the others to be ready to travel, as they would all be moving out before long. Apparently there seemed to be some disagreement within the group as some wanted to get rid of the white men, whereas the others realized this could cause them a lot of problems. The compromise was to take them along, even though they were obviously not welcome. The donkeys were tolerated, plodding along with them as they left.

"These guys must understand donkeys at least," Charlie mumbled. "Or maybe they've seen white men on horses before and know what to expect." He was thankful as the donkeys were his most valuable possession as well as his two best friends.

They started to move again, heading across a flat section of land, covered with smaller bushes, scrub trees and swampy areas. By noon they were again into more hills and ravines, as they had to cross several creeks, mainly small ones, but others quite large. Still overcast, the clouds were much higher now, allowing them to see more of the surrounding country and beyond.

"I'll bet this is the Sombrio River." Charlie ventured as they crossed yet another creek.

"What is the Sombrio River?" she asked, "And how do you know that?"

"That's one of them Spanish rivers we passed . . . it means sad river . . . on our way around on the Maggie M." he explained. "You might not remember, it runs out near a point of land called Sombrio Point, almost to Port San Juan. From where we've been, we must be up on the table land quite near where that river starts, almost like we've gone around in a circle."

Margaret listened, trying to figure out the location in

her mind. A new respect for Charlie was developing, it was becoming clear the man knew what he was doing and was very aware of his surroundings when he travelled.

Dragging along their captives was slowing them down, frustrating several of the renegades. Kane had been listening to several arguments during the day, but Pock Face had kept a tight rein on the group. By nightfall, the arguments had heated up, indicating they had only travelled half the distance they had planned. They were again tied to small trees, this time closer together.

"We got to make a move soon" Charlie whispered to the others. "I figure if we can take off, they probably won't bother to come after us if what Kane told us is true."

"But what if they do come after us?" Margaret argued. "You saw what they did to Thomas, they have no qualms about killing us all." Memories of the clash and Thomas' fate brought new tears to her eyes. Forcing back her sobs, she allowed the anger to rise within her, a rigid frown replacing her fear.

Kane settled the argument by offering the most sensible approach. "Do nothing now . . . wait until morning. Eat first, then rest, new plan will come."

They settled down for the night, using their packs as pillows, giving them some degree of comfort. Thankful the rain had finally stopped completely, they did not take long to drift off into a deep sleep.

Chapter 59

Pain.

Very slowly, Thomas moved his head, almost buried in the wet mat of leaves and fir needles. Waves of pain stabbed him again.

Darkness.

Caked with blood, his eyes wouldn't open. Moving his hand up to his face, he tried to wipe off the clotted blood and dirt from his face so he could open his eyes again.

"Blind!" he panicked. Fumbling around, he saw nothing. The darkness was total. Turning over to lie on his pack, he raised his head slightly and could barely make out the outline of the trees against the lightening sky. Relief and oblivion came together as he passed out.

Cold.

All he could think of was cold. His body shivered violently in the filthy drenched garments.

"Cold . . . must cover up . . . cold.. " his feverish words came and went as he drifted in and out of consciousness. Delirium subdued him . . . he was back in his bed . . . must pull up covers. His arms thrashed around, looking for anything with which to cover up. Leaves, twigs and small branches within reach were all dragged towards him, eventually covering his body. Each struggle took more and more out of him, each time causing him to pass out for longer periods.

The day came, then the night. Then the day again. The rain had stopped, allowing some of the moisture to evaporate from his clothes. Consciousness slowly returned, together with a powerful thirst. Dragging himself closer to the creek, he drank deeply of the cool liquid, replenishing some of the fluids lost. He turned over on his back then faded again.

The night came again, then the day. Slowly, as the dawn lightened the area, he became aware of his surroundings. He could see down the slope to the main river bank where they had last camped. That is where he must go, he thought. He had no idea where the rest of them would be at this point, but he knew he couldn't help them unless he helped himself first. His head still throbbed. Reaching up, he touched the side of his head. Pain! Caked with blood, he could feel the outlines of a large flap of skin and hair that had almost been ripped completely off. After his fall down the slope, his head being jammed into the soggy mat of leaves must have held the skin back in place for the last few days while he slept. His arms and back were chafed by his pack's straps, not meant to be worn steady for three or four days. Struggling to get it off, he suddenly remembered his food and clothes inside! Reaching in, he pulled out the soggy remains of some ship's biscuit and jerky. Hunger suddenly became foremost in his mind as he stuffed pieces of it in his mouth, almost choking as he wolfed it down. His hunger held at bay, he drank deeply from the creek again, looking around trying to plan his next move. He looked down the small ravine where the creek ran down towards the San Juan River. Struggling to his feet, his legs folded, too weak to support him. He rested for a short time, then slowly crawled and skidded himself down the slope towards the river. Most of the distance was covered with a mat of needles, so the travelling was easy. He had covered most of the distance when fatigue subdued him and he slept once more.

It was dark when he awoke. His head wasn't quite as painful, so he tried to wash off some of the debris stuck to his hair. Fumbling around in the dark, he pulled a shirt out of his pack, tearing it in half. Part of the cloth he dipped in the creek, using it to wash off the caked blood and dirt from his head. Cautiously dabbing at his wounds, he eventually had to stop as he could feel fresh blood starting to flow. Using the remainder of his shirt, he wrapped it around his head as best he could to hold the skin in place, and keep the dirt and flies off the wound. Exhausted by his efforts, he drank some water and slept once more.

The sun filtered through the trees, lifting his spirits as it woke him. Breakfasting on creek water and the remainder of his soggy biscuit and jerky, he once again struggled to his feet to try travelling down the slope. Weak and unsteady, he carefully picked his way down to the river, using a heavy stick for support. As he approached the river bed, he spotted a large patch of salmon berries, common in the area. Moving among the bushes, he feasted on the large sweet berries, filling his stomach with the energy giving food it craved for. As he started to leave one of the bushes, he came face to face with a small deer that had been drinking water from the river.   "Well,   my little friend," Thomas said softly to the animal, "I guess we're both living off the land now." Realizing the deer was much better prepared and adapted to this life, he turned again and headed down the river, the deer carrying on with his drink. "Interesting," he thought, "That deer didn't know I was there until we almost bumped into each other. I must have lost the scent of man and smell more like the forest now." He decided to remember this, sure that the information could help him later.

Moving down the river, he made note which pools held

good sized trout as well as which sand bars had fresh water clams. His hunger was satisfied now, but he knew that availability of food would be important to his survival. Luckily, the summer provided ample bounty in the berries and seeds he could harvest. The river and ocean shore would provide the rest.

It took the rest of the day to reach the beach where they had arrived. The surf continued to pound on the long sandy beach at the end of the bay. Seagulls screamed overhead, fighting over morsels of clam meat. After finding a clam on the beach, one of them had flown high, dropping the small mollusc to the rocks to break its shell, not noticing a competitor flying in to share in his bounty. Small sandpipers ran up and down the beach, their little cries competing with the surf. Thomas knew the sea breezes could be cool during the night, and he did not want to be caught out in the rain again, so he began to build a shelter from the collection of driftwood scattered along the beach. Although very tired, he could feel his strength returning as his body started to mend. By the time he had his shelter made and had feasted on more berries and river water, he was drained. Crawling into his small lean-to, he quickly fell into a deep, untroubled sleep.

Chapter 60

At first light the band was up and moving, packing their gear to leave. They roused the prisoners to allow them to pack up. Charlie spent more time than usual packing the donkeys, moving slower, tying every knot more deliberately. Frustrated with the delay, Pock Face finally came over to try to speed them up. Without using Kane as a translator, he barked out some commands, which meant nothing to Charlie so he continued to pack, a little slower than before, knowing that what he was doing would provoke a confrontation.

He didn't have to wait long. Enraged at the Charlie's show of defiance, Pock Face moved quickly towards him. Not prepared for what came next, Charlie watched in horror as Pock Face swung his heavy cheetoolth, hitting one of the donkeys between the eyes. The animal dropped like a rock, kicking weakly on the ground. As the final spasms of death ceased, Charlie's abhorrence turned to rage. Turning to Pock Face, he grabbed his club and they both went down, struggling for possession. The club was lost in the shuffle and they were on their feet again, Charlie swinging at the tall Indian with both fists.

The fight was short lived. Before Charlie had a chance to do any damage, two of the others grabbed Charlie from behind and held his arms. Inflamed by Charlie's attack, Pock Face forgot his club and slowly pulled out his skinning knife, intending to remove Charlie's hide, piece by piece.

When the knife appeared, Margaret screamed, visions of her son returning. Kane started to move, shouting something at the pair, but was quickly held back by the others. Sobbing violently, Margaret stepped towards Pock Face, hysterically screaming curses and threats at the tall man. Shaking her fists, she attacked him, still wailing loudly and swinging wildly as he backed off, surprised at the assault from this fiery haired woman. Face to face, they met in a brief struggle, Margaret pounding his chest with her fists. Trying to grab Margaret around the throat, he pulled the necklace out of her blouse, where it dropped between her breasts. Pock Face's eyes became large as he spotted the coin, his scarred face blanching in terror. The other renegades looked closer to see the large gold coin as it flashed in the sun. They started yelling at once, gesturing wildly at the coin, and its red haired bearer. Within seconds they had disappeared, the three explorers left standing by themselves in the wild plateau of the west coast wilderness.

"What in hell was that all about?" Charlie spat out first. "I've never seen the likes of it, and I thought we were all goners!"

Kane answered, trying to make sense of it as he translated.

"They mention sacred spot, or forbidden spot . . . your coin means old gods come to . . . curse them? Think you a god from soldiers with metal clothes . . . get revenge."

They tried to make sense out of Kane's words, but the translation too complex for his knowledge of the language. As Kane repeated his translation, it suddenly came to her.

"That's it,' she blurted, "It's something to do with the Spanish soldiers . . . soldiers with metal clothes."

"What Spanish soldiers?" Charlie asked suspiciously, "How the hell did the Spanish get involved with this? You never mentioned anything about Spanish soldiers before."

"Don't you see?" she answered, "The coins, they're Spanish! The Spanish must have brought the coins ashore years ago to find a hiding place while they rebuilt their ship. The local natives must have massacred them, either before or after they were all infected with small-pox. The small-pox must represent some kind of curse . . . a revenge for killing the soldiers."

Kane nodded, agreeing with her summary of his words.

"Maybe the coin represents something, maybe they think whoever wears one represents the dead soldiers from years past."

Charlie's eyes grew smaller as he listened to Margaret's explanation, an idea forming in his mind.

"That's the "deposit of gold" we're looking for, isn't it?" he asked finally, seeing the confirmation in Margaret's face. "Somehow, your first husband must have learned about it, or found it. I don't know how, but he managed to get his hands on some of those coins, the one you have." His head went back in a hearty laugh. "My God woman, when you said you wanted to go looking for gold, I had no idea!"

There was no reason to deny it, and Margaret now needed Charlie's help more than ever. She agreed with the miner, filling in more of the details to the story.

"So you see, Mr. Croghan, I couldn't very well ask you to go on a wild chase for some Spanish treasure, you would have laughed at me!"

"Yes, I probably would have." he agreed.

"From the actions of those Indians, they must know where the gold is . . . it must be treated as a shrine or some sacred place." The words echoed in her memory. "That's it!" she remembered, pulling her notes from deep in her pocket. "Here it is . . . in Adam's notes . . . "arrived some sacred place wh . . . cave and steps" ."

"Let me see that." Charlie demanded, grabbing her notes. "I didn't know you had maps and notes like this." he mumbled as he leafed through the pages. "There's not much to go on here, but it could, at least, point us in the right direction." He paused, looking around them as he kept referring to the notes. "Right . . ." he said, obviously satisfied with what he saw.

"What, Mr. Croghan," Margaret asked, "Do you see something important?"

"Yes . . . and no, I'm just looking at the drawings he made. It looks like we're on the right ridge, from the shape and layout of these mountains he drew. 'Course, depends on how good an artist he was." He paused a moment then continued, "And for God's sake woman, stop calling me Mr. Croghan!"

"Yes Charlie," Margaret answered meekly. Then more defiantly she added "And he was a good artist, for your information. If he drew something, then that's the way it was. Unfortunately, those are the copies that I drew, but I'm sure I copied them accurately."

Looking around, they could see the plateau they were on continue for miles, broken periodically by occasional outcroppings and ravines. As she thought about the task ahead, Margaret suddenly realized the magnitude of what they were trying to do.

"My God," she said in wonder. "We could wander around up here for years and never find what we're looking for!"

"I suppose we could," answered Charlie. "But if we stick close to his notes and the map, we might narrow it down. I think we'll carry on along the ridge and look for the twin peak landmark he mentions, that way at least we'll be gettin' close."

He then turned to the grim task of removing the packs

and gear from the dead donkey. Margaret and Kane helped, saying nothing as they distributed the supplies between themselves and the remaining donkey.

The sun was mid-sky by the time they began to move. In contrast with the wet and cold of the past few days, the direct sun felt good, warming their spirits as well as their bodies as they started again on their expedition.

Within hours, they were almost hoping for some clouds or rain. There were few trees to offer shelter from the direct sun as they made their way along the ridge. The heat was intense, drying up the moisture from the meadows and scrub bushes around them, turning the entire plateau into a hazy steam bath. By mid afternoon, the mist had disappeared, replaced by the unobstructed intensity of the sun. Damp clothes that were removed earlier were now put back on to prevent sunburn, adding to their discomfort.

The terrain fascinated Margaret, now used to the dense forests and tall trees of the coastal areas. The expanse before them had changed dramatically, almost like a different country. The largest trees now were small scrub pines, willows and other smaller trees and shrubs. Large marsh areas were covered in a variety of grasses, bull-rushes and occasional cattails. The recent rains had replenished many of the pools and swamp areas, forcing them to detour around, not knowing how deep some of them were.

As they walked through the grasses, the mosquitoes and small flies were disturbed, attacking them with a vengeance. Kane was the only one not bothered by them. When he was asked about it, he took out a small leather bag, tightly tied with thongs. Unwrapping the top of the container, he stuck his finger in and removed a large gob of grease, oolichan grease! Margaret turned in repulsion, the fishy stench nauseating her.

"I didn't know you used that stuff Kane." she asked him.

"All my people do," he answered, "Not so much now, but when flies get bad, works good!"

Margaret had her doubts as to which would be worse, the flies and mosquitoes, or the overpowering fetor of the rancid grease. She had her answer soon after as the little pests became more numerous and aggressive, driving them to desperate measures. As she was already surrounded by the smell, she thought she might as well be getting some of the benefits. Meekly, she asked Kane if she could try some, and before long, the three of them continued their hike, smelling very fishy but happily mosquito free.

Chapter 61

Screams of seagulls aroused him from a deep sleep as they fought over the remains of a fish on the beach near his shelter. Looking out between the pieces of weathered wood, the rugged beauty of the area held him spellbound. The surf was high, roaring along the beach as it died in thunderous crashes on the sand. Enormous clouds of spray and mist billowed up, illuminated by the rising sun behind him, creating a hazy glow over the entire bay. The air was fresh and cool, laced with the aroma of the Pacific, spread in front of him for thousands of miles. He couldn't help thinking of Mark and the rest of the crew on the Shanghai Lady, still sailing out there somewhere, possibly in China by now.

The seagulls pulled his attention back to the present where their argument over the fish continued. Leaving the shelter, he walked down the beach, relishing the freshness of the morning. Working his way along the rocky south shore, he found a small tidal pool where he knelt down to wash himself. The crude bandage applied to his head had dried to his hair, making it difficult to remove. Dunking his head in the small pool, he managed to soak his head enough to remove the cloth strips. The jagged wound was healing in spots, but was still raw and bleeding along one edge. Carefully washing the whole area with the salt water, he then rewrapped his head with clean strips of cloth. The little pool he had washed in consisted of a small depression in the rocky shore where sea water had been trapped when the tide had fallen. Looking around, he saw many similar basins of all sizes and shapes, from small ones holding a few cups of water, to large ponds ten to twenty feet long. Besides capturing the sea water, these small lagoons held a variety of sea life. When he knelt down to wash, small fish scattered for shelter, hiding beneath small shell fragments and pebbles at the bottom. Crabs scurried for shelter among the seaweeds along the sides. A variety of shellfish either clung to the sides or were buried in the sand and mud on the bottom of the larger pools.

"Here's my breakfast!" he said to himself as he reached for a large abalone deep in the pool. As his hand approached the ruddy shell, he noticed it tighten its grip on the rock, making it impossible to move. Moving on to another pool, he tried again, but could not pull the animal off fast enough. Realizing what the creatures were doing, he knew he had to get under the shell before it tightened up the large muscle that it used to stick on the rocks. He headed back to his shelter to get his knife, determined to have abalone for his breakfast. Armed with his short rigging knife, he returned to the area and hunted for a good sized abalone. When he spotted one, he knelt down beside the pool, careful not to disturb the creature. He slowly moved his knife toward the animal, quickly sliding the blade between the rock and the flesh of the abalone, prying it off. Pleased with his success, he carried on, pulling off several more to carry back for his meal.

Once back to his shelter, he realized he had no fire to cook the delicacy and would have to eat them raw. Cleaning the flesh out of the shell, he placed the large muscle on a log, where he then pounded it with a rock, tenderizing the tough flesh as Kane had taught them. He then tentatively tried some, biting off a small piece, chewing it slowly. Although different in taste than when cooked, he found it pleasant enough. His hunger demanding more, he finished the first one and then another, pleased with his progress. Heading back to the river, he drank deeply of the cool water, then finished his breakfast with some fresh berries.

Fully satisfied, he surveyed his surroundings, wondering what to do next. Knowing that Jonathan would not be returning for some time, he tried to calculate how long he would have to survive. He knew he had been unconscious or delirious for several days, so he tried adding up how much time had elapsed since their arrival. Surprised by the results, he figured that at least a week, almost two weeks had passed. This left him between two to three weeks to wait for the schooner to show up, a long time to spend alone on the beach. He realized he could not walk back to Fort Victoria along the shoreline as much of it was the rocky bases of cliffs beaten constantly by the ocean surf. He knew nothing of the territory to the east, over the mountains between him and the other side of the island so he would not want to try that route. Left with the only alternative, he decided to stay where he was, explore the area and survive the best he could.   During the first two days, he spent wandering idly along the beach, picking up extra driftwood for his shelter, hunting for fresh berry patches and fishing pools. He found another small river running into the bay at the north end of the beach, providing more trout fishing holes. Climbing some small hills around the bay, he discovered large huckleberry and salal bushes, providing even more food for his larder. By spreading the huckleberries out on pieces of driftwood in the sun, he found he could dry the berries into small beads of sweet treats he could carry in a canvas bag for future use. The salal berries were pounded and dried into cakes that Kane had called 'yama', a pleasant and sustaining food supply.

He had been there four days before he found the house. As he had not seen a soul since his arrival, he had not expected to find any habitation of any kind. The large Indian longhouse was impressive. Larger than any of the houses in the Songhees village, enormous cedar logs supported other logs that made up the main roof beams. The inhabitants had elaborately carved the two largest logs to form the entrance to the structure. The front of the house was carved and painted with totems and legendary figures, creating a colourful facade looking out over the Pacific.

Wandering in and around the structure, Thomas expected to meet its inhabitants at every corner. His shouts echoed through the empty structure as he called out for someone. Realizing they were all gone, probably to their summer fishing or hunting grounds, he felt a sense of disappointment. Any other time of the year he could have met these people, perhaps received some help.

Fascinated by the construction of the main building and other items scattered about, he wandered around, inspecting the structure and the grounds surrounding it. Large fish drying and smoking racks were set up along a grassy area, close to the beach. Something caught his eye, almost hidden behind some logs on the beach. Investigating, he pulled aside some shrubs, revealing the pointed bow of a small two-man dugout canoe! Thomas was jubilant, looking forward to having something he could explore the shoreline with. As he pulled the long canoe from the shrubs, he suddenly realized this could be his way home! Remembering the short trip out, he knew it was possible to paddle his way back! Looking around, he soon found some paddles, long pointed ones carved and painted with elaborate designs similar to those on the longhouse.

Struggling with the heavy vessel, he pulled it down the beach to the water, threw in the paddles and shoved it out until it floated. Elation turned to disappointment as he noticed water pouring in a long crack in the bottom of the canoe. Thinking about how he was going to patch it, he walked into the water, pulling the canoe behind him as he headed back to his shelter.

When he approached his shelter, he looked around for a place to leave the canoe for the night, not wanting to lose it when the tide came in. As he tried to pull it up the beach, he noticed the crack was much smaller than he thought. "Of course," he thought, remembering some lessons Jonathan and Kane had taught him. "The wood is soaking up the water and is swelling up!" He then piled the canoe with wet seaweed for the night to keep it wet and by the following morning, the crack was almost sealed.

Excitement returned to his life, he now had a project, a purpose. The calm routine of his beach life was replaced by the planning and preparation for his voyage home!

Chapter 62

The weather stayed clear, the sun hot. The San Juan Ridge was flatter terrain, much of it open country with little shelter, so their progress was hot and dry. Flies, mosquitoes, bees and wasps attacked the intruders, resulting in constant aggravation, itchy bites, painful stings and a lot of disorder and panic. The wasps brought the most concern as they often built their nests in the ground or a rotten log, making them difficult to detect before stepping on them. Concerned that the donkey might run off, Charlie tightened up his rein on the animal, ready to hold it back if it bolted.

The foliage intrigued Margaret, so different from the coastal rain forests they had travelled through. They tried to avoid the low, marshy areas filled with bull-rushes and tall cattails, later fighting their way around tall bushes of Oregon Grape, with its prickly leaves similar to holly. Margaret was used to seeing this plant around Fort Victoria, but it stood only one to two feet high. These giants were sometimes over six feet high with a spread of branches of similar magnitude. With painstaking care, they avoided the large patches of stinging nettles, now even more painful when their skin was hot and sensitive. The low ground in the shady creek gulleys was home to the large salal bushes, loaded with the peculiar berries they ate with relish. Other berry bushes grew in profusion, offering them a variety of treats and sustenance, as well as slowing their progress. These included huckleberries, blueberries, and the low growing blackberries, all adding to their diet of dried jerky, biscuits and the occasional feast of bacon and beans. Kane gathered some 'quanoose', a bulb that he said was a favourite of many of his people. Margaret recognized the quanoose as the camas bulb, common around the Fort Victoria area.

After almost a week of wandering around the ridge, they decided to rest for a day or two and try to pinpoint their location. Making camp by one of the many creeks in the area, Charlie brought down a deer with his rifle early the following morning.

"If we are going to be here for awhile, we might as well eat well." he told them. Although the small animal provided more than they needed, the fresh meat was a welcome change, keeping them satisfied for a few days.

The rest was welcome and appreciated. It gave them a chance to wash some clothes as well as themselves. The hot, dirty travel had taken its toll on all of them, Margaret in particular. During the first afternoon while Charlie and Kane hiked up one of the local peaks to check for landmarks, Margaret took advantage of being alone and headed down to the creek for a wash. Stripping off her clothes to wash them as well, she stepped in, shivering as she scrubbed and rinsed her body with the cool water. Looking down at her body, she thought of Mark, and what he would say if he saw her now. Lean and muscular, she was trimmer now than she had been since her teens. The creamy white of her body contrasted sharply with the swarthy brown of her arms and freckled face, now tanned from the constant exposure to the hot sun. She then attacked her hair with a bar of soap, painfully picking out pieces of wood, leaves and debris from the weeks of travel.

Refreshed with the cleansing, she then started on her clothes, still standing in the creek.

"Well, well, a wood nymph no doubt!" Charlie's words startled her. He was standing high on the bank, leering down at her. Quickly, she grabbed her dry clothes, covering her body as she struggled to put them on.

"What are you doing here?" she cried desperately. Awkwardly replacing her clothes, her anger overcame her fear of the man. "Get out of here, you dirty man!"

"Don't get so uppity with me lady! You ought to be thankful. We just got back to camp and when we didn't find you, we started to look around. You should be a little more observant, there's bears around here."

Still fumbling to put on her clothes, Margaret looked around quickly, thinking of what Charlie had just told her.

"Oh," she mumbled, looking around quickly, "I didn't know."

"And besides, if I wanted to look at your bare ass lady, I wouldn't have said anything, would I?" he sneered, eyes still evaluating her body.

Margaret flushed again, both embarrassed and furious with him, promising herself never to provide him with an opportunity to shame her again.

Kane greeted them as they returned to camp, noting Margaret's discomfort, suspecting the reason for it. He moved closer to Margaret, concern in his voice.

"You all right, Tlul-cul-ma?" he asked.

"Yes, fine, Thank you Kane." she answered, trying not to let him know how upset she was with Charlie. She knew the two men barely tolerated each other and she didn't want to provoke another confrontation. Smiling weakly, she tried to change the subject, interested in the results of their exploration.

"Well, did you two find anything up the hill?" she asked.

Charlie answered, eager to offer his suggestions.

"The only thing we could see up there is more of what we see down here! We did get a better view of the ocean, but it didn't confirm anything. Let me look at those notes again and I'll show you somethin'." he offered.

Margaret pulled the notes from her pack, opening them up and spreading them out on the grass. Charlie picked them over, looking for something specific. Spotting it, he grabbed two of the sketches, smoothing them out to inspect them closer.

"Yeah, just as I thought . . . see here . . . his sketch of the Juan de Fuca strait? See the mountains across there? Those are the ones we see now, so we must be pretty close to the right angle" pointing out across the ocean to the south. "Now this one," he continued, "Is a bit of a puzzle. These two peaks he mentioned... there isn't a two peak mountain around here as far as we can see."

"But how . . . there must be," Margaret interrupted. "He wouldn't have made up something like that."

"I agree," Charlie added, holding the paper up towards the hills behind them. "But maybe we're just looking at it wrong. Remember now, this is a man that's injured, unconscious much of the time, his point of view will be a little different from ours."

"Yes" Margaret agreed, "But what are you getting at, how will that help us?"

" I think we're thinking wrong. These aren't big mountain peaks he's drawn here, there're probably some local hills . . . maybe just a rock outcropping."

Margaret thought it over and had to agree. Worried that their quest might be halted, she looked at Charlie, hoping he had more answers.

"But what are you saying Charlie?" she asked. "Do you have an idea . . . a plan?"

"I sure do . . . it came to me when we were up on the hill. We've been out too far . . . too far away from the mountains on this ridge. I know," he added quickly, "we did that so we could look back at the mountain for the peaks. We'll have to get a couple of miles closer and travel along the base of the hills. We have to look for small peaks, rock chunks, something that looks like this," pointing to the drawing.

It sounded reasonable to Margaret, now willing to try anything. Looking towards the hills they had been inspecting closely, she had a feeling this could be the answer. Rather than travel up and down the slopes and through the marshes of the ridge, they should have been hugging the base of the mountains, watching for the landmarks.

Another day of rest helped refresh them, as well as allowing their laundry to dry. They picked extra berries for the food supply they carried and feasted on the deer as much as they could while in camp as it couldn't be taken with them.

Before falling asleep that evening, Margaret wondered what the next days would bring as they started again on their quest.

Chapter 63

A few days later, he was ready to go. Soaked with sea water, the wood in the bottom of the canoe had swollen enough to seal the crack. Although confident the trip would only take two to three days at the most, Thomas knew enough to prepare for the worst. He had gathered several large clam shells for scooping out the water if the crack leaked more than he expected. He filled his canteen with fresh water, knowing the container held enough to last one day, and there would be plenty of small creeks along the route to refill it.

Foraging around the Indian Longhouse, he found a piece of netting, woven from fine strips of cedar bark. He then lashed it in the canoe, securing all loose items under it so they would not go overboard if the canoe capsized. The extra days had given him more time to recover his strength while he practised his paddling and stocked up on extra supplies. He added to his stock of dried berries and yama, which would supplement his diet on the trip. He then wrapped some clams and a few extra abalones in wet seaweed to keep them cool and fresh in the bottom of the small vessel. Not sure how much time or what conditions he would be facing, he felt he should bring as much as possible with him.

The sun was barely over the trees to the east when he finally convinced himself he was ready to go. Lashing down the extra paddle, his pack and canteen, he pushed off from shore and started his journey. Sticking to the south shore where they had arrived, he avoided the rough water and dangerous surf of the east end of the inlet. Once well clear of the shore, he had no problems overcoming the large swells rolling in from the ocean and was soon well out in the bay.

The sun had climbed halfway up the sky when Thomas started his turn around the point, skirting the rocks at the head of the bay. To his right lay the open Pacific, nothing between himself and Japan or China. Ahead lay the large mountain range behind Cape Flattery. Turning some more, he now travelled in a southeast, almost easterly direction along the shore towards Sooke and eventually, Fort Victoria. From time to time he paused, arms aching from the unfamiliar work. His legs started aching as they cramped up from crouching and knees chafed from the constant exposure to sea water and rubbing on the cedar bottom of the canoe. His shirt dripped with sweat from his exertion, but to remove it would result in a serious sunburn.

By noon he was ready for a rest. The water was calm and the sun hot as he pulled out his canteen for a well deserved drink. Some small pieces of abalone and some dried berries made up the rest of his meal, restoring his energy. He relaxed, leaning back against his pack, relishing the break.

A loud "whoosh" and fishy spray of moisture startled him as a large black object broke the water beside his canoe. Before he had a chance to see what it was, it had slipped beneath the waves, leaving him frozen with fright. Within seconds another broke the water on the other side of the canoe, again spouting a large cloud of smelly spray. Thomas realized they were Blackfish, the large killer whales that frequented the coastal waters all around Vancouver's Island and the coast of British Columbia. He had spotted large groups or "pods" of them many times as they passed Fort Victoria or when he travelled on the Shanghai Lady up to Jensen's Mill. Kane had told him many stories about the Blackfish, the most interesting of which was that the Indians would venture out in canoes to hunt this animal! Larger than his canoe, Thomas shuddered as he thought of the damage the animal could do to his small boat if provoked. Terrified but fascinated by the large beasts, he could do nothing but watch as they passed by. Estimating the pod at about a dozen, he noticed a variety of action. Two of the larger ones further out appeared to be either having a fight or playing, Thomas could not decide, as they cavorted around, sometimes leaping completely out of the water. Their white bellies flashed in the sun as they turned slightly, falling back in the water with a huge splash, instantly disappearing beneath the surface. Others appeared to be checking out the shoreline as they paused, their bodies rising vertically out of the water, holding themselves halfway out for a considerable time like they were looking him over. He trembled as they passed under his canoe, their sleek black bodies slipping beneath the waves, the tall dorsal fin waving slightly, barely submerging before they crossed beneath him. Thomas watched in mute fascination, fervently hoping they would not miss-judge the distance and slice his small vessel in two with the large fin. It was over in minutes. The group quickly left him behind as they continued along the straits toward Fort Victoria. His fear transformed to awe, leaving him with a feeling of fascination and respect for the large animals, now understanding the Indians' reverence for them. He continued to watch them as they disappeared, small clouds of sunlit spray flickering on the horizon.

His attention returned to the shoreline, changed slightly from when he stopped for his meal. Remembering he had not paddled of almost an hour, he suddenly realized he was drifting along in the right direction!

"Of course!" he told himself. "The tide's already turned so she'll be running into the Straits most of the afternoon!" Encouraged by this stroke of luck, he started paddling again, knowing the tidal current could add at least two to three knots to his speed. Rather than hug the shoreline as he had been doing, he boldly struck out towards the centre of the channel, to pick up an even stronger current. Later that afternoon, he figured he must have travelled almost twenty-five miles. The sun was getting low and he knew the tide would be changing before long, so he headed in closer to shore, not wanting to get swept out to sea by the ebbing tide. He picked a gravel beach near a river to land, paddling into the entrance to the river mouth to secure his canoe at the high water level. Exhausted, but pleased with his progress, Thomas wasted little time with his evening meal and finding a spot to stretch out for the night.

The raucous gulps and cries of a raven roused him from a deep sleep early the following morning. The large black bird sat on the top of a bare snag near his camp, looking down and scolding the intruder. Thomas tried to shut out the noise and go back to sleep, but the black sentry would not be content until his victim was completely awake and standing up. Either startled by the man or satisfied with his results, the raven flew away, leaving Thomas standing on the beach looking forward to an exciting day.

Now fully awake and anxious to continue his journey, he enjoyed a quick swim in the river, washing off the previous day's sweat in the cool water. Chewing on another abalone and some yama, he looked forward to when he could sit down to a full cooked meal. Drinking deeply of the river water, he then refilled his canteen and packed the canoe to leave.

Knowing the current would now be running out toward the ocean, he kept very close to shore, lessening the effect of the ebbing tide. He passed giant beds of kelp, the long stemmed seaweed anchored to the bottom with its bulbous top and long rippling leaves floating on the surface. The early morning antics of sea otters amused him as he watched them fishing for their breakfast in the kelp. Surfacing with a small crab or a clam, they would turn on their backs, cracking the shells on a rock they held on their tummy.

The cool freshness of the morning soon became a furnace, as the sun rose high, reflecting off the water's surface as well as blazing down directly. Thomas kept soaking the bandage to cool his head and ease the itching of the healing wound. The salt water trickled down out under his shirt, running down his chest and back. It then mingled with his sweat and soaked his clothes, burning and aggravating his raw, chafed skin. Paddling east all morning into the sun, his eyes now burned as the reflection off the water blinded him.

The sun was well past its zenith when he passed the inlet near Sooke and continued around the point. Spurred on by the closeness of his goal, he renewed his efforts, looking for signs of civilization, paddling faster. Before long he had passed yet another inlet without seeing anyone on shore. As he rounded another large point he started entering a narrow inlet and he could see the farmhouse up on the hill. Somebody had already spotted him and was on their way down to meet him as the small canoe ground to a halt on the fine gravel beach.

Chapter 64

The early morning air was refreshingly cool as they headed towards the hills to the north. The ground rose slightly as they approached the first hills, making them thankful they had started before the sun became unbearable. Before long they were travelling southeast again, trying to stay close to the edge of the mountains. Their progress was much slower and difficult as the ground was rougher and the trees more plentiful. Although the extra trees made their travelling a lot cooler, it also complicated the search for the landmarks. To make sure they did not miss the peaks again, they would pause each time the trees became dense, to scout around for a better vantage point to see the shape of the mountains. This extra activity slowed them down, but the slower pace was welcome in the cool trees.

By noon that day they had established a good system and were confident they could cover most of the ridge in a couple more days. Margaret was concerned at how much time they had spent with so little to show. It was almost time for Jonathan to return to Port San Juan to pick them up and they hadn't even covered the main ridge yet! Even if they started right now, she knew it would take at almost two weeks to get back to the rendezvous point, so she hoped they would not wait too long, but return to Fort Victoria and come back later. Constant checking with Adam's notes and maps did nothing to help. His references were vague and the sketches too incomplete to help. By that night they were exhausted, having stretched their efforts more than usual. Making camp by a little stream, they made some tea, had a light supper and turned in early.

Margaret woke with a start, a dirty hand over her mouth and another on her breast, tearing at her clothes. Twisting away, she rolled over, out of his grip.

"Kane!" she choked, trying to call out to her friend.

"Your faithful savage has gone for a walk, so don't bother trying to call. You and I have a little unfinished business and I figure you're just what I want right now!" Before she had a chance to get on her feet, he was on her again, groping at her underclothes. During the hot weather, she had been wearing very little while sleeping, a habit she now regretted. Holding her down, he ripped off the light chemise she wore, bearing her breasts in the dim moonlight. Small rocks and gravel ground into her back as he wrestled with her, the reek of his breath gagging her. His hands groped over her body as he buried his head between her breasts, unaffected by the punches and scratches Margaret rained on his head. Reaching down her body, her felt around between her legs for the prize he sought. Fully enflamed by what he found, he fumbled around in the dim light, trying to remove his own underclothes while Margaret struggled to escape. The air was still heavy and warm from the scorching sun earlier in the day, quickly heating them up. The fetid stench of his sweat soaked body permeated the air, making her gasp for breath.

Suddenly, she felt his body stiffen as his head snapped up, his face inches from Margaret's, a confused look in his eyes. Margaret glanced down slightly and quickly understood as a long knife pushed upward on his neck, now stretched tight by the brown hand that pulled back his hair. A single drop of blood swelled on the edge of the knife, finally trickling down his neck.

"You want this man to die, Tlul-cul-ma?" Kane's familiar voice asked.

Her relief turned to horror as she realized Kane was serious, and it would only take a slight nod of her head to end Charlie Croghan's life.

"No," she replied quickly, "No more! We've seen enough killing and violence on this trip." sobbing heavily.

As he let him go, Charlie spun around, fire in his eyes, ready to kill.

"You filthy savage!" he hissed. "I told you once before if you ever touched me, I'd kill you!"

Margaret started pulling on her clothes, thinking the incident was finished. As Kane reached down to help her to her feet, a thunderous roar shattered the tranquillity of the night. Kane spun around, almost pulling Margaret over. He turned, looking at Margaret in disbelief, his eyes wide, as the hole in his shoulder oozed blood. His mouth opened, trying to say something as he crumpled to the ground and silence closed about them again.

Margaret stood there, too shocked to move as she looked down at her friend. Dropping to her knees, she knelt beside Kane, examining his shoulder. The entrance hole was small enough, considering the large calibre slug that Charlie used. Turning him over slightly, she could see the massive exit hole the piece of lead made as it tore through his body. He was still breathing, but unconscious and in shock from the trauma. Concern rapidly turned to fury as she spun around to face his assailant. Charlie was standing there, his rifle still in his hands, a look of shock on his face.

"I didn't mean to kill him . . . I only wanted to warn him." he started blubbering meaningless words, his eyes fixed on Kane's body.

Margaret turned again, grabbing Kane's hunting knife, and pointed it at Charlie.

"He's not dead yet, you rotten son of a bitch! Get that fire going and pass me my pack, we've got to stop this bleeding!" Turning Kane on his face, she used his knife to cut away the remains of his shirt from the gaping wound. "At least the bullet went right through," she said. "No bones broken, so it should heal well," not totally convinced.

Charlie started to move, quickly throwing some dry branches on the fire to illuminate the area. He then brought her pack, a guilty look on his face.

"Grab that end," she said to him, handing him the tail of one of her blouses. Wielding Kane's knife, she cut the garment into large strips, coming threateningly close to Charlie's hands as she cut. She then sent Charlie to gather some bark from the small willow trees scattered along the creek. Cutting the strips into small pieces that she pounded to a pulp between two rocks.

"Oh Kane, your medicine better work," she muttered to herself as she tried to remember the Indian tricks Kane had taught her in Victoria. Working some of the bark pulp into a small pad, she placed it on the entrance wound, holding it down until she could bind it. As she worked, her anger surfaced again, boiling over at the futility of the act.

"Oh God, Charlie . . . why? You might have killed him . . . over nothing! Don't you think we've had enough violence on this trip? Poor Kane," she added, now wrapping the strips on his wound to hold the willow bark on the wound. "He's twice the man you'll ever be, Charlie Croghan." she choked out, barely able to control herself. Fully incensed, Margaret continued her tirade.

"What's more," waving Kane's knife at him, "If you ever touch me again, I'll cut out your liver, you rotten bastard!"

Slowly, she regained her composure and calmed down, scarcely believing what she had said to him. Plugging the large hole with another pad of willow bark, she continued to wrap the strips around Kane's shoulder to hold it on.

Charlie said nothing, putting away his rifle and walking over to his donkey. The eastern sky had already begun to lighten, so he mechanically started to pack the gear, saying nothing.

"We can't leave now." she said quickly as she realized he was packing. "Kane can't travel in this condition, we'll have to lay up here for a day or so."

The day passed slowly, each sombre and quiet. Little was said as they mechanically moved around the camp, drinking tea and keeping their eye on Kane. It was late afternoon when Kane opened his eyes, mumbling something in his native language. Seeing Margaret, he relaxed and fell into a deep sleep.

Chapter 65

"Oh, you're a white man!" the farmer exclaimed as he approached Thomas. "From your rig I took you for one of them injuns from Port San . . ." he paused a moment, looking at Thomas intently. "Why you're . . . you're that young boat builder fella from the Fort! Your mother runs that little store."

"Thomas Manson, yes." Thomas answered, reaching out to shake hands. "Exactly where . . .?"

"Tom Blinkhorn, pleased to meet ya. This is Metchosin . . ."

"Of course!" Thomas remembered. "This is Captain Cooper's place . . . or it was."

"That's right," Blinkhorn agreed, "We took charge of the farm last year after shipping in on the Tory." He paused a moment, looking Thomas over. "Jeez, Tom, you look like Hell! How come you're out here and in that rig?"

Thomas partially explained his situation, telling Blinkhorn that he had become separated from the main expedition and he had been injured. He didn't mention anything about the renegade Indians in case it would alarm the locals and most likely cause further trouble.

"Is there a way I could get a ride into Fort Victoria?" he asked, knowing it would be faster than the canoe.

"Why sure, we ride in once a week for supplies. You can get a lift with us on Saturday."

Thomas had to ask him how long that would be as he had lost track of the days.

"Three more days, today's Wednesday."

Thomas groaned, frustrated at the delays. "I hate to be a bother, Mr. Blinkhorn, but my need is a little urgent. Is there any chance I might borrow a horse to ride in myself?"

"Why of course, how foolish of me! I might have known you wouldn't want to sit around here . . . Oh my! What am I thinking of? You must be starved, probably could use a clean dressing on that head of yours as well." He turned to go back up the hill, pulling on Thomas' sleeve. "Come along, my wife probably has something for you. Leave that injun dugout here, we'll pull it up and stow it later on. You can pick it up again some other time."

The walked up to the farmhouse Thomas had spotted from the water. Anne Blinkhorn was delighted as she greeted them at the door, visitors to their farm being rare. As they were talking, Thomas caught sight of another person in the room. Mrs. Blinkhorn noticed Thomas' glance and turned, all excited.

"Oh goodness, where are my manners?" she cried, pulling over a pretty young girl, scarcely Thomas' age. "Thomas, this our niece, Martha Cheney. She arrived last year as well and is staying with us."

Thomas flushed, ashamed at his own unkempt, filthy appearance. Mumbling a greeting, he bowed slightly at the girl, charmed by her dark hair and flashing eyes.

Mrs. Blinkhorn pulled his attention away, in a flap about Thomas' head. Before long, she had him at the table in front of a steaming bowl of venison stew, while she worked on his head, changing the dressing. Thomas dug in, pausing only when she wanted to wrap his head again. The hot stew with fresh baked bread filled Thomas' dreams as well as his stomach. His hunger surpassed his interest in Martha's eyes, so he scarcely noticed she had left the room. Few questions were asked about the expedition, as the Blinkhorns were more interested in the happenings at the Fort, especially " . . . and what is going on between the Douglas girl and that Dr. Helmcken?"

"You probably know more of what's going on than I do." Thomas replied when asked. "I haven't been there for a few weeks, and if you go every week . . ."

"Of course! What am I thinking of?" Mrs. Blinkhorn continued to flutter around Thomas, not used to visitors this far out. Thomas promised they would all come out to visit as soon as his mother returned. The thoughts of his mother flooded back, in the hands of the savages. He had tried not to worry too much, convincing himself they would either escape or talk some sense into their captors. He knew he had to get back to Fort Victoria and talk with Jonathan before the Maggie M. sailed for Port San Juan.

"Thank you, Mrs. Blinkhorn. That was wonderful! You're the answer to a hungry man's dreams." Thomas rose from the table, anxious to continue. "I hope you don't think it rude of me but the sun's still high and if I get going now, I should be home before dark."

They agreed, reluctantly releasing their guest to continue his journey. After supplying him with a horse, they were soon waving goodbye as Thomas trotted down the dirt path towards the Fort.

It was a rough and twisty trail, barely wide enough for a horse, thought Thomas, wondering how they managed to bring the wagons into town for supplies. As he got closer to the Fort, he passed more new farms being worked by the recent colonist brought over by the Hudson's Bay Company. Thomas reflected on how his own life could have been so different, so much like these workers if fate had not dealt them a twisted hand.

It was almost dark when the horse finally plodded up the trail along the inlet. As the last time he saw the area their home and store was a pile of ashes barely cool from the fire, he was not prepared for what he saw. Now a large building stood on the same site, complete with the sign, Manson & Holland, General Merchandise. He dismounted in front of the store, preparing to enter. The door burst open, Andrew flying out.

"Thomas! My God, what happened? Where..."

"Andrew! You don't have any idea how good it is to see you!"

"But where . . .?"

"In good time, Andrew" he replied as he threw his arms around his brother.

He then noticed the tall man watching them from the front porch, vaguely familiar. The familiarity finally hit him, taking his breath away.

"Uncle Kenneth . . . wha . . . when . . ." he stammered.

"Hello lad! How are ye?" his uncle asked as he approached, arms outstretched. After some large hugs, he stepped back, appraising his nephew.

"Good God lad, you've grown! The life over here must be agreein' with ye." He looked around, noticing only the horse. "Where's your mother lad, I thought she was with you from what the others tell me" pointing to Andrew and Jonathan, who had also arrived.

"Let's go inside, we've a lot to talk about." Thomas said grimly, scarcely knowing where to start. The others followed him in, questions coming fast.

Inside the store was much larger than the original one. The shelves were almost empty, most of the stock lost in the fire. The living quarters had been expanded to provide rooms for Ah Fong's family. Thomas was impressed with the results they had accomplished during the weeks he had been absent.

Po lyan and Li Ching were both rushing about, torn between trying to listen to the news and preparing food and drink for Thomas. Sitting down to a much appreciated cup of tea, Thomas related the entire story to the group, side-stepping references to his father's notes about Spanish gold. They listened intently, fascinated by the entire tale, especially his survival and return to Fort Victoria.

"So you don't know what became of them after that?" Kenneth asked finally.

"No, but I have a feeling if they don't try to fight like I did, they might be all right. I figure we'll have to return to Port San Juan like we agreed, in hopes that they make it."

"We've already been there." Jonathan interrupted. "We went back as agreed, hung around for two days, and decided to come back here for more supplies. We're heading out again tomorrow, this time with the Shanghai Lady as well."

"The Lady's back, already?"

"Yes, she arrived two days ago. Mark's up at the Fort now, should be back shortly."

Thomas couldn't believe it, both losing another week somewhere, and having the Lady back so soon. He turned to his uncle with a few questions of his own.

"I can't believe you're here, Uncle Kenneth! Mother will be so surprised."

"Well that's what I hoped to do, but when the ship came in last week, you two were off running around the mountains somewhere." He went on to tell Thomas some details of his voyage on the Falmouth. After telling his tale, he turned and waved at the building around them. "I'm amazed at your progress so far, though, the fire must have been disappointing."

Before he had a chance to respond, the door flew open and Mark rushed in.

"Thomas! My God lad, what happened to you, are you all right? Where are they, lad . . . what's happened?" Concern pained his face as he listened to Thomas' tale, interrupted by the occasional "Damn, I told her to wait." Thomas knew that Mark was aware of the real reason for the trip, not to check out some made up story about "gold deposits". Arranging to take both Mark and Kenneth aside, he told them everything about the trip, including the promising start to their search, based on his father's notes. Mark was not surprised, nodding as Thomas spoke. To Kenneth, it was too much.

"What are ye sayin' lad? Do you mean your Mother has gone on some wild treasure hunt in that uncivilized territory with a wild Indian and an unscrupulous miner with nothing to go on but the ravings of a delirious man?" Kenneth was furious, not understanding how the family could have let this happen. Mark stepped in, trying to calm the distraught man, explaining that part of the trouble was because of the stories that Mark had told her during their trip, stories confirmed by the Spanish coins. They talked further into the night, finally confirming what they had already planned for the next day, they would leave together for the west coast.

Chapter 66

Dawn found Kane awake and struggling to get up. Margaret tried to calm him and hold him down, but he staggered to his feet, pain creasing his face. Breaking into a sweat, his legs started to fold, forcing him to sit down quickly.

"At least have something to eat." Margaret scolded him, offering some biscuits with tea and fresh berries. "You've lost a lot of blood, and you have to build up your energy again." They all had the same, again relishing the food now they saw that Kane was mending. Before long, Kane was on his feet.

"Kane travel" he said, favouring his shoulder.

"Why don't you rest some more," she protested, "You'll feel much better tomorrow." He ignored her, staggering over to pack his own gear.

"Here, let me help you at least." she offered. "First let me bind that a little tighter. If you're going to travel, you'll have to have it tight." With that, she bound extra strips around his shoulder, pulling his arm close to his chest to help ease the wound. Against her wishes, they were soon packed and ready to go.

The morning passed quickly, Margaret scarcely conscious of walking, her attention on Kane. The entire trip had become a disaster, a quest for gold for which she had sacrificed her son, then almost a good friend. She should have listened to Mark, Oh God, how she should have! He said it would not be easy, but no, she knew better. Her strong-headed beliefs had got her into trouble before, this time it was catastrophic.

Their progress was much slower, allowing Kane to follow with less effort. After the initial shock wore off, Margaret knew the pain must have been severe. He managed to keep up, teeth clenched and face streaming sweat as they plodded along, and Margaret knew he couldn't continue too long. Each time they stopped, she checked his wound to make sure it hadn't opened.   Charlie   was   also quiet, mechanically moving along, leading the donkey. Up and down the hills and ravines, they rested more often, always looking up, hoping to spot the twin peaks they had sought for so long.

Late in the day they rested on a knoll, high enough to look over the Strait of Juan de Fuca. The mountains to the south were sharp and clear in the distance, the air freshened by a westerly from the ocean. As they looked out, enjoying the view, they spotted some tiny sails, barely visible on the ocean before them. At first she thought it was Shanghai Lady, but on closer inspection, realized they were the sails of a much larger vessel, heading out to sea! Fascinated by the sight, they watched until the tiny sails disappeared over the horizon. Adam's notes convinced them that they were close to the area where he had drawn the sketches of the mountains.

"We'd better make camp here," Charlie said, turning to check the hills again, "Before it gets dark . . . Wha . . . Quick! Look up there!" he said to Margaret, pointing up the slope.

She turned to look, wondering what had excited him. They had noticed a small outcropping of rock above them when they stopped to enjoy the view. Now there was two! Margaret looked again, moving several feet away to get a different view.

"My God, I wouldn't have believed it!" she murmured. "Do you think that's what Adam saw?" she asked Charlie.

The sun was low in the western sky, casting long shadows as it tinted the landscape a pinky hue. As it shone on the small pinnacle above them, the silhouette and shadows it cast on the cliff beside it combined to form the appearance of two peaks. It was so convincing, it almost had them fooled, so the effect on a semi-conscious man would be total. Kane too, was fascinated by the sight, his tired eyes blinking in the receding light, trying to figure it out.

Margaret stood still, transfixed by the sight, convinced that this was what they had been seeking for weeks. She shivered as she realized how close they came to missing it, how easy it would have been to carry on rather than stop to watch that ship.

"This must only be visible for a very short time each day, even then, only under very special conditions." she said to the others, scarcely believing their luck. They agreed, transfixed by the sight for a few more minutes until the illusion faded, leaving a solitary outcropping of rock.

They started talking at once, each offering an opinion. Darkness closed around them, cancelling any plans to investigate further until the morning. Again, a cold supper satisfied their tired bodies before fading into an exhausted sleep.

Early morning found them around the fire, drinking tea and waiting for the sun. Margaret was surprised that Kane's wound was already starting to heal, apparently helped by the willow bark poultice. By first light, they had broken their fast and were packed, ready for travel.

They were confident they were very close, but decided to take all their gear with them until they actually found something. Now constantly referring to Adam's notes, they tried to plan what direction they should move to find their goal.

"He mentions that the two peaks were to the north," Charlie offered, "So we should just keep moving south of here." He read the notes again and added "He also says there was water nearby, probably another creek."

"Remember Charlie, that was in April or May, when the spring rains are almost constant. Unless it was a good sized creek, it might be all dried up now."

"Right!"

"So we should be looking for the large hill, that wouldn't change." Margaret added, realizing that could be a problem as the entire area was covered with hills.

To cover the area better, they spread out, walking through the bush over a hundred yard width. Oregon Grapes flourished on the dry rocks and red, sandy soil, while thick Salal bushes filled the low, shadier areas in the ravines. The vegetation and rough ground either slowed them down or completely blocked their progress and they would frequently lose sight of each other.

Kane spotted it first. They had only gone a couple of hundred yards when he called out to them.

"Tlul-cul-ma, come quick! Kane think this is what we look for."

Margaret couldn't believe the words. They both converged on Kane as fast as they could. At first Margaret thought he must be mistaken. Kane stood in one spot, looking at some rocks and bushes. She realized how lucky they were that Kane had spotted it, sure that she or Charlie would have walked right past. Berry bushes and small shrubs almost covered the site in front of them. The face of the rocks were cracked and split, widening as it approached ground level to a small opening, barely large enough for a man to enter. On either side of the opening, almost hidden in the bushes, two grim sentinels stood guard. The skeletons of two armour-clad Spanish soldiers slumped against the rocks, still clutching long pikes at a rakish angle. Between the two guards, at the threshold of the entrance, they could see the first of several steps leading into the darkness.

Margaret's heart was in her throat as she realized what they had found. Although each had hoped for success, each knew within themselves how remote their chances were. This was it! She turned to Charlie, already tethering his donkey so he could investigate the cave.

"Charlie, I think this is it! Should we all go in, or should one of us stay out here?"

"Let's see what we're faced with first." he countered as he approached the entrance.

"Kane not go in!" Kane spoke out defiantly. "This is sacred place for some of my people, not good."

"But Kane," Margaret quickly explained to him, "These were Spanish soldiers that probably were shipwrecked and hid their cargo in this cave. They can't hurt you now." she added, trying to lessen the sacred aspect.

"No good, these men with wooden feet, they kill many of my people. They die. Then my people get white man's disease."

Margaret knew the story well, the arrival of the white man and his gift of small-pox to the natives. She smiled at the reference to "the men with wooden feet", the early name Indians had for the Spanish, because of the leather boots they wore. Not familiar with the hard, stiff kind of leather, they thought they were made of wood.

While they were talking, Charlie had entered the cave, disappearing into the shadows beyond the opening. A low whistle sounded, followed by a loud hoot. Before they could follow, Charlie appeared at the entrance, his eyes glazed and a large grin creasing his face. He held out his hands, brimming over with Spanish pieces-of-eight!

Chapter 67

Low clouds scudded along over the Fort, driven by the southeaster blowing in from the Strait. The glass had fallen swiftly overnight, confirmation of the weather system they were just starting to experience.

"We'd better get going" Mark said as they met at the dock the next morning. "If this keeps up, she's going to be pretty messy by the time we reach Port San Juan."

The small group divided, carrying their gear to their respective ships, ready to cast off. Kenneth joined Mark on the Shanghai Lady while Thomas went with Jonathan again on the Maggie M. Expecting heavy weather, Jonathan had recruited another of Mark's crew to give them a hand on the smaller boat. Leaving Ah Fong behind served a multiple purpose. He was a natural to run the store, especially to organize all the new supplies they had brought back from China. They also wanted someone to ward off any direct inquiries from James Douglas or any other Fort official. He also would have to supply some reasonable excuse why the entire family had left the safety of Fort Victoria and headed out in two ships to the west coast. The last thing they wanted to do was to provoke a confrontation between the Company or the colonists and the Indians. Previous mischief by the natives had resulted in swift action from Mr. Douglas, who in one case had sent the S.S. Beaver with armed men to deal with them. In another case involving the killing of a local shepherd, he called out a detachment of blue jackets and marines from the H.M.S. Thetis to track down and hang the guilty native. Mark had discussed these incidents with the rest of the group and they decided they would try to keep the matter quiet until they knew exactly what had happened.

Once clear of the protection of the harbour, the heavy swells pounded them, adding to the fury of the wind whipped waves. Swells born in the far reaches of Puget Sound had many miles of "fetch' to build up before pounding themselves to death on the rocks of southern Vancouver's Island.

Putting the wind and swells on their port quarter, both captains tried to raise enough sail to ease the sickening motion the seas gave their vessels without driving them under, yet take advantage of the wind for best possible speed. With the larger vessel, Mark had his crew ease the sheets from time to time, so the others could keep up.

"That Maggie's a spirited little thing, wouldn't you say Billie?" Mark commented to his mate.

"She is for sure, skipper, but I'm just as glad to be here if you don't mind... I got that kind of sailin' out o' my blood years ago!" They cringed as they watched the Maggie take another wave broadside, drenching everyone on deck.

Before long, they turned slightly as they passed around the point near Sooke, putting the main force of the storm directly behind them. They watched as Jonathan swung the schooner slightly, easing the main sheets to sail "wing and wing", the mainsail on one side and the foresail balancing it on the other.

"Come on Billie, let's loose the foresail or they're going to pass us!"

Not wasting any time, Billie soon had the large foresail, the "workhorse" square-sail, pulling the Shanghai Lady along at breakneck speeds.

The rain started about mid-afternoon, as they rounded

the point and headed into the long inlet at Port San Juan. Now familiar with the bay, Thomas and Jonathan led the way to the small cove where they had stopped before, knowing there was good anchorage for the Lady as well. Once anchored, they rafted the two vessels together, allowing them to meet for tea on the larger ship. Although sheltered from the winds, the area seemed to attract the rains.

Thomas looked around, memories flooding back. "This is what is was like when we started" he explained to the others. "You've never seen rain until you get your belly-full of this!"

Later in the afternoon, Mark and Thomas went ashore in a small boat to see if anyone had been around since Thomas had left.

"This is the San Juan River" Thomas explained as they grew closer to the wide mouth. "The water is low now from the dry weather, but the river-bed is almost level and spreads out quite a bit. There are sand and gravel bars for several miles up stream, past where we turned up the hill . . . way ahead up there to the right."

As they walked around, the rain soon drenched Mark and he quickly realizing how wretched the group must have been after travelling in this for several days. Further searching turned up nothing, the area deserted since Thomas had left.

"Let's get back to the ship" Mark said abruptly. "We're not going to find anything more here, we'll just have to wait."

On the ship, the atmosphere was gloomy. Already the incessant rain had dampened their spirits as well as their bodies. Meeting for supper on the Lady, they talked over the problem and offered suggestions.

"We should arm a small party and head out to find them!" Thomas immediately offered.

"No, dammit!" Mark countered. "That'll get us into more trouble! I want to get Maggie back as much as any of you, but we must be honest with ourselves. They've been up there for weeks, and we haven't any idea where. If we go tramping around, we could end up the same way, either lost or in trouble with this band of renegades."

Thomas had to agree, not wanting to remain idle. "But what can we do?" he asked, frustrated.

"Think!" Mark said firmly, spreading a chart out on the table. "I agree, this chart doesn't show any inland details on the south part of the island, but it does give you an idea of how large an area we're faced with." He marked off the section of the island from Port San Juan to just west of Sooke. "We're talking more than thirty miles here . . . in one of the wildest, roughest territories around! We could spend a lifetime along that ridge and never find them."

"So Mark, are you saying it's hopeless . . . we're wasting our time?" asked Kenneth.

"No, I said think! We have to put ourselves in their position. If you were either lost, injured, out of food, or just wanted to go home, what would you do? They might be too far to return to this spot, or unable to do so. They might even be closer to Sooke. You must remember one thing about that ridge, remember Thomas? Your father kept referring to it in his diary . . . he could see the ocean most of the time!"

Thomas looked confused, wondering what that had to do with the problem. Kenneth picked up on it right away.

"Of course! If there was a problem, or they wanted the fastest way out, they could head down to the nearest shore." He paused, not knowing what came next. "But then what would they do, they don't have a boat?"

"No, but they have a better chance of being spotted by one coming by from Barkley's Sound or some other port up the coast."

Thomas agreed, but added cautiously " . . . heading down to the nearest shore isn't as easy as you might think in this country. It could take days just to find a spot to get around some of those cliffs we passed, a few miles back." They talked into the evening, finally agreeing on a plan.

The soggy dawn found both ships raising anchor to sail out of the long bay. Their plan was to sail along the coast, each ship covering a section of the shore from Sooke to Port San Juan. Even one or two sweeps per day would cover the area as well as ease their minds.

The rain lingered, sometimes a heavy mist, other times in torrents. After weeks of hot, dry weather, the decks of both ships allowed enough of the rain through to make life miserable below as well as on deck. The wind had steadied, making the routine sailing part of the task much easier. The jagged shore, sheer cliffs and treed slopes often disappeared in sheets of rain and low cloud. Hesitant to move any closer to the certain death of the pounding surf, they frequently missed long sections of the beach, hoping to see it during the next pass. As they completed their pass, they would return to meet the other ship, also finishing their run. Nothing to report, they would turn and repeat the chore, each night returning to Port San Juan. Hopes faded as their anticipation was washed away by the relentless rain.

On the third day of their coastal quest, the rain eased slightly and the sun broke through the southern clouds, lifting their spirits. That afternoon, one of the Lady's crew spotted smoke, drifting up through the trees along the shore.

Chapter 68

She froze, eyes locked on the coins, the sun glistening off their golden surface. Charlie laughed, pouring the coins from one hand to the other, letting them overflow to the ground. Margaret stood transfixed, watching them fall, hitting the dry ground with little puffs of dust.

"We've hit the jackpot . . . there's tons of it in there! I can't believe it!" Charlie was screaming.

She didn't hear him, her attention locked on the coins. The discovery wrenched her soul, bringing to the surface the grief and anguish of the past year. Sobbing violently, she collapsed to her knees, grovelling in the dust for the coins. Pounding her fists on the ground, she relived the grief of her husband and son's death, as well as the filth, suffering and the violence of the search . . . all for these small pieces of metal! All her life she had struggled to make a living, to succeed at whatever they did, a struggle mainly for money. Now it was all so meaningless. Here was all the money she could ever want, but she felt empty, her husband and son dead, nobody with whom she could share the joy. She realized that by leaving before Mark returned, she had even cheated him out of this moment.

"Oh Mark, my love, I'm so sorry," she thought. Wiping the dust and tears from her eyes, she slowly stood up, resolving to change. Now that she had found the gold, she would replace the chase with the enjoyment and fulfilment of what was left of her family.

Charlie was already unpacking the donkey, digging out burlap sacks and leather bags to load their booty. Kane remained outside, fascinated by the actions of his white companions while he rested on the ground to ease his wound.

Margaret entered the cave, stooping slightly as she stepped down the steps through the opening in the rocks. Three steps led down to the dirt floor of a large chamber, dimly lit from the light that filtered through the entrance crevice. She had read about natural limestone caves but had never seen one. Stalactites covered the ceiling, ranging from several inches to almost a foot in length, some with their tips glistening with yet another drop of limewater. As her eyes became accustomed to the faint light, she finally spotted the treasure, stacked in a dry area at one side of the room. She caught her breath as she realized how much there was. Large chests lined an area against the wall, a couple broken open, coins spilling onto the floor. Piles of bars, ingots of gold and silver, were stacked next to the chests, material the Spanish had not yet melted down for their coins. Other decorative artefacts littered the collection . . . gold cups, plates, bowls, small statues and primitive figures, all fashioned with the skill and artistry of master goldsmiths. She caught her breath, overwhelmed by the sight. So much, she thought, and from what Mark had told her, but a small fraction of the treasures plundered from the Inca and Aztec civilizations to the south.

She scarcely had time to take it all in when Charlie arrived and started to fill his sacks with coins.

"We can't take but a fraction of it." he said, shovelling coins in with his hand. "We'll have to come back for the rest later." The words hit Margaret as absurd.

"Come back?" she said, incredulous. "You expect me to come back to this hell-hole?"

"Well, you don't have to come back, now that I know

where it is. I'll have to get a couple more donkeys or some mules and try to come in from Sooke . . . shouldn't be too far."

The thought of Charlie walking off with the rest of this treasure disturbed Margaret. She resolved that she would arrange for someone else to come as well, someone she could trust.

The rest of the afternoon was occupied by trying to decide what to take and what to leave. Before they packed completely, they decided to camp there and start fresh in the morning. This gave Margaret a chance to check Kane's dressing. The exit wound was becoming inflamed around the edges, a bad sign. Asking Kane for some help, she tried various poultice mixtures and pads of leaves to stop the infection. The pain had eased a little after she was finished, but she could see that her native friend was still in a lot of trouble.

By the time they turned in, an almost forgotten sound of rain drops started around them. The large drops spattered off the big salal leaves with loud plops, while richocheting off the Spanish helmets with metallic clinks. At first it was refreshing after the long dry spell they had suffered. Before long, the old memories of their first sodden days in Port San Juan flooded back. Rather than remain out in the open and get drenched, they decided to sleep in the cave. At first Kane would not go in, but when he realized Margaret would be in the cave alone with Charlie, he relented and packed his bedroll to move inside.

It was a troubled, sleepless night. Kane's wound throbbed with pain, robbing him of sleep most of the night. For the other two, visions of gold and silver treasure filled their minds, and the future it would buy.

The rain continued all night, increasing in the early

morning as the winds started. Tossing around in a fretful dream, Margaret awoke suddenly to screams outside the cave. Jumping up quickly, she poked the embers of the fire to provide some light. Charlie was fast asleep, Kane was lying in his roll, watching her, a serious look on his face.

"What was that?" Margaret gasped. "It sounded like someone screaming."

"Kane say not sleep here, not good!" he repeated to Margaret, "Spirit voices say go away!"

Then the noise repeated. The long scream ended in a wailing sound, this time familiar to Margaret.

"Oh God, it's just a tree, rubbing in the wind." she said, relieved. As the wind increased, two trees outside the cave struck up a constant rubbing, sounding like everything from a dying animal to a tortured violin. Kane's words were not lost on her however, and she knew she would feel a lot better when they had left this place. Looking around, she tried to picture Adam's last days, probably spent right here.

Daybreak found them packing their gear, sacrificing as much of the heavy items as possible, making room for the gold. By the time they left, everyone had full pockets and pack, as well as carrying an extra sack with a few gold artefacts. Charlie loaded the donkey with as much as he thought it could bear. Margaret felt sorry for the beast, visibly sagging.

As they were leaving, Margaret started to think about how they would get back, a thought they had not dwelled upon.

"It'll take too long to get back to Port San Juan." she offered.

"Probably longer to go to Sooke, and we don't know

what the country's like that way... what do you suggest?" Charlie asked.

"Is there any way we could head down to the shoreline below us? It's already past the time when Jonathan was supposed to pick us up, but maybe we could see him as they went by, or hail one of the other ships coming down from up island."

"Not a bad idea . . . could be rough, but at least it's all down hill." Charlie agreed. With that, they started their homeward journey.

Chapter 69

Heading south towards the ocean, they found the storm had cloaked all landmarks in a thick shroud of fog and low cloud. The rain persisted, varying from a constant drizzle to violent downpours, made worse by the violent winds. At first they continued to follow the slope of the land as it dropped slightly towards the flatter meadows. By noon they were still travelling through the marshes, now soggy with the rain. Large areas were flooded and rapidly softening, making progress difficult and increasingly dangerous. The extra weight they carried slowed them down, their sodden packs constantly shifting and sliding across drenched clothes, chafing their skin. The donkey staggered along, barely able to keep his footing in the mud and wet grasses. Struggling with his own pack, Charlie no longer lead the donkey, but let the animal go ahead with the rope loosely draped back and tied around his waist. By occasionally prodding the animal, he kept it moving, breaking a path for them.

Visibility remained limited throughout the day as the low clouds drifted by, seldom lifting to treetop height. The storm masked sight, sound and scent, allowing them to spot more game... deer, sometimes large groups, as well as the occasional elk and black bear. Their senses diminished, the animals rarely detected the intruders until they were much closer than usual. Progress slow, they finally spotted the ocean late in the day, a faded view through a break in the gloomy overcast around them. The view quickly disappeared as the clouds again closed around them.

Margaret's skill at fire-making was improving, so when they made camp, she quickly found some dry fuel under the trees and soon had a warm fire crackling. Kane's shoulder was inflamed, the bandage soaked with both rain and blood. Margaret worked on it again, trying to clean and poultice the wound with available materials. The fire lifted their spirits, already waterlogged by the first day of travel. Hot tea warmed their bodies chilled by the cold rain and violent winds. Their small tents and damp blankets provided meagre protection and comfort for their cold bodies and aching muscles. The loss of rest the previous night and the demanding travel of the day finally took over, dropping them into a dreamless sleep.

By dawn the next day the rain had eased to a steady drizzle, still enough to keep them soaked, but the thinner clouds allowed more light to filter through to boost their spirits. Charlie had his gear packed and the donkey ready to go before the others had scarcely eaten. He must have thought they were getting closer to finding a way out as his sullen disposition of the previous day turned into active aggression, taunting the others to hurry or he would leave them. Margaret was worried about Kane's shoulder, not wanting to rush her morning inspection and bandaging. Although she didn't think Charlie was serious, she knew he had the bulk of the gold on the donkey, she felt he would have liked to leave them behind, and claim the entire donkey-load as his own.

"Don't be a fool, Charlie" Margaret answered him, continuing with Kane's shoulder. "You won't go anywhere without us! If you showed up in Fort Victoria with that gold, you'd have a few questions to answer."

"They know what it's like here, I'll just say you all died on the trail or were killed by injuns, like young Tom." The memory flooded back, hurting Margaret, but stiffening her resolve. She knew now that Charlie was a coward, especially afraid of being taunted by others.

"And besides," she continued, wanting to give him something to think about, "If Kane dies, they'll hang you for murder. You know how James Douglas is about things like that."

Indeed Charlie did know, having seen some of the justice handed out by the Chief Factor and Governor. He fumbled around with the donkey again, trying to save face.

"I was only joking, but if you guys don't get going pretty soon, I'll leave you!" he sneered.   Margaret   smiled slightly, but knew inwardly she would have to be extra careful with Mr. Croghan. She had heard the tales of gold fever and what it could do to a man, but with a man like Charlie, no telling what could happen. Once she finished her bandaging, it wasn't long before they were ready to go.

All morning the land slanted downward to the ocean and by noon they had arrived at the top of a steep bluff that dropped off to the beach. The precipice was too high and too steep to climb down, so they turned, following the top of the ridge to find a better spot to descend. The hill was covered in salal, Oregon Grape and scattered arbutus trees, making progress slow and difficult. The rain had eased again, but the wind whipped over the edge of the bluff, surrounding them with a turbulent back-eddy. The noise and confusion made communications difficult as they followed Charlie and his donkey single file.

They were carefully picking their way around a rock bluff on their high side, trying to stay away from the slippery edge of the cliff below them when Margaret heard the donkey let out a loud braying snort. Looking ahead through some bushes between her and Charlie, she spotted a large cougar on a rock above him, spitting and snarling down at the trespassers. Before she could say or do anything, the large mountain lion leaped down to ground level and immediately disappeared into the bush. The group had apparently surprised the big cat and it only wanted to get away as quickly as possible. The surprise was too much for the donkey. Already alarmed by the proximity of the predator, it panicked when the animal leaped down to the ground in front of them. Trying to rear up on its hind legs, one leg slipped sideways, too close to the loose rocks and gravel at the edge of the precipice. As the gravel started to move, the foot skidded over the edge. Trying to take the weight, the other foot followed, as the two front hoofs clawed desperately for a grip on the level ground. Charlie had the rope tight, straining to pull the animal back up from the edge. Margaret could see what was happening, but was too far behind them to help. The donkey's eyes were wide with fright as its front hoofs scratched and clawed at the ground, kicking out stones and mud as they vainly tried to grip the ledge. Within seconds they had lost, the extra weight of the gold too much for the small animal. Before either could recover, the donkey's front feet disappeared over the edge as it tumbled down the precipice. Before he realized he was still tied to his beast, Charlie followed quickly over the edge, his screams cut short about half way down the rocky cliff.

Silence descended on the scene. Even the wind paused momentarily, shocked by the event. Margaret and Kane rushed to the edge, not sure what they would find. They could see nothing from where they stood, the victims had obviously fell right to the bottom, past the rocks she could see halfway down the slope. Turning to Kane, she saw a satisfied smile on broad face.

"Charlie man a bad man. Fool many men, but not fool Pacheenaht Gods! Good thing he gone, too bad donkey animal go too, good animal."

Margaret couldn't believe what he was saying, but as she thought about it, she couldn't help agreeing with Kane's philosophy. As she thought more about all the trouble and grief they had experienced, she began to wonder for the first time if she would get out of this alive herself.

Most of the gold now lay somewhere at the bottom of the cliff, on a west coast beach. Looking around, they still had the same problem they were working on before, trying to find a way to the bottom. Without the donkey, they could now try a more difficult route down, one they could climb down, on hands and knees if necessary. They persevered, finding a possible route later that afternoon, less than a mile from the accident. Kane's shoulder allowed little use of his arm, slowing their descent. Step by step, they picked their way down, plagued by loose rocks, mud slides and small streams from the rain. Windfall logs and broken branches entangled the area, adding dangerous hazards to confuse their efforts. Margaret could see the pain in Kane's face, wincing visibly as each step or drop jarred his shoulder. The light was fading, making each step more hazardous and difficult. The bottom of the cliff was becoming harder to see, fading in the deepening gloom below them. Not wanting to be caught on the slope in the darkness, they renewed their efforts, taking more chances and shortcuts to cover the remaining ground. The Pacheenaht Gods were smiling on Kane and his companion as they finally set foot on the beach at the foot of the cliff in complete darkness, collapsing with exhaustion.

Chapter 70

It was still dark when she opened her eyes. She could hear the waves pounding on the beach, very close. Not knowing if she was above the high water mark, she painfully dragged herself higher up the gravel shore, collapsing again behind a log.

The second time she awoke, she smelled wood smoke. Opening one eye, she spotted Kane feeding some driftwood to a fire on the beach. She tried to move. Cold muscles objected painfully or would not respond at all. Her wet clothes chilled her body, now worse as she moved upright into the cool breeze from the ocean.

The rain had stopped, but a foggy mist surrounded them, limiting visibility to a few hundred feet. She joined Kane beside the fire to enjoy the warmth and dry her clothes.

"Thank you Kane, this fire's wonderful!" she mumbled gratefully. "How is your shoulder this morning?"

He winced slightly as he moved his arm, showing the movement he didn't have the day before. "Much better today. Extra work coming down hill must help." Margaret smiled, knowing the climb had almost killed them. She was also relieved, knowing how serious his wound could have been if the infection had continued. They kept the fire much hotter than usual, drying the clothes they wore as well as their packs and personal gear. Margaret gathered some salmon berries growing along a nearby creek while Kane cooked some clams found in the sand at low water. As they didn't have the pots and kettle normally carried by the donkey, they had to improvise for their breakfast.

"I think the first thing we should do is find that donkey." Margaret said as she chewed noisily on a steamed clam. "God, it would be wonderful to have a cup of tea right now, but we'll wait until later! Besides, I don't want to lose track of that gold, now that we've gone through all of this."

"Kane not want gold . . . Tlul-cul-ma keep." Kane's fear of the Spanish gold became apparent each time they discussed the subject.

"But you deserve a share of the treasure, Kane." Margaret tried to convince him. "We decided that when we started, we would all share."

"No! Kane not understand then . . . not want yellow metal from white men with metal clothes . . . bad medicine."

Nothing Margaret could say could change his mind. In one way, she understood and almost agreed with the simple logic behind his decision. She had enough violence and hardship on this trip and did not want to push her luck or possibly invoke the wrath of the Spanish spirits any more than she had to.

"Well, we'll head back and try to find them anyway. Charlie Croghan was not a good man, but he deserves a Christian burial if we can find him."

With their hunger satisfied and clothes dry, they set off up the beach, feeling better than they had in weeks. Gulls flew in through the mist, hunting for their breakfast along the beach as the tide dropped. Hundreds of wood ducks and cormorants swam in large groups just off shore, half under water most of the time. The shore was strewn with immense heaps of giant kelp and other seaweeds, torn loose by the recent storm and cast up on the beach. Kane kept Margaret fascinated as he described much of the wildlife to her, and how his people gathered and used each item. With the tide low, they walked along the beach, much easier than the travelling they had been doing.

By noon they had worked their way around a rocky point to get to the area where they thought the donkey had fallen. The beach kept narrowing as they rounded the corner, tapering to nothing by the time got to the other side of the point. The shoreline became solid rock again, dropping off into a small inlet. At the bottom of the cliff there was no beach, the ocean ending right at the cliff base.

"Oh my God!" Margaret cried. "If the donkey came down here, we'll never find it." fearing the worst. Just then she spotted one of their packs floating in the inlet, washed against the rocks at the far end. "Look Kane, over there!" pointing to the debris.

Kane had already spotted it and was trying to figure out a way to get to it. "Come Tlul-cul-ma, help drag log." he called to Margaret as he tried to pull a log down from the high water mark.

Struggling with the log, they managed to get it into the water. Straddling the log like a canoe, Kane carefully paddled with his good arm, trying to manoeuvre the makeshift vessel around into the bay. As he approached the end of the bay, Kane picked up the small pack, a light one with only a few clothes. Looking up the cliff, he spotted the gruesome sight. A bloody trail was traced on the cliff, accentuated by bits of hair and clothing where both Charlie and his donkey had come down. The cliff continued vertically into the water, so it was obvious they must have ended their fall at the bottom of the small inlet, loaded down with the gold.

Kane returned to Margaret, explaining what he had found. Dumbfounded, she sat down on the beach, not believing what he was telling her.

"You mean it's all gone?" she asked incredulously. "You

mean all of this has been for nothing, for just a few more coins?" She broke down again, weeping violently. Kane didn't know what to do, so he finally helped her up to take her back along the beach to where they had started. Gathering more driftwood, he started another fire to warm them both up.

Margaret finally recovered, but remained depressed at the uselessness of their expedition. They chose to stay where they were and set up camp. A small creek trickled down the hill nearby, supplying them with ample fresh water. They pitched the tents on high ground and established a full camp, not knowing how long they would be there.

The following day the weather had not changed. Margaret was worried the light rain and the misty fog would continue, severely limiting their chances of spotting a passing ship. Knowing their chances were very slim, she and Kane gathered as much firewood as possible, ready to throw on the fire as a signal, the only way they could be seen. They kept the fire burning constantly, ready for that purpose.

The clouds did not lift all day, depressing them both. Kane warned Margaret that the rain and fog could continue for weeks on the west coast, something she did not want to hear. Satisfied with another meal of baked clams, steamed crabs and many cups of steaming tea, they turned in again for a full night of dreamless sleep.

The third day dawned a little brighter, but still plagued with occasional drizzle and low cloud. Margaret talked with Kane about other ways out, whether they could walk along the beach to Sooke. From what she learned, she decided to stay and take her chances on a passing ship. Besides, she was loathe to risk any further disasters by trying to travel along the rocky beach. They talked for hours, each taking turns watching the ocean, hoping the shroud of mist would clear.

A little past noon, the clouds broke, letting sunlight filter down to ground level. It was so long since their last sunny day, Margaret enjoyed the feeling once again. Their view of the ocean cleared as well, opening an unclouded view of the Juan de Fuca Straits and across to the large mountain range above the far shore. Their vigilance increased, now with something to watch. Less than an hour later, Margaret was surprised when Kane yelled, he had spotted a ship!

She looked, at first not believing what she saw. Could that be the Shanghai Lady? Rather than try to figure it out, she yelled to Kane to get the wood. Rushing around, they piled the extra wood on the fire, quickly building it up to a roaring blaze. To add to the smoke, they then dragged on some fresh cut branches of fir and cedar trees. The green boughs sizzled loudly as they hit the hot flames, soon consumed in a tower of smoke and flame. Each wet branch sent another cloud of smoke straight up, above the trees. At each effort, they would turn to the ocean, trying to determine if their signal was succeeding. If that was the Lady, then Margaret knew they were looking for them and they had a better chance than trying to flag down a passing ship.

"Look Tlul-cul-ma, they turn." Kane yelled.

"Oh God, I think you're right Kane." she answered, feeling the relief flood through her. She watched closely as the ship turned, gybing around to come closer to the shore for a better look. She grabbed Kane, overjoyed at their luck. Waving her jacket over her head, she ran up and down the beach, making sure they saw it was them.

The ship hove to, dropping anchor not far off shore.

She could barely make out who was on board, but she knew that Mark would lead the shore party as soon as the boat was launched. She was right, as she watched Mark and two others row the small boat towards them. She recognized Billy Guthrie as the second man, but it wasn't until the boat ground to a halt on the beach that she realized who the third one was... her brother Kenneth!

Chapter 71

The reunion was a joyous one, everyone hugging, kissing or shaking hands. Margaret's astonishment at seeing her brother almost overcame her relief of their rescue.

"Oh Kenneth, it's so good to see you, when did you arrive?" she asked finally.

"At least two weeks now," he replied, "I've been kicking around that old Fort with nobody to talk to." Knowing her brother, Margaret didn't believe a word. She knew that by now, he would have a complete knowledge of the activities and business prospects available in the entire area.

She turned again to Mark, hugging him furiously. At first he responded, then quickly stood back, his nose wrinkled in distaste.

"Belay that, lady! You smell like an old fishwife," he laughed, "I'm not sure I can take too much of this."

Margaret suddenly realized how she must look and smell. Weeks of sweat, wood smoke, mouldy clothes and oolichan grease mingled in a pungent cloud around her. Although she had tried to wash in the creek, her hair hung in filthy strands, and feeding the rescue fire had covered her with ashes and pitch from the trees. As she tried to offer some explanations, memories flooded back, many very unpleasant.

"Oh, my God . . . Thomas!" she cried, "Thomas is dead!" sobbing violently in Marks arms.

"No Maggie, he's not." Mark answered quickly. "He made it out . . . injured, but all right. In fact he should be here shortly when the Maggie M. returns from that last run."

She wasn't sure she heard him correctly. "No, we saw him killed by the Indians . . ." It slowly penetrated, "Do you mean he survived that?" she asked, afraid to believe what she was hearing.

"Yes Maggie, you'll see. He's frantic about you as well, not knowing if you survived that brush with those renegades. I often told you, you're all a bunch of survivors" he answered.

Turning to Kane, Mark saw the bloody bandage around his shoulder. "Thanks Kane, for bringing her back. It looks like you all have some stories to tell here," he added. "And where might be our tenacious Mr. Croghan?" he asked, noticing his absence.

Margaret explained the accident, not mentioning any of the troubles she had with Charlie. As Mark motioned for them to return to the boat, Margaret suddenly remembered the reason they were there.

"Come here Mr. Holland." she commanded, "I want you to see something." Reaching into her pack, she pulled out a handful of her treasure, the coins glistening in the bright sunlight. Mark froze, his eyes wide, chin sagging.

"Wha . . . where . . . how?" he stammered. He turned to Margaret, tears in his eyes, beaming with delight. "Oh Maggie, it's true . . . and you found it! Oh, my God, I can't believe it!"

Margaret stopped him, tears in her eyes. "Oh Mark, don't get too excited, this is all we have left! Mind you, it's a lot more than what we had when we started. We've probably enough here to make things comfortable for awhile." Mark looked at her closely, questions forming. "Oh it's there alright . . ." she added, "and we had a good portion. Unfortunately, the late Mr. Croghan took almost the entire load to the bottom of the sea with him!"

Grabbing her brother's arm, she added "See Kenneth, I told you there were fortunes to be made over here" laughing at her brother's amazement. Turning again to Mark, she continued her tale, right up to their disappointing discovery on the beach.

Stowing the rest of their gear in the small boat, she took one more quick look around her before they climbed in and pushed off.

As they approached the larger ship, she spotted the Maggie M. closing quickly on them, a familiar figure standing at the bow. She couldn't believe Thomas was safe, after weeks of thinking he was dead. The small schooner rounded up close enough to the Lady for Thomas to leap off, then bore away in the freshening breeze.

Thomas helped his mother over the side of the Shanghai Lady, hugging her fiercely as they wept. The questions came in torrents, promising many hours of answers for a long time to come, tales of hardship and terror in a savagely beautiful country.

Mark and Billie wasted little time getting the ship under way. The sun was dipping low in the sky behind them as a light westerly gently pushed the little brigantine along the Strait of Juan de Fuca. Standing beside Mark at the wheel, Margaret couldn't help thinking of the first day they arrived, sailing the same route. Mark purposely steered the vessel further south to delay their arrival at the Fort.

"I think we need some time together Margaret, before the rest of the crowd gets to you" Mark explained. "The rest of the crew wants a little celebration tonight, so we'll just drift around in this breeze for the night."

Truly, it was a night to celebrate, a night few of them would forget.

It was late the following morning when they turned into the entrance to the harbour. Margaret couldn't help thinking how familiar the view was now, returning home. How her life had changed! Watching the shoreline slip by, she counted her blessings. She had Mark, her sons, a new daughter and now her brother to share her life. For the first time, she had a strange feeling, one of contentment and happiness.

Even as these feelings filled her, the faint stirrings of new ideas, new concepts started to take shape, new challenges for this west coast wilderness and the future of Fort Victoria.

THE END